Dear Cynthia,

Thanks for your support!

Noël

SECRETS CHANGE EVERYTHING

Thanks so much
Hope you enjoy the book
and let us know
Take care.
Maggie

BY

MAGGIE BRANATH

AND

NOËL F. CARACCIO

ISBN: 1481201700

ISBN 13: 9781481201704

DEDICATION

To my parents, Frances (Fannie) and Fred Branath, who did their best to love and encourage me, despite many obstacles. You made me strong and independent.
To my grandmother, Sarah Holicky, (Nanny), who taught me all the good things in life and for whom I am named. I am (Nanny) to my two beautiful grandchildren, Charlotte and Oliver.
To Lois Ellison, thank you for always having a place for me when I ran away from home, even if it was just across the street. You taught me the importance of being responsible for my own actions; they are the only ones you can control. Thanks for our afternoon cup of tea.
To my dog, Tina Bean, you will always be in my heart.
I love you and miss all of you,
Maggie

To my parents, Ann and Sal Caraccio, who showed me the meaning of unconditional love, and that you can achieve whatever you set your mind to.
To my niece and nephew, Kate and Dan Centofanti, whom I love as much as if you were my own children. I know you two can achieve great things.
Noël

ACKNOWLEDGMENTS

To my co-author, Noël, a.k.a. "EGG" for being the pushiest, Type A and perfectionist throughout the writing of this book, for which I am so grateful. Our ideas, collaboration, laughter and tears made this journey worth every word.

To Denise Galkin, for her never ending support and encouragement with the book and in my life.

To Vickie Thomson, no matter the years or miles, you are never far.

To Sam, my family, friends, Rye PT, patients and clients of Essential Healthworks, for being so supportive and encouraging of my efforts to write this novel. I am forever grateful.

To Jo-Anne Travers for her patience, her input and thoughts about the book. Now you can read the final, and I do mean the final, manuscript.

I am so very thankful to all of you and for your belief in me!

Maggie

To my co-author, Maggie , for her never ending wellspring of ideas for the story, and for nicknaming me "EGG," English Grammar Guru. We "fought" about the words and concepts, but ultimately came to a consensus and strengthened our friendship.

To Sal Albanese and Fred Whalen, who each graciously lent us their vacation homes so we had a place to write, away from the daily distractions at home.

To Jo-Anne Travers, who good naturedly read multiple drafts of the manuscript in varying degrees of completion, and gave us her thoughts and comments.

To Richard Lavsky, for all your help and patience with our multiple computer problems. Without you, we would be stuck somewhere in cyberspace.

To Brenda and Joe Morra, who were the ultimate referees on the questions of grammar and usage.

To Sandy Schoeneman, for encouraging me for years that I was stronger than I thought.

Thanks so much to all of you!

Noël

CHAPTER I

The only person who definitely knows I'm here is my daughter, Abby. The irony of the situation is that the person I kept the secret from is the only one who can see and hear me. Abby and I didn't get on all that well when I was alive, until the last few months of my life. I loved her for her feisty attitude as a little girl, which carried over as she became a grown woman. I wish I had told her, and I regret that I didn't. We were like oil and water; I was the same with my mother. But I have this feeling that I'm supposed to be here, wherever "here" is now, and set things straight with Abby. Don't get me wrong, setting things straight with Abby is not about apologizing. It's just about the secret I kept and why I kept it. I'm hoping she'll forgive me.

I certainly had my share of failings, and now I regret that my smoking and drinking got in the way of almost everything in my life. Night after night, I would sit on the couch in the living room, and I would be thinking of the life I wanted rather than the one I had. I loved my daughters, and Fred was a good husband. All I know was that I wanted more and I never knew how to make it happen. I'd be drinking one Black Label beer after another. As I cracked the pop-top on the can, it made a "whoosh" sound. It was that sound which usually got Abby up from her bed. As young as she was, I think around eight or ten years old, she would come downstairs angry and ready for a fight. God knows, as a kid Abby dumped as much of my beer and alcohol down the drain as went down my throat. Wherever that drainpipe flowed to, I'm sure there were some fish under the influence. However, it didn't stop me from drinking! Now I wish I had the courage or strength to do something about it, but the truth is I didn't, until the last few years of my life. By then I had no choice but to discontinue these vices because I had done considerable damage to myself. Dead is where the damage left me. When I was younger, I really didn't consider them as "vices." So puritanical and so judgmental. I did the best I could. Wouldn't it be wonderful if we could envision the future and therefore be able to change the past?

It's amazing how your own baggage can damage you when you don't deal with it, can't face it, or don't give a damn. My daughters both suffered yet handled it in different ways. Donna, my older daughter, retreated into herself; she was painfully quiet and timid. You wouldn't even know she was in the house at times. I believe she thought that if she was very quiet, very good, always listened to me, and never caused one bit of trouble, the tension and the fighting in the house would end. Looking back, there were many times Donna never should have listened to me. I could be threateningly convincing, a trait I projected only on Donna because I knew I could. I essentially forced Donna into marrying her first husband, even though I knew she really didn't want to go through with it. I didn't care much for my future son-in-law, too much whining and way too lazy. However, I thought his parents were good people, and would take care of Donna, even if he didn't. Maybe I wouldn't have forced Donna to marry the S.O.B. if my judgment wasn't impaired because of how much alcohol was floating around in my bloodstream. On the other hand, my younger daughter, Abby, handled things completely differently from her sister. She was loud, brash, and defiant! Abby *never* listened to me. We locked horns on just about everything from my alcoholism to the end of the alphabet. She was the one who wanted the drunken drama to stop. God knows, I wish

I could have given my girls what they wanted, peace and a sober mother.

Until the last few months of my life, I hadn't paid much attention to heaven or the afterlife. I wouldn't have called myself a religious person, although I became a "somewhat devout Catholic," primarily because I wanted to raise my two daughters with some sense of belonging to an organized religion. I know, I know, a "somewhat devout Catholic" is a contradiction in terms. I believed in a higher being, mostly because of my mother's mother, my beloved Grandma Brown, who came from the back woods of Minnesota.

As an adult, I actually dabbled in a few religions prior to Catholicism. I was interested in Judaism for a while, but I couldn't get a handle on what they believed. Four Jews had six opinions. I tried to be an Episcopalian for a while, but they were too lily white and hoity-toity for me. I believe the queen of England is an Episcopalian. Buddhism was too esoteric. Is organized religion truly the "opium of the people?" Not that any religion or prayers seemed to help me with my destructive habits; that's for sure. You'd also think that whoever laid out the master plan of the universe would have given a little more thought to our departure from this world, so that you'd have some idea of what to expect.

In the last three months of my life, Abby came back home in the beginning of May to take care of me. Spring is my favorite time of year, when life renews itself—a form of starting over. Don't I wish. But in reality, every day you do get a new chance to start over. Do you think you can, or do you think you can't? The question is, do you take the chance and make the change or not? After all my years on earth, I realized life is the sum total of choices—the choices you make in the life you've been given. Yup, just choices. I learned too late that every choice you make has a cascading effect on your next choice and the one after that.

The summer that I died, my condition had worsened significantly. When I had any color, my skin had a greenish pallor. I spent virtually all day tethered to an oxygen tank, and unfortunately, my conversations with Abby were dramatically reduced because my breathing was so labored. Abby now did most of the talking and described her life in Colorado with her husband and two children. Abby was able to fill in the details since she was spending more time with me than she ever had in our prior brief phone conversations. I listened, some days more attentively than others, depending on my energy level. At my request, Abby left Colorado to come and help me. Her husband, Jerry, stayed behind with the kids to tie up the loose ends. They would all eventually move to New York. I was happy that Abby came back to help. As it turned out, that summer was to be my last.

The summer went by fast, partially because so many of the days were the same. We got up; Abby made breakfast; she helped me get washed and cleaned up; she did some housework and usually went for a run to clear her head. Abby then took her father with her to do some errands and get him out of the house. I had to keep reminding myself that this was very hard on Fred as well. He would never say anything or lose his temper. He was a good man and a better father. I'm glad he asked me to marry him. I heard Abby ask him many times how he was doing, and the answer was invariably, "I'm doing fine. Let's just take good care of your mother."

I also overheard Abby ask her father, "Do you realize that you've been married for fifty years? You've been married for two-thirds of your life. Do you even remember what it was like not to have Mom in your life?"

With some heartfelt sarcasm, Fred answered, "Really, fifty years? My, how time flies. Your Aunt Rita set us up on a blind date to go on a ski trip in the beginning of January. You remember all the stories your mother used to tell about the two of them being inseparable. Anyway, that ski trip was the beginning, and we were married six months later on June 30. How's that for a whirlwind courtship? Sometimes your heart knows these things way before your head. Funny, isn't it?"

"Dad, did you know that Mom still has her skis in the basement? They're warped, but she kept them for some reason. Now I know why."

"I bet it surprises you that your mother is sentimental. Underneath that gruff exterior lies the heart of a real softie. Only a very few people get to see that side of her, and then only occasionally. Do you realize that you're an awful lot like your mother? You and your mother could never see beyond your differences to see how much alike you two are."

On August 3 of that last summer, I called Abby into the bedroom and asked her to stay with me. She sat on the edge of the bed and held my hand. She remarked that my hands were like ice. She then checked my oxygen level. Abby looked into my eyes, and I looked directly into hers. She kissed me on the cheek and told me that she loved me. I nodded and said in a throaty whisper, "You know how much I love you. We fought the way we did because we are who we are. It's just us. I don't want you to have any regrets. It's never the 'what ifs' that matter."

Abby stayed in my room for two days; she slept in the rocking chair, which she had moved next to the bed. This was the same rocking chair that I had rocked my two daughters in when they were infants and my mother used for me. Periodically, I would open my eyes to see her sitting next to me. It was comforting. The cycle of life was beginning to come full circle. Fred would come in and check on us, and sometimes he took Abby's place in the rocking chair when she went to take a shower or if she went into the kitchen to prepare a meal.

On the third day prior to my death, in the late morning, I awoke, or so I thought, and found myself watching this scenario unfold before me, as if, floating from above...strange, very strange. I think I may have made some sound that had awakened Abby. She saw that I was not breathing. I could hear the hum of the oxygen tank, and she frantically checked for a pulse. She screamed for Fred to come in. He burst into the room, and she said, "I can't get a pulse; she's not responding!"

Fred grabbed my shoulders and picked me up off the pillows and pulled me to his chest. He then wrapped his arms around me and, rocking me back and forth, and yelled, "Frances! Frances!" He laid me back down on the pillows and shook my shoulders again, as he continued to scream over and over, "Frances, wake up! Come back—come back to me!"

I wanted to speak, but I couldn't, or maybe they couldn't hear me.

The whole incident probably only took less than a minute. However, it seemed like everything was in slow motion and warp speed at the same time.

All of a sudden, I was back, not floating anymore. I sat bolt upright, and with a huge breath, my eyes popped open. In the next breath, and with my eyes closed, I said, "Shit, the light...so bright...and the colors, so vivid...They were...I was on my way... for a moment." I faintly heard Abby tell her father I was "back."

When my eyes fluttered open again, I could see Fred and Abby looking at each other in absolute amazement. Neither one of them said a word to the other. What exactly had happened?

I didn't know at the time those were the last words I'd ever speak prior to my death. I lay back down, and my eyes closed slowly. My breathing was still labored, but steady. Abby told Fred to stay with me, and Abby ran into the kitchen to call the doctor. The doctor arrived within twenty minutes. He listened to my chest with the stethoscope and then turned to Abby and said, "Your mother needs to be in the hospital right now."

I had never clarified with Abby what my wishes were about dying at home. That was a mistake I would dearly regret. I had been in and out of the hospital several times before Abby returned from Colorado to take care of me that summer. I did not want to return to the hospital yet again...to die.

Abby said that she, Fred, and the doctor all thought it best that I go back to the hospital. I didn't have enough strength to fight that decision. Abby kept trying to reassure me that everything would be all right.

They called the Rivertown volunteer ambulance corps, which arrived within minutes to take me to the hospital. Fred went in the ambulance with me, and Abby followed behind in the car.

Within minutes, I was ensconced in a small cubicle in the emergency room, with no fewer than five medical personnel moving efficiently around me. I was quickly intubated. Abby leaned over the bed and said that the color in my cheeks had returned. I almost felt healthy—if I could just ignore the tube that was shoved down my throat. I perked up and was more alert than I had been in weeks because of the increased oxygen levels. If I had realized how important oxygen was, I would have stopped my cigarette smoking years earlier.

Abby continued to reassure me, but now, with my heightened awareness came increasing anger. Still feeling very weak, my hands shook as I motioned for pen and paper. I scribbled in bold letters, "You lied. It won't be OK. HOME."

Abby looked so upset and responded, "I'm so sorry, Mom. The doctor thought you'd be better off in the hospital, and Dad thought so, too."

I will never forget the pain in Abby's eyes as she looked at me, her eyes filling up with tears. It dawned on me that this was the final leg of the journey, and I was going to spend it in the hospital. She told her father to stay with me, that she'd be right back. I wanted to scream for Abby to come back as she bolted out of the emergency room and down the hall.

I think Abby finally realized when I scribbled the note to her in the emergency room that I had asked her to come back from Colorado not only to help me physically, but also to make the important and agonizing decisions, because Fred could no longer make them. I didn't want her to think she had failed me.

CHAPTER 2

If Abby thought that life had been difficult with her mother, Fannie, sick at home, having her in the hospital was far more difficult. Frances preferred to be called "Fannie," which was the nickname her Grandma Brown had called her as a young child. Abby was now spending a lot of the day in the hospital and running back and forth to check on her father at the house. Fred came to visit Fannie in the hospital, but he didn't have the stamina to stay the whole day, nor did he want to. It was too emotionally draining for him.

After Fannie was stabilized in the emergency room, she was transferred to the intensive care unit. The next day the pulmonologist approached Abby and said he had conferred with the surgeon, and they both felt Fannie needed a tracheotomy. They needed Fred's consent. Fred really didn't quite understand the implications of this decision and looked to Abby for an explanation. As hard as this was, since the doctor felt this was in Fannie's best interest, Fred signed the consent form.

Despite the doctors' best efforts, Fannie continued on a downward spiral. One morning as Abby was sitting in the hospital room with her mother, Fannie started having a severe epileptic grand mal seizure due to an allergic reaction to the medication. Abby ran out of Fannie's room, yelling for the nurse. The nurse paged one of the doctors, who prescribed Dilantin. Eventually, the seizures ended, but Abby was clearly frazzled by them. It was now another thing to have to worry about.

Abby had had seizures as a child, and so when Fannie was stabilized and more coherent, Abby said to her, "Mom, you scared the living hell out of me. Now I understand what it must have been like for you to feel helpless when I was having the seizures."

Fannie picked up the pad of paper and pen Abby had given her to communicate with since the tracheotomy. Fannie scribbled, "Yes, scared. Did the best I could. So did you."

The combination of medicines for the emphysema and the seizures then caused Fannie to have a bleeding ulcer. In addition to that, her stomach was badly distended, and she was in a great deal of pain. The doctor told Abby that Fannie needed surgery sooner rather than later to repair the bleeding ulcer.

That afternoon Abby was walking alongside the gurney as they wheeled Fannie toward the operating room. Abby was holding her hand and telling her yet again that everything would be all right. Abby wasn't sure she really believed what she was telling Fannie, but what choice did she have? Fannie smiled at Abby and blew her a kiss as the doors to the operating room opened. Abby called to her and said again as she had every day, "I love you. I'll be here when you wake up." The doors closed, and Fannie was gone.

About three hours later, Abby was awakened by the doctor, who came to find her in the waiting room. He told Abby that the surgery had gone well, and they had repaired the bleeding ulcer. Abby could see Fannie in the recovery room shortly. The doctor continued, "The problem is that when a patient reaches a certain age and something happens, whether it be due to disease or injury, medicine can only do so much. Complications arise, which make a good outcome difficult, if not impossible, to achieve. There's a snowball effect. It's like trying to pull someone back after they've fallen over a cliff. Sometimes you just can't reel them back in. In your mother's case, there are far too many complications for us to get the outcome we would like. Do you understand what I'm saying?"

Unfortunately, Abby understood all too well. Less than a week after the conversation with the surgeon, Fannie died.

CHAPTER 3

Abby left the hospital at about eight thirty the night before Fannie died. Fannie had been very alert that day. After Fannie's death, one of Abby's friends told her that often hours before a person dies they become much more aware and lucid. The radial pulse diminishes, and the pulse in the carotid arteries becomes almost impossible to detect. She was right in both cases. Had Abby known this at the time, she would not have left Fannie's hospital room. Abby told her mother that she wanted to check on her father and take care of a few things at home.

Fannie's eyes were intently following Abby around the room. Abby leaned in to kiss her mother and told her that she loved her and that she'd be back early the next morning.

About six thirty the following morning, the hospital called and said that Fannie had died. Abby started to tremble and hung up the phone. Abby went upstairs to her father's room to tell him and asked him if he wanted to go to the hospital with her. He said he'd stay at the house and wait for Abby to come back. Abby said, "Are you sure you want to stay here, Dad?" Fred replied, with tears forming in the corners of his eyes, "I've seen your mother in her best light, and that's the way I want to remember her." With that Abby hugged him tightly and then left for the hospital.

Abby had a gold 1972 357 Pontiac Le Mans—a screamer! It was the last year they made "three on the tree." A normal ride to the hospital would have taken a good twenty minutes. That morning Abby made it in ten.

When Abby went into Fannie's hospital room, she noticed that the ever-present respirator was gone from the room as well as all the other life-support equipment, including the pulse oxygen monitor and the intravenous poles. Fannie was lying peacefully in the bed, and the tracheotomy tube had been removed and her hair had been combed. Abby bent down to kiss her on the forehead, and when she did, she could feel how cold Fannie had become already. Abby wanted to be there with her mother, to hold her hand and tell her again that everything would be all right. Abby wanted to tell her that it was OK to go. Abby *needed* to be there with her when Fannie took her last breath. Abby didn't want her mother to die alone. She felt she had made the wrong decision to admit Fannie to the hospital against her wishes, and now Fannie had died alone.

Abby sat down in the chair next to her mother's bed and took her hand. The waves of grief started to pour over Abby, and she started to sob. She was crying for her mother; she was crying for herself. She was just crying because she had to. Abby felt there was still so much she wanted to know about her mother and so much Abby wanted to tell her.

Abby was so grateful for the time she had had with mother. They both tried to make up for the years they had missed being with each other. Abby had missed out on knowing her mother as an equal, instead of just knowing her through a child's eyes. Her gratitude still didn't take away her feeling of failure to make the right decision about taking her mother to the hospital and not being with her when she died. Abby realized that sometimes even though it feels like it's not enough, all you can do is your best...and then you have to let it go.

CHAPTER 4

Seventeen Years Later

It had been a beautiful day at the beach—Silver Beach to be exact, not too far from Seaside Heights, known for its boardwalk restaurants and amusement park. Adam, at just five years old, loved the kiddie rides. He always smiled, laughed and screamed, "Faster, more faster!" Rick and Jennifer had bought a vacation house at Silver Beach with her parents. Rick couldn't have asked for better in-laws, especially since his own parents had passed away. The house was one block from the beach, and it was large enough to have some alone time if you needed it, and big enough to gather the troops. It had a wrap-around porch with more than enough Adirondack chairs to sit in. The porch just made you want to kick back, put your bare feet on the porch rail, and tilt back a cold one.

Rick had just gotten off the phone with his boss. He was needed back at the law firm for an emergency. A client was in the midst of a battle over a corporate merger and acquisition, and Steve Goldrick, the managing partner, was calling in the best associates. There went the rest of Rick's vacation. He knew his heading back to Manhattan wasn't going to go over well with Jennifer or Adam. Rick could already imagine the disappointment on Adam's face. Rick thought he would break the news to Jennifer after they all finished dinner. No need to ruin a good barbeque.

The next morning Rick, Jennifer and Adam went for an early morning walk on the beach. Adam enjoyed looking for tiny crabs and shells washed up on the sand. He was running away from the surf making its way to the beach and then chasing it back to where it met the ocean. Adam would turn around every once in a while to see where his parents were and say, "See, Daddy, the wave can't catch me." Rick would yell back, "That's 'cause you're too fast for the wave!" Rick was content and happy with his life. "I am one lucky son of a bitch," he thought.

Rick finished loading up the car and was saying his good-byes. Jennifer said, "Drive carefully and call when you get home—promise."

"Yes…I promise," said Rick. "Are you going to leave tomorrow or stay until Sunday?" he asked.

"Mom said she wanted to head home on Sunday, so she'll be there for her board meeting, without having to rush home on Monday. It's just not the same here without the 'Grillmaster,' so I will see you, as she pointed a finger at him, "on Sunday and be ready for some fun in the bedroom."

Rick leaned over and grabbed Jen tight. "Fun sounds good," he whispered in her ear. He then kissed her and picked up Adam, who had just run over to his dad with arms outstretched.

"You looked like an airplane coming at me; what am I a runway?" Rick said as he picked Adam up and twirled him around.

"Daddy, you're funny. You're a people, not a runway."

Adam hugged Rick tightly. "See ya Sunday. Love ya, buddy."

"You too, Daddy," Adam replied as he ran toward the house.

Rick's ride to Manhattan was uneventful and quick. Surprisingly, not much traffic. He breezed through the Lincoln Tunnel and made his way across town to the office. Work was work—time for the game face. Rick worked Wednesday through Friday and part of the weekend in a flurry of activity for Monday and the next onslaught in the war for the corporation. As Sunday morning turned to Sunday afternoon, Rick was surprised that he hadn't heard from Jennifer. Rick tried Jen several times on the cell phone, but each time the voicemail came on. They were either on their way or more likely stuck in the Sunday afternoon traffic on the Garden State Parkway, "shore traffic." It was on a par with the traffic on the Tappan Zee Bridge and the George Washington Bridge during holidays or rush hour. Just sitting in that traffic made ya wanna jump off the bridge. If the jump didn't kill ya, you could probably swim faster across the Hudson. Rick was beginning to get concerned, but he tried to tell himself that Jen just forgot to turn her cell phone on.

Rick left the office at about three o'clock on Sunday afternoon and arrived home in less than an hour, since most of the traffic was coming east into Manhattan. As Rick pulled into his driveway, he noticed a police car pulling up behind him. He had an overwhelmingly sick feeling rising up from deep inside. Why haven't I heard from Jennifer by now? She always called. Did something happen to Adam? Why the hell is a cop pulling into my driveway? This can't be good. Oh fuck, he has that look on his face—something has happened! So many thoughts tumbled through his head in a split second. Rick and the officer got out of their cars at the same time.

"Mr. Singleton?" the officer asked in a very deep voice that reminded Rick of a very young country-western singer on *American Idol*. Jennifer was so hooked on that show. "Yes, I'm Rick Singleton. What's going on?"

"I'm afraid I have some bad news; can we go inside?"

"Just tell me now! What is it? What happened?" Rick could feel the bile rise in his throat.

"There's been an accident, and your wife and son are in the hospital. Why don't you let me take you to the hospital? Is there someone you can call to have them meet us there?"

"How bad is it—just fuckin' tell me." Rick began to pace, his hands to his temples and brushing the hair back from his face.

"All I know is that they are seriously injured; we need to get to St. Barnabas Hospital—now. While we are on the way, why don't you call someone to meet you there?"

On the way to the hospital, Rick called Jason, his older brother. "Jas, it's me; there's been an accident. Jennifer and Adam are at St. Barn. It's bad. I don't really know any details except they were hit by a car crossing the center line. Meet me there."

CHAPTER 5

Abby looked out the window above her bed. All she had to do was roll over in the morning, and she could see the most beautiful sunrise. Since it was so early, she was able to see the brilliant white glow of the full moon and the shadows the moon cast on the trees. For whatever reason, she couldn't sleep, and the alarm clock on the nightstand just continued to blink the minutes away. It was early September, and the nights were cooling down with the unmistakable feel of autumn. She lay still for a few minutes, feeling the breeze as it blew the curtains above her head, and she could feel the night air on her face and arms.

Abby finally decided that any hope of getting back to sleep was futile. She was beginning to work up a sweat from rolling over so many times trying to get comfortable; she decided to get up and go downstairs to the kitchen. She looked over at Tina Bean, her big beautiful black Lab. Tina had found Abby when Tina was about a year and a half old. It was a time in Abby's life after Jerry had died, and she was trying to keep everything together for herself and the kids. Abby had been having a conversation "in her head" with her deceased mother. Abby asked her mother for a sign, and Abby wanted to know if her mother had heard her. Seconds later, a big black Labrador was standing at the kitchen door. Abby had checked around at vet offices and shelters to see if Tina had run away or belonged to anyone else, but nothing was found. Abby guessed that Tina's purpose was to just be, to be in Abby's life with her and her children. Abby strongly believed that her mother had everything to do with Tina's sudden appearance, even though Fannie had been dead for many years. Abby looked at Tina as she was curled up sleeping and thought how cute she must have been as a puppy. Abby had missed that part of Tina's life, but she was so thankful that they shared the rest of their lives. Tina was sleeping soundly next to Abby on the bed. God only knew how many sheep or maybe dog biscuits Tina was counting. All of the dogs and cats she had ever acquired had slept in her bed. "Where else were they going to sleep?" she would say to her mother. It was a good thing her husband, Jerry, had an understanding and an affinity for animals as well. He would have loved Tina. All Abby had to do was put one foot on the floor, and Tina popped her head up. That particular morning, as Abby started to get out of bed, Tina looked at Abby as if to say, "Do you know what time it is? It's still dark. Even I, who likes to wake you up early, don't want to get up before the crack of dawn." Tina gave Abby the equivalent of a dog shrug and jumped off the bed.

Abby threw on shorts, T-shirt, sweatshirt, and sneakers and started her descent down the stairs with Tina at her heels. Abby stood at the kitchen counter and poured herself a glass of water and got a biscuit for Tina. Since they were up anyway, Abby decided to go for a walk. "Tina, do you want to come along for a walk?" Stupid question to ask, Abby thought to herself. Since Tina never wanted to miss anything, she began to wag her tail and waited by the sliding glass door in anticipation. "Here's some carbs for the run," Abby said, and tossed her the biscuit.

Because it was so early and they had so much time, Abby thought it would be great to drive to a trail in the woods where they could see the deer feeding in the early morning. The trail had been cleared by the town to create a path along the river for running or biking or for a very early stroll in the morning. Some mornings it was absolutely breathtaking to see the sun rise. Abby opened the passenger side door, and Tina practically knocked Abby over in her haste to get in the car.

About fifteen minutes later, they parked at the start of the trail that would lead them to the bridge where there were picnic tables and great places to fish along the river. Here was a place bustling with activity during the summer months, and as soon as school started in the fall, the activity dwindled to a few hardcore folk. Abby and Tina got out of the car, and Abby grabbed her flashlight and looked at her cell phone. She realized she should have plugged it in to charge—only one bar left and no car charger. She stuffed her cell phone and the flashlight in her jacket pocket along with a poop bag and some doggie treats. Abby thought it was extraordinarily bright as Tina trotted next to her in the moonlight.

Abby was thinking how different this place looked and sounded from all the activity that was usually going on during the summer. It was so nice to be here by themselves. She thought they'd walk across the bridge and get to the trail before the sun came up so they could see the sky change color. After that, they'd take a run.

They could hear the water coming off the falls and running downstream. Abby knew she could hear those sounds during the day, but they were certainly more prominent now. Abby mused that the sounds of nature got drowned out by the sounds of people. The rush of water was quite audible, almost loud. Abby remembered her father telling her that this was one of the roughest spots of water around for miles because the river narrowed considerably at this point. The current was very strong, and only experienced kayakers or canoers were able to maneuver through without mishap. It was really considered a treacherous spot, in sharp contrast to the gorgeous view from the bridge.

Abby loved it that this spot was tucked away only a few miles from her house, yet it was somewhat of a local tourist attraction. Sometimes that was good and bad. Abby thought back to when she was about twelve or thirteen and a bunch of high school seniors got drunk one night and drove up here. One kid was so drunk that his friends dared him to climb up on the bridge, and like an idiot he took the dare. He got part way up the side of the bridge, lost his balance, and fell in. His friends panicked when they saw him fall in, and one kid dove in to try to save him. Your chances of surviving if you fall off the bridge are slim to none. It was a double tragedy since both boys drowned, and they didn't find their bodies downstream for a few days. The rest of the boys just watched in horror as they lost two friends in a matter of seconds.

Abby and Tina were moving across the bridge at a pretty good pace, when all of a sudden Tina came to a sudden stop. Abby had been somewhat lost in thought, and so it took her a few more paces before she realized that Tina had stopped walking and had fallen behind her. It was Tina's body language that startled her and then scared her. The first thing that flashed through her mind was that there was someone else on the bridge who might hurt them. For a second, Abby regretted walking in the dark on a deserted bridge with no means of protection and a dead cell phone. She didn't want to become a crime statistic, nor did she want to be in the headlines in tomorrow's newspapers. She knew Tina would try to protect her, but that would do little good against a person with a gun or a knife. The thoughts raced through her mind in fractions of a second, but she had yet to accurately assess the threat because she didn't know who or what the threat was. The dark only made it worse.

All her senses were heightened, and she froze in place straining to hear or see something. Out of the corner of her eye, she tried to find Tina. She wasn't sure if it was safe to turn all the way around to look for Tina, because Abby still wasn't sure where the danger actually was. Her thoughts were racing through her mind at a frenzied pace. With the fear she felt, she understood what it meant when people said that the hair stood up on their arms, because she could literally feel the hair standing at attention.

The man up on the bridge felt empty and hollow during the four months after the accident. There was nothing left now that they were gone. As he wrestled with his demons, he agonized over and over. What is it about life and death? I know I just want to die, because I don't want to be here without them. The man sat quietly. He could feel a slight breeze on his face and could hear the leaves rustling at the tree tops. He could also hear the rush of the water far below.

How long have I been here? Doesn't matter now, does it? It will be quick, the dive straight down. My neck will snap like a twig on impact. Three seconds, that's all. One thousand one, one thousand two, one thousand…And it will be the end and on to a new beginning

The man on the bridge had been startled from his thoughts by the barking dog. Why did these people have to come along now and disturb him? He needed to think everything through. He needed quiet; he longed for deafening quiet. He needed to be with his family.

Tina first started with a low growl, which gave way to frantic barking. She lunged ahead of Abby toward the side of the bridge. It probably took another three to five seconds for the situation to become clear to Abby based on where Tina was going. Abby realized that there was danger and it was almost palpable, but the danger wasn't to her. She had glanced at the bridge stanchions quickly at first, believing that the danger was coming at them from the bridge deck itself, when in fact, the danger was way above them. Abby now took a longer look up toward the apex of the bridge, and her eye caught what had made Tina crazy. Someone was up on the scaffolding used by the repair crews and was leaning precariously over the edge toward the water. Realizing at this time of the early morning that there were no trucks or repair people in sight, Abby decided 911 was the only choice to make. She automatically reached into her pocket to grab her cell, but the screen was completely black.

"Shit, I don't need this now—no, not now!" She then shouted, "Hey, are you OK up there?" Even as the words were coming out of her mouth, Abby knew they were stupid, but she seemed powerless to stop them. What else was she going to say? She knew immediately that the person was not part of a repair crew. The bridge was bathed only in moonlight and not in high intensity lights.

If Tina hadn't started barking so loudly, Abby might have startled the person by calling up to him. As she focused on the person, she was pretty sure from the build and the haircut that it was a man. He looked to have sandy-colored or blond hair. Even from that distance, he appeared to be tall and fairly lean. He had on dark pants, maybe jeans, and a light-colored T-shirt. The more she focused, the more detail she saw.

He didn't answer Abby, so she yelled louder this time, again knowing full well that he had heard her voice ringing up to him in the still night air.

"What the hell are you doing up there?" It was much less polite, but much more accurate.

"Just leave me alone and go away." Definitely a man's voice responding.

"No one is on scaffolding near the top of a bridge in the middle of the night if everything is fine. Can you come down off the scaffolding?"

Abby had seen enough police shows to know that if someone is that far up on a bridge, that most probably jumping is the main thing on their mind. But in movies, the negotiator is Denzel Washington who has been on the police force for twenty-five years, and a hostage negotiator for the last fifteen of them. It didn't seem to Abby that he had any hostages, which was at least one plus in this situation. The extremely large minus was that they were in the middle of a bridge in the middle of the night, and she was here by herself with a potential jumper, a black Lab, a flashlight, and a dead cell phone. She had no way to call for help, and unless Tina was going to pull a Lassie and find help and find it quickly, Abby was stuck in a situation she was very, very ill equipped to handle. She was so afraid of saying the wrong thing—something that would encourage his jumping.

Abby felt as if the air was being constricted in her chest, and when she spoke again, the voice that came out didn't sound like hers, but she was at least able to say something.

"My name is Abby, and this is my dog, Tina. We came out for a walk because I couldn't sleep. Can you tell me your name?"

Abby listened in the stillness of the early morning for a response. Nothing.

"Aw, come on, don't make me stand here like a stupid jackass and talk to you, and you won't tell me your name."

"Look, I told you before, just go away."

"Let's stop bullshitting each other; you're not fine, and I'm not going away." To Abby's surprise, there was actually annoyance in her voice.

The man heard the annoyance too, because he said, "My name is Rick! Now leave me the hell alone. I don't want your help or anything else. Go away—now!

"Thanks for telling me your name, Rick." Like Rick's your real name, she thought to herself. "Right now I'm not sure what either of us is doing here, but I really don't think I can just leave. I have absolutely no idea what I'm supposed to say or not say to you, so can we just talk for a few minutes? Somehow I don't think that it's sheer coincidence that I took a walk on this bridge this morning and you're up there. Look, I'm not a cop; I just want you to talk to me. Please, your life is important to me."

"Go away and leave me alone!"

"Sorry, Rick, it's not happening. Tina and I are staying. Can't you at least tell me what made you so upset?"

There was silence for what was probably a few seconds, but seemed like an eternity.

CHAPTER 6

Abby thought she saw something move to her left, out of the corner of her eye. She was hoping that maybe a cop had come along or someone with a cell phone who could quietly call for help and get her out of here. No such luck. She turned to her left and saw nothing.

Although she saw nothing, she heard something. It was hard to describe, since it didn't seem she was hearing it through her ears, but somehow hearing it inside her head. The "something" seemed to surround her.

"Abby, I'm here beside you."

"Oh my God…who's beside me? You sound like, like… like…Mom?"

"Yeah, it's me, your Mother."

Abby looked at Tina, and then Abby did a three sixty! Abby was squinting as though this would somehow make whatever it was come into better view, and her arms were swinging out away from her body as though she was looking for something to grab on to or touch.

"Where are you, Mom?"

"Don't freak out. Just because you can't see me doesn't mean I'm not here."

"How the hell are you here? You're not here because... you're dead!"

Abby's mind was racing, not unlike her heart. She looked at Tina, whose head was cocked and ears were at point, listening intently, and she was keeping her eyes focused on Abby. Abby thought, "What the fuck is going on?"

"Abby, you need to tell him that I tried and almost succeeded in committing suicide, but thank God, your father was around to save me. Tell him how glad you were that I didn't die."

"What are you talking about? Tell the guy on the bridge what? Why? What the hell am I doing?"

On the bridge, far above Abby and Tina, Rick was standing looking into the dark water. He just wanted to be alone, to have some quiet. He could hear the woman's voice and her muffled words as if she were talking to someone. Maybe it was her dog. He didn't much care. He needed to think and say good-bye to the life he had known. He smiled as he thought about his family. He was ready to see his wife and son very soon.

"I want you to tell him I didn't die."

"Yes, I am glad for that, but why am I even answering you and why the hell are you here now? You're dead! You didn't bother to show up when my husband died, but you show up now...This can't be real. Couldn't you just send another dog? Oh dear God, I must be having a seizure or something." Abby looked at Tina again. "Am I having a seizure or a hallucination?"

"I think now is quite a good time to show up and talk to you. You survived Jerry's death and even flourished despite the pain you felt from losing him. Now, right at this moment, you're in over your head. You have to save Rick. Just tell him what I just told you. Do it and don't argue."

"Don't argue? Are you for real? We've always done that. But I'll tell him; I don't want him to jump and plunge to his death while I'm talking to my dead mother!"

Abby and Tina stood on the bridge almost frozen, looking at one another, Tina's head still cocked to one side and her ears on alert. Abby could not believe what she was hearing—or maybe it was all in her head. Was it really her mother raised from the dead? Abby began to sway side to side, shifting her weight from one foot to the other, trying to think things through, something she always did when she was uncertain.

"Hey, Rick, it's Abby again. I know...another stupid comment from me, because there's no one else here but us. I get what you're going through. My mom tried to commit suicide when I was ten years old. Mom thought she had no other way to get rid of her demons, except to kill herself. To this day I can remember how terrified I was. Mom later told me she was glad she hadn't succeeded."

Abby stopped the freight train of words only long enough to take a breath.

Rick heard Abby far below him. He really thought he should just go ahead and jump and not answer her; he didn't care what she said, but the words came out anyway, "You're lying. That never happened. "

"Rick, I swear that's the truth. My mother tried to slash her wrists. My father carried her out of the house, bleeding profusely, while my sister, my grandmother and I watched in horror. We cleaned up her blood in the bathroom. That is not something you can make up or ever forget."

"Well, my situation is very different."

"It may be, but I bet the intense pain is the same."

"Abby, tell him that you know he feels that there is nothing more for him to live for because he lost his wife and son."

"God, Mom, is that true? Jesus, really?"

"Rick, I know you think your life is over because you lost your wife and little boy."

"How the hell do you know that? I don't know who you are, and you don't know me."

"Honestly, Rick, I'm not really sure how I know that, but I just seemed to know."

Abby was afraid to tell him that her dead mother was talking to her for fear he would think she was crazier than he was—and he was the one wanting to jump off a bridge. Maybe she should be the one up there.

Abby heard Rick begin to weep loudly. In a panic, she thought, "Oh, God, did I just say something that's literally going to push him over the edge?"

"Mom, I don't think that was the right thing to say. He's definitely getting more agitated. What should I do?"

"Abby, keep talking to him. He feels absolutely miserable, but at least he still feels something."

"I know the pain you feel, Rick," Abby continued with a knot in her throat. "I felt the same way you do now when my husband died. I felt alone, sometimes scared, and thought leaving this world would be the answer. But I didn't. Because no matter how much pain I felt, I knew how much pain I would cause to others who loved me and needed me if I went through with it. Rick, please, just tell me what happened. Please tell me what happened."

"It's my fault; they're dead because of me." He spoke without hesitation and with conviction. Abby could hear the pain and anger in his voice.

"Rick, what did you do? Can't you tell me?"

"My job! It's always been my job," he fairly shrieked at Abby. Then he said in a barely audible voice, but loud enough that Abby could still hear, "I'm sorry about your husband."

"What the hell do I say now, Mom?"

"Abby, ask him to tell you about his wife and son; what were they like?"

"Rick, tell me about your wife. What did she look like?"

Abby waited. She waited a little bit longer for what she hoped would be an answer and not the "whoosh" of his going downward to an almost certain death. Even though the moon was full, the darkness of the situation seemed to surround them.

Abby's question started Rick reminiscing in his head about the first time he met Jennifer. She was a lanky five nine and very athletic looking. She was a volleyball player in college at Stanford and damn good. They were in their junior year, and Rick had gone with a friend whose girlfriend was on the team. Jennifer had her hair pulled back in a ponytail, and what jumped out at him were her gorgeous green eyes, the kind you could get lost in.

Just as Abby was about to ask him again, Rick spoke. "She was beautiful, but it doesn't matter anymore. She's gone."

Abby answered, "Jennifer is still in your heart, and she will be always. Tell me about your son."

Fannie said, "Just keep him talking. If he's still talking, he's not jumping." In a more muffled tone, she said, "Lucky it's not rush hour. What a goddamn mess this place would be."

Abby heard Rick stifle a sob. "Rick…talk to me about your son."

"He's my little buddy. He just turned five, and he can really hit a baseball. He loved baseball."

For a second, Rick's voice was animated and then reality caught up to him, and his voice trailed off.

"Oh my God, they're dead! How can I live without them?"

Fannie said calmly to Abby, "Change the subject and keep him talking." Abby looked up at Rick. She could see him standing very close to the edge of the scaffolding, almost as a silhouette in the moonlit night.

"Rick, do you work here or in New York City?"

"It's my fucking job that caused this whole thing! It's the goddam law firm! I had to work a shit load of hours. They pay you a bundle of money, but they think they own you."

"What is it that the law firm did?"

"I worked too much, and I wasn't home enough. We had the big house and the big mortgage and Jennifer wanted to stay home with Adam. If I hadn't gone back to work early from vacation, they'd still be alive."

"Why, what happened?"

"I got a call. I drove back early from vacation to the office. In my job, you can't say no to a partner."

There was another long pause, and Abby waited for Rick to continue. Abby could tell how hard it was for Rick to speak, his voice breaking between words and sentences. "A truck hit them on the way home from our summer house. The guy had a massive heart attack at the wheel and came across the yellow line. If only I hadn't gone back to work early and I'd have driven them home, they'd still be alive."

"This is not your fault. It was an accident. You had no control over this. This was a horrible, horrible accident that you certainly didn't cause." The tension of the situation now had Abby pacing back and forth as she was speaking to him.

"Abby, tell him it wasn't meant for him to die in that car crash, but your paths were definitely meant to cross."

"Paths cross? What the hell does that mean?"

"Abby, who's there?"

"Just me and my dog, Tina. I often talk to her when I'm in the midst of a crisis...uh, I mean, dilemma. She makes a good sounding board, right, girl?" Tina sat, looking at Abby, and then to Rick up on the bridge as if she understood what was happening.

Abby noticed that the darkness that surrounded them was beginning to diminish slightly as the stars were moving to the west. With that, the sun would be fast approaching. She had to get him down off the bridge. She wanted him to live to see the sun rise again and the new day, and every day thereafter.

"Abby, ask him if he can sit down for a few minutes on the scaffolding. Tell him that you've got two bottles of water in your jacket because you were going to run."

Abby absentmindedly reached into her jacket pocket and found two bottles of water. Where the hell did they come from? Had she put the bottles into her jacket before she left the house and not remembered it?

"Mom, where did the water come from?" Abby spoke in more of a whisper, or at least tried. It was difficult to speak softly when it came to the conversations between her and her mother.

Fannie smiled. "Oh, for the love of God, Abby, sometimes you can be so annoying. Who cares at this moment in time where the water came from—just talk to him, would you?"

"Hey, Rick, can you sit down for a few minutes while we're talking? I've got a couple bottles of water with me, and I thought maybe you would like a drink. Please just step back and sit down for a minute."

"It doesn't matter if I'm thirsty when I jump."

Good point for his side. Abby could see Rick look down at her and Tina. She could certainly understand the pain, but she wanted him to try to look beyond it. "Mom, how do I answer that?"

"Tell him that you're not through talking to him and that, for a lawyer, he hasn't done a very good job of convincing you that it's the right thing if he jumps."

"Mom, I was looking for words of wisdom, not sarcasm. Suppose he says he doesn't care if I'm convinced."

"Abby, you don't know what he's going to answer you until he actually answers you. Tell him what I said."

"Rick, look, I think a few minutes of talking one way or the other isn't going to matter, so just humor me. Frankly, you haven't done a good job of convincing me it's the right thing to jump." Abby finished talking and held her breath, hoping Fannie was right and she wasn't baiting him to jump.

Rick was beginning to get agitated. "You know, you're really a pain in the ass. This isn't some oral argument that I have to win. I guess you didn't hear me before; I want to be with my family and be left alone."

Abby wasn't sure if she heard him exhale or if she just wanted to hear it. "I get that, but now is not the time. You have other family and friends who love you."

Rick sat down and realized how tired he was. His thoughts were like a deck of cards that had been tossed in the air, leaving his memories of the past scattered. And why is this woman here? Nothing made sense. He tried to swallow and lick his lips, but his mouth was dry. He realized he had been sweating, a lot. Am I rational? The next thing he said was "Do you think you can throw one of those bottles up to me?" His mind flashed back to the question of his own rationality: I guess not, since I'm asking for water when there's plenty below, he thought.

"No matter how strong I am, even if I had an arm like the Packers quarterback, Aaron Rogers, I couldn't throw a bottle that high."

"Then just forget it."

"No, I'm gonna bring you up a water!"

Abby said, "Fuck, Mom, now that I said that I actually have to get my ass up there and bring him the water." She added, "Rick, whether you like it or not, I'm coming up there."

Fannie answered her, "Now, Abby, don't get testy, and watch your language. It's not that high up. You're a great athlete, and you have wonderful balance. I can remember how good you were at gymnastics on the balance beam."

"Mom, that was more than forty years ago, and the balance beam was a couple of feet off the ground. It didn't matter if I fell off. It certainly will matter if I fall off the bridge, don't you think? I hadn't planned to join you in the afterlife quite this soon, or do you want me there now?"

"Abby, I'm telling you, you'll be fine. You have an opening now with him. You have to take it."

"Mom, can't you just bring the water to him for me? I really don't want to go up there. You're already dead, so it won't matter if you fall. Do you catch my drift here?"

"Abby, remember you already said you'd go up there. I know you can do this, and he needs you. You've got to try. He won't be able to see or hear me, anyway. Besides, imagine how freaked out he'd be if he thought he was talking to someone on the other side."

"And what makes you think I'm not freaked out by all this dead mother chatter?" She then cast her voice back up above her. "Hey, Rick, I told you: no matter how good an arm I have, I'm not going to be able to throw this bottle high enough to reach you. It would make a lot more sense if you came down, had some water, and we continued talking."

"I came here to jump because my life is over without Jennifer and Adam, and that's what I'm going to do."

As Abby started for the side of the bridge, she said, "Mom, just to refresh your very short memory, it was Donna, your only other daughter, who was the much better gymnast. Remember, I was the swimmer! Why don't you just go find Donna and talk to her from the dead? Get her to go up on the bridge."

"Now, Abby, you're just being snotty. Go ahead. Start climbing. And to quote Dr. Seuss, 'Today is your day; your mountain is waiting, so get on your way."

"My mountain...what...Dr. Seuss of all people? What's next—*The Cat in the Hat*?" Abby turned her head in disgust. "I can't believe this. All right, I'll go, but I don't have to like it—shit! I'm not sure it's the right thing to do. I don't want him to jump because I went up there to give him a bottle of water he didn't want in the first place." She added again,

"Rick, stay where you are." "Yeah, like he's going somewhere else, other than jump. Really brilliant," Abby thought to herself. No response from above. Abby said under her breath, "Please, God, don't let him jump. And please don't let me fall!"

Abby got to the side of the bridge and took a deep breath. The first step made her realize she was really doing this. She was climbing up the side of the bridge, above the river, to get close to a jumper she had never met until about forty-five minutes ago. Abby thought, "Why am I listening to my dead mother now when I never listened to her when she was alive? Why is she talking to me now in my head?"

Fannie answered her, "Because I can."

As Abby took the first huge step and hoisted herself up, Tina started barking furiously again. Tina had stopped barking when Fannie was talking with Abby. She was almost sure Tina could hear Fannie as well. Abby looked at her watch, hoping somebody would come by soon, really soon. Abby turned her head and looked over her shoulder as she called down to Tina, "I'm OK; settle down. It's OK—all right, girl. Sit, wait." Tina did exactly that. She sat...and she waited, never taking her eyes off Abby.

Abby was actually thinking to herself that she had to just put one foot in front of the other and pay attention to where each foot was going. Don't look down; look up. Her breathing was a little ragged. She knew she wasn't out of shape because she could run three miles and not be winded. It had to be the fear and adrenaline. Her hands began to hurt, and she realized she was gripping the heavy wire cables so tightly that she was white-knuckled. Her arms began to fatigue from pulling herself upward and forward. She certainly had a newfound respect for all those bridge workers. They must have nerves of steel and be half crazy—no, maybe all the way crazy.

Abby couldn't stop the thoughts that were zooming around in her brain. She wondered why this bridge didn't have more safety precautions and why it was so easy for people to have access to climb the bridge. Her brain also noted with particular clarity that she had never climbed up a bridge, and more importantly, she didn't have on a safety harness.

Ironically, despite the fact that Abby was climbing higher on the bridge, the sounds from ground level intensified. She could distinctly hear the sound of the rushing water even though it was so far below her. She could hear the sounds of a few cars and the low rumbling of the trucks on Route 59, a few miles away. Why were there no cars on this bridge tonight? It reminded her of all the sounds she heard when she was hot air ballooning in Colorado. Abby would much rather have been hot air ballooning, than be on this bridge. Frankly, she would rather have been anywhere else than where she was now.

Abby could hear her heart pounding. She also noticed that it was far windier up here than it had been on the bridge deck. It felt as if the temperature had dropped fifteen degrees, and it was bordering on cold, but it didn't stop the beads of sweat starting to form around her temples. What was ragged breathing a few minutes ago had now become heaving breaths. The droplets of sweat made it feel as if she had tiny bugs crawling down her cheeks. Fear can do a lot to the human body.

Rick was standing on the stanchion, still far above Abby and her climb, imprisoned in his own misery. Thoughts were still swirling in his head like a raging tornado that left only a bottomless abyss. He was mourning for the life he once had.

Abby took another step, and then her foot slipped. Simple as that—her foot slipped. She didn't know what it slipped on or if her foot caught on something. It took a fraction of a second, but to her it felt like the proverbial slow-motion scene in the movies. The next thing she knew she was over the edge of the bridge and hanging on literally for dear life. She screamed and screamed again. Tina went into a frenzy of barking, but it sounded far away.

Rick was startled from his trance by a piercing scream. It came from somewhere below him.

Abby was trying to get a toehold on something to pull herself up and back onto the railing and stanchion. There was nothing there. If her heart had been pounding before from adrenaline, it was nothing to what was happening now. She felt as if she had gotten a jolt of electricity into her heart. Her body perceived the danger nanoseconds before her brain processed it and went into warp speed. She could also feel the pain above her eye. For a minute, she thought it was just sweat. From the thickness and taste, she realized it was blood.

All of a sudden, her brain kicked back in, and rational thought began to take shape through the adrenaline haze. How long could she last dangling over the edge of a bridge and hanging on by her arms? Her shoulders felt as though there were tearing at the joint from grabbing the suspension cable to prevent her fall. There would certainly come a moment when her strength would give out, and she would plunge to her death. Abby was totally and completely terrorized by the thought of eventually letting go and falling. It didn't seem possible that she could be even more terrorized by the thought of falling to her death, but she was. Abby heard screaming, and she realized she was the one doing the screaming. She tried again desperately to get a toehold so that she could have something to push off against or support herself so all her body weight was not hanging solely by her arms. Nothing. Come on, come on. Still nothing, oh please God! "Please don't let me die!" she screamed.

Rick started yelling, "Abby, oh my God, Abby!" Abby could distinguish the terror in his voice, too.

"Rick, help me! I can't pull myself back up."

"Abby, hang on!" Rick screamed, as he cupped his hands around his mouth. "I'm coming down to get you. Hang on. I'm not going to let you die."

"Abby, hold on; it's only going to be a few seconds until Rick gets to you. Focus. Think of how strong you are. You can do this; I know you can."

"Abby, I'm coming. Don't let go. I'm coming as fast as I can."

Abby didn't know how long it took for Rick to get to her. It could have been several seconds, or it could have been a few minutes since Abby was more than halfway up to the top when she slipped.

Abby saw Rick before she felt him. He was about three feet away, and he started to bend over and get himself into a prone position so that he was lying down on the ramp. Abby realized he was trying to give himself as much leverage as he could to pull her up without his being dragged over the side of the bridge.

She felt a huge hand grab her arm. He started going hand over hand on her arm, then grabbed the back of her sweatshirt to hoist her up. Eventually, he got enough of her upper torso raised up so that she could fall over onto the stanchion. They both lay there for a few seconds gasping for air.

"You OK? Did you break anything when you fell? You have a big gash on your forehead."

Abby felt her forehead with her left hand. She could feel the good-size gash the fall had given her and the thick blood oozing from it. Even reaching up to touch the gash made her arm feel like lead.

"I'm OK…I think. I need to stay here for a few minutes to catch my breath."

"You're bleeding pretty badly from the gash. You don't feel it? You may be going into shock."

He reached into his pants pocket and took out a wad of tissues. "Hold them up to your forehead and see if you can stop the bleeding."

"Thanks, Rick. I really don't know how long I could have lasted. You saved my life. I couldn't pull myself up."

"Don't mention it. You wouldn't have been climbing up on the bridge in the first place if I hadn't been up at the top. You stopped me; you saved my life."

"Look, it's OK, if we can make it down together the rest of the way. We *are* going down the rest of the way together, aren't we? I'm not too sure I'm so steady on my feet after this."

"Yeah, we'll go down together. Any chance you still have that water?"

"Well, believe it or not, I still have one bottle left. The other bottle must have taken a dive into the water like we almost did. Want some?"

They each took a swig of water and looked at each other up close for the first time. He was handsome, with chiseled features, but there was a tired and profoundly sad aura that seemed to permeate his whole being, and rightly so. Now that Abby was sitting right next to him and looking at him full face, there was something about him that looked so familiar. He evoked something in her memory...something that she couldn't quite place. There were fleeting thoughts that ran through her mind, but she couldn't seem to put them in any order that made sense. They sat there for a time in silence.

"Let's start down now. I've had enough of heights for today and probably the rest of my life. Rick, why don't you lead the way down? If you look over there to the east, you can see the sky is beginning to lighten. The sun will be up soon, and you've lived to see it. I guess there's a reason we're both here for the start of this new day."

Abby noticed that the sky was turning from a deep sapphire to subtle golden and pink hues. She was so happy that this night was coming to a close. Darkness was giving way to light. Maybe some of the darkness and pain Rick felt was giving way to a ray of hope in his life.

As they both reached the bridge deck, Tina bounded over to Abby and she knelt down on one knee and hugged her around the neck, thankful to be alive. They were, as they say, on terra firma.

Abby could see the pain etched in Rick's face as she looked at him standing next to her. Words were not going to be enough. The only thing she could do was hug him, not just because she thought he needed it, but because she needed a hug as well. He hugged her back. Rick let go of Abby for a moment and looked at her. "I kept telling you I don't have any reason to go on living. Everyone I love the most is dead."

Abby took Rick's hand, and they sat down on the concrete and metal decking of the bridge. "That's not true! Look, Rick, I almost got killed up there a few minutes ago. I keep telling you that I was meant to be here, in this very place tonight for some reason. That reason was you were not meant to die. I know your wife and son didn't want you to die...because they love you. They wouldn't want you to feel this way. You will find another reason or purpose to gather your strength to move on. Rick, I didn't want you to die." With that Tina came over to Rick and laid her head in his lap, and looked up at him with her big brown eyes. As they all sat there together, Abby put her arm around Rick's shoulder. She knew that words were not going to comfort him at this point, but she hoped this simple gesture would.

In a few minutes, Abby heard the wail of the sirens. At first, the sound was faint, but then she realized that the police and the EMTs were getting much closer. She told him that he would be OK, and she would be there if he needed her. Help had arrived. She let the two EMTs walk him toward a gurney. They sat him down on the gurney and covered him with a blanket. Rick looked at Abby, but his eyes looked tired and almost vacant.

"Rick, it's going to be OK. Let them take care of you." She was walked over to the gurney to be near him.

Abby barely got the sentence out, when one of the other EMTs came over to her and asked about the cut on her forehead. She explained how it happened and told him she was all right. He insisted on cleaning the wound and putting on a butterfly bandage to help keep the wound closed until they got to the emergency room.

The trooper walked over to Abby and said he'd like to talk to her and take her statement. The trooper asked, "Are you related to this young man? What's his name?"

Abby realized that she had saved this young man's life, and she didn't even know something as basic as his last name or how old he was.

The trooper continued asking a series of questions about Rick. She answered to the best of her ability. Abby saw the EMTs hoist the gurney into the ambulance. Finally, the questions ceased, and Abby began feel very weary.

Abby knew she should call her daughter, Maizie, to let her know what had happened. She also thought she should call her friend Denise to come get Tina.

As tired as Abby was, she asked the trooper the question about how they knew to come to the bridge. The trooper said that someone heard some loud screaming and barking coming from the vicinity of the bridge and called 911.

Fannie said to Abby, "There are some discoveries about your past you will uncover as the result of your connection to Rick."

Abby moved a few feet away from the troopers and all the commotion so that she could answer her Mother. "So what's the discovery and connection, Mom?"

"Just remember that the choices we make each day determine the lives we live."

"And what the hell is that supposed to mean...you sound like a fortune cookie. Mom, if you weren't already dead, I'd have to kill you."

CHAPTER 7

The door opened to the room in the hospital where Rick was sitting. A short, but not too short, black man walked in carrying a tablet and a yellow legal pad. He walked over to the client chair that Rick was sitting in and held out his hand. "Mr. Singleton, I'm Dr. Torrey Burke. I'm one of the attending physicians, and I've been asked to speak to you." Once they shook hands, Dr. Burke walked around to the far side of the desk and sat down. He took out a pen from his jacket pocket and put it on top of the legal pad.

For some bizarre reason, Rick wondered why the doctor had a yellow legal pad instead of the white legal pads they used in the firm to be environmentally conscious. What a stupid thing to think about, Rick thought to himself, at this particular moment in his life when he had tried to kill himself.

"Can I call you Rich or Richard?" Dr. Burke asked.

"You can call me Rick."

"OK, Rick, would you please tell me what happened?"

As Rick started to tell Dr. Burke about Jennifer and Adam, he got a few sentences out before he choked back tears. Dr. Burke listened attentively and nodded his head as he made some notes. He let Rick catch his breath a few times as Rick tried to continue. At one point, Dr. Burke got up from the desk and walked over to a shelf and grabbed a tissue box and handed it gently to Rick.

Rick wasn't sure how long the session had lasted, but it reminded him of the tea kettle they had on the stove in their kitchen. All of a sudden, the kettle seemed to come alive as the steam came screeching out of the spout. This was what he felt was happening to him in the session. The "kettle" started boiling over, and he was spewing out the pain of his loss to Dr. Burke.

Abby wasn't sure if going to see Rick in the hospital was the right thing to do. For some unknown reason, she felt strangely responsible for Rick. She might have had it wrong. In some cultures, the person whose life is saved is indebted to the person who saved him for the rest of their lives. Abby seemed to have it backward, because she felt she needed to reach out to him and make the first move. She couldn't explain it, but she now felt responsible for him. Would he want to see her? Would she be the visible reminder of a night that he might want to forget? Would he actually be pleased that she had stopped him from plummeting to his death? Was his pain any less now? Would death have been a release from that pain?

Abby waited about three days, and she wrestled with those questions the whole time. She often spoke out loud to her mother. "Mom, can you help me out here? Do you think I should go see Rick or will it make things worse?" Abby asked herself the question over and over without coming to a definitive answer. She asked Fannie the same questions over and over as well, but Fannie wasn't exactly being forthcoming. Quite the contrary, if Fannie knew the answer, she wasn't talking, at least to Abby.

"Hey, Mom, how about just giving me a sign? Something—anything would be good. I know you can do that." That must have been the right way to phrase it, because Fannie did give Abby a sign.

Abby was absentmindedly flipping through her mail, lost in her thoughts, when something jolted her. There staring her in the face was a flyer for a new business. It read, "J&R Flooring," and in smaller print at the bottom, "Rick and Jen Olsen, Owners."

"OK, Mom, that was a pretty direct answer. I'll go see Rick on Friday."

When Friday rolled around, Abby was much more certain that it was the right thing to do to go see Rick, and not just because of the flyer in the mail. She wasn't sure if he was having a lot of visitors because he had never answered the question she asked him that night on the bridge whether his parents or Jennifer's parents were still alive. Abby didn't know if he had siblings or a ton of good friends. She wasn't sure how, or even if, he'd agree to see her, but Abby was determined to try. Even though she had been through such an intense situation with Rick, she hadn't bothered to ask his full name, but as she watched Rick being shepherded in to the ambulance, she overheard Rick tell the EMT his name.

Abby pulled the car into a parking space not far from the door of the hospital and got out. It was a beautiful day with the sun warming the earth and the cumulus clouds so large that they looked like enormous cotton balls clearly defined against the blue sky. Abby turned to Tina to say she didn't know what the rules of the hospital were and whether she could come in. "The windows are rolled down, so there's lots of fresh air. You stay, and I'll be back." Abby gave Tina some water, her chew toy and a big scratchy pat on the head. Abby walked toward the front entrance of the hospital with a box filled with her famous homemade chocolate chip cookies in one hand and two paperbacks in the other. Would he like the food for the mind or the food for the body, or maybe both? Abby really knew so little about him, and he about her, yet she did feel somehow connected. This visit could prove incredibly interesting, or it could be an unmitigated disaster. She would know soon enough.

Tina gave Abby that "I'll be patient look" as Abby left her in the car and walked purposefully toward the building.

Abby walked up to the front desk and asked the receptionist if she could see Rick Singleton. The receptionist asked for her name, and Abby realized she didn't know how to identify herself.

"I'm his friend, Abby." God, she hoped he thought that was right, and he thought she was his friend.

"I'll call him. Why don't you just have a seat and give him a minute."

As Abby went to sit down on the floral print sofa, she wondered whether he was free to wander around on his own, or whether he would appear with an attendant, sort of like something from *One Flew over the Cuckoo's Nest*.

In less than five minutes, the door to the left of the receptionist opened, and out walked Rick in a pair of navy blue sweatpants, and a white T-shirt with a picture of Michael Phelps in four different colors on the front. He had a towel around his neck, and his sandy blond hair looked wet, as if he had been working out. His eyes darted around the reception area until he saw Abby, and then his face lit up.

"Abby, I couldn't believe when they said it was you who was here. It's so good to see you on level ground." And with that he gave her a smirk and walked over to hug her. "How's the gash on your forehead? I can see you still have stitches."

"I get the stitches out tomorrow. The plastic surgeon said that he doesn't think there will be much of a scar left. I really thought I was going to be a dead ringer for Harry Potter. Now all I need are those glasses."

Rick said, "It really doesn't look that bad."

"I'm glad you're telling me it doesn't look bad. I brought you a few goodies. I wasn't quite sure of your taste in novels or food. I took a shot. Hope you like them."

"Wow, thanks. How about we go inside and get a cup of coffee in the coffee shop? It's pretty nice for the nuthouse."

He led Abby down a long corridor with brightly colored paintings on the walls. They made a left turn and walked through a set of double doors into the coffee shop. The décor was a cross between Starbucks and Dunkin' Donuts as if whoever decorated it couldn't decide what they wanted it to be. Maybe the decorator in the hospital was schizophrenic, Abby thought to herself. Could this be hospital humor?

They each got a cup of coffee and sat down at a booth by the window that overlooked a garden. It didn't look as sterile as the typical hospital cafeteria, with plastic everything. It had some wooden tables and chairs and the sun streamed in from the skylights and big windows. The garden was well manicured, and the landscaper had a good eye for color and shape.

"Here, I brought you some of my homemade chocolate chip cookies. They're the best – if I do say so myself. They're quite a job to make, because shelling enough pistachios to make the cookies takes forever. Fresh is best when it comes to the ingredients for my cookies. I make about seven hundred cookies for Christmas each year. The number just keeps growing. You're lucky this is the fall, so you didn't have to be on a waiting list. Oh, God, I'm droning on and I don't mean to."

"Abby, you're not droning on. This was so nice of you to think of me and come see me, and then to top it off, you bring one of my favorites. It's a good thing that they have a workout room here, or, speaking of Christmas, I'd be looking like Santa. The food isn't all that bad either. But with these cookies, I'll have to work out twelve hours a day."

"No segue here, but I was wondering if you saw the article in the local new about us? I'm sure that's not going to go over too well with the partners in my law firm. Won't be good for the image of the firm."

Abby replied, "I saw it, too. Sometimes these things have a way of blowing over. I'm sure you're a good lawyer, and the firm will want to keep a good lawyer like you. So am I allowed to ask you how you're doing, or is that against some rule?"

"Actually, it depends. It depends on a lot of things, like the day, what I'm talking to the psychiatrist about, and how I'm doing with the medication. It's better living through chemistry."

"I can see a difference in you already from the night at the bridge. You look better. I hope you feel that way, too."

"Sometimes I feel like I'm going to be swallowed up by the pain, like it's some monster. When I first wake up, I think everyone is OK and everything was as it used to be. Then I realize why I'm here and what happened."

Abby leaned across the table and gently laid her hand on top of his forearm. "It's a myth that time heals all wounds. It doesn't, but time will allow you to reflect and gain perspective. You won't always think of the accident, but you will begin to remember all the joy and laughter that you shared with Jennifer and Adam."

"Thanks for being here and for saying those words. I only hope they come true."

"If you don't mind my asking a personal question, do you have any siblings? What about your parents? You haven't told me anything about the rest of your family."

"My parents are deceased, but I have an older brother, Jason, who lives in Saddle River, New Jersey. He's an architect. We grew up in London and lived there for fifteen years when I was a kid, right near your name sake, Abbey Road."

"I'm sorry about your parents," said Abby quietly. "Where do you live?"

"I live in Alpine, New Jersey. Not too bad a commute to New York City, but as I said, I doubt I'll go back to the firm. Hell, knowing them, they wouldn't even want me back. Not the image that the firm wants to project that one of the lawyers wanted to off himself. The doctor says that I'll probably be discharged in a few days. Going home will be tough because it's not going to feel like home anymore. Everything in that house will be a reminder of Jennifer and Adam—that's the reality of it. That's one of the things I need to figure out. Where else can I go except home...at least for now?"

"What about your brother? Can you stay with him for a while?"

"Jason has been up to see me a few times already. We're pretty close. He offered to let me stay with him and his family. I'm considering it, but he has a wife and two kids. I'm not sure how that's going to work either. I don't know if I feel up to the organized chaos in his house. Everything takes a lot of effort for me. I guess I'll figure it out soon enough."

"So where do you live, Abby?"

"I live in Rivertown. I've lived there for most of my life except for the years we lived in Colorado. I mostly raised the kids in Rivertown. My daughter, Maizie, now lives in Stamford and works in White Plains as a paralegal. Single, but always looking. My son, Scott, lives in Boston doing a residency in orthopedics. It's a long haul, but he's a smart guy and very determined."

"I remember your saying that your husband passed away? Can I ask what happened?"

"Jerry died fifteen years ago of pancreatic cancer. We were told he would have about three to six months, but he was gone in about a month. Three weeks, six days. In his case, everything happened so fast after the diagnosis, and the tumors kept growing throughout his body. I still miss him very much. I always will."

Rick said in a soft voice, "I'm sorry."

"You don't forget; you just go on."

Just as they were about to leave the coffee shop, in walked a young man in a suit with his tie open. He walked right over to their table, and Rick got up to hug him.

Rick turned toward Abby and said, "Abby, this is my brother, Jason. Jason, this is Abby."

Jason extended his hand and a warm smile to Abby, but it was clear that Jason was trying to place who she was.

Abby said to him, "It's nice to meet you. Rick was just filling me in on the family." Abby frankly didn't know what to tell Jason about who she was, because she wasn't sure what Rick had already told him or planned to tell him.

Rick saw the quizzical look on Jason's face; it was obvious that Jason couldn't place Abby at all.

Rick said, "Abby is the person who found me on the bridge and managed to convince me that the quickest way down off the bridge was not the best one."

Jason gave Abby another smile and said, "You must be his guardian angel. In any case, I'm really, really glad to meet you, and that you came along when you did. Both of us don't know how to thank you enough."

"I was in the right place at the right time. If the truth be known, we literally saved each other in more ways than one."

"No, that's being way too modest from what Rick tells me. It's also so good of you to come to see him. Let me get a cup of coffee, and I'll be right back."

Jason returned with a huge Styrofoam cup of coffee in hand and sat down. Rick said, "It's only because he drove all this way to see me that I'm going to give him one, and only one, of your cookies, Abby."

Jason looked at the assortment of cookies and snatched two. "I'm still your older brother. I get to have more. I'm taking two cookies just to spite him."

Jason wolfed down the cookies and most of the coffee in a very short space of time. He looked haggard, too. As Abby watched him across the table, it appeared that Rick's crisis had taken a toll on him as well. Jason was not as tall as Rick and perhaps a little heftier. Rick had lost some weight over the last several weeks since the fatal crash. Rick said that he had been working out to try to exhaust himself so that he could get some sleep. Jason had wavy, dark hair and light brown eyes. All in all, quite nice looking, but there didn't seem to be very much of a family resemblance.

"Listen, Bro, since Abby is here, I am going to cut out early, if that's OK with you. I have to submit the renderings to the client first thing in the morning. I'll be back tomorrow in the late afternoon."

Rick appeared to be OK with that.

Jason shook Abby's hand and said again how grateful he was to her. He gave her a quick hug and said, "I hope this is not the last time I see you, Abby."

"I hope not, too. Rick is lucky to have a brother like you who makes the trek to see him every day, when you seem to have a full plate."

Rick gave Jason a hug, and Jason was like a blur as he left the coffee shop.

"I'll call you tonight, Rick," he tossed over his shoulder.

"Now that the whirling dervish is gone, let's go outside. I just have to sign out."

Fannie was sitting at an adjacent table watching what was going on and listening intently to the conversation among Rick, Abby and Jason. She was in one of her "states" where she could see what was going on, yet no one else knew she was there. She was pleasantly surprised to see how well he looked today. It was just good to see him. It's amazing how fast time passes, yet she would have recognized him anywhere. She also thought, it was a shame—so close and yet so far.

A few days later Rick was signed out of the hospital for good.

CHAPTER 8

Rick walked through the parking lot to the psychiatrist's office. He was glad to be out of the hospital, but so many thoughts continued to haunt him. "Does time really heal all wounds? I fucking doubt it. There are more whys and what ifs than there are answers. I know I need to go on; I want to, but the fucking guilt—*stop...*" he thought. As Rick waited in the anteroom of the doctor's office, he looked at his watch, and as the number turned to 10:00 a.m., the door to the office opened, and Dr. Burke came out. "Morning, Rick, come on in."

Dr. Burke was impeccably dressed, as when Rick had first seen him in the hospital. Dr. Burke had on a navy blue blazer and a light blue shirt with a blue and black tie. He was a soft spoken man with dark brown eyes. Rick realized that Dr. Burke was younger than he had originally thought. Rick pegged him to be about forty-five years old. Rick laughed to himself every time he saw Dr. Burke. When Rick was told originally he was going to meet with Dr. Burke, Rick was expecting a redheaded Irishman. Rick was totally taken aback when they first met, since the doctor was a good-looking black man. Maybe there was some hidden Irish lineage back in time.

Rick walked into the office, which was a good size and was clearly less Spartan than the room where Rick had first met with the doctor, and this office had some personal touches. The interview room where Rick had first met with Dr. Burke in the hospital was the epitome of sterile. Rick's eyes wandered around the office for a few seconds and saw a few abstract paintings, a signed Ansel Adams print, and a pair of basketball pictures of the glory days of the Knicks. On the table next to the doctor's chair was a picture of a set of twin boys decked out in Little League uniforms and a second picture of an older girl in a soccer uniform, presumably the Burke kids. The picture of the twins made Rick swallow a lump in his throat, thinking that he would never see Adam in a Little League uniform. The doctor had followed Rick's eyes to the pictures, and he said, "I get some very interesting comments when people see the pictures. Sometimes it surprises me what people say. Your eyes have said it all. Do you want to talk about Adam? How do you feel this morning?"

"I feel lousy. I'm exhausted, yet I can't sleep. I close my eyes, and all I can visualize is Adam and Jennifer pinned inside the car and screaming for help. I should have been there!" And then more softly, he said, as if to himself, "I should have been there."

The doctor looked at Rick and said gently, "How could you possibly have known that something terrible was going to happen? We all go in the car literally thousands of times each year, and we get to our destinations without anything happening. No one could have predicted anything like this. It was a nice day in the summer, no snow or rain. The other driver had a heart attack."

"It doesn't matter. If I had been there, I could have saved them."

"Not necessarily so, Rick. You could have been pinned in the car, too, or you could have been dead yourself. You could have been knocked unconscious and not been able to help yourself or them."

"But suppose I wasn't pinned or dead. I could have gotten them out of the car."

"You don't know that, Rick. You're torturing yourself with 'maybe' or 'might have.' No one knows what would have happened."

Rick didn't answer; he put his head between his hands.

Dr. Burke let a few more seconds elapse and then continued, "Rick, whether you know it or not, you're asking the question humankind has asked since we were able to reason. Why do bad things happen to good people? It doesn't matter if you're a religious person or not."

Rick looked up from where his head had been between his hands.

Dr. Burke continued, "Probably every priest, rabbi, minister, Buddhist monk, shaman, guru and philosopher who ever lived have asked this very question. Unfortunately, I don't think the smartest people on the face of the earth have ever had an answer to it. It seems to be a hazard of being a part of the human race. It's something that rears its ugly head, and we have to live with it."

"Great, just great. Now we're talking philosophy. This isn't some abstract philosophical theory; this was my wife and son we're talking about!" he said through clenched teeth.

Dr. Burke held Rick's gaze through the outburst. A few long seconds ensued with neither of them saying anything. Finally, Dr. Burke said very slowly and very quietly, "I get it that this is not some abstract problem. I know this is very painful for you. You can beat yourself up, or you can choose to live on."

The sessions continued. Rick struggled with survivor's guilt. Why had he been spared and Jennifer and Adam hadn't? Why had he been called back to work, which ironically saved him?

The sessions continued. Some days good, some days bad, some days they laughed a little over some funny things that had happened, and other days Rick cried or raged at life. But the sessions continued, and Dr. Burke was able to see the progress before Rick did. Finally, one day Rick realized that there were more good days than bad days, and the bad days weren't as bad as they once had been.

After seeing Dr. Burke for a number of months, one day Rick mentioned the name "Maizie." It was the first time that a ray of sunlight was peeking through the darkness. At first Rick was tentative about even mentioning her. Ironically, with the ray of sunlight came another round of survivor's guilt. How could he possibly go on with his life and be happy with another woman? Wasn't this disloyal to Jennifer? Was he allowed to be happy? How could he be happy with Jennifer and Adam in their graves?

Questions, always more questions. And the sessions continued.

CHAPTER 9

About three weeks had passed since Abby's visit to Rick at the hospital, and to be honest, she was glad that her life had settled back to what she had come to know as normal. She was back in the routine of working with her clients, going out with friends, and seeing her daughter, Maizie, who called regularly and came for dinner once a week, sometimes with friends and sometimes by herself. Abby's son, Scott, always seemed to be on duty as an orthopedic resident, so their conversations were brief and not nearly as frequent as she would have liked. Abby sent him care packages on a regular basis, and while he did protest that he was no longer a kid away at summer camp, he also mentioned in the next breath that he loved the cookies. Abby derived tremendous satisfaction from baking, and since her cookies were such a hit with people, it was a way to stay connected to friends and family not within striking distance. Scott could never seem to choose a favorite, so he always got a big assortment. It did occur to Abby that not choosing a favorite might have just been a ploy to get a bigger container of cookies. She always felt that Mrs. Fields had beaten her to the punch but Abby felt her chocolate chip cookies were far superior.

Abby learned to cook at an early age, especially from her grandmother, whom she always called "Nana." Nana was her mother's mother, to be distinguished from her father's mother, whom she called "Other Nana," even to her face. Nana was conscious of the environment long before it was fashionable. She grew her own fruits and vegetables, and Abby was a somewhat willing participant in going to pick the raspberries, because she would be rewarded with Nana's warm raspberry bread pudding.

Abby came home from seeing clients one day and saw the light blinking contentedly on her home answering machine. She had been particularly busy with clients and was glad that it was her answering machine at home with messages and not her business phone. She flipped through the mail, fed Tina and the cats, and brewed herself a cup of mint tea. The first message was from the dentist's office confirming her appointment, but it was the second message that made her stop short and pay attention.

"Hi, Abby, it's Rick. I'm calling to say hi and tell you I'm out of the hospital. I thought I'd ask if I could go for a run with you and Tina. Give me a call back when you get a chance. "Bye." Click.

Abby somewhat surprised herself because she could feel the smile widening on her face. His voice sounded animated and not flat. That certainly was a good sign. She knew she had taken a chance going to the hospital unannounced and that he might have chosen not to see her. Even if he saw her at the hospital, that might have been enough for him. She listened to the message again to check her original thesis that he did sound better.

CHAPTER 10

Abby brushed the grill clean and cleared the dishes, which went into the dishwasher, and she pushed the start button. Abby sat down on the couch and grabbed the remote control and turned on the television. She dialed Rick's number and waited. A little flutter of anxiety flashed over her. What was that about? After a few rings, his voicemail clicked in. She left him a message with both her home and cell phone numbers. As she hung up, she made a mental note that she was leaving a message on his cell phone and not at his house. She presumed that meant he had not gone back to live at home. Was he staying at Jason's house?

About an hour later, the phone rang and interrupted Abby's multitasking, which included watching television, reading a novel, and playing with Tina and the cats. It was Maizie.

"Hi, Mom, it's me. You sound tired. What's happening?"

"Hi, honey. Yeah, I am tired. It was a long day; I had quite a few clients today all wanting me to give them a miracle cure for their financial woes. What's going on with you?"

"Not much. I just came back from taking a yoga class."

Abby asked, as she always did, "So, any 'eligibles' at the gym?"

It was good-natured bantering that had been going on forever. Abby always teased Maizie about it, and Maizie usually gave evasive answers. Abby heard an exasperated sigh on the other end of the phone.

"Mom, I told you, when I have something to tell you, I will. When Mr. Right comes along, I'll certainly let you know when we set a date for the wedding."

"OK, OK, you're Ms. Independent. I understand that. I would, however, like to know *before* you set the wedding date because I could be busy."

"Then you'd just have to miss the wedding."

Maizie would best be described as "vibrant colors." Think of flaming reds, sun-drenched yellows, and bold blues. The palette of colors described not only her show-stopping attire, but the colors also reflected her personality.

"Who raised such a smartass liberated woman? It certainly couldn't have been me. Want to come for dinner on Tuesday?"

They chatted about a few more things, and Maizie said Tuesday would be fine for dinner.

"Let me know on Monday if you have a craving for something for dinner. Love you."

"Love you, too, Mom. Bye."

It was getting late, and Abby headed upstairs to go to bed, with Tina in tow. Scott said it was the three-foot rule. Tina was never more than three feet away from Abby. It occurred to her as she was brushing her teeth that Rick had not called back. That was good. Maybe he was out and doing something fun.

CHAPTER 11

It was about nine thirty in the morning when Abby returned from her spin class. She was barely able to make her way from the front door to the kitchen with all the weaving in and out, in order not to step on the fur balls, a/k/a, the cats. This was retribution for not having fed them before she left for class. Tina greeted Abby and ran for her food bowl and sat down with patience written all over her. Abby went to the kitchen pantry and retrieved a couple of cans of cat food and a container of beef and rice from the refrigerator for Tina.

"All right, you guys, if you trip me and I fall down, you'll be waiting a lot longer for your food. You understand? Feisty, get off the counter!" Abby often wondered how and when she became known as the dog and cat woman of the neighborhood. Oh well, she thought, she could be called worse.

Abby was finally able to wrestle the cans open and fill the bowls, and all were happy. She was headed for the shower when the phone rang. She had one hand on the refrigerator door to get a bottle of water and grabbed the phone with the other, not paying very much attention.

"Hi, Abby, it's Rick. I'm glad I caught you. I wasn't sure how early I could call you without waking you up, and then I figured it might be too late and you'd left for work."

"Well, your sense of timing is impeccable. Not only did you catch me before I went to work, you probably caught me on the only day this week I don't have to leave early. I just came back from a spin class. So how are you doing?"

"OK, I know I sound like a walking cliché, but it's one day at a time. I was calling to see if I could take up your offer to go for a run. I've been running so much lately by myself that you'd think my iPod was growing out of my ears."

"Well, I know a good audiologist you can see for the iPod ailment. Seriously, I'd love to go for a run with you. Thursday is a good day for me."

Rick countered, "Let me see if I can squeeze you in to my extremely busy schedule. Yep, I can definitely squeeze you in. Where should we go? Where do you like to run?"

"How about around the reservoir? I'll meet you at the entrance where they have the huge boulder with the sign in front."

He wasn't sure where that was, so Abby gave him directions.

Abby went upstairs to take a shower, and Tina bounded up the stairs behind her. As Abby was about to walk into the bedroom, she turned because she thought she saw something out of the corner of her eye. Maybe it was just the way the sunlight was coming through the windows. Tina stopped and cocked her head to the side.

"Hi, Abby, it's Mom."

"Jesus, Mom, you scared the shit out of me. What are you doing here? No one's up on a bridge, no one's dropping water bottles in a raging river, and no one's falling over the edge of a bridge to their death. This is hardly enough excitement for you."

"Abby, Abby, Abby—you are always so cynical. I would think that you'd be happy to hear from me. Dead mothers visiting their daughters is not exactly a common phenomenon, and people are generally thrilled. Especially since what I told you the night on the bridge is coming true. Somehow I get the sense that you, on the other hand, would rather have a root canal than a visit from me, your Beloved Mother." Abby made a face in response.

"OK, Abby, now I'm being serious. You helped Rick when he was in the midst of a crisis, and you're helping him again in a much less dramatic way. That should make you feel good. Well, you're going running with him, aren't you? That's a good start."

"Mom, how do you know that?"

"Mothers always know these things."

"Oh, for God's sake, give me a break. Mom, I can hear you in my head, but I can't see you? I want to see you. Can I?"

"It's hard to describe. I'm a disembodied soul. If you're ready to see me, you can, but it's going to be the way you want to remember me."

"Do you mean I can visualize you any way I want?"

"It's just what you said, 'visualize' being the key word. It's up to you. It's your mind and your memory of me. It's not what I actually am anymore. Don't you understand that I'm not in a physical body? Your need to see me is because that's what you're used to on earth. It may be a little strange, and it's going to take some getting used to."

"OK, then I guess I'll visualize you during happier times when I was younger and so were you."

"A very good choice."

Fannie didn't quite know all the ins and outs of being in the state she was in. It had never been made clear to her if there were some "rules" that now governed her being. She knew she had died, and she wasn't what she was when she had been on earth. Nothing felt the same to her as when she was alive. Nothing felt bad. In fact, she couldn't really feel anything. It felt something akin to being submerged in water, without the water. Sometimes she missed being able to actually feel things against her skin. However, she could "think" about being in a particular location, and then she was "there." It seemed that her existence, whatever it was, was still about the people who were left behind in the living world, and she was somehow connected to them. She just didn't know exactly how.

"How am I hearing you? Are you speaking to me in my head, or am I actually hearing you through my ears? I'm talking to you out loud, aren't I?" Abby asked, still somewhat puzzled by all of it.

"You are talking to me out loud, because again, that's what you're used to. You could think in your mind what you wanted to say to me and I'd understand you. You think that you're hearing me as if I were speaking to you the way I did when I was alive, but that's not what's really happening. Frankly, it doesn't matter at all, so don't worry about it. You do realize that we're communicating and understanding each other very well, even the sarcastic remarks. I just know that I am able to talk to you; it happens, that's all I know."

"I still don't quite get it."

"Abby, don't miss the point. As I said, you're not going to figure this out intellectually. It is what it is. It works the way I told you. I don't know how or why. I think it's a big picture kind of thing."

"Abby, I'm leaving now, but I'll be around. I want you to stay connected to Rick and help him. I'll keep an eye on things."

All of a sudden, Abby felt a little panicky.

"Mom, promise me you'll come back and talk to me again."

Fannie didn't answer for a second.

"Mom, do you promise? I need you to promise me. There are a lot of things we need to discuss. There are so many things that were left unsaid between us. I came back from Colorado to help you because you asked me to and I loved you. The worst part was that I wasn't even there at the hospital when you died. I really wanted to be there for you…Do you hear me?"

The words poured out in a torrent, and Abby was surprised by the ferocity of the feelings. She only took a breath because she heard her own voice crack. Fannie heard it, too.

"Abby, it's OK, and I did hear you. I know we had lots of issues between us, but I also know what you did for me in the months before I died. I will come back."

CHAPTER 12

Thursday, was a beautiful autumn day, despite the fact that it was early November. It was cool in the morning, but as the sun came up, it fairly kissed the earth with its warmth. This was the perfect day to drive with the sun roof open and the radio turned up in the car. The sky was an azure color with barely a cloud. Today's sky reminded Abby of September 11, 2001, also a beautiful morning, until tragedy hit.

Everything had gone well with Abby's clients today. Even the traffic on the Tappan Zee Bridge was cooperating. Abby enjoyed the view of the Palisades in the distance. She made it home in almost record-breaking time, since she drove like Mario Andretti. Tina and the cats were happy to see her.

"Tina, I'm going to change my clothes, and then we're going for a run. We're going to meet Rick at the reservoir." Tina gave Abby that "I'm always ready to go" look.

Abby changed her clothes and put on her running sneakers. She even had a few minutes to spare before she and Tina had to leave. The answering machine was blinking, and she realized she had not checked it when she came in. As she listened to the messages, she was pleased that there was no message from Rick saying he was backing out. She would have been disappointed if he had cancelled.

"C'mon, Tina, it's time to go." There was something about Tina that gave Abby the impression that whenever they got in the car together Tina thought they were headed for an adventure. Tina never hesitated, and she always appeared to be taking in all the sights as they drove. It was the simple joys that dogs loved and made them happy. Maybe we humans should follow suit, Abby thought.

They arrived at the reservoir, and there were plenty of parking spaces. It wasn't deserted, but it looked as if they'd have areas around the reservoir all to themselves. It made it much nicer not having to weave in and out of so many people running and biking.

Tina and Abby got out of the car and walked toward the bench near the large boulder. The boulder was the Rockland County equivalent of meeting in front of the clock in the center of Grand Central Terminal. Everyone met here whether this was your first trip to the reservoir or the twentieth. Since the morning on the bridge with Rick, Abby had become very conscious of making sure she had her cell phone with her and that it was always charged.

Abby thought that maybe it was one of those connections that Fannie talked about with Rick. Nothing is ever a coincidence. If the cell phone had been charged that morning, she would have called 911 for help and bowed out as soon as the police arrived. She doubted she would have waited around once the police were there, thinking there was nothing more that she could do, and not wanting to be around if things had not gone well. She also could have saved herself the scare of a lifetime. Thanks again, Mom, for more good advice! Fannie made suggestions, some of them good and some outrageous. They fought about them, and ultimately they had détente. The bridge incident definitely typified their relationship.

Abby was doing her stretching as these thoughts about coincidences played through her head. She heard a friendly voice call out from about twenty yards. She looked up quickly and into the sun, but she looked again. With his baseball cap pulled down on his head, and a fast glance on Abby's part, Rick looked a little like her son, Scott. Perhaps they had similar builds.

Fannie was over near the boulder waiting for Rick as well. Today she was not visible to Abby, but she was here nonetheless. Fannie thought to herself how extraordinary it was that she could be in a place, yet no one else had to know she was there, if she didn't choose to make her presence felt. Fannie's mother used to laugh and say she wanted to be the little fly on the wall, so she could overhear other people's conversations. Fannie thought this state of being—whatever state this was—was better than being the little fly, and she didn't have to worry about a fly swatter.

"Hi, Abby, you ready to run? Glad to see you're coming with us, Tina," Rick said as he patted her on the head.

Rick was stretching as they talked, and when he was ready, Abby pointed in the direction they should go. The first part of the run was mostly flat, which was good to get into a rhythm. She figured that she'd let him set the pace for the run, and she hoped she could keep up. Rick was young enough to be her son.

As they continued running, Abby asked, "Do you think you'd like to go to back to work as an attorney?"

"Honestly, I'm not sure. My firm is being pretty decent and put me on paid leave, but deep down, I think they're just being politically correct. No one has officially contacted me to say how long the leave is for and how long they're going to pay me. But if I were to call them and say I'd like to come back tomorrow, I think they'd run for the hills. That's why I think nothing is in writing. I don't have a real good feeling that they'll take me back, or if they do, I'll never see another interesting or challenging case again. They probably would have me in the local small claims courts doing two-thousand-dollar cases."

"Think you might like to go out on your own and open your own firm at some time in the future?"

There was no immediate answer from him, and Abby hoped she hadn't overstepped. "I suppose it's a possibility. Who knows? I'm not sure I want to practice law anymore."He grinned a little. "Want to hire me to crunch some numbers for you since you're the financial adviser? You'd be surprised how good I am with the calculator."

"You might be a tad expensive for me."

They both chuckled, and they ran in silence after that for a few more minutes. He broke the silence.

"OK, enough about me. Tell me a little more about you. Anything has to be more interesting than my life. Wait—that came out wrong."

"For a lawyer, you certainly have a way with words. There's not all that much to tell. I have a private practice as a certified financial adviser. I enjoy helping people to become financially independent. It probably is somewhat like being a lawyer, with people relying on you."

"It's true that people rely on us, and we do help them, but we're not always connected to them. As a lawyer, a lot of times you're picking up the pieces of what they've done wrong and trying to do the best you can to get them out of a mess that they've created."

Rick changed the subject and said, "I know you said you have two grown kids, one an orthopedist and one a paralegal. You said you'd been widowed for a long time. That must have been very hard to raise two kids alone. It must have been painful for all of you."

"You're right; it hurt so much to lose him. It was devastating for all of us. I think that our brain lets our memories of the ones we loved remain, but the pain of that loss fades. It just takes time."

"I hope so...And you never remarried, even though it was a long time ago? You're an attractive, vital woman. There must been a line of men stretching for a mile outside your house."

"No, no line stretching for a mile. Not even a hundred yard dash to get to me. When the kids were young, I was a little wary of bringing a new man into the house, and I frankly think some guys were turned off when they saw I came with two kids. Some guys just weren't right. I got used to my life as it was, and I'm really happy. I'm not sure I'd even want to be involved with someone now if it meant that I had to change my life or make a lot of compromises. I like the freedom, but I'm still always open to the possibility that I'll meet someone that I can share the rest of my life with—preferably, tall, good-looking and with lots of money. "

"Interesting...I think you will meet someone when the time is right, and you'll get both—love and money."

"From your mouth to God's ear. And I hope the same happens for you. Life has a way of changing you. No, I think I take that back. Life has a way of changing how you look at things."

"You've really thought about this a lot, haven't you?"

"What I've had is a lot of time to take a step back and see things from different perspectives. Now I'm beginning to sound like I should be writing for Oprah. OK, I'm saved by the reservoir. We've done the whole loop around, and we're back to where we started."

"Abby, I really enjoyed running with you and Tina."

They walked back to the parking lot together with Tina close behind, and Abby handed him a bottle of water from her car. Ah, the infamous water bottles!

CHAPTER 13

It was one of those bleak January days where you'd like to be anywhere but New York City. There was a slight rain, and the temperature was about thirty-five degrees. Thank God, just warm enough that the rain wasn't freezing on the roads and sidewalk, but just cold enough to be miserable. No matter what you wore to stay warm, the dampness seeped through, and you became chilled. The snow had been on the ground long enough that it was frozen solid and no longer anything close to white. It was now dark grey in places and was littered with specks of pavement, sand, and bits of garbage. The snow was lying there as an impediment to all who dared to cross the street. Even crossing at the crosswalk was a challenge. Whatever melting had gone on had nowhere to go and was dammed up between the mountains of snow on either side of the crosswalk. You could step off the curb into ankle-deep frigid water, or you could go skating into midair and make a perfect video for YouTube. The embarrassment of being on YouTube was the better alternative to ending up at the Hospital for Special Surgery.

Rick gingerly picked his way up Fifth Avenue dodging the rain, the other pedestrians, and the traffic. He arrived at the building where the law firm was located and walked into the lobby. The first thing that struck him was the royal blue runner laid down on the highly polished marble floor—certainly different from the drab, steel gray runner of last year at this time.

Rick walked up to the guard at the front desk and showed him his badge with his picture on it. Rick thought he still looked like the picture on the badge except that he had gotten leaner and stronger from the workouts and running. He also had a little more gray hair than he wanted.

"Hello, Mr. Singleton, nice to see you."

"Hi, Bill, nice to see you, too."

"Did you have a nice holiday? Will you be coming back to work now?"

Rick steeled himself to give the rehearsed answer he had been practicing. He knew he was going to be asked these questions, and it seemed better if he had a pat answer to give.

"The holidays were fine, Bill. I may well be coming back to work. See you later."

Rick turned and headed purposefully in the direction of the elevators. Since it was ten in the morning, the elevator was practically empty, and he zoomed up to the fifty-first floor. The elevator doors opened into the reception area of the law firm, which occupied the entire floor. Above the receptionist's desk was an extremely large brass sign with the name "Braddock, Lindsay, Goldrick and Schoeneman" and spotlights on the name. As he walked toward the receptionist, he could hear the familiar sound of Martha answering the phone, "Braddock, Lindsay, Goldrick and Schoeneman, how may I direct your call?"

"Good morning, Martha, still spitting out all four names?"

"Mr. Singleton, so nice to see you. How are you? I'm waiting for the day when your name follows Mr. Schoeneman."

"I'm doing much better. Thanks for your card and thoughtfulness. I have an appointment with Mr. Goldrick."

There was an awkward moment of hesitation when neither Rick nor Martha knew what to do. Should Rick just walk in as he had always done or should he wait to be announced?

Martha broke the ice and said, "Why don't you just go on in, and I'll buzz Mr. Goldrick's secretary to let them know you're on the way in."

Rick winked at her and said, "Thanks for making me feel welcome. See you on the way out."

As Rick walked through yet another set of doors that led to the offices and conference rooms, he hesitated and considered whether to go to his own office first. He thought better of it and continued on to his appointment.

Rick knew that he was going to have to walk the whole length of the hallway because, as the managing partner, Steve Goldrick's office was about as far away from the receptionist as was humanly possible. You didn't get to be managing partner in a prestigious New York City law firm of close to seventy-five attorneys without bringing in megabucks and representing very large powerful corporations, wealthy foreign investors, and high-profile clients. On any given day, it was not surprising to see a contingent of Asian businessmen ensconced in one of the large conference rooms buying Manhattan real estate or a sheik negotiating dollars for oil. If you worked at the firm, you learned very quickly not to react when you saw Oscar and Grammy winners, sports figures, or super models who had graced the covers of *Sports Illustrated* and *Vogue* walking down the halls of Braddock, Lindsay, Goldrick and Schoeneman.

Rick stopped along the hallway and poked his head into his friend Jack's office. "Hey, Rick, seeing Stevie Wonder today? I heard he closed the deal with Waterman Real Estate yesterday. He's in a good mood. Lucky you."

Steve Goldrick got the title of "Stevie Wonder," not because he was black, nor could he sing. The legend started about thirty years ago, when one of the young associates had called him that because Steve had pulled off some of the most impossible verdicts against all odds. He always had his associates "wondering" how the hell he did it.

"Stop by on your way out and let me know how you did. Let's catch a few brews sometime soon."

"Good to know Stevie Wonder's in a good mood. I'll catch ya on my way out, one way or another."

Rick reached the inner sanctum at the end of the hallway. Rick said to Steve Goldrick's secretary, "Hello, Helen, I'm sure you know I am here to see Steve; hope you're well."

"Yes, Mr. Singleton, I am aware of your appointment with Mr. Goldrick. He's on the phone, but he shouldn't be long. Why don't you just have a seat, and I'll let him know you're here." There was no hesitation or small talk with Helen; she was all business. Without further ado, she plugged herself back in to the headset and proceeded to start typing at breakneck speed as if her surroundings and any human beings ceased to exist.

Meanwhile, Steve hung up the phone. He was composing himself for the meeting with Rick. Steve thought what a mess it was. Why did that Abby Parker woman have to be the one to rescue Mr. Suicidal off the bridge…of all people…her. And what a mess Rick made for the firm. Thank God his old friends weren't alive to see these events take place. It wasn't going to be pretty.

In less than five minutes from when Rick sat down, Steve Goldrick appeared at the door to his office. Steve Goldrick was almost a caricature of a successful lawyer as portrayed by Hollywood. He was over six feet tall, with striking blue eyes. His hair was not just cut, but professionally styled, perhaps even colored, with the top of his ears perfectly covered by his hair. There was a little bit of grey showing at the temples, and to his dismay, he had somewhat of a receding hair line. The grey around the temples was probably measured to inspire confidence in the clients as well as a certain dignity. He wanted to project that he had been in the practice of law long enough to have acquired vast experience, but not so long as to be tired or out of touch.

His shirt was a very pale and almost unnoticeable blue. The shirt was impeccably starched and had French cuffs with not-too-large, gold cufflinks with a large *G* on them, undoubtedly to emphasize his last name. His initials were also embroidered on the cuff of the shirt. He had on a navy blue Armani suit with a faint pinstripe. He had on the proverbial power tie. In this era of the casual workplace, Steve Goldrick was the antithesis of that ethic. He had strongly vetoed casual Fridays, asserting that the law firm was never casual, and was always serious about its commitment to its clients. His philosophy was that you only had one chance to make a first impression, and that first impression was never to be forgotten. Steve Goldrick wanted his clients to be in awe after their first meeting with him.

To look at Steve, you'd think he had been born with the silver spoon in his mouth. Nothing could have been further from the truth. Steve was the epitome of the self-made man. Steve's father had been a New York City cop who rose to the rank of captain before his death. Although his father was immensely proud of being a New York City police captain, he knew that the way to live the American dream was for his kids to be educated. One of his sons became a New York City cop, but two of his other children became professionals, Steve and his brother, Ray. Ray became a well-known sports agent. It worked out well for both Steve and Ray, who were able to refer clients to each other. Might as well keep it in the family.

Steve was the product of Holy Cross College, a good Jesuit institution, which he attended on scholarship and then went on to graduate from Fordham Law School, number one in his class. Steve ignored the offer of the *Fordham Law Review*, much to the dismay of his professors in law school, who tried to convince him that Law Review was a ticket to a job with a big law firm. Steve declined, saying he was working his way through law school and couldn't waste his time writing absurd articles. He once said to the faculty adviser of Law Review that the big firms could kiss his ass and would do so one day when he was a partner in his own firm. Despite his defection from Law Review, a federal judge in the prestigious Southern District of New York was so charmed by Steve at the interview that he offered him a clerkship the next day. It probably didn't hurt that Steve's family and the judge's family both came from County Donegal, in Ireland, and that the judge's father had also been a New York City cop. Steve had the ability to find the common ground with whoever he was talking to, and pretty soon, they were swapping stories.

After the clerkship in the Southern District, Steve's rise in law firms was close to meteoric. His first job after the clerkship was for a firm in Manhattan that primarily did litigation. Steve was a hard worker and extremely thorough in his work. Talk about luck and being in the right place at the right time. After a few years of toiling in the firm, Steve was the second chair on a big case. The partner trying the case dropped dead of a heart attack after about eight days of trial. After the shock wore off, the partners were going to ask for a mistrial and an adjournment for three months so another partner could get up to speed on the case. The client refused. He told the partners that he had every confidence in Steve and that he wanted Steve to finish trying the case. Even though Steve was only several years out of law school, he finished the case and won. And the rest, as they say, is history.

Steve came out of his office to greet Rick.

"Rick, great to see you. Come on in."

"Hi, Steve, good to see you, too. Thanks for seeing me."

As Rick stepped into the "inner sanctum," and although he had been there many times, he was once again struck by the sheer opulence of the office, its size and the view of the Manhattan skyline. Even in the rain, the view of Central Park was breath-taking. The office was so large that there was enough room for a conference table and another area with a leather couch and chairs and an oval-shaped, glass coffee table.

There were pictures of Steve with his arm around Mayor Giuliani, very soon after September 11, both with fireman's hats on and looking very sober, and pictures of Mayor Giuliani in happier times with Steve, both of them with Yankees caps on. Steve was every bit an equal opportunity picture taker, so there were pictures of Steve with Mayor Bloomberg, both of them in tuxedos, and a picture of Steve with his arm around Ed Koch, with the caption, "How'm I doing?" There was a separate wall for sports figures and celebrities, including Michael Jordan, Eli Manning, and Derek Jeter.

Steve motioned Rick to a client chair opposite his desk. Always maneuvering for position, Steve set up the meeting in a more formal way, keeping Rick across the desk from him and Steve in a position of power.

"So, how are you feeling, Rick? What have you been doing with yourself for the past few months?"

Rick knew that he was going to have to be honest with Steve and that the rehearsed answers he had given to the receptionist and the secretaries were not going to fly with him. Steve was a very shrewd judge of character, and his ability to size up people and his opponents was an enormous help to him.

"I think that while I'll never stop feeling the loss of Jennifer and Adam, I can cope with the pain. I've been seeing a psychiatrist who's helped me. It's a long process. Although it sounds like a truism, I think it gets a little better every day."

Steve nodded, but didn't say anything. He continued to stare directly into Rick's eyes as if there were some words written there that he could read. Rick felt that since Steve wasn't saying anything that he ought to fill the silence.

"Steve, I want you to know how much I appreciate it that the firm put me on paid leave all these months. It was terrific that I didn't have to worry about money. I know this had to be your doing as the managing partner, and I really thank you for it."

"Actually, Rick, although it was my idea, I didn't have a very difficult job selling it to the Executive Committee. Everyone was sympathetic about what happened."

"Being on paid leave gave me a chance to catch my breath. I started running—never was much of a runner before this—but I find it helps a lot to clear my head. I now find I really enjoy it."

"Running was something I could never really take to. I found it too boring. I still play basketball, and I'm now eligible for GLIB. Do you know what that stands for?"

"No, what?"

"Geriatric Lawyers in Basketball. Never thought I'd reach that age to be in GLIB, but it's fun. Some of these guys are really serious. We played Wednesday night, and one guy broke his nose when he was hit with his opponent's elbow. The game is just as intense as I remember it in college." Steve cleared his throat and continued, "Let's talk about your future with the firm."

"I definitely am ready to come back to work full-time. I feel confident and much stronger mentally and physically."

"That's good to know, but there are a lot of things to consider, especially since I'm the managing partner. You know we were supportive of you, and that's why we paid you your full salary while you were out. However, you also know this firm is a pressure cooker. I don't want the stress to become too much for you. We've reassigned all your cases to other attorneys, and of course you know that your secretary is now working for John Hubbard."

"I'm ready to start with some new cases and new clients. In fact, a fresh start might be better for everyone."

"Rick, your situation was discussed at length at the partnership meeting. We feel that what happened to Jennifer and Adam was a terrible tragedy and what you had to endure must have been god-awful. The problem is that we have to be responsive to our clients and their needs. The partners feel that a client is just not going to be happy with a lead attorney who tried to commit suicide. I'm not going to insult you by putting you on crappy cases, yet the partners don't feel comfortable bringing you back to your previous position. Paying you while you were out was one thing, but letting you come back to work in a high-powered law firm with huge clients is quite another."

"Steve, I've been here since I graduated from law school, and you know how hard I've worked for this firm. I went through one of the worst things that could happen to anyone, but it doesn't mean I can't recover from it. I'll take a crappy case, and I'll prove you wrong."

"Don't think that this all wasn't hashed and rehashed at the partnership meeting. There were some people who were in favor of letting you come back on a trial basis, but the majority of the partners felt it was a bad idea. We have to think about the reputation of the firm. It wasn't good for the firm to have one of our senior associates try to commit suicide. The story was in the papers. The clients whose matters you were directly responsible for were really shaken up. It took a lot of hand holding for us to keep them as clients and not have them jump ship. Rick, believe me, if it were only up to me, I'd take a chance on you, but it's not only my decision. There's no way to sugarcoat this, and I'm sorry. We'll help you with an out placement firm, and we'll pay for it. We'll pay your salary for another three months, and you can use me for a recommendation."

Rick sat back in his chair for a moment after Steve stopped speaking. For a second Rick thought he had been punched, because it was the same sensation. He wasn't ready to be fired or let go, not just yet.

"Steve, I know this hasn't been easy for you or for the firm, and believe me, I certainly appreciate what you've done for me.

I don't want to appear ungrateful. But rather than just hand me some money, I'd like to come back. I think I can be an asset to the firm. I know I can."

Steve had tilted forward in his big, leather office chair as he was speaking, but once he finished, he tilted backward, as if his body language was giving away the fact that he wanted to be as far away from Rick as possible, literally and figuratively. When Steve didn't respond, Rick picked up the ball and ran with it.

"Look, I'm not minimizing that this was a bad situation for everybody. But it's over. I've put it behind me, and I think the firm can do the same. You don't have to let me work with the same clients. Obviously, I understand that they would be skittish. Let me work on some of the new matters with new clients. I get it that I may not be the senior person on a case for a while until I prove myself again."

"Rick, I told you, if it was only up to me, I'd say it's OK to come back. But you know it's not only up to me. This situation didn't even stay in the Executive Committee. It went before the full partnership. Based on the reaction of the clients whose matters you were working on at the time—and I told you, their reactions were not good—the firm doesn't want to chance it that another client finds out about it and bolts. You know as well as I do that clients are often selfish bastards. Yeah, they say they care about us, not only as their attorneys but as their 'trusted advisers.' Do you think a client wants his 'trusted adviser' in a mental hospital? The loyalty from clients only goes as far as the next bad decision from a court or a bill they think is too high. It's not like what it was years ago, Rick."

"You want to talk about loyalty, Steve? Let's talk about loyalty," Rick shot back at him. "I missed lots of family functions because the firm needed me on a case. I came in lots of times to bail people out. You called me, and I cut short my vacation and came back because an important client had an emergency. I did it because I was loyal to this firm. It's my job, and it's what I'm paid to do. But I lost the two people who were the most important to me. So now I see what my loyalty got me with this firm."

Perhaps for the first time in a long time, Steve looked uncomfortable and possibly not in control, a feeling he certainly didn't embrace. He was the consummate negotiator, who always wanted the upper hand.

"Lower your voice and get a hold of yourself," he hissed. "We all know it was a terrible accident, but you can't pin this on the firm."

Steve looked at Rick and his eyes narrowed. "No one can know if you had been with them whether the accident could have been avoided. You all might have died. As for loyalty to the firm, this firm was very loyal to you. We compensated you, and compensated you god-damn well, for your time. That's how a firm shows its employees its loyalty. I never saw you turn down a paycheck or a bonus, nor should you. Law is a noble profession, but don't kid yourself, we're all in this for the money. Surely that fact hasn't escaped you."

Steve realized that he wasn't getting anywhere with Rick with sarcasm or authoritative intimidation, so he tried a different tack.

"I get it that you're upset—very understandable. If you want, I can take one more run at the partners, but I'm not sure it would do any good. Do you want me to try?"

"Yes, I do, Steve. I know that if you're pulling for me, things can get done that otherwise wouldn't happen. I know how much power and influence you wield around here." Rick was upset, but not so much that he didn't know that flattery was a big carrot for Steve. Right now, Rick wasn't above a little groveling. Rick said, "I'm sorry about the outburst, Steve. I didn't mean to lose my temper, but this is important to me. I would really appreciate it if you would bring this up again with the Executive Committee."

"OK, but no promises as to the outcome, Rick. We have an Executive Committee meeting coming up. I'll send up the trial balloon with them and see if I can rally some support to bring this issue up to the partners again. I'll let you know how it goes with them, and that will be a good indication. I'm writing this down on my list of items to discuss at the Executive Committee meeting." Steve made a show of uncapping his Mont Blanc pen and writing in his day timer.

Steve rose and put out his hand. The message was clear; the meeting was over. They shook hands, and Steve walked Rick out of his office.

"I'll be in touch, but give me some time. This might not happen as quickly as you would like."

Steve walked back into his office and shut the door. He sat down at his desk and ripped off the page from the day timer where he had just written Rick's name below the agenda of items for the Executive Committee. He crumpled the sheet of paper into a wad and threw it into the garbage pail next to his desk.

Fannie had been sitting in the other client chair next to Rick. She had watched this whole scenario play out. There was something vaguely familiar about Mr. Goldrick. Fannie thought to herself, yeah, he's about the right age, same name, too much of a coincidence. You're him. You're the one who set it up. I remember now.

Neither Steve nor Rick had been aware that Fannie was there. Fannie was not in the least pleased as to how the conversation had gone. As Steve threw the piece of paper in the garbage pail, he knocked over the mug of coffee on his desk. Before he could do anything, the black contents, looking like the rapids of Niagara Falls, splashed onto the contracts and papers on Steve's desk and continued to flow onto the Persian rug below. Steve cursed and Fannie smiled.

CHAPTER 14

Abby had finished cleaning up the kitchen from dinner and put everything she could possibly load into the dishwasher. She sat down to watch television after a long week, and the show *Medium* was starting. The first scene finished, and they started running the opening credits. She thought she heard someone say her name, but it was faint. The second time she heard her name, there was no mistaking it.

Fannie's ability to move about with just a thought, or so it seemed, and appear in the place she was thinking of boggled her mind. She wasn't used to "life" in this new dimension. "Hi, Abby, do you have some time to talk?" Fannie thought coming while *Medium* was on was a wonderful 'coincidence' as they say. "You and I know there are no 'coincidences,' but I thought *Medium* would put you in the right mood for us to talk." She definitely smirked as she said that.

"You've been very quiet lately, Mom. I didn't know what to make of that."

"Really, nothing at all. I keep my eye on things, and you know me, I'm not one to meddle."

"Mom, can you really, truly say that with a straight face? Don't get me started again about Rick and that night on the bridge. If you'd look in the dictionary under *meddling*, there would be a picture of you."

"Pick, pick, pick, pick. I'm going to ignore your sarcasm. When you were a kid, you so loved the TV show *Topper*. Remember George and Marion Kirby who were ghosts who would appear to Topper?"

"Yes, I do, but as I remember, Mom, they were constantly getting him into precarious situations. Not unlike you."

"Abby, enough! I have to tell you something. Rick told you he was going to have a meeting with the managing partner of his firm. Well, he had the meeting yesterday. They have no intention of taking him back, but they made it seem as if they would reconsider it."

"How the hell do you know this?"

"Let's just say I was a fly on the wall."

"A fly on the wall...where?"

"In the managing partner's office. His name is Steve Goldrick."

"Why were you there, Mom? Why were you spying on Rick?"

"I wasn't spying! I just wanted to check up on Rick...you know, see how things are going."

"And you just had to fly or transport yourself or whatever it is you do over here to inform me of this piece of information... because?"

"Because I thought you might be interested in how things went with Rick's meeting."

"Mom, sitting in on Rick's meeting goes way beyond just being 'interested.' You're way out of line doing that. I could have waited for him to tell me if he wanted me to know. Did it ever occur to you that you were eavesdropping on a very private conversation?"

"Well, it wasn't like I was eavesdropping at all. You make it sound like I was hiding behind the door with my ear pressed up to it. It certainly wasn't like that!"

"Mom, sometimes you can be so dense. No, you weren't hiding behind the door, but you might as well have. Answer one question for me. Did they know you were there?" Abby quickly answered her own rhetorical question. "Of course they didn't!"

"The methodology is not what's important. What's important is that they're playing games with Rick, and he thinks this Steve guy is looking out for him. The only person Steve is looking out for is Steve."

"I get it that you like Rick, and so do I, but I still don't get it why you are so involved with him. We can talk until I'm blue in the face, and you're not going to answer my questions if you don't want to."

"I assume Rick will tell you about the meeting. Mention to him that he should think about what to do if the firm doesn't take him back."

"He's a pretty smart guy. I assume that he's considered that alternative. It's probably a fifty-fifty proposition the way he describes the firm. I think they're mostly concerned with their bottom line."

"Well, if you heard that man, Steve Goldrick, talk, he could sell you the Brooklyn Bridge. I really think he led Rick to believe that he was going to personally put himself on the line to help Rick. It's just not so. I think Rick bought his whole Mr. Sincere act."

"Look, I really don't think that there's much we can do about this—especially since technically we aren't supposed to know what really went on at the meeting."

"True, I hadn't thought of it exactly that way."

"Mom, you still haven't answered why you're so invested in Rick. He's a nice guy, I admit that, but why are you doing this?"

"He's hurting, and I don't see that anyone is looking out for him. I thought I could do that."

"Mom, he has a brother and lots of good friends to help him. So answer me, why you?"

"You've heard of six degrees of separation, haven't you? Well, I think Rick is going to be someone who may lead you to something important in your life."

"Mom, what the hell does that mean? Do you think this is some sort of joke and so you're speaking in riddles?"

"Abby, sometimes things in life come in strange ways, and you just have to let them happen. We're not always in control, in case you haven't yet figured that out."

"OK, the white flag is raised in surrender. I give up. We're dancing around, and you're still not giving me any specifics."

"You don't need any specifics. Here is a very nice young man who's had more tragedy bombard him than most people have in their entire lives. He deserves some help."

"Ya know, Mom, you just may be getting warm and fuzzy from the other side. Next thing I know you'll be baking cupcakes with sprinkles on top and giving cotton candy to little kids at the zoo. I can't wait to see that."

"Stop it. You know I can be sweet as sugar if I want to. It's just that I didn't want to most of the time. It wouldn't have been good for my image."

"Face it, Mom. You were more like a cactus than a teddy bear. I still want us to talk about us."

"OK, but not now. I have things to accomplish. But I promise you, I will be back, and we'll have time to talk. I've learned from the other side that promises are not made or taken lightly. Love you, Abby. Bye."

With that she was gone, but a part of Abby truly believed that Fannie would come back and they would deal with the unfinished business, however painful it might be.

CHAPTER 15

Friday night rolled around cold and clear. The temperature was in the mid-twenties, and the stars were unbelievably bright in the night sky. The phone rang, and it was Maizie.

"Hi, it's me. I'm on my way, but the traffic is awful. We're crawling across the Tappan Zee. Who are all these people, and why do they have to be on the Bridge with me now?"

"I know. Fridays are a bear on the bridge. How much longer?"

"I'd say a good twenty-five minutes the way we're going, but if we pick up the pace, I'll call you to let you know."

"No hurry, honey. I kind of factored in the Friday night traffic, so dinner is not quite ready, but the wine is uncorked and breathing. I'm watching the news and just about to have a little wine. You get here when you get here. No big rush."

Abby loved her dinners with her daughter. Usually, Maizie came for dinner midweek, but tonight was an added treat. Maizie wanted to go shopping tomorrow at Woodbury Commons, where there were outlets galore. Woodbury Commons was about a half hour from Abby's house, so Maizie was going to spend the night, and they'd go shopping together tomorrow. Occasionally, Maizie came with a friend, but mostly it was just the two of them. They talked about everything from friends to work to politics to shopping and bargains. Some nights they watched *Jeopardy!*, and some nights they rented a movie, but mostly they just talked. Abby realized now how much she missed doing anything like this with her mother. Living in Colorado two thousand miles away wasn't exactly conducive to having dinner together. As Abby looked back, she had to admit that even if she had lived close to her parents, she probably would not have come for dinner on a regular basis. Abby and Fannie couldn't seem to get past the superficial differences. They got stuck there. Especially with what had happened to Abby as a teenager, Abby wished that it had changed things for the better between them, but in reality, it hadn't. Now as a mother with an adult daughter, Abby realized what she and her mother both missed. Since Fannie had been appearing to Abby recently, Fannie certainly was on her mind.

Abby heard the car door slam in the driveway, and Tina bounded to the front door to greet Maizie. As Abby opened the door, Maizie swooped in with a very large purse over her shoulder, a carry bag, a loaf of French bread under her arm and a cake box.

"Afraid I wasn't going to feed you?" Abby asked, looking at the goodies. Maizie looked at Tina and said, "Hey, old girl, how ya doing? Let me get rid of all this stuff." They walked to the kitchen, and Maizie put down the packages on the table. She then turned and sat on the floor to greet Tina, playing with her and giving her some hugs. Even the fur balls came to get in on some pats, scratches and treats.

As Maizie worked her way up from the floor, and stepping gingerly so as not to step on anyone's tail, she said to her mother, "I went past the bakery today, and the bread was sitting there in the window beckoning to me. Once I walked inside, it was game over. I saw this apple pie that had just come out of the oven, and I could smell it. You're lucky that I didn't eat everything on the way here. You don't have to indulge in any of this good stuff, if you have that much self-control."

"Which, you know, I don't. Does this mean that we have to eat it all tonight, or can we save some for tomorrow?"

Abby finished the final preparations for dinner, and they sat down to eat shortly after Maizie arrived. They had barely started eating when Maizie became very quiet. She put her fork down and looked at Abby.

"What? That is not a happy look."

"We got some news today in the office. I'm barely processing it. When I said I was going past the bakery today, it was because I needed to get out and get some air. About three thirty today, the partners called all the staff and the associates into the conference room. No one knew what to make of it, and the mood in the conference room was so tense you could have cut it with a knife."

Abby waited for Maizie to take a breath and continue. "The firm is breaking up. Apparently, one group of partners is breaking off to form their own new firm. Jeff, for whom I work, is not going with them. After this bombshell, they said each partner would speak personally to the associates and the staff that worked for him. It was amazing that they kept something like this quiet. This is the kind of thing that spreads like wildfire through the firm. Anyway, from what I can gather, Jeff is not one of the big producers in the firm. I guess the partners have been fighting among themselves about the split up of the profits and the whole thing came to a head."

"So where does that leave you, honey?"

"I'm not sure. Jeff has something lined up for himself where he would be in-house counsel to a corporation. He's not sure if he's going to be able to take any of the associates or paralegals with him. He says he should know toward the end of next week, but there's a very real possibility that I could be out of a job in a very short time. It's so unreal, and it's so scary with the job market the way it is."

She finally stopped to take a breath. Before Abby could say anything, she could see the tears welling up in Maizie's eyes.

Abby leaned across the table and laid her hand on Maizie's. "Let's not jump the gun; you don't know if Jeff is going to be able to take you with him. You know the old adage about hoping for the best and preparing for the worst. You're going to have to sit on your hands for a little bit until things get decided. Did Jeff give you any indication or hint of which way it would go for you?"

"No, he's playing it close to the vest. He says it's up to the chief in-house counsel how many people they think they need. I can't imagine that they'll be able to absorb everyone. I don't know how much clout Jeff has."

"How are you set for rent?"

"I'm probably OK for about two months or so, which is about the same time the lease comes up for renewal. After that I won't be able to keep the apartment if I'm not working. I'll have to tell my roommate that I won't be able to renew the lease."

"Look, Maizie, if push comes to shove, and I know you don't want to do this, you can live here for a while if you need to. That should take some of the financial burden off you…And truth be told, I wouldn't mind the company."

"Thanks Mom, I may take you up on the offer. You still have lots of room in the shed and garage, right?"

"Yes, we can always pile more stuff in there if we have to. This isn't your fault; it wasn't anything you did. If things don't work out, if you want, I can ask around with some of my clients to see whether they or anyone they know is looking for a paralegal."

"This is not a great economy. I don't think a lot of law firms are hiring."

"True, but people move away or get pregnant or change careers. You're still getting way ahead of yourself."

It was going to be a long night; every time Abby thought things had calmed down; Maizie would get agitated again and repeat the whole story. Probably the not knowing was worse than the reality of the situation because Maizie's imagination was running wild. Mercifully, the ten o'clock news came on, and exhaustion took over for both of them. They decided to have some of the delicious apple pie that Maizie had bought, with a cup of chamomile and mint tea, and then head for bed. Abby knew the respite would only be temporary, and Maizie would be up worrying early the next morning.

CHAPTER 16

The next morning dawned, and what awakened Abby was not the sunlight, but the rich smell of coffee wafting into her room. OK, not surprising, that Maizie couldn't sleep and was up early. Abby stayed in bed for another ten minutes or so, trying to collect her thoughts and think of something new to say to relieve Maizie's anxiety.

As Abby walked into the kitchen, Hurricane Maizie was busy stirring pancake batter as if her life depended on it. Strawberries were washed and neatly cut to go into the batter. The bacon was beginning to sizzle in the frying pan.

"Did I wake you? I really was trying to be quiet."

"No, it was the smell of the coffee that got me. While you're making breakfast, I'm going downstairs. I have something I want to show you."

Abby returned from the basement with three large photo albums.

"I was down in the basement last week looking for something, and I found these. I hadn't looked at them in a long time. I want you to see these after we have breakfast."

They sat in the kitchen where the sun was streaming through the windows and illuminating the flowers that were in a clear glass vase on the table. The bright colors of the cut flowers looked as though they had a spotlight on them. Abby and Maizie sat and ate strawberry pancakes with the maple-smoked bacon. They didn't care about the calories—just a good hearty breakfast!

Before Abby had finished her last pancake, Maizie jumped up from the table and grabbed the top photo album. She brought it over to the table and practically laid it in the dish with the maple syrup.

"Can I finish my last bite of pancake, and then I'll show you the pictures of Nana and Poppy."

"OK, Mom, I'll get us another cup of coffee and we'll look at photos and you can tell me everything."

Maizie had randomly opened the album to a picture of Abby with her mom. The picture had Fannie and Abby sitting on the couch in the living room. The tubes from the oxygen tank were draped around Fannie's frail body and led to her nose. Abby had her arm around Fannie for support.

"Wow, Nana looks so sad and very sick."

"She was Maiz. That picture was taken right before she went into the hospital."

"How old was she in that picture?'

"Believe it or not, she was only seventy-five. Mom does look much older than she actually was. Amazing how too much drinking and smoking can take their toll."

"Is this when you left Colorado and arrived in New York and Scott and I stayed with Dad? Had you and Daddy planned on coming back?"

"Yes, we wanted to stay in Colorado, but Mom called saying she was so sick and asked that I come back to help out. I never realized that I was ever going to stay here in New York permanently. Your dad stayed behind in Colorado to take care of you two, the house and the cats. When I realized that going back to Colorado was not in the cards, we put the house on the market and made the move to New York."

"What did Nana say to you that made you up and leave Colorado?"

"I didn't feel that I had a choice. I could hear the urgency in her voice. Knowing how independent your grandmother was, she would never have called me to come home unless her health had declined dramatically within such a short period of time. The decision to go home was made very easy for me when your grandmother said she was dying and didn't have much time left, but it certainly wasn't easy for me to leave you, Scott, and Daddy."

Abby could remember almost verbatim what was said that day when her mother had called. She now recounted it in detail to Maizie.

"It was about eleven o'clock in the morning, and the phone rang. I was somewhat distracted as I picked up the phone, not thinking about much else except how nice a day it was going to be to take a long bike ride. I was pleasantly surprised to hear my mother's voice on the other end of the phone. Mom and I talked about twice a month on the phone and we mailed each other pictures and letters on a regular basis. This was well before cell phones, texting and iPads became everyone's appendage."

Abby continued, "We talked about your Aunt Donna and your cousin, Rachael, in California. Mom talked about what was happening in the neighborhood in Rivertown and about local politics. Then there was a long pause on the phone, and I waited for Mom to say something else. When she started to speak again, I knew from the tone of her voice that something was very wrong. Mom said, 'I need you to come home right now. My illness has progressed to the point that I can't manage, and your father and I really need your help. I'm not sure how much time I have left and there are so many things we should discuss.'

"I was completely dumbfounded by Mom's words. I gathered my thoughts a little, wanting to ask so many questions. I was finally able to say a few words and asked, 'How did your condition deteriorate so quickly from the last time we spoke? I know that you've been having a lot of trouble breathing, but what happened? Have you been to the doctor to see if there should be any changes in your medication or something else you should do?'

"Mom said, 'I have been seeing the doctor, and there is nothing more to be done. I'm dying. It's that simple and I want you here.' I was shocked after what Mom said; I couldn't believe it. I mean, you know it will happen someday, but to hear it from her like that..."

Maizie watched her mother as Abby recounted the story. Maizie could see how much pain there still was even after all this time. She wanted to give her mom a hug but instead watched Abby's face as Abby continued the story.

Abby said, 'Mom, there is always something that can be done. Maybe we'll see another doctor or a specialist and get more information when I get back to New York.'

"From Mom's hesitation at the other end of the phone, I realized that there was so much that I didn't know about Mom's illness and discussing anything further was futile. Once Mom made up her mind, that was it."

"Mom said, 'I've sent you the money for the plane ticket. It should arrive in a day or so. Just come home. Let me know what flight you're going to take.'

"I said to Mom, 'You sent me the money for the plane ticket before you even called me? You just assumed that I'd come home? It's so like you to be sure of everything.'

"Mom gave a soft chuckle into the phone. 'Abby, even though we never saw eye to eye on a lot of things, and we fought like cats and dogs—no pun intended, God knows we've had enough of all those critters—I knew I could count on you, and that's why I'm calling you now.'

"Mom said she was tired and out of breath and wanted to end the phone call. In any case, Mom had certainly given me an awful lot to think about, for both of us. I told her I'd make the flight reservations and let her know when I'd be there."

"All I said was 'I'll see you. You know I love you, and I'll be there for you tomorrow.'

"With that, I heard Mom say, 'OK, see you tomorrow,' and she hung up."

Maizie said, "That was pretty blunt with what Nana said to you and must have been so hard to hear."

Abby said, "I was afraid for Mom, for her life or how little time she had left. I was afraid for myself for what I would find when I arrived. I was anxious about leaving Daddy and the two of you in Colorado. I knew I would miss you terribly."

Maizie said in a soft voice, "I hope I never hear you tell me you're dying, at least not over the phone."

They continued to talk about Abby's return to New York from Colorado. Abby said, "Some of what went on when I came back was absolutely heart wrenching, because of Mom's condition. She was so much weaker than I thought she would be, but on the other hand, she was still stubborn as hell. Some of the stories are comical, because Mom and Dad were so set in their ways that I practically had to dynamite them to get them to change even the smallest thing in the house." Abby continued on as she and Maizie flipped through the pictures in the photo albums.

Maizie asked, "What happened once you were actually back in New York? Tell me some of the things that happened. I'd love to hear more about when you first got back. I wish I had gotten to know Nana and Papa. You've said they were characters."

Abby responded, "It's always seemed to me that people's personalities don't change just because they get older; they just get more pronounced. That's clearly what happened with Nana and Poppy."

Abby began to tell Maizie about her summer in New York before Fannie died. As the story unfolded, it became like a film reel in her mind, a movie of her life.

Back in New York, Abby got out of bed and went downstairs to make some coffee and see what was going on this morning. Maybe the situation and the condition in her parents' house wouldn't look as bad in the morning light and after she'd had a good night's sleep. Unfortunately, her hopes were dashed as she walked into the kitchen. The kitchen was still a mess, and the piles of papers on the dining room table hadn't gotten any smaller overnight. As Abby realized there was no coffeemaker in sight on the kitchen counter, she proceeded to rummage through the cabinets, looking for anything that resembled a brewing object. Not finding anything and having searched through the entire kitchen, Abby decided to ask her mother if they had one.

Abby went to peek in on her mother. Fannie was sitting propped up in the bed on three pillows, sleeping with the two prongs of oxygen still in her nose. Her breath was raspy and shallow. She was in such a light sleep that even though Abby never actually walked into the room, the sound of her footstep on the floor just outside the room was enough to wake her. Fannie opened her eyes and smiled at Abby.

"You're up early. I'm surprised you're awake. I thought your body clock would be on Colorado time. How did you sleep?" Fannie asked.

"I'm OK, Mom. Believe it or not, it was kind of a surprise to wake up in my old room and my old bed. Do you and Dad have a coffeemaker? I looked around and didn't find one. I really need some caffeine."

Fannie replied, "No, we don't have one of those coffeemakers. The doctor said no caffeine, so all we drink is instant Sanka. I think we have some jars downstairs, if you want to check."

"I did, Mom, there are about twelve jars down there. Are you stocking up for some reason?"

"No, we just pick them up whenever they go on sale."

"Is the Sanka on sale all the time? Sure looks like it. Well, I guess I'll have to go buy a coffeemaker and some real coffee."

"Well, then I guess you will since our Sanka doesn't satisfy your taste."

"Nice attitude, Mom, this early in the morning."

"I'm not the one with the attitude."

"OK, then I'll go to the deli for coffee. Do you want any decaf?"

"I'm perfectly fine with the Sanka."

"All right, back in a few with real coffee for me then."

Abby returned from the deli with two large cups of hot, caffeine-filled coffee. Two cups were going to awaken her senses enough to start the day.

"Two cups—that enough caffeine for you? I heard on the radio that too much caffeine isn't good for you. That's why the doctor took us off the caffeine," Fannie said.

"Yes, it might be enough caffeine for now, and I'm sure the doctor has you on decaf for other reasons as well. Would you like some breakfast?" Abby thought changing the subject might be a good idea at this point.

Fannie said that she'd like to have breakfast. However, what Fannie wanted to do and what she was able to do were two very different things. Fannie was so weak that the act of swinging her feet over the side of the bed and trying to put her weight on her feet was a very big effort. Abby stepped forward to help. She was helping Fannie get to her feet with one hand, while trying to maneuver the tube leading from the oxygen tank to the prongs in Fannie's nostrils with the other hand. It took a few minutes to master that activity, and then they began the slow journey from the bedroom to the dining room. Fannie half shuffled and half leaned on Abby to get into the dining room. When they finally reached the dining room, which was only a few feet from the bedroom, Fannie slumped into the nearest chair.

Abby simply couldn't believe that getting out of bed and walking a few feet into the dining room was so exhausting to her mom. She was literally gasping for air and it was so difficult for Abby to watch. Fannie was also tethered to the oxygen tank in the bedroom by the tube. It seemed absolutely ridiculous to Abby that her mother was limited by the length of the oxygen tube. To be limited by your illness was one thing, but to be limited by the length of a tube was quite another.

"Mom, do you know that there are portable oxygen tanks that weigh almost nothing and that would allow you to move about much more freely? We can speak to the doctor to order a different oxygen tank. I'm planning on calling your doctor this morning, so we can make an appointment to go see him and discuss your treatment and maybe changing your medications to see if they will make you feel better."

Even though Fannie was exhausted from getting out of bed and the short walk to the dining room, she jerked her head up to look at Abby. "Now, don't start with me, Abby! You're not even here twenty-four hours and already you're stirring things up. Can't you leave well enough alone? I don't want to start fighting with you right away. You can't just come home and try to take over everything."

Abby couldn't believe what she was hearing. What was the point of coming here if not to help her mother? Clearly, her mother wasn't doing well and she had reached out to Abby to come home and help. Abby wasn't going to sit by and watch her mother get worse if anything could be done to help her.

Abby looked her mother right in the eye. "Are you kidding me, Mom? We're going to do everything possible to help you. We're going to see your doctor and any other doctor we can think of to battle this disease. I'm not fighting with you; I'm telling you. This is not open for discussion. You can't ask for my help and then hamstring me. I didn't come all this way and upset my entire life to do nothing. You knew that about me and how I handle things when you called me."

Fannie didn't answer Abby's outburst. Abby wasn't quite sure what her mom was thinking, whether she was trying to think up an answer or was stunned by Abby's strong response. Was she was actually agreeing with Abby? Fannie wasn't one to hold back her opinions, nor was she at all shy about saying exactly what was on her mind. Certainly, her mom hadn't held back in her call to Abby to get her to come back from Colorado. Abby thought it was very much like waiting for the other shoe to drop, but the shoe might very well drop on your head or get thrown across the room at you.

The second skirmish of the day over, Abby said to Fannie, "What would you like for breakfast?"

"Just some coffee would be good. If you're going to make eggs for yourself, then I'll have one, too."

Abby made a mental note that her mom would never again help her make breakfast or make any other meal for that matter, given her mother's condition. Abby would miss that.

"Eggs are a great idea; I was thinking of having some myself. How about some toast to go with the eggs?"

"No, thanks, that would be too much to eat," Fannie responded.

Abby's father, Fred, was sitting at the far end of the dining room table. He was settled into his breakfast routine. This included a large red bowl filled with Total cereal, a banana, two pieces of whole wheat toast, and a cup of Sanka with milk and sugar. He would usually help Fannie to the table. Abby and her father had been up early that morning, so Abby told him she would help her mother get up.

Fred said, with more than a little sarcasm in his voice, "Nice to see you two getting along so well; it's just like old times around here. Glad you're home, Abby."

"Me too, Dad."

Abby made yet another mental note to hang back and see what she could learn about her mother's physical condition by her responses. It was clearly not a good sign that it took so much effort to get her mom into the living room from the bedroom. It also didn't seem like one egg and toast was a huge meal, but Fannie had already dismissed it as being too much to eat.

Maybe that was part of her mom's problem. She just wasn't getting enough nutrition. Her mom certainly looked much thinner than Abby remembered her. Abby also didn't ever remember her mother looking this frail. Perhaps if Abby got enough calories into her mother, Fannie would perk up and return to her old self. Abby could see this as a vicious downward spiral. Fannie was too weak to cook, so she wasn't getting enough to eat. The less she ate, the weaker she became. Abby thought if she could reverse this, maybe her mother would really get better, or at least mostly back to her old self. It seemed like a good plan, until she thought it through. Yes, nutrition was a part of the problem, but it wasn't the biggest part of the problem. The little voice in her head was screaming at her that she was denying the truth. Her mom had emphysema, and it was her lungs that were giving out. Abby could try to feed her mom all she wanted, but unless her mom's doctor or some specialist could come up with a new course of treatment or some new, even experimental, medication, her mom probably wasn't going to make it.

Abby wondered how many times in the past two and a half days she had fought back tears. Here was yet another time.

If Fannie had been sitting in the dining room when Abby started to clean out the kitchen, there would have been another fight between them. Since there had already been two fights before nine o'clock, Abby had decided to wait until a little later in the day for fight number three.

Although the kitchen had always been small, Fannie had managed very well in the confined space. The present condition of the kitchen was just more proof to Abby that her mom was much sicker than she had let on and that she had not been well for longer than most people knew. If her mom had been well, things would never have deteriorated as much as they had. It was also proof that her father's health was failing as well, because he seemed not to notice the mess; if he did notice, he didn't have the capacity to do much about it. It was beyond him. Abby was stunned at the quick deterioration of the house—and her parents.

Abby's plan was to start at one end of the kitchen and work her way toward the other end; it seemed pretty simple and logical. The most obvious place to start was with what looked to be about fifty cans of soup. Armed with a big black garbage bag, Abby, for some perverse reason, decided to actually count the cans of soup. Her estimate wasn't far off. There were forty-seven cans of soup, most of them Campbell's. This was worse than the twelve jars of Sanka. As Abby started to go through the cans, it wasn't too difficult to weed them out. More than half of the cans had long since expired, so they could be pitched into the black garbage bag. Then there were a number of cans that had bulges in them, so they weren't fit to eat either. That was all they needed—to either get botulism or food poisoning, two very unappealing choices. And, in Fannie's weakened condition, Fannie might never recover from a bout of either one.

Moving forward in the battle to reclaim the kitchen, Abby then attacked the cereal boxes. It was pretty much the same routine. As she examined the boxes, there were more that had expired than were still good. Abby totally hated to think of what a mouthful of stale cereal would taste like first thing in the morning. If there were only two people living in the house, exactly how much did they think they could possibly eat that they had stockpiled that much food? Were they expecting a famine, a plague of locusts that would wipe out the food supply, or perhaps a nuclear explosion?

The refrigerator was next. This was a truly scary scene. Abby had already moved on to the third big, black garbage bag, so now she was finally glad of one thing her parents had stockpiled—the big garbage bags. On the top shelf in the refrigerator, there were several packages of cheese that looked as if they were growing penicillin. Out! Then there was a package of hot dogs that had a slightly green hue beneath the packaging. Out again! There were some grapes in the back of the refrigerator that had shriveled very badly. Out yet again! By the time Abby was finished with the refrigerator, another two black garbage bags had been filled. However, Abby now was able to see the back of the refrigerator and had made room for some fresh food. Abby took the shelves out of the refrigerator to wash in the kitchen sink. For the first time in her life, she was grateful for the yellow Playtex gloves her mother kept next to the sink to do the dishes. Abby used to make fun of them when she was a kid. It was strange how things could stay the same, yet maybe it was your perspective that changed as you aged a bit. By the time Abby was finished washing the shelves, there was something resembling a small oil slick in the sink.

Then Abby moved on to the cabinets beneath the counters. There were an amazing number of pots and pans of all shapes and sizes shoved into the cabinets without regard to the size of the item. Didn't anyone ever hear of stacking with the largest things on the bottom and the smallest on the top? After the first three cabinets, where things seemed to fling themselves out of the cabinet with a vengeance as soon as the door was opened, Abby had enough sense to open the cabinet door part way and hold it with her knee to let the pile shift so that it didn't come cascading down onto her foot.

Maizie was listening attentively as Abby told the story about her first few days back from Colorado. Maizie said, "I'm sorry to hear things were such a mess for them and that they waited that long to call you. It must have been so hard for everyone. Some of the stories are so funny, and I guess I'll be throwing out Sanka, soup and cereal for you in a few years. Do they even make instant Sanka anymore?"

Both Maizie and Abby had enjoyed their time looking through the photo albums and would save the rest of the stories for another time. Maizie knew her mother certainly had other stories to tell.

CHAPTER 17

Abby could see that Maizie was stalling and didn't really want to leave to head back to her apartment. Normally, she'd want to get on the road to beat the traffic going back over the Tappan Zee Bridge on a Sunday. Tonight she was willing to stay for dinner and then decided to do her laundry. It seemed that by staying here and prolonging the weekend, she was somehow denying the problems that were waiting for her at work. Mom to the rescue.

Abby said to Maizie, "Look, I know how upsetting the breakup of the firm is for you, but somehow these things have a way of working out. You still don't know for sure whether you'll be able to go to the new place with your boss."

Maizie responded, "What could possibly make you think this is going to work out? Jeff is not negotiating from a position of strength. I really don't have a good feeling about this."

Abby could hear the annoyance in Maizie's voice, so maybe it was time for Abby to shut up. It brought her back to sparring with her own mother. Abby loved her mother, but it didn't take much to get them arguing. The problem with her mother was she always had to have the last word, or maybe it was Abby who had to have the last word.

Hearing Maizie's voice brought Abby back to the present moment and out of her thoughts. Maizie said with a hound dog face and a long sigh, "I suppose I might as well go home. And don't say it's all for the best. It sounds like *Candide*. It's all for the best in this best of all possible worlds."

Abby started to laugh, despite herself, which, thank God, made Maizie laugh, too.

"I'm outta here; love ya. I'll call you when I get home."

With that, Hurricane Maizie swept out of the house. Now it was Abby's turn to breathe a sigh of relief. It was almost as if she had been holding her breath the whole weekend. The tension in the house dropped palpably.

Abby made herself a cup of tea, and sat down to read the paper, with one eye; she kept an eye on TV with the other. Mostly, she was thinking about Maizie.

Maizie hadn't been gone more than a half hour when Abby heard her mother. Now she understood what it meant to be the sandwiched generation. Oh, God, now it's Hurricane Fannie. That's where Maizie got the theatrics. It was in the genes.

Fannie said in a sarcastic tone, "It's not so easy being a mom, is it? Your kids think you're wrong even when you're right. There is a certain irony that you have a daughter who's got a mind of her own and a mouth to go with it. Remind you of anyone you know?"

"I raised her to be independent, and it's OK with me if she mouths off now and then. She's scared now and with good cause. She can't be as perfect as I was as a kid." Abby couldn't say that with a straight face.

"Abby, I think they call it 'revisionist history.' You change the history after the fact to suit yourself. You were a handful from the time you were a little thing. And you were fearless. Nothing and no one intimidated you."

"Well, then the apple didn't fall far from the tree, Mom."

"That's not entirely true. So many things that are open to women now were not available to women when I was young. I would have liked a career like yours. I always felt hemmed in by what I couldn't do."

"I can understand being unhappy about feeling like your options were limited because you were a woman. That really stinks. When you think about it now, it's so absurd. What else made you so unhappy, Mom?"

"There were a lot of things. We'll talk about them another time."

"No way, Mom, you're not just bailing out on me now. You started a serious discussion, and we should continue it. We could never talk about these things when you were alive. Let's talk about it now."

"No, it's not important. Nothing can change the past, and I'm not in this world anymore. There's no point to this."

"You don't get it, do you, Mom? This is not all about you. I want to understand what went on in your life and why you were so unhappy. Your unhappiness directly affected everyone in the house as we were growing up. You didn't exist in isolation. You didn't live alone. You were the most important part of our family; you were Dad's wife and our mother. The things you did impacted us."

Fannie paused a minute to consider Abby's remarks but didn't say anything. She looked intently at Abby. Finally, she said, "I never really thought about how many my actions impacted everyone. I was pretty wrapped up in my own problems, and you and your sister seemed to be doing fine. Maybe that was all an act on your part, and I wanted to believe it was so. I'll come back, and we'll have that conversation."

With that having been said, and a lot more not having been said, Fannie just wasn't there anymore.

"Damn it, Mom, are you still here? Can you hear me? Can you?"

Abby thought, as she stood and looked around the room, while pointing her finger to the ceiling, as if that was where Fannie had disappeared to, that this would be the most incredibly useful tool for those people who are still alive. When the going gets tough, just go. No explanations, no messy situations. Just go. Infuriating, for those left behind. "Will things ever change, Mom?"

CHAPTER 18

It was precisely 7:30 a.m. according to the hands on the chrome and mahogany clock on the conference room wall, and Steve Goldrick started the Executive Committee meeting. Everyone was there, except for one partner who was in California on firm business. He was on the speaker phone, even though it was 4:30 in California. Fortunately, it was not a video conference because no one really wanted to know if he was in bed in his underwear, or if he was in bed with someone else. He sounded reasonably awake, and that was good enough. The meetings started exactly on time, since Steve had become the managing partner, and with very few exceptions, ended before nine. It was a privilege and a coveted position to be on the Executive Committee because it wielded incredible power. Nothing was a more perfect indication of a partner's status in the firm and being a strong source of business and billing than being on the Executive Committee.

Steve delegated tasks and projects to the members and expected—no, demanded—that they be finished on time. All reports were submitted to Steve and disseminated to the other members in advance of the meeting; everyone was to have read and become familiar with the report before the meeting.

There were six members of the Executive Committee. All were high-powered, opinionated lawyers, and yet, incredibly enough,

Steve managed to get them through a healthy agenda in an hour and a half. There was only one woman on the Committee, and she was not a token. She earned her way on by landing one of the movie studios as a client, and the billings were astronomical. Danielle Bevan understood the importance of being the first woman on the Committee, and despite her billings, she was not taken with herself; she had been a good choice and a breath of fresh air on the Committee. Although she probably wouldn't have admitted it out loud, she knew this sent a good message to the other women in the firm and an even stronger message to the men—things always changed, even in the seat of power.

Dannie Bevan would have deceived a casual onlooker. Dannie had a head of flaming red hair that was God given. Her red hair only served to accentuate her stunning cornflower-blue eyes. At first glance one might have thought she had just finished a photo shoot that would grace the pages of *Vogue*. She often surprised her opponents in the courtroom and boardroom by her personality and tenacity. Despite her beauty she was definitely a lawyer to be reckoned with. There was an intensity that fairly emanated from her. Her presence had been honed by a few years in her youth as an actress doing commercials on TV. She hawked everything from teen acne medicine to toys to lip balm to breakfast cereal. Her career as an actress hadn't been very successful by Hollywood standards, but she learned enough as an actress to be able to mesmerize a jury. She was always well put together, and every outfit was accessorized to the hilt, with matching jewelry and an assortment of Coach purses for every occasion.

Steve opened the meeting. "OK, first thing is the increase in our health insurance premiums. These insurance guys are really crazy. They want a thirty percent increase. Bob, what's happening with this?"

"I spoke to our agent last week. I told him to lean on the insurance company and tell them there's no way we're paying a thirty percent increase, with what we're already paying in premiums. With all the people we have on the policy, including the professional staff and the non-professional staff and their families,

I told him they have to do better—hell, a lot better—or we're going somewhere else. I don't care who takes the poison, but I told him it better not be us. I swear I could hear him gulp on the other end of the phone. We still have plenty of time before the renewal comes due. I had my secretary call two other agents and tell them we might want to make a move. They're salivating. I'll have some more definite numbers for our next meeting. Steve will give you my report in advance."

"Thanks, Bob, next up is office space. Ted, you're up."

Ted Schoeneman put on his reading glasses and looked down at his legal pad. "The landlord sent a letter saying there is additional space available on the floor below us. They want to know if we're interested in taking it. He showed me around the space last week. He's working up the numbers for me, but there are other more basic questions. Do we want to take more space? This is one of those snowballing questions. How does this impact our bottom line? Are we ready to hire some new people to fill this space? Do we have enough billings to fill this? Do we think we have new clients that require more attorneys and staff? Those are the main questions we need to answer. Of secondary importance is do we want to split the firm onto two floors? I think this possible new space raises a bunch of questions we have to think about. Steve and I should huddle when we have some answers and decide how much time to allocate at a future meeting and when."

"How much space is available, and how long do we have before the landlord wants an answer?" Dannie asked. "We've done remarkably well in the recession, but we could lose a big client at any time, and I don't know if we should be stretching ourselves too thin."

Steve tapped his pen on the table, loudly, and leaned forward, placing his elbows on the table as well. He intervened and refused to let the train become a runaway and hijack his meeting.

"Dannie," Steve said, "Ted said we need to pull a lot more data together before we discuss this. Let's move on."

Dannie spun her head around to look at Steve. She looked straight at him; she was not to be deterred. "I asked a question that's simple enough. How much space is available, and how long do we have before the landlord wants an answer?" she spat out with some annoyance in her voice.

As Fannie looked around the conference room table at the members of the Committee, she walked over to one of the massive windows and leaned against its frame with her arms folded in front of her. She said, "Impressive, Dannie, don't let Goldrick push you around. You're the only woman on this Committee, and you've earned it." Fannie shifted her position in the conference room from over near the window to right next to Steve's chair. Fannie looked directly at him; she was remembering more about Steve the more she saw of him.

Dannie pointedly took off her glasses and put them down on the table. She purposely looked at Ted and not at Steve.

Ted said, "The landlord would love us to commit right away. He says he'll hold off showing it for about two weeks, and in that time he'll work up the numbers and get them to me. There are two possibilities as to the square footage, depending on how we might want the space configured."

Steve jumped in again and said impatiently, "OK, let's move on. We can't make any decisions without a lot more info, which we don't have now. We have other items to discuss." Steve suddenly felt like a rush of cold air hit him, and asked, "Is there a window open?" Everyone else in the room just looked at one another and in almost perfect unison said, "No." Fannie then walked back to her position by the window.

Three more agenda items came up and were rapidly dispatched. Except for the hiccup on the new space, Steve thought the meeting moved along well.

Steve said, "Last item, before we adjourn. It's 8:50, and we're wasting billable hours, so let's finish up. Rick Singleton. I had a meeting with him last week. I told him what we decided and gave him the package we're offering him. He didn't take it all that well. Wanted me to bring it up again at the Executive Committee meeting. I'm bringing it up. We're not changing our mind. I wanted to make him think we're 'sympathetic and New Age.'"

Before Steve could say, "We're done," Dannie jumped in and said, "Why don't we reconsider? He was a very good attorney when he was here. He worked with me on a few projects, and he's a smart and savvy guy. I have enough work on a number of projects for the studio; I could use him."

Fannie turned her head and gazed in Dannie's direction and then back to Steve. Fannie thought it was only fair that someone represent Rick since he couldn't be here himself.

Steve gave Dannie a look that would have made most people cower.

"We talked about this, and it's decided," Steve said again emphatically.

"If it was decided, then why are you bringing this up again? The guy had enough chutzpah to come in and talk to you and try to change your mind. You can be very intimidating if you want to, Steve. The guy has guts. I'm telling you I have work for him, so he wouldn't have to be here twiddling his thumbs. I have billable hours for him."

There was clearly exasperation in Steve's voice. "I told you, and in case you forgot, and you were here, we already decided this." Steve said the last sentence through clenched teeth.

"I remember the discussion, but Rick has been through an awful lot, and he hasn't drowned. We should all be thankful that none of us has had to go through what he's been through. His head is still above water. Let's throw him a lifeline instead of an anchor."

Fannie wished Dannie knew she was there and was cheering her on.

"Just because you lost the vote last time, doesn't change what the vote was. If I recall, there was a very lengthy discussion about it," Steve said.

Steve was about to go on when Bob motioned to Steve by putting his own hand on his shirt pocket. Steve looked down at his shirt pocket and yelled, "Shit."

The top of his Montblanc pen was off, and there was an ever-growing pool of black ink on his otherwise pristine white shirt pocket. The shirt was ruined, and Steve stomped out of the room. He had a client meeting in an hour and he wasn't sure if he had a clean shirt in his office closet. The Executive Committee meeting was over.

Fannie was standing back in the corner of the room near the window again. She was looking at the cap of Steve's pen which was right by her foot, far away from where it had been. The pen had been bleeding into Steve's expensive shirt. Fannie smiled and thought to herself that the big blob on Steve's shirt looked like something from a Rorschach test. Let Steve figure out what the blob represented and how it got there.

The remaining members of the Executive Committee gathered up their things and stood up to go. Ted told Andy, on the conference call in California, who had no idea why Steve was yelling, what had happened. At least three people in the room had smirks on their faces.

Dannie said before anyone else left the room, "Since we're adjourned without a decision about Rick, I'll ask Steve to put it back on the agenda for the next meeting. He'll love it. I'll just make sure I have my asbestos suit on when I talk about it with Steve. I'm getting a little tired of this firm being run as an autocracy."

Fannie said to the now empty room, "Dannie, you're the one with the guts. I really like that about you. This is Rick's life we're talking about here! Steve'll get his."

CHAPTER 19

With all that was going on with Maizie, Abby decided that perhaps she should do some scouting around in the attic and basement to see if she could start to move some things and throw out others. She needed to make room for what appeared to be the inevitable move of Hurricane Maizie and her possessions back into the house. The situation in Maizie's law firm with Jeff was not looking good. It did not appear that there would be a place for Maizie. She was by turns resigned to the situation on some days and wildly upset on others. The job market was not strong, and so she and Abby might have to hunker down together for quite a while. Secretly, Abby enjoyed the thought that Maizie would come back to live with her for a time, but the mother in Abby didn't want Maizie to be so unhappy.

Abby dragged a trunk across the attic floor. The damn thing was heavy; she was never going to be able to get it down the stairs by herself without her pulling a muscle or throwing her back out. She pulled up an old rocking chair and moved it next to the trunk. Abby started digging around in there. There were a host of items piled in what seemed like no particular order. There was her mother's high school diploma from Haverstraw High School, three basketball trophies, a pair of Abby's baby shoes, and on and on. As Abby continued rummaging through the memorabilia, she came across some yellowed newspapers from 1963 of President Kennedy's assassination and clippings of her high school swim meets. Did her mother think they were of equal importance? Abby noticed that below the newspapers were packets of letters tied with ribbon. She picked them up and put them on her lap.

There were letters addressed to her mother from her high school friend, Rita. She and Fannie had been inseparable all through high school and throughout their lives. Although she was not Abby's aunt by blood or marriage, Abby and her sister always called her Aunt Rita. Abby didn't find out until she was about ten years old that Aunt Rita wasn't really her aunt. Abby never gave it a second thought. Her mother and Aunt Rita had played on the basketball team together in high school, and the team had apparently won some local championships, which was amazing. Her mother was only about five foot three standing on tiptoes, and Aunt Rita was shorter than that, so they must have been very quick and agile. Abby had such fond memories of Aunt Rita, and when Abby saw Aunt Rita's name on the return envelopes, Abby decided to indulge and revel in the memories from the past.

Fannie, sitting on the cedar chest in the attic, the one that she and Fred had received as a wedding present, watched as Abby rummaged through the trunk. Distressed, Fannie suddenly realized there was something at the bottom of the trunk that was never meant to be seen by anyone but her and her husband. Fannie had always meant to dispose of the letters long before her death, but periodically she would go up to the attic when she knew she was alone in the house and read them. The letters gave her comfort about decisions she had made long ago. While reading the letters, she did not feel alone, but she did miss her friend Rita. In her current state of being, or non-being, Fannie felt alone, and she wondered about the repercussions those decisions had all these years later.

When Fannie had taken sick, her decline in health was rapid. She had other more pressing things to worry about. Somehow the letters had totally slipped her mind, and they were never disposed of as she'd planned. The truth was going to come to light this way whether she wanted it to or not. Fannie realized that she was powerless to stop Fate, and that this revelation was meant to be.

Fannie knew the time had come to speak up or remain silent. She chose silence. Abby would discover a past that was connected to the present and would change the future as each letter was opened.

CHAPTER 20

Rick was rooting around his desk, looking for a bank statement, when he saw Dannie's business card. Rick wasn't even sure why he had it, but he stopped what he was doing and looked intently at the business card and smiled. His first thought was that she was stunningly beautiful and amazingly smart. In an instant, he chastised himself for thinking of her physical beauty over her brains. OK, she was amazingly smart and stunningly beautiful. Perhaps that was the right order.

As he was dialing her number, a thought flashed through his brain. Could she help him, or was he putting her in a precarious situation? He quickly ended the call and took a deep breath. He needed to think about this for a second before he did something he would regret.

He walked into the kitchen to get a glass of water while staring at his cell phone. I need help, and maybe she could be the ally I need. It would be good to talk to her anyway, since it's been so long. Despite how busy she was, Dannie was always willing to spend a few minutes to help me with a question about a case.

Fanny was standing in the kitchen and observing Rick. She said aloud to Rick, "Just go dial the phone number and talk to Dannie. She can have a very big influence on your future. Now go. Dial!" It was too bad that Rick couldn't hear her.

"I have the feeling that this is the right thing to do. I'll call her directly and avoid the receptionist." Plausible deniability. He grabbed his cell, scrolled down to her number and called her directly.

Dannie picked up the phone on the second ring.

"Hi, Rick, how the hell are you?" she laughed.

"Hanging in there, Dannie. How about you?"

"I'm doing fine. New clients, same old shit. It's good to hear your voice. You've been in my thoughts even though I haven't been very good at keeping in touch. It's not an excuse, but I get so busy around here that I lose track of time."

"It's OK, Dannie. I understand. So you're still really busy—that's great in this economy."

"Actually, I wish you were back here working, Rick. I miss having you around. I liked having you work on my matters. Some of the other people around here are less thorough than you. That puts more of a burden on me. It's important to work with someone you can trust."

"Speaking of trust, can I ask you something in confidence about the firm? I don't want to put you in an awkward position."

"I won't know until you ask. Let me just shut the door to my office." She was back a few seconds later and said, "OK, fire away."

"Did you know that I had a meeting with Steve?"

"Yes, I heard. And...?"

"When I met with Steve, he told me that the partners had voted no on my coming back. Then we talked some more, and Steve said he would revisit it at the Executive Committee and go to bat for me. He said he didn't quite know how long it would take to get back to me."

Dannie adopted a sarcastic and quizzical tone. "Steve said what? He said he'd go to bat for you? What an asshole bastard he is! The only bat Steve used in the Executive Committee was to bash you. I said we should revisit this again, and I'm going to have a battle with Steve over this. Frankly, I'm getting tired of working with a dictator."

"Rick, now I'm going to tell you something else in confidence; I need your word that you'll keep this completely quiet.

I'm thinking very seriously about leaving the firm. I have enough business that I can start my own firm, and I'll need to take some people with me. I'm going to hand pick who I want, and there aren't going to be that many people. You know, lean and mean to start. If you're ready to come back to work full time, why don't you and I have dinner to discuss this matter. Are you interested?"

"Interested? God yes! Dannie, this couldn't have come at a better time for me. I couldn't tell if Steve was stringing me along, and maybe it's time for a change. Hard to believe I'm saying that with all the changes that have gone on in my life, but this would definitely be a change for the better. When can we meet?"

Fannie smiled as Rick hung up the phone. "I told you so, Rick. It's good that you listened to me, even if you can't hear me."

CHAPTER 21

The dinner with Dannie went well, and as they say, the deal was sealed. Dannie was much further on in her plan to leave the firm than she had let on in the phone conversation. She had talked to the people she was going to take with her. Her close friend, Christopher McKay, was leaving his firm, and Chris and Dannie were going to be partners. Chris was bringing seven attorneys with him to the new firm, and Dannie, with Rick agreeing to come, would bring six. Chris and Dannie had apparently spoken to two other attorneys from another firm that Chris had tried cases against and been impressed with, and they were considering the offers. The new office space was under negotiation in White Plains, a suburb of New York City. All the attorneys lived in Westchester or Rockland, and the move out of New York City would save everyone a commute and would save the new firm considerable rent. Dannie's question at the last Executive Committee meeting about the cost of new space was partially an exercise in comparison shopping about rents, but it was also to find out about how much time she had before she had to tell the old firm about her departure. Dannie was decent enough that she was not going to let the old firm commit to new office space and then tell them she was leaving. That was something she just could not do to her soon-to-be former partners. Dannie also knew that breaking off from a firm caused enough animosity in and of itself, and she didn't want to add any more fuel to the fire.

Dannie and Rick decided that Rick would send in his resignation, and he agreed to help her with the transition to the new office space. Since Rick wasn't working, he could be available to meet with the contractor building out the new space, and take some burden off Dannie. Rick knew it couldn't hurt to extend himself on behalf of his new boss. Frankly, Rick was happy for something of substance to occupy himself, since sitting around only made him morose and dwell on the past.

Rick completed his resignation letter and signed it. Originally, he thought this would be a painful process because it was another chapter that was closing in his life. Lately, he had begun to see with his psychiatrist that endings aren't always bad or painful. Certainly, Dannie had made this ending much more of a non-event, and he was looking forward to being in the new firm with people he liked and who liked him.

Rick called Abby to tell her what was going on. He hadn't spoken to her in about three weeks with all that was happening, and he felt a little guilty because she was always so willing to help him. His idea was to invite her to dinner to celebrate his new beginning. Rick didn't verbalize it that much, but he was eternally grateful to Abby for risking her own life and refusing to give up on him. He would never be able to adequately repay her, but he wanted her to be a part of his life, and he wanted to give her good news for once.

"Hi, Abby, it's Rick. Sorry I haven't been in touch in a few weeks, but there's been a lot going on. All good stuff. I was hoping that I could take you out for dinner on Friday to tell you about it. Give me a buzz when you get back." Rick hung up the phone and, for the first time in a long time, felt some peace. He could exhale.

Abby got home about an hour after Rick left the phone message. This was a good surprise, perhaps the yin and the yang of it. Rick sounded happy in the message, but Maizie was depressed.

Abby called Rick back immediately, eager for some good news since her house felt as if a pall had descended on it.

"Hi, Rick, it's Abby. I was so happy to hear your message. What's the great news?"

"I have a job with one of the partners who's leaving the old firm and starting her own firm. I had done a pretty good amount of work with her, and she likes me and respects my work. An added bonus is that the new firm will be in White Plains, so there's no more schlepping to New York City."

"Rick, that's fantastic! I am so happy for you. This sounds like the start of something really good."

"I need to celebrate; I can't believe I just said that. But I'm really pumped about this; it's good."

The tumblers of Abby's mind went into overdrive. Rick and a new firm in White Plains? Maizie in need of a job as a paralegal. The fortuitous meeting of a need and a resource.

"Rick, I have an idea. My daughter, Maizie, is here. Why don't you come for dinner on Friday night? We'll have a celebration in your honor."

CHAPTER 22

Abby was sitting on her grandmother's old rocking chair. It was made of maple. It had a high back with carvings of hearts, ribbons, and small doves. The armrests were wide and worn from all the years of use, and the rocker had a distinctive squeak as you rocked backward. Abby held the yellowed letters in her lap. She gently untied the green ribbon—no particular fancy shade of green, just green. Abby remembered that green was her mother's favorite color. Oddly enough, she still recognized Aunt Rita's handwriting on the envelopes after all these years. Some of the postmarks were from England. Abby opened the letter on the top, which had the oldest postmark. The ink was faded but still legible.

Dear Fannie,

July 10, 1973

It's hard to believe that we're actually in England. So many unbelievable things have happened in the past few months that sometimes I wake up in the middle of the night and look out the window to make sure this is real and not part of my dreams. I'm going to stay for a few months to help Caroline get settled in the new house and help with the baby. Jonathan has started his new job and is working a lot of hours. I let them sleep at night when the baby cries. It sounds so selfless, but actually, I love having him all to myself.

I'm sending a few pictures of him, but they don't do him justice. He's much cuter than that. He now recognizes us and gets excited when we walk into the room. When I'm alone at night with "our little boy," I tell him all about his other grandmother.

I feel better about this every day and that we did the right thing. Caroline wants me to tell you how much she appreciates what you did for them. You will always have a special place in all of our hearts. You know that you already have a special place in my heart. You are the sister I never had.

I will keep my promise and write to you every single week while I'm here to tell you all about "our little boy."

Love always,

Rita

Abby looked at the pictures of a cute little baby. He had wispy light hair in the pictures and big brown eyes with long eyelashes. Abby wondered what Aunt Rita meant that she and Mom did the right thing.

Abby opened the next letter. There was another picture of presumably the same little boy.

Dear Fannie,

October 16, 1974

I took your suggestion and sent you some colored photos. "Our little boy" is growing in leaps and bounds and is walking, and he learned he can run. He has a contagious giggle that makes you laugh as well. His laugh reminds me of Abby when she was a baby.

Got to run, but wanted to get the pictures in the mail to you today. We have an appointment with the pediatrician today. I'll give you all the new info on him.

Love always,

Rita

Abby read through a few more letters and looked at more pictures of "our little boy." She thought it was strange that Aunt Rita never referred to him by name and on the back of each picture was just his age. Abby skimmed through a number of letters because she was beginning to recognize a pattern. She began to feel anxious; she couldn't read through the letters fast enough.

Dear Fannie:

September 8, 1978

"Our little boy" started school today. Caroline sent these pictures to me and asked that I send some to you. Doesn't he look adorable in his little uniform for school? I miss him so much.

The great news is that Caroline and Jonathan will be moving back to the US in two months. I can't wait! Would you like to meet "our little boy" once they're back? Do you want to come with me? Caroline would love it if you could bring yourself to meet him.

Love always,

Rita

Abby didn't quite know what to make of this letter. Why would Aunt Rita ask her mother whether she could bring herself to meet their "little boy"? Why wouldn't her mother have jumped at the chance to meet this little boy whose every move had been chronicled so carefully by Aunt Rita to Mom? It just didn't make sense, or maybe it did.

Then Abby looked at the five pictures that had been included in the letter. Abby actually gasped. This little boy in the school uniform was the spitting image of Maizie as a kindergartner! The house of cards began to collapse. Now all the intrigue and vague references in the letters made sense. This was her child, her son whom she had given up for adoption when she was fifteen years old.

Abby sat in the chair, rocking back and forth, holding the letters and photos in her lap. So many memories of what had happened during that period in her life came flooding back. How many "periods" in a person's life are there? She felt confused, her memory foggy—was this really true? She remembered seeing the tall man that came into the hospital room with the adoption papers for her to sign. She'd never forget the smell of the cologne or aftershave, whatever it was he wore, and he was dressed in a fancy suit.

Other images began to form in her mind as she remembered that day. She realized that she had buried so many of those memories, except for one. Her mother was sitting in the corner of the room and rose from the chair as Aunt Rita walked quietly into the room. Aunt Rita walked to the side of the bed and kissed Abby on the forehead. Aunt Rita said in a soft voice as she leaned close to Abby, "Everything will be OK and so will you. It took a lot of strength and courage to do this, and I am so proud of you." Aunt Rita turned from Abby and went over to Fannie. Fannie and Aunt Rita spoke in whispers to each other. They nodded and Aunt Rita left. Abby looked across the hallway through the open door of her room. Abby saw her father standing there, watching his little girl, as if he needed to be ready in a moment's notice to rescue her, to pick up the pieces. He looked sad to her.

The hazy memories that swirled around in her head began to clear. Abby now felt anger—and lots of it. "Mom...Mom...Mom! I need you here...Now! I need some answers! Goddamn it, are you here?"

Abby rose abruptly from the rocking chair, and the letters dropped from her hand and her lap like autumn leaves falling to the ground.

"Yes, Abby I'm here, and I have been watching you read the letters. This wasn't exactly how things were supposed to happen. I wanted to tell you myself many times, but it was just never the right time."

"What the hell is that supposed to mean? In all these years, you couldn't find a right time?" Abby exploded. This was just the first part of the explosion, and there was clearly more to come. Abby was literally red in the face. "Is this boy my child? How could you do this? How could you keep this from me?"

Abby bent down and picked up one of the photos, a little faded and yellow. This was her son. Abby clearly knew it; she didn't have to ask. She remembered the day she gave birth at fifteen. Thankfully short labor, four pushes and there he was. Her mother and father were with her. She also remembered the boy who had gotten her that way. He was a prick! She was nothing but a checkmark on the locker room wall. When she told him, all he said was "How do you know it's mine? And if you are pregnant, it's your fault. I don't want anything to do with you. I gotta go to practice." He just turned and walked away. Abby tried to run after him and say something, anything, but he just pushed her away and screamed at her to leave him alone. The birth certificate said, "Father unknown."

Abby continued to rant as if talking to herself. "We never talked about it. You never asked me if I was OK or if I needed your shoulder to cry on. You acted like this child never mattered to you. Like he was just an article of clothing that could be discarded. Now I find out that you knew everything that went on in his life. Why did you and Aunt Rita keep this a secret from me? You acted as if once the decision was made and the baby was taken out of the hospital that it was all over. Well, it wasn't over for me. It definitely was *not* over for me. We never talked about it; it was like nothing had happened."

Abby exploded with a torrent of words, "I worried every single day what happened to him, where he was and who was taking care of him. You didn't think I had the right to know what happened to my son? Who appointed you God? You were fine. You knew the details of his life. Didn't it ever occur to you that I might want to know, too? Are you such a coward that you couldn't once have owned up to what you did."

As Abby finished screaming, she was shaking, and she sank back into the chair and began to sob violently.

Fannie knew that virtually anything she said to Abby now was going to be of no consequence, and no logical explanation would suffice. Fannie decided to stay invisible. Fannie only let her voice be heard.

"Abby, I understand that you're upset and you have a right to be. But I thought that I was doing the best thing for you, my beautiful daughter, who was an unmarried teenage girl. Your life would have been a hand-to-mouth existence, just scraping by. I certainly thought the baby had the right to be raised by two parents who desperately wanted a child. Not that you wouldn't have loved him and done the best you could for him. But here was a wonderful chance to give the baby a good life with every opportunity that you as a teenage mother would not have been able to. I knew Caroline from the time she was a little girl, and of course Rita and I were like sisters. You couldn't pick a better home for that child. Was that so terrible?"

"You still don't get it. You convinced me to give up the baby and sever all ties and go on with my life. But you lied for almost forty years, and you've been lying from the grave. You didn't sever the ties. You kept those ties, and you kept them from me."

Abby had been pacing back and forth during her assault at Fannie. The letters strewn on the floor were under her feet, but she held tightly to the photo.

"C'mon, I want to show you something."

Abby climbed down the attic stairs and stomped down the hall into her bedroom. Tina looked at her, and Tina could feel the anger emanating from Abby. Tina followed behind Abby with her tail down. When they reached the bedroom, Tina sat by the window and waited, wondering what was coming next. The sun streaming through the skylight and the warmth in the bedroom made it an inviting place, in sharp contrast to Abby's own dark mood. Abby yanked open the bottom drawer of her night table. The ferocity of the way she pulled the drawer open made a few things from the top of the night table spill onto the floor. Abby got down on one knee and pulled out a small plastic photo album from underneath a book that was lodged in the drawer. Abby flipped open the photo album and shoved it toward Fannie.

"Look at it! Look at the fucking pictures!"

What Fannie saw truly surprised her. Inside were three pictures. The first was a close-up of the baby with a little, light blue cap on his head used for newborns, and his eyes were closed. The second was a close-up of a very young Abby holding the baby and looking directly at him. His eyes were open, and even though Fannie knew that a newborn couldn't focus, he appeared to be staring directly at Abby and smiling. A connection had been made. The third picture was of Fannie and Fred standing next to Abby's bed in the hospital. Fannie was holding the baby with a wistful smile of her face and Fred had his arm around Fannie. Had it not been for the circumstance, this would have been the perfect family photo.

"These pictures are beautiful. You've kept them all these years," Fannie said as her voice trailed off. Fannie not only stared at Abby, the baby and Fred in the picture, but also at herself. She looked around the room and her eyes focused on the mirror above the dresser. She had forgotten what she looked like when she had been alive. She then looked in the mirror, but saw no reflection of herself, only Abby's reflection. How could this be? Have I been dead this long, that I can't remember what I looked like? I was tethered to this earth and my family. Now I feel as if the ropes have frayed. Am I being torn away from my life, as I once knew it? No, not yet; I'm not ready! Fannie wanted to be in the here and now, with her daughter. She wanted to hold Abby in her arms and to make everything alright between them. The problem was she couldn't. That time had passed and it might be too late. She hoped it wasn't.

Abby began again, her voice sounding less angry, more spent, "I've kept this secret to myself all these years. I never told Jerry; I never told Scott or Maizie that I had a child, but every single day of my life, I looked at these three pictures and worried and wondered what happened to my son. Was he OK? Was he having a good life? Was he healthy? Did he marry? Did he have any children of his own? Did he make something of himself? I wrestled with those questions every day of my life. And goddamn it, you knew all the answers and kept them to yourself. How selfish can you be?"

"I wasn't being selfish. The truth is I gave up my grandson! Every letter I opened from Aunt Rita brought me and your father happiness, but sadness as well. Sacrifice is never easy. Giving up someone you love makes you reluctantly change direction.

Abby looked in the direction of Fannie's voice, "So, Mom, do you still know where he is? Is he healthy? Did he turn out well?"

"The answer is yes to all three questions."

"What—you can't elaborate a little more?"

"I could, but I can't."

"You could, but you can't? You know I might want to meet him or at least see him."

"Be careful because there is a lot to consider. You know that you can't just spring this on Scott and Maizie, especially since you've never said one word to either one of them."

"You know, Mom, I've had enough. I can't think anymore. Leave and leave me alone for a while. I need to process all that you told me and didn't tell me."

Abby walked around the room and was thankful she was alone. She walked to the bed and sat down. She looked at the pictures for a long time. She then looked at Tina and called to her. Abby reached out to Tina and hugged her around the neck. Abby realized she wasn't totally alone and was thankful that Tina was there to comfort her. After the tears stopped, Abby then went back to the attic and gathered up all the letters and pictures that had fallen to the floor. She neatly put every one of them in order and tied them gently with the green ribbon.

CHAPTER 23

A few days later, it was getting toward seven in the evening, and Rick was due in about twenty minutes. Being busy with work and worrying about Maizie were good diversions for Abby, even though the letters and this newfound information continued to haunt her. She was finally satisfied that her son had gone to a couple she knew, and who wanted children. She wished that she hadn't had to worry about him for all these years for no reason.

"Hey, Maiz, where are you? You dressed yet? Rick's going to be here any minute."

"I'll be down in a minute, Mom. I guess with all the running around we did today—I sat down on the bed, and I fell asleep for a few minutes. I'm just putting on my makeup, and then I'll be down."

A few minutes later, Maizie bounded down the stairs and into the kitchen.

"OK, all set. What can I do to help?"

"You can finish the salad and open the wine. Look, I know you're independent and you're a grown-up—blah, blah, blah—but I'm going to work the conversation around to your being a paralegal and recently unemployed, and then you can run with the ball."

"Oh, for God's sake, Mom, could you be any more obvious? Unless the man is a total moron, he's going to figure out what you're doing."

"Even if he does, it couldn't hurt to let him know that you're looking for a job. He's going into a new firm, and they're bound to need staff. Not all the staff from the firm in the City is going to want to come to White Plains to work. Make sure you tell him about how experienced you are, too."

"I won't say anything. I'll just sit on your lap and be the dummy, and you can be the ventriloquist. You tell me when to move my mouth."

Abby threw the dish towel at her.

"He's a really nice and smart guy. You could do a lot worse than to work in his new firm. It's not like there's a lot of jobs out there in this economy. Don't be stupid; take advantage of a good opportunity when it practically gets dropped in your lap."

A few minutes later the doorbell rang, and Abby opened the door to Rick, a bouquet of flowers and two bottles of wine.

Abby kissed him on the cheek and ushered him into the foyer.

"Rick, it's so good to see you. You look great. This is my daughter, Maizie."

Rick reached out his hand to her. "Maizie, it's so nice to finally meet you. I feel that I already know you, from all that I hear about you from Abby. I can certainly see the family resemblance."

Maizie responded, "Rick, do not believe a word she says. I can only imagine what she's told you about me. You probably thought I was a cross between Wonder Woman and Mother Theresa."

They all laughed, but Rick added quickly, "Moms have a license to do that, but in your case, she wasn't that far off." Maizie actually blushed.

"OK, enough with the Mom bashing. Who wants a glass of wine? Rick, do you want to open one of the bottles of red you brought and one of the whites over there on the counter?"

Rick replied as he opened the wine, "If we have a few minutes before dinner, I'd like to see the rest of your garden. My grandmother really liked to garden, and I used to help her when

I was a kid. Plus, I think she liked the slave labor. She was a little bit of a thing, about the size of the shovel. I was a tall string bean as a kid, and she was so short that we must have been a sight together. She was a great lady. It's funny the things that stick out and you remember from being a kid."

Rick had a faraway look, and it seemed he was doing some private reminiscing. Maizie watched him for those fleeting seconds. She thought how good-looking he was and working with him would be even better. Maizie interrupted the silence that was settling over the room. "She sounds wonderful. Is she still alive?"

Abby gave Maizie a withering look and then Maizie realized what she had said. This was supposed to be a celebration for Rick and his new job, and the last thing they needed to discuss with Rick was death.

Maizie was quick to pick up on Abby's look, and so she said, "You would have liked my grandmother, too. She was 'vertically challenged,' but she was a pistol. Ironically, she was a good basketball player in high school. I guess we've evolved a little since then, height wise, that is."

Rick said, "No, my grandmother passed. I still miss her."

Abby wasn't sure if what came out of her mouth was lame or profound. She heard herself saying, "It's a tribute to the people you love that the memories are still so vivid."

Rick nodded and made a point of walking over to look at the deck and opened the porch door to walk out there. If he needed a moment to compose himself, then this was his way of taking it.

Maizie mouthed to Abby, "I'm sorry."

Abby nodded to her that it was OK and said in a voice loud enough to raise the dead, no pun intended, and so that Rick would know she was coming, sort of like hide and seek. "Rick, let me show you the sunflowers and the rest of my garden."

After a few minutes of showing Rick the garden, Abby said to him, "Let's go back up on the deck and have something to drink and some hors d'oeuvres."

They sat down on the wicker couch and chairs that were positioned around the outdoor fireplace.

Rick said, "I'm always fascinated by nature. I'm really impressed with your garden. I always promised myself that I was going to plant a garden, but I never got around to actually doing it. I had planned to plant one with Adam because I thought he'd get a kick out of it. I could sort of see myself letting Adam dig in the garden as I had done with my grandmother. As a little boy, I was intrigued by the worms, since they always had a direction to go in. I always wondered how they got there with no eyes. Besides, what kid doesn't love to get dirty?"

This was the first time Abby heard him mention Adam by name. Maybe there was a little healing going on.

Rick said, "I'm ready for those hors d'oeuvres and a glass of wine. Where's Maizie? Doesn't she come on the garden tour?"

"No, she doesn't. She grew up with the gardening, but I began to find her on the deck working on her tan instead of the garden."

Maizie had brought all the hors d'oeuvres onto the deck and was sitting on the love seat with a glass of wine in hand. She got up to pour some wine and said, "Just put the money for the tour in the jar over there."Then without further ado, she turned the conversation in a completely new direction. "Mom tells me you're starting in a new law firm in White Plains. That's exciting. When do you start?"

For a person who thought Abby was too pushy, this was certainly a surprise coming out of Maizie's mouth.

Rick seemed more than happy to talk about the new firm. "I think it's going to be good. I had enough of the politics and the bullshit of the firm in the City. We all want to make money, but at Goldrick, money and the bottom line are a religion. At the new firm, there will be two partners to start, and I know Dannie Bevan very well. She's one hell of a lawyer. I think it's an opportunity for me. For some reason, I always had this nagging doubt that I would ever be made a partner in the old firm. I've worked on matters before with Dannie, and I know she has confidence in my ability. It's a chance to start over."

Maizie responded, "That sounds like a good deal. Have you ever worked in White Plains before? It's undergone such a transformation in the past few years. There was never anything happening at night in White Plains and now Mamaroneck Avenue is restaurant row. It's great. Some night if you're free, you can come over and meet me, and you can check it out. It would be fun, and I also have a group of friends that meet for drinks on Thursdays."

It was a good thing that Abby was wiping her mouth with her napkin, because the baked brie that was in her mouth would have fallen on the floor as her jaw dropped open. Here was Abby's daughter, who hated it if Abby told her friends anything good about Maizie because Maizie thought it was bragging. Then Maizie was not pleased that Rick was invited to dinner because it seemed too obvious to her that she needed a job as a paralegal and he was a lawyer in a new firm needing staff. Now Maizie was inviting Rick to meet her and some friends for drinks. Some spirit must have inhabited Maizie's body. Oh God, was this Fannie?

Rick looked at Maizie, smiling, and answered, "Sounds like a plan; I might just take you up on that offer. It'd be a good way to get to know the area and you. Um, I'm thinking of moving to Westchester, so I won't have that horrendous commute across the bridge. Jersey is just too long a commute. There's nothing keeping me in Jersey anyway. Do you know any good real estate brokers that you can recommend? You seem to know a lot people, and you're familiar with the different towns in the area."

"Where are you thinking about looking?"

"Probably Rye or Rye Brook. Maybe even Harrison. I like the idea of moving to a new place, but I dread the thought of making the move and packing. I don't think that I can just call in movers and tell them to move everything in the house, without my sorting through things. I don't want as big a house as I have now. I might even want a condo."

Maizie then piped up, "You know, I'm out of work for a while, so I wouldn't mind helping you by packing up the more impersonal things like kitchen supplies or linens and then helping you decide what of the other things you want and packing those for you. I could wrap pictures for you and put them all in a few boxes, and when you have time, you can decide what you want in your new place."

Abby thought, as she watched the volley of conversation, who was this alien in my daughter's body? If I had even so much as suggested this to her, she would have been screaming that I was demeaning her by suggesting that she take a job that was beneath her or that I was trying to run her life. Was this boredom or perhaps hormones around a handsome young man? Easy answer.

As they sat down to dinner, Maizie and Rick were already talking about dates the following week for her to start helping him because he wanted to be settled into his new place, if possible, before he started work. To his credit, Rick said up front, "I really appreciate it that you'll help me, but we have to be clear that I'm paying you for this work. Should we agree to an hourly rate? How about seventy-five dollars an hour?"

Maizie raised her eyebrows, her eyes opened wide, and she quickly thought that this was an absurdly overpriced offer. "Seventy-five an hour? That's too much. Fifty an hour will do fine. I'm very efficient. Wait until you see how much I can get done in an afternoon."

Abby almost laughed out loud. She could see how much Maizie had done in less than an hour! Even if he hadn't moved into his new place by the time he started his new job, it didn't matter. Maizie worked in Westchester, and Hurricane Maizie would blow into the new place and arrange things. In that respect, she very much reminded Abby of Fannie. They both wanted to be in control. Abby had learned the hard way as an adult that there is no control. There is only the illusion of control.

CHAPTER 24

The following morning Abby was up early and went for a run with Tina. When she came back, Maizie was sitting at the kitchen table with a mug of tea in front of her. She got up and poured a mug of coffee for Abby.

Abby sat down at the kitchen table with Maizie. "You seemed particularly chipper last night when Rick was around. For someone who didn't want to stay for dinner when I invited Rick, you seemed to be having a very good time."

"God, Mom, do you ever give up? I have to admit you were right—for once. He's a very nice guy, but do you always have to make a federal case out of every little thing?"

"You and I clearly differ on what is a 'little thing.' I'm glad you like him, too. Did I understand correctly that you're going to help him clean out his house and pack up things for him?"

"Yeah, since I'm not working, I thought it would be something good to do to keep me busy and I won't mind picking up some cash."

"And his being a handsome, eligible lawyer had nothing whatsoever to do with your offer."

"You're so jaded; I really need the cash, really," Maizie said, smiling at her mother.

Abby replied, "You couldn't even keep a straight face when you said that." They both laughed. Abby continued, "You two were having such a good time last night that I didn't even need to be there. But I do want to say something serious to you. I think he's a sweet guy, too, and very handsome, but I want you to remember that you're walking into a very difficult situation. That house has got to be chock full of memories. I don't think any of us, including Rick himself, is going to know how he's going to react to dismantling the house, with pictures of his deceased wife and son. Just visualize trying to clean out Adam's room. This is going to be a very tough go. Are you sure that you're prepared to do this?"

Maizie paused for a long moment and looked down into her mug of tea as if she were going to be reading answers in the tea leaves. "I did think about it, but maybe not hard enough. I was kind of thinking that I'd do a lot of the cleaning out when Rick wasn't there. There has to be some stuff in the house that is just everyday household items like towels or linens that I'm sure Rick is not attached to. I thought once I got the process going that I'd pack up the more personal things and label the boxes, and he could make decisions about them once he's in the new house and in whatever time frame he wanted. I think either today or tomorrow, I'll give Rick a call and see if I can go over and meet him at the house to sort of get the lay of the land. I need to figure out how big a job this is going to be and how many boxes I need." Maizie told her mother she was going to Lowe's to buy some tape, labels and boxes and to see what else she needed.

Shortly after Maizie left, Abby was sitting at the kitchen table balancing her checkbook. She suddenly had a strange feeling as though someone was hovering over her. She put her pen down and clasped her hands in front of her, just to keep from throwing the pen.

"Well, well, well, look who decided to appear?" Abby said with sarcasm in her voice as turned in her chair. "I don't want you here after what you kept from me. Do you understand?"

"I do, but I'm here anyway."

"I'm so fucking angry at you! Don't you get it? You continue to either change the subject or not discuss anything at all. I am just plain pissed! Do you think I can just forget all you put me through? Anything that you didn't want to talk about, and that was pretty much everything of any consequence, was buried and never discussed again."

"I'm sorry that you're angry with me. I can't change what happened or the past. That's the strange thing about life. It very often doesn't work out the way we wanted it to or the way we anticipated."

"Really! Ya think? It would have been nice if we could have talked about these 'life-changing' events instead of pretending that they hadn't occurred. Nothing ever got resolved in our house because we never dealt with anything. So why are you here now, Mom?"

"I was happy to see that you and Maizie had dinner with Rick. How's her job hunting coming, not that I really need to ask."

Abby fired back, "Then don't."

"Funny how the offspring have lots of the same traits as their parents. She's independent and fiery, and she's going to do things her way. Remind you of anyone you know?"

Abby thought to herself, Maizie does have a lot of the same character traits as me, and I'm not sure if that's good or bad.

Abby said, as some of the sarcasm and anger left her voice, "I learned from some of our battles. As I look back now, some things were not even worth fighting over. What was the matter with us that neither of us could see that? How come neither of us could ever back down?"

Fannie thought about it for a moment and said, "We are... alike, whether you want to believe it or not. We each had to learn on our own terms. That's just how we were."

Abby answered, "Do you remember the time right after I came home from Colorado to take care of you—we had a battle over a coffeemaker and instant Sanka? It was the first morning I was home. What was so damn important about Sanka when you were dying of emphysema?"

Fannie laughed out loud. "The two of us were so pigheaded. Your father came into the room just then, and I can remember his saying to us that he was so glad that we're 'getting along as well as we always did.' Your father was very insightful in his own quiet way. He tried talking to me to get me to back down on unimportant things, but somehow in the heat of the argument with you, I couldn't keep my promise to him. Then he and I would get into an argument, and things would spiral further out of control. If I had ever been truly honest with myself, I would have acknowledged that my drinking had a lot to do with the problem. I know now that alcoholism is a very selfish disease. I don't think I ever said out loud to you that I was sorry for what I did, but I should have."

Abby stopped looking at her hands and looked up at Fannie. "We left much too much unsaid between us before you died."

CHAPTER 25

It was the proverbial catch-22. Abby wasn't sure if she enjoyed or was even happy with her conversation with Fannie, even though she knew that lots of people would "kill" for the opportunity to have even one more chance to talk to a deceased parent. On the other hand, it always seemed that the conversations with her mother never totally answered her questions and usually left her agitated.

"Hey, Maiz, come on down here and help me hang these new curtains." Maizie bolted down the stairs.

"Was that quick or what?" Maizie said as she grabbed the other end of the curtain rod.

Abby asked, "I was thinking about Rick and wondered if you talked to him again about helping him with the house?"

"Yeah, I did. I'm going over there day after tomorrow. I thought it would be good if he was there the first time I went to the house. I don't feel comfortable just wandering around his house unless he's there. He's been sort of overseeing the build out of the space for the firm in White Plains, so I had to coordinate it with his schedule."

"Maiz, I said this to you before, I think this could be an emotionally charged situation. Why do you want to put yourself in the middle of this? If you like him, why don't you just invite him out? But honestly, honey, I don't even know if he's ready for another serious relationship with what he's been through."

"Mom, I think you're really jumping the gun here. I'm looking at this as a good deed for someone who needs help. He offered to pay me and I can use the money."

"That's true, but I also get the sense that you like him and would like to date him, especially with the flirting going on between you. It was like I was watching a rally in tennis. But this might not be the best circumstance under which you get to know him."

Maizie answered a little defensively, "Who says I want to date him? That's your projection."

Abby retorted, "Well, are you interested in dating him? It seemed that way."

"God, I was just being myself and being friendly. You've been out of circulation way too long. Men and women can actually enjoy each other's company as friends and nothing else comes of it. Why do you always have to make this into a dating thing?"

"Maiz, if you want to get to know him or date him, that's one thing, but it's an entirely different thing to put yourself in the midst of Rick's pain for no reason. I just can't see why you feel so strongly about this when you hardly know him."

"It's not that I don't hear you, Mom, but I think you're exaggerating this whole thing out of proportion. If you're this upset about it, I'll promise you this: if it feels like I'm walking into something bad or if I'm in over my head, I'll stay a day or two and then tell him it's just too big a job for one person. I'll also tell him I'm job hunting and that I have interviews. I get it that I have to have an escape hatch. I can always get out before I get to the really emotional stuff. Does that make you feel any better? I have my mother's smarts and foresight, you know."

"OK, flattery will get you everywhere. I'm glad you understand why I was worried. But I'm your mother, and I will always worry about you no matter how old each of us is. It's because I love you."

"I know that, Mom. I really do. I hope that someday I'll be as good a mother to my own kids as you are. I know it sounds corny, but I mean it. OK, now the love fest is over; can we clean up the kitchen?"

It wasn't exactly the result Abby had hoped for, but it seemed that Maizie had heard her and that she had considered the potential problems before she jumped in. She was being reasonable and mature, and Abby felt she had to believe in Maizie's good judgment. Even if Abby didn't believe in Maizie's good judgment, what more could she do? She couldn't exactly tie her to the refrigerator.

Two days later, Maizie was up early, and Abby heard her in the shower. This was the big day of the meeting with Rick. Abby was watching The Today Show and eating breakfast when Maizie came into the kitchen. Abby had to suppress a smirk, or maybe even a full-blown smile. Maizie was dressed. Oh boy, was she dressed! She had on a turquoise cashmere sweater and enough jewelry to blind you if the sunlight caught the bling in just the right light. She threw a leather jacket, which looked buttery soft, over the back of her chair. If only all movers looked like this, no one would ever change residences for fear of getting their clothes dirty. Abby sincerely hoped that Rick lived in a museum with no dust or dirt on anything that could sully the designer clothes. Abby couldn't remember the slogan of Allied Van Lines being, 'Date the movers in the designer clothes.'

Maizie asked, "How do I look? Think I overdid it?"

Abby said, "Well, does a bear shit in the woods? I'd say, yes, but it looks good on you!"

"OK. I'm off to Rick's house; see ya tonight." With that, Maizie was gone.

Abby got in the car about an hour after Maizie had left and headed toward Westchester, thinking about the clients she would see today and which of their financial issues she had to focus on. All of a sudden, Fannie started talking and scared the crap out of Abby. Abby jerked in her seat and let out a scream.

"You scared the hell out of me. I'm lucky I didn't have an accident."

"What do you want me to do? Blow a trumpet to announce myself or talk to you through the GPS? 'Recalculating, recalculating, and by the way, this is your mother talking.' You still don't seem to get it that I'm dead, and there are limited ways I can speak to you."

"I was deep in thought. What do you want?"

"So I see that Maizie is going to Rick's house today. Did you try to talk her out of it?"

"Of course I did. What—you didn't know that? She is being reasonable and told me that she may tell him it's too big a job for one person. There's not much more I can do than that. She's an adult and she's not being impetuous. Look, Mom, there's nothing more I can say to her on the subject. Is there something else going on with this that you're not telling me? Is that why you're all fired up about this?"

"It's a bad idea."

"Mom, you're not answering me. Why is it such a bad idea that you keep harping on it?"

"I can't tell you everything about this. I just can't. Sometimes it's better if all the facts do not come out. I say this because there are a lot of things that need to be considered here."

"Mom, you won't tell me the truth even now, even from the grave. You dangle bits and pieces of information in front of me, but don't come clean on the whole situation. What am I supposed to do? This is so ridiculous."

"Abby, I'm not doing this to be mean or spiteful, but there is so much going on."

"Is Maizie going to be in some danger? Is Rick a rapist or a serial killer? I'm not kidding—answer me!"

"No, nothing like that. There's no danger to Maizie. I can't go into the rest of it. You have to trust me on this. These things will all work out in time."

Yet again, Fannie was gone without giving Abby the answers, and she was making Abby crazy. Abby was screaming at the GPS. Apparently, Fannie was recalculating. Abby had several primal screams in the car. The person stopped at the traffic light next to her may have thought she was crazy and was happy when the light turned green and he could speed away. Abby thought her mother could have that effect on anyone, but especially on her.

CHAPTER 26

Maizie drove herself to Rick's house, and as she pulled up the driveway, she saw a beautiful, center hall Colonial. Rick's long hours at the firm had paid off financially. Maizie could now understand better the crushing sense of obligation since Rick had to pay a huge mortgage and steep real estate taxes. Maizie found herself making a mental note not to make this mistake if she got married. Maizie also understood that this house was very large for three people, and now with Rick rattling around in it alone, it must have seemed like a mausoleum.

She wanted to get to know Rick better, and for some unknown reason, it felt as if he belonged in her life. Maizie continued to ruminate, and the fact that Rick was in their lives at all was pretty amazing, if you thought about it. Her mother stumbles on a stranger who's about to jump off a bridge. Her mother manages to keep him calm enough so that he doesn't jump, and then she goes up on the bridge, slips, and falls over the edge, and he saves her. Then on top of it all, he turns out to be a normal, lovely guy who wants to be connected to her family. And now she finds herself wanting to be connected to him. You can't make this stuff up.

Maizie pulled up into the driveway and turned off the ignition. She grabbed the rearview mirror and pointed it in her direction, so she could check to make sure there were no smudges. She wanted to look perfect. She stepped out of the car and smoothed her sweater and pants, grabbed her jacket and purse and sashayed up to the door. Maizie rang the doorbell. Rick answered the door quickly, since he had been watching for her and noticed her arrival. When he answered the door, he was dressed in a pair of navy blue sweat pants and a light blue golf shirt, which showed off his biceps and his tan. Despite himself, Rick gave her the once over with his eyes. When Rick said to Maizie, "You look great today," that was a cover for what was actually going on in his mind, which was, "How gorgeous is this woman who wants to come clean out my house!"

"Did you have any trouble finding the house?"

"No, no trouble at all. Just some rush hour traffic to contend with."

"Come on in. I made some fresh coffee."

Maizie wanted to act nonchalant as she followed Rick into the kitchen, but the house was pristine. There was a huge chandelier that hung over the foyer and reflected the sunlight on the second floor walls. The marble on the floor in the foyer had a high gloss and looked as if it had been recently buffed and polished. The kitchen was behind the foyer on the other side of double mahogany doors. The kitchen looked out over a well-manicured lawn through two huge sliding glass doors.

"What a beautiful view."

"Yeah, I like to sit out on the deck and watch the sunset."

The deck had stairs that led down to a very large, custom-made stone patio that had a huge stone fireplace and grill. Next to the grill was a counter area, with a wet bar and refrigerator.

As Maizie was standing in front of the sliding glass doors, she surveyed the backyard. She couldn't help but notice the trampoline with the mesh siding. It was, of course, for Adam. She also noticed that to the left side of the backyard, a patch of grass had been replaced by a square of blacktop with a basketball net. Was this for Adam or for Rick or perhaps both? She could feel the lump in her throat.

Rick handed her a mug of coffee with the steam curling out of the mug. "You take it with milk and no sugar, right?"

"How did you know that?"

"That's how you took it the night I had dinner with you and Abby. Want some breakfast?"

"Thanks, but I grabbed some breakfast already. Uh, have you given any thought to where you want me to start cleaning out the house?"

It was an abrupt change of subject, but Maizie didn't want the flirting to start in the first five minutes.

"I thought I'd show you around the house and let you make that decision. The extra bedrooms upstairs might be one good place to start because there isn't that much junk in them to box up. Come on upstairs with me. I even made the bed in my room and picked up the dirty clothes off the floor."

Maizie wasn't sure if he was kidding or serious about the dirty clothes on the floor. Everything on the first floor looked to be neat and in place, but she didn't know what to expect on the second floor. Maizie had dated one divorced guy whose main floor in the house looked like a museum, but the second floor looked like a tornado had swept through if you didn't see the house on the exact day that the cleaning woman had been there. Maizie was afraid to go to his house during the two weeks that the cleaning woman was on vacation. She honestly couldn't understand how one person living alone in a house and working all day could make such a mess of things.

They climbed the winding staircase to the second floor. As they walked down the hall, Rick pointed to the left. "That's Adam's room, and these two rooms are guest bedrooms. I use the fourth bedroom as an office, and over here is the master bedroom suite."

The words "master bedroom suite" rang in her ears, as they walked down a long hallway past the other rooms and bathrooms. It wasn't just a master bedroom, but a master bedroom suite. How many rooms were in the suite? What did it all matter now, since he had no one left to share it with?

Rick led her into the two guest bedrooms—nicely appointed, but clearly guest bedrooms with no particular theme to them.

One room was done in shades of seashore blues, and the other had the colors reminiscent of a desert sunset.

"There are things stored in the closets and the dressers that I really don't need or care about. There are extra blankets and sheets. I'd like you to make a decision to keep a few sets of sheets and a few blankets and pillows, but the rest of the stuff can be boxed up and given to the Salvation Army or Goodwill. As far as I'm concerned, this is all impersonal stuff that I'd be happy to get rid of and hope someone would make good use of it. I definitely do not want to cart this to my new house. Oh, by the way, I wouldn't mind a tax deduction for the things they take, especially if they take some furniture. The lawyer in me is always there."

They moved fairly quickly to the bedroom that doubled as an office. The door was open and they walked right in. Maizie should have been prepared for what she saw, but she wasn't. The walls were lined with pictures and they were so poignant. There was a picture of Rick in a hospital gown holding his newborn son. There were pictures of Rick beaming at the camera, holding Adam in his arms as an infant. There were pictures of Rick holding Adam as a toddler, each holding a melting ice cream cone. Most of Adam's chocolate ice cream cone looked to be on Rick's white Ralph Lauren shirt.

There were several pictures of Adam's birthday, complete with party hats and birthday cake, and Rick and Jennifer flanking Adam. There were pictures of Rick, Jennifer, and Adam at the beach and on the deck of a boat, all tan and all wearing Yankee baseball caps. There were pictures of Rick and his brother, Jason, although much younger, at a black-tie event sitting at a table with other people similarly attired. One woman looked oddly familiar to Maizie.

On another wall, there were shelves holding a series of trophies. There were a number of volleyball trophies, which were Jennifer's. There were a number of swimming trophies with male figures, so they were Rick's. There were two tennis trophies, again with male figures on the top.

There was another wall with college degrees side by side for Rick and Jennifer from Stamford. Maizie realized that she had preceded Rick into his office and had walked around looking at the pictures and diplomas. All of a sudden, she realized what she had done. Rick was standing over near the desk and laptop, watching her walk around the room.

"I'm sorry. I was mesmerized by these pictures; they're beautiful. I didn't mean to gape, but they're so special."

"They are. Some days I just sit here and look at them and they bring back such wonderful memories. And then there are the worse days where I can't look around the room, so I take my laptop down into the den or kitchen."

He gently ushered Maizie out of the office and back down the hall to the guest bedrooms. "What do you think about starting here?"

"I didn't know the house would be so large. This is a huge job for one person."

"It is. My feeling is that you should do as much as you can or as much as you want. I'll be back and forth between here and White Plains trying to keep an eye on the build out for the firm and doing some house or condo hunting. I also have to start moving some of my files out of storage from the firm in New York City. Anything you do will be a big help to me because I'm starting to get a lot busier. If it's OK with you, I'll give you a key and you can come in and work even if I'm not here. It's up to you—how much you can do."

"OK, I can get started tomorrow, but I am job hunting so I'll need to work around that. And I'm going to do some work as a paralegal for a firm in New City on a part-time basis. I don't exactly know how much time I can spend on this. Is that OK, or do you want to get movers?"

"Look, do as much as you can and if it gets to be too much for you, I can then make other arrangements with movers. So ya wanna do this?"

"Yes."

They walked down the stairs and toward the front door. Rick walked Maizie to the car and opened the door.

"See you tomorrow. Um, as gorgeous as you look, I'm a pretty casual guy and there has to be some dust in the house."

Maizie smiled as she got in the car and rolled down the window. Rick leaned in to the car and said, "Thanks for doing this. It will be a big help to me."

"You're helping me out too, Rick. Actually, we'll be helping each other. I gotta run. See you tomorrow." Maizie tapped Rick to move his forearm so that she could roll up the window. Rick seemed in no hurry to move his arm.

As Maizie drove home, she replayed the conversations in her head. Why had she said to Rick that she was job hunting and that she had part-time work with a firm in New City? The job hunting was real, but was certainly not taking up much of her time. The part-time work with a law firm was a total fabrication. Why had she said that? She definitely had wanted to go see Rick, and she had steeled herself for an emotional time, so she didn't think that was it. So what was it?

CHAPTER 27

Maizie arrived at Rick's house at ten o'clock the next morning, as she said she would. She rang the doorbell and Rick opened the door after only a few seconds. Today Rick was again dressed casually, but much more dressed up than the day before. He had on a pair of khaki pants, a blue oxford cloth shirt and loafers. Blue was apparently a favored color, conservative yet it did show off his eyes and his tan, Maizie observed in one quick look at his clothes. She remembered that he'd had a blue shirt on the night he came to dinner, too. Maizie chastised herself for being so involved with every detail about him, yet she couldn't seem to help herself. She was definitely drawn to him, even as she tried to deny it to herself.

"Hi, Maiz, come on in. I'm just finishing breakfast and the coffee's fresh. Want some cereal or a bagel?"

Maizie again noted in a split second that he called her 'Maiz,' which only her mother and brother called her. There was a degree of familiarity between them that Maizie liked, but yet was somewhat unsettling considering the few times that they had been together.

"I'll always say yes to coffee, but I ate, thanks."

By now they were in the kitchen and Rick opened a cabinet above the counter where the coffeemaker sat. "There are the mugs. While I'm gone, help yourself to anything you want in the refrigerator or in the cabinets. Help yourself to anything you want for lunch. I also want to show you how to work the central air because the house is zoned. It gets much hotter upstairs."

Maizie caught herself being a little disappointed that Rick was going to be gone at least through lunch and maybe longer.

Rick sat down at the table and said, "Kellogg's Frosted Flakes are one of my real weaknesses. It's something my brother and I ate as kids and neither one of us has ever been able to break the habit. Since Jason and I grew up in England as little boys, you'd think that I would have grown up eating scones or porridge, or something terribly British. Jason and I had battles with my mom over breakfast. My grandmother came back from one of her trips to the States, with a few boxes of Frosted Flakes with Tony the Tiger on the front of the box. Once Jason and I tasted the Frosted Flakes, that's all we ate. My mother and grandmother rationalized it that at least we were eating something for breakfast, and the milk was good for us, if not the Frosted Flakes. If the truth be told, I think they got tired of fighting with us every morning. So if you see several boxes of Frosted Flakes in the cabinet, it's not that I'm anticipating a nuclear holocaust and I'm hoarding the stuff." Rick grinned a very sheepish grin.

"Rick, I think it's a sweet story, no pun intended. I bet you and Jason were really cute little boys. Am I going to come across pictures of you two?"

"They're here somewhere, I guess."

"Am I more appropriately attired for sorting and packing than I was yesterday?" Maizie knew exactly what she was saying to Rick. If he hadn't already noticed her outfit, now she was calling attention to it. Today she had on jeans and a printed T-shirt, both of which showed off her figure. No bling today, just a simple necklace, and her hair was pulled back in a ponytail.

"As Tony the Tiger would say, 'You look grrreat! OK, enough with Tony; I'm really not obsessed with him, just with the cereal."

"So where are you headed today?" Again, Maizie realized it was a pushy question, but she also knew that he could give her a vague answer if he chose.

"I have a meeting with Dannie Bevan who's starting the new firm. We're going to start going over cases that she's taking with her from the old firm. I may possibly meet with Chris, her new partner, if he can get free. We decided it would be a good thing for me to get to know him a little better. That's why I'm not sure how long I'll be gone. The meeting will be a lot shorter if he doesn't make it, but then we'll have to find another day to meet. I also have to start setting up appointments with realtors to look at houses or condos, too."

Maizie was surprised with how forthcoming he was with the information. She knew he could have answered her that he had a meeting or that he had an appointment with no further explanation. That would have been polite, but nothing more.

"I know a few realtors that I like. If you don't have someone you're working with already, I'd be happy to give you their names."

"OK, just write down their names for me."

"Rick, I hope this isn't too pushy, but you know I'm job hunting. I don't know if your new firm has done all its hiring for paralegals. Perhaps some of the people who work at the old firm won't want to commute to Westchester. Is there a way that I could submit my résumé to the firm?"

There she had said it, and it was out in the open. Maizie thought, did there come a point in life when you turned into your mother? Had she reached that point?

"I don't think we've filled all the staff positions. You've been job hunting, so obviously you have a résumé. Bring a few copies tomorrow. I'd like us to hire top-notch people and you're sharp. That's what we want. It won't hurt if I put in a good word for you."

He winked at Maizie again.

"Thanks, Rick, I'd really appreciate it. The job market isn't that great. I'd rather stay in a firm in White Plains if I could. There are a lot of people applying for very few jobs. I just happened to be in the wrong place working for a partner who wasn't that great a producer and who isn't going to the new firm."

"Maiz, firms break up all the time. Look what's happening with us. We're starting a new firm."

Fannie was sitting in the corner of the room nearest the sliding glass doors watching the two of them as the conversation unfolded. She wished that she could have had a cigarette in hand as she watched the conversation. One of those drawbacks about being dead. Now that she thought about it, she wouldn't have minded having a cold beer once in a while either. It was a little early for a drink, even for her, but the cigarettes had always settled her nerves and gave her something to do with her hands. Back to the current situation. She knew Maizie was smart, but she didn't know that she was shrewd as well. Fannie was getting a kick out of how Maizie had massaged the conversation to just where she wanted it. Fannie thought that Maizie inherited those good traits from her, not Abby. Maizie was a little more street smart and savvy, just like her grandmother. Fannie wished that she could have read Maizie's thoughts. At first it seemed to Fannie that Maizie was interested in Rick on a romantic level, but now Fannie was convinced that Maizie was playing him a little to get what she wanted. Smart, Fannie thought.

CHAPTER 28

Rick arrived at Dannie Bevan's house in Rye and he liked what he saw. It was a big house with the backyard facing Long Island Sound. It was a sunny day and there were huge clouds in an azure sky, which only enhanced the view and color of the water. Rick thought it was a very good sign that he was going to a law firm with a partner who was very prosperous. Rick remembered handling a case when he was a young lawyer a number of years ago, with co-counsel from another firm. Rick thought the guy was a mediocre lawyer until he happened to get out of the car in the parking lot of the courthouse and had parked right next to his co-counsel. His co-counsel was driving a bomb of a car, with duct tape holding the mirror on the driver's side to the door. Right then and there, as a young associate, Rick decided that he wanted to be with the successful and hard-driving lawyers and not the bozos who drove around in pieces of shit.

Rick rang the doorbell and Dannie opened the door. "Hey, Rick, come on in."

"Hi, Dannie, nice digs here, and what a view of the water."

"Yeah, and taxes to go with it."

Dannie had on a pair of jeans, a bright yellow shirt and sandals, and her glasses were perched on top of her head. She ushered Rick into the dining room to the left of the foyer. There was a laptop open on the huge dining room table and there were files neatly stacked on top on the buffet. There were also files stacked on several of the dining room chairs. Lots of files. Even with the files all over the place, the dining room was impressive. The furniture was expensive; the dining room table could seat twelve without the leaves open. There was a huge chandelier with lots of crystal which looked to Rick to be Venetian glass. The room was a formal dining room—in sharp contrast to how Rick perceived Dannie to be. Hard driving, but somewhat casual.

Dannie said, "Rob is out of town, so I took this opportunity to unpack some boxes and see what's actually here. Rob hates it when I mess up any other part of the house with files or boxes from the office, other than in my own office. He gets antsy if either I or the kids leave 'crap,' as he calls it, around the house. His mother is obsessive-compulsive, and obviously he has that genetic trait. Most of the time he's fighting a losing battle, but to keep peace, I try to cooperate somewhat." Dannie laughed a nervous laugh as she finished her narrative.

"Hey, Dannie, I couldn't care less. Everyone works differently, and you do what works best for you. No one has ever accused you of not working productively."

"I'm having my secretary, Gwen, come in four days a week to help me until we can get into the new space. The move better happen fast or Rob will have a nervous breakdown with the mess. Frankly, I got tired of commuting to the City, and I couldn't stand the tension in the office any more. It just seemed easier for me not to be there and run into my soon to be ex-partners on a daily basis."

"Dannie, I was at the new office yesterday, and the contractor is saying they should be finished by the end of next week."

"I know, I know; I went over there day before yesterday. They really have been making progress, but it's like waiting for your due date. The doctor says everything is progressing nicely, but he's not the one having the baby. Same thing here. The contractor says everything's going well, but he's not the one waiting around for something to happen."

"Don't take offense, Rick. I had to see for myself. You know we type A personalities can't sit back and wait for things to happen. We always have to push. I don't mean to step on any toes, but you can see that I won't be able to function here for that long, without getting a divorce!"

"No offense taken. I can understand why trying to function on your dining room table, no matter how large and spacious it may be, is not the optimal way to practice law. Hopefully, this'll be coming to a rapid end."

"The associates still working at the firm are feeling the pressure, too. I think they all want to get the hell outta there. I'd like you to do a few things for me, please, and I want you to take over several cases. It would be a big help if you would take over the supervision of the files from the old firm. I need the active files to be moved together and the closed-out files in storage need to be moved as well. I'll give you the list of the files we want to take and the list of the clients who have already consented to our taking their files with us."

"Hey, Dannie, do you expect Steve Goldrick to give us a hard time about any files that we don't have signed consents from clients?"

"I absolutely do expect that! It's just his way of being a complete prick. He knows we're going to leave and there's nothing he can do about, but he can make it as difficult as possible to do it. I'm having Gwen e-mail the clients who have not yet signed the consents for us to take their files and send them another consent to sign. Would you check in with her today and see how many are still outstanding? Give her a call on her cell and see where we are with that. Do you think you can get the contractor to get the file room ready earlier than the attorneys' offices, so we can get the files in first? The closed out files in storage need to go to a new storage facility."

"Yeah, I can take care of that. No problem. The file room probably only needs a coat of primer and one coat of paint. Is the landlord OK with moving the files in early? Has someone spoken to him?"

"Good point, Rick. Gwen probably never even thought about that. Can you work all this out? I'm starting to get crazy with all these details and trying to keep two big deals both happening simultaneously, which, by the way, are taking a tremendous amount of my time. If you can orchestrate all this and keep me out of it, I will be eternally grateful. I'll write any checks you need, but just keep things moving through the pipeline and have us come out on the other side and be able to move in to the new office!"

"Don't get freaked out, Dannie. I can handle this. Moving is always a big deal, so let's try not to make it feel like a root canal as well."

"Good point, Rick. If this move goes smoothly, I owe you big time!"

Dannie and Rick had been playing musical chairs around the dining room table while organizing some of Dannie's files for Rick to take. They both decided to sit for a minute, and Dannie leaned over closer to Rick and put her hand on his. Rick was a little surprised by the gesture. He was even more surprised that her hand lingered on his for an extra moment. He didn't quite know what to do or how to react, if at all. Almost as quickly as her hand was on his, it was gone.

Dannie said, "Want a soda or iced tea?"

"Yeah, an iced tea would be great if it's not the sweetened kind."

"You're so sweet for helping; you don't need any extra," she laughed.

It was an innocuous enough remark, except that it followed shortly after her putting her hand over his. He decided to just let it go without comment.

"Where's Chris? I thought he was going to be here today, too."

"He was going to be here, but he had to be in the Supreme Court in Manhattan. He thought the case was going to be adjourned to next week, but the judge wanted them there today. Chris was not a happy camper over that."

Chris McKay was a very good trial attorney and a partner in a firm in White Plains. He and Dannie had been friends since law school. They always had talked about going into practice together, but the time had never been right until now. Chris and Dannie had dated for a short period of time while they were in law school, but then they broke up and each married someone else. Chris felt it was one of the big mistakes of his life to let Dannie slip away.

Dannie's response was so quick and without hesitation that Rick felt that her answer was genuine.

"I'd really like an opportunity to get to meet with Chris sooner rather than later, Dannie. I hardly know him, and I just think it's really important that we get to know each other. He and I need to be comfortable with each other. You've laid it out for me that I'm going to be the most senior attorney after you and Chris. I know what you think that entails, but I want to make sure that he feels the same way. I want to iron out any glitches before we get started in the new firm."

"Fair enough, Rick. I'll probably talk to him tonight. Why don't the three of us have lunch in the next day or two?"

"That's good, Dannie. I really want this to work out. By the way, have you filled all the paralegal positions? I have a résumé from a woman who has worked as a paralegal for almost ten years. The firm broke up and her immediate boss was a casualty. He saved his own ass and became in-house counsel, but threw everybody else overboard. I don't think he took any of the people who worked for him directly. Would you want to interview her?"

"Actually, I don't have time to do that. Why don't you and Gwen interview her? Gwen told me the other day that there are a few people who say coming to White Plains is just too far. Gwen has some guidelines for salaries. If you and Gwen like someone enough to want to hire her and you've checked all the references, then I want to meet her. I don't have the time or the patience to sit through a parade of losers or people with random body piercings."

Rick nodded and laughed out loud. "So you want to meet the people who have uniform body piercings, but not those with random body piercings? Dannie, you are such a piece of work. I can't decide if you're a princess or a slave driver. Maybe even the queen."

Dannie was able to laugh at herself. "There are worse things, and believe me, I've been called them. I've learned to rely heavily on my own instincts, which are pretty damn good. I don't want to be told what to do by some damn Executive Committee, which is code for male ego trips."

"Dannie, I would've liked to have sat in on the Executive Committee meetings—just to see you and Steve Goldrick go at it. It would have been worth the price of admission."

"Some days it was tolerable. Toward the end, I sometimes baited him just to make him crazy. Talk about a dictator."

"Dannie, it's getting late, so let's go over the files you want me to work on."

When Rick got home, he sat at his desk in his office and started to go through the matters Dannie had given him to work on. He felt as if there was a new surge of life and excitement motivating him. It was a far cry from what he felt after Jennifer's and Adam's deaths. He could barely be responsible for himself and wondered more times than not why his life was worth living. In that split second before he was ready to end it all, something or someone stopped him. He didn't feel much like socializing and begged off from most social engagements. He saw his brother, Jason, and some friends here and there, but it mostly revolved around sports of some kind, because he wasn't ready talk about or answer people's questions about Jennifer or Adam or discuss his attempt to end it all. In Rick's reflections about his attempted suicide, he realized that ultimately it was Abby who stopped him. Even before Abby stopped him, he thought he could feel some kind of presence near him, but he still hadn't been able to figure it out completely.

He was excited about a new start in a new firm with people he liked. He liked Dannie's choice of associates to come to the new firm, and he had always respected Dannie. He knew she had gone to bat for him in the old firm and that took guts, because it wasn't the popular position to take.

He also was now willing to admit to himself that he got a kick out of Maizie. That was almost in spite of himself. For the first time in a long time, he began to notice things, even little things that he didn't have enough psychic energy to pay attention to after Jennifer and Adam's deaths. He noticed how green Maizie's eyes were, and while she was wandering around his office looking at the pictures and the trophies, he found himself looking at how soft her hair looked, and how perfect the back of her neck looked when she had her hair up. She was so full of life, and she fairly exuded energy and excitement. He wanted to come out of the land of the living dead and come back into the light. A few months ago the light would have blinded him, but now he wanted to venture out into it. He knew Maizie was flirting with him, and now he might even be interested in flirting back. He surprised himself that he brought her up in his conversation with Dannie and vouched for Maizie when he hadn't even seen her résumé or checked her recommendations. He wanted to be around her and see what happened. He could work things out to get her hired, but she wouldn't work for him. Too obvious and too messy. But he was interested. It felt as if he was finally breathing again after holding his breath for so long.

And then there was Dannie. She was a force to be reckoned with. He wasn't sure what, if anything, to make of Dannie's touching his hand. He was sure, well fairly sure, that her putting her hand on his was purposeful, and that the touch lasted a few seconds too long to be inadvertent. He had almost immediately tested what was going on by asking Dannie about why Chris had not come to meet with them at Dannie's house. Dannie's answer was so rapid and without hesitation that he believed Chris was stuck in court. He was waiting to see what Dannie's next move was. Would she, in fact, set up the lunch meeting as she said?

His opinion of Dannie's husband, Rob, was that he was a smart enough guy but, frankly, a little nerdy. He was never quite sure what Dannie saw in Rob, but there truly was no accounting for taste. Dannie was extremely successful in her own right, so he didn't think she necessarily needed his money. She might even have been the more successful one in the marriage. He wasn't sure what Rob brought to the marriage that would have interested Dannie. He was of average height and average looks. Nothing more. When Rick had an opportunity to socialize with Rob at the Christmas parties, or once in a while when they had been at a barbecue together, Rick found that he had very little in common with Rob. Rob liked to talk about stamp collecting and wines, and he had an extensive wine collection. Rick thought that at least with the wines you could learn the difference between an oaky Chardonnay and a fruity Pinot Grigio. As far as the stamp collecting, Rick knew there were people who had a passion for it, but he was certainly not one of them, and at those times he'd have to excuse himself and walk away. Her two kids looked more like her, and Rick hadn't been around them long enough to get whose personality they inherited. Dannie was a ball of fire; she possessed almost boundless energy. Unless one of them had changed an awful lot, Rick couldn't imagine what had attracted them to each other in the first place.

The phone rang and jolted him out of his reverie. He had taken to screening his calls, but when he looked at the caller ID, he was pleasantly surprised. It was Maizie.

"Hi, Maizie, how are you?"

"Hi, Rick. I wasn't sure I'd catch you home. I thought I'd come over and do some work if that's good for you. I don't have your cell number."

"When do you want to come over? I'm just looking through some files that Dannie Bevan gave me to start working on."

"I'd like to start around eleven if that's good for you and wouldn't bother you."

"Yeah, come on over. Maybe we'll both work for a while and have some lunch together."

There was a moment of silence on the other end of the phone. He thought to himself that he was so lame. What kind of stupid line was that—to ask her to come have lunch? She'd think he was a dork. Then he had a much better idea, and he recovered.

"It's going to be in the nineties today. Why don't we eat lunch by the pool and then go for a swim." There, much less lame. Plus he'd get to see Maizie in a bathing suit.

"Yeah, sounds great. I really need to do some work because it's a much bigger job than I originally estimated."

Maizie was now pleased with herself. She would appear to be responsible in Rick's eyes, and she could do a few hours of work and get paid for seeing Rick in a bathing suit. All in all, it would be a good day's work, and she hadn't been too pushy. It was all so "innocent."

"Great, I'll see you about eleven."

CHAPTER 29

Steve Goldrick was sitting at his desk revising affidavits on one of his litigation matters, when his cell phone rang. He looked at the number and saw that it was his daughter, Gabriella. He wasn't sure if this call was business or personal, but hoped it was the latter, because having any issue with the business only meant headaches. He answered, "Hi, honey, how's it going?"

Gabriella replied, "Doing fine, on the way to the airport to pick up the 'package.' I called the airline a little while ago, and the flight is on time, for once. I'll meet the flight myself. Listen, I got a call, and I need some information from the prior file we had on the 'package.' We need to retrieve the file from storage. There was a fire at the facility; unfortunately, the records were lost. Good thing we have a backup. Can you get Helen to do it? We need it pretty fast."

Steve replied, "Sure, give me the name, but let me get a big piece of paper first. I swear I have never seen so many consonants in one name. Who the hell puts an *s* followed by a *z* in a name?"

Gabriella spelled the name for Steve and asked him how long it would take for Helen to get her the file. "I don't need the whole file, probably just a few pages, which she could e-mail to me."

Steve said he'd speak to Helen to see how fast she could get the file and have Helen call Gabriella back. As soon as Steve hung up, Steve buzzed Helen and asked her to come in to his office. Helen came right in and closed the door behind her. Steve handed her the piece of paper. "Helen, Gabby needs some information from this file because they lost the files in a fire. Didn't these jackasses ever hear of backing up data on a computer? Can you call Gabby back and tell her when you can go get the file?"

Helen took the piece of paper from Steve and said, "It depends on what you want me to do about revising the affidavits. Are they going to be ready for the next draft now? If not, I can go get the file on my way back from lunch."

"I still have some more revisions to give you, but I can wait until this afternoon. It would be better if you got the file for Gabby. Just call her back and tell her."

Helen turned on her heel, opened the door and disappeared almost in one fell swoop. Steve marveled to himself about Helen. She was the most efficient person he had ever met, and in some respects, she was the stereotype of the perfect secretary—down to the reading glasses hanging on a cord around her neck. She had been with Steve forever, and she was as loyal as a Labrador Retriever, but Helen was also incredibly smart and savvy. Not much in the way of personality, but Steve wasn't looking for a friend, just a loyal secretary who knew how to get things done for him and could keep her mouth shut. Helen had done all that and more. Even Steve, whose expectations were colossal, had to admit that Helen had far exceeded his.

As Steve picked up his reading glasses and went back to work on the affidavits, he paused for a second and looked up from the affidavits and put the glasses down on the desk. This has been a long run, Steve thought, and quite a lucrative one. He probably would shut down the business in a few years when he retired, but by that time both Helen and Gabby would be very well situated financially. We've been careful and we've meticulous and that's why this has lasted so long. But on the other hand, there have been considerable risks as well. That's why the fees have to be so high, because there are a lot of people who have their hands out all along the way. It also crossed Steve's mind that if Helen said she wanted to retire, he might have to close down the business. It would be too risky and too time consuming to find and train a new employee.

Helen took a car service to Yonkers, where the storage facility was located. One of the things she liked about Mr. Goldrick was that he didn't skimp on anything. He knew how to reward people for their service to him. No disgusting yellow cab to Yonkers for her.

As Helen walked into the huge gray building, she showed her ID to the person behind the desk. Helen didn't come to the building as much as she had years ago, since the business was getting tougher, and with computers and cross matching, you had to be more discrete. Helen gave the number of the box she wanted to the receptionist, who picked up the phone and gave the number to a file clerk. Within a few minutes, the file clerk appeared with a large "Trans-file" box and asked Helen to follow him to a small private room down the hall, not unlike the bank procedure when going to open a safe deposit box. The file clerk said, "When you're finished, ma'am, just call the receptionist on the phone on the wall, and I'll come back to get the box." Helen nodded in agreement. Helen opened the lid on the box and started to shuffle through the files. While looking for the file, she mused about the years she had been doing this and was grateful for this business that Mr. Goldrick had asked her to be a part of. It had been a lifesaver for her and her family. Although she made a very good salary at the law firm, this extracurricular business was definitely major icing on the cake. It put all three of her kids through college, paid off her mortgage, and she and Jack were able to purchase a vacation home. No one was any the wiser in the law firm, since Helen knew enough not to flaunt her wealth, and wealth was what she had, thanks to Mr. Goldrick.

Fannie somehow found herself in the room with Helen at the storage facility. It seemed a minute ago she was in Steve's office. She wondered again how it happened. She stood next to Helen as Helen went through the files. Fannie wondered if she would recognize the file if she saw it or if it was even in this box. Fannie observed Helen as she retrieved the file she was looking for. This file looked fairly new...Still in business after all these years, Fannie thought, but not for long.

Helen looked at the file and put it in her briefcase. She put the lid back on the box and walked to the phone on the wall. In a few minutes, the file clerk appeared silently at the door. Helen pointed to the box. "Thank you, I'm finished," she said to the clerk. Knowing Helen was unable to hear her, Fannie said out loud, as she followed Helen out the door, "You might be finished, but I'm not. I guess you missed the green tag on the back of the box…too bad."

CHAPTER 30

Rick was in the kitchen waiting for Maizie to arrive, and he was chopping up salad and ham, turkey, tomatoes and avocados and anything else he could find for his rendition of Cobb salad. He wanted to make a good impression on her, of that he was certain. It kind of surprised him he was so conscious of everything he did that related to Maizie. She was beginning to make him feel as though he was in back high school going on a first date. These feelings were definitely a revelation, but he hoped that Jennifer would understand. His desire to move forward with his life was beginning to be stronger than the survivor's guilt he had felt for a long time. It seemed that all the work with Dr. Burke was beginning to take root.

Rick had left the door ajar, so Maizie let herself in and called out, "Hi, Rick, it's me. Where are you?"

As Maizie found her way into the kitchen, she stopped for a moment to comment as she watched Rick chopping away and looking as though he should be on the Food Network. "Boy, look at you, a man of many talents. I didn't know you like to cook."

"I enjoy cooking, and I learned a lot from my mother and grandmother. I think I told you that I was a picky eater as a kid, so my mother used to let me help her cook, with the hope that I'd like some of the things we made together. Sometimes it worked and sometimes it didn't. When I met Jennifer, she liked to cook, and I liked being with her. We had a lot of good times together in the kitchen." A slight smile appeared across Rick's face as he remembered those times. "We both enjoyed entertaining and our friends enjoyed our culinary genius as well."

"Is this one of the 'culinary genius creations' that you're making now? Should I get a pad of paper and a pen and write everything down?"

"No. You should come one night for dinner when I'm actually making something that requires cooking, grilling, or basting. One never knows what goes into those recipes."

Maizie laughed. "Can I set the table or do something to help?"

"Yeah, I thought we'd eat out by the pool. You can take the plates and silverware out."

As Maizie picked up the plates and headed for the door, she brushed up against Rick's arm.

"Sorry." Actually, she wasn't sorry at all. There was something about him that she was so attracted to that she wanted to touch him, even if she had to make it seem inadvertent.

As they sat down to have lunch, Maizie glanced around and the scene was something out of a Pottery Barn summer catalogue, with the pool, the table, the umbrella and the plants, all color coordinated and all picture perfect. It was a contemporary look, but had a very comfortable feel.

"When you put the house on the market, make sure the realtor has lots of pictures of the pool setting. It's beautifully put together and very relaxing. This would be a great selling point for the house. Have you actually listed the house with a realtor? If that's the case, I better get moving a lot faster with the cleaning out."

"I'm getting close. I don't want to commute for very long to White Plains because the Tappan Zee Bridge is a bear. Speaking of the new firm, I need your résumé. I spoke to Dannie and she's leaving the hiring of the remainder of the staff positions to me and her secretary. Of course, Dannie will have the final say, but I think that she'll go with what we recommend."

"I just updated it, and it's in a folder in my car. Let me go get it."

Maizie returned in a moment with several copies of the résumé in hand. They were printed on a light silver-colored bond with script type and looked very professional. Maizie handed them to Rick with a manila folder underneath them and a large black paper clip holding them to the folder. Maizie so wanted this job, not only for the job's sake, but for a chance to be around Rick on a daily basis. She had changed the color of the bond several times and the type as well. She had even considered the color of the large paper clip. When she stopped to think about this, it had seemed very adolescent even to her, and she would never have admitted this to anyone else. Originally, she tried telling herself that she was just being professional and thorough in order to get the job, which was partially true, but in reality that was only a small part of what was going on inside her.

She handed the résumés to Rick, who promptly sat down on one of the kitchen chairs and began reading. Maizie thought it took him a long time to get to the second page, and the clock on the wall above Rick's head seemed to be making a really loud, almost pounding sound. As Rick turned the page, Maizie realized that she was holding her breath, and what she was hearing was her own heartbeat.

"Very impressive résumé. With all the experience you list here, I would have thought you were a much older woman."

Maizie's face fell. "Does it appear that I'm too flighty or not serious enough?"

"Maiz, lighten up. I'm kidding. Your résumé is impressive. I think I just said that to you about ten seconds ago. I'm very willing to give this to Dannie's secretary and have you come in for an interview. There is nothing not to like here. Calm down. Do you need a Valium before I call Dannie's secretary?"

Maizie exhaled and sat down in another chair across the table from Rick.

"No on the Valium, but it's just that I really want this job. I never thought I'd say this, but I miss working. I miss the interaction with the other staff members and the attorneys. I detest telling people that I'm unemployed, even though it wasn't my fault and it's temporary—at least I hope so. It seems in this economy that it's more than ever about who you know, rather than what you know."

Rick was somewhat struck by Maizie's comment and her naiveté. "I hate to tell you this, kid, but it's always been that way. How do you think the 'good old boys network' got started?"

Maizie stopped to take a breath, and it looked as if she might start to cry. Rick leaned across the table and took her hand. He liked the feeling of her hand; it was soft and a good fit for his hand. As he leaned a little closer, he got a whiff of a citrusy scent in her hair, which he found enticing, along with the rest of the package.

Maizie looked at Rick holding her hand, and she liked it. She attentively looked at Rick's face as he began to speak.

"Maizie, I told you before that I'd help you get this job, and I will. We certainly want people like you who care about the clients and their problems. We want people for whom the clients are not just names on a file. Clients sense that, too."

He wanted to lean all the way across the table and kiss her. He wanted that so badly that he could almost taste her lips on his, but he caught himself. His elbow hit a bowl of blueberries as he slid his hand across the table and they fell onto the kitchen floor and rolled in every possible direction, as if escapees from prison. The bowl hit the floor and fortunately didn't shatter, but the blueberries threatened to commit suicide under his shoes.

"Shit, oh sorry, Maizie. That was dumb. Let me clean them up before we smash them into the floor."

Rick didn't care one wit about smashing the blueberries to pieces, but he did care about smashing the mood in the room to pieces.

Maizie was doing her utmost not to laugh as Rick picked his way precariously among the blueberries. He looked like a cross between a flamenco dancer and a high-wire artist. It didn't matter what he did, he was slaughtering blueberries left and right. The more he squished them, the funnier it got, until Maizie couldn't stand it any longer and burst out laughing. Maizie thought she should try to do something to help him, but once she started laughing, she could barely get the words out,

"Rick, let me help you." With that she stepped off the stool and smashed yet more blueberries. Rick looked up at her from the floor and he couldn't help but laugh at the situation too. Maizie added, after catching her breath, "I didn't know you had such good moves. We should go dancing sometime." With that Rick tossed some blueberries at her.

Fannie was watching this interchange between Maizie and Rick with mixed emotions. She was clearly getting an idea what direction this "friendship"—now relationship—was going. The blueberries were a diversion, but they were not going to be enough. It appeared that the ship was about to sail, if, in fact, it had not done so already.

After they finished the free-for-all, cleaned up, and finally ate some lunch, Rick and Maizie sat there for a while and enjoyed their time together. They laughed and told stories of family folklore, and both realized that they enjoyed themselves more than they wanted to admit. Finally, after a long time had passed, Rick said, "I'm going to make a call right now to Dannie's secretary and you are going to call her in the next five minutes. So get ready to dial yourself a new job."

He winked and smiled at Maizie. She smiled back at him, and there was a tear in the corner of her eye. She was overcome with emotion and tried to wipe the tear away casually, but he saw it. He saw everything, and he so liked what he saw.

Rick switched into his business voice on the phone. "Hi, Gwen, it's Rick...Good. How are things going today? Sorry I missed you at Dannie's the other day...Listen, I have a résumé of a paralegal who I think is going to be terrific for us. We have some mutual friends, so I've had a chat with her already. Her name is Maizie Evers. She's got great experience, and she worked as a paralegal at a firm in White Plains until they had a bloody coup and the firm broke up. Dannie wanted us to see some candidates and do some weeding out before she saw anybody. I think she wants to see only the people we feel good enough about to hire. I'm going to e-mail you Maizie's résumé, and I told her I was going to call you right now and that she should follow up. Expect a call from her in the next few minutes, because I told her to call you directly, and I want to set up an interview for her...Yeah, I can be available any time you want the rest of this week except Thursday. Set it up for around nine thirty or ten...Great, give me a call later this afternoon because I'm headed out to meet someone for lunch now...Yeah, let me know the day and time. Thanks, Gwen. 'Bye."

"You should wait about five minutes and call her and set up the appointment." Rick walked to the kitchen and Maizie picked up the cell and dialed Gwen's number.

CHAPTER 31

Dannie had asked Rick to be the prime moving force in getting the new office up and running and being the liaison to her. She had given him lots of latitude in what needed to be done, and almost any decision he made was fine with her. If it involved a lot of money, he always ran it by her first, but so far she had agreed with every decision he'd made. He had to admit that it was rewarding to be working with someone who sought his opinion and valued his ideas, unlike the firm in the City.

One of the things that Dannie had asked Rick to do was coordinate moving the active files from the firm in New York City to the new office. Dannie's secretary, Gwen, had located the movers, but Dannie wanted Rick to review the contract with the movers and troubleshoot any problems with the old firm if they were being difficult about coughing up client files, both active and closed. At first he thought he was going to hate doing this because of Steve Goldrick. As he was thinking about this, it occurred to him that this shouldn't be making him uneasy or anxious because he had Dannie's full support. That was becoming clearer to him on a daily basis. Dannie seemed pleased with him about virtually everything he was doing, which only gave him more confidence to make more decisions.

He was going to use that confidence that Dannie had in him to get the job for Maizie. It was a win-win situation. He would look good in Maizie's eyes, Maizie would get a great job in an up-and-coming firm, and Dannie would get a wonderful employee. If the truth be known, he wanted Maizie around him on a daily basis. Having her as a paralegal in the firm would allow him to see her in all aspects of life as she dealt with clients, their emotions, both good and bad. Nothing was more volatile than a client in the midst of litigation. If you lit a match around a client during a trial, the whole room might go up in smoke. It wasn't much different with the attorneys trying the case either.

A few of the rooms in the new office were finished, even though the new furniture hadn't yet arrived completely. There was a small conference room that had been freshly painted and had a table, albeit a large aluminum one, with a table cloth on it to hide the aluminum, and some nondescript chairs. Maizie seemed excited to be there for the interview, so she wouldn't have cared if she had been interviewed in the bathroom.

Rick had told Dannie's secretary, Gwen, how much he liked Maizie's résumé, so unless Maizie came in tattooed head to toe and spit on Rick's shoes with chewing tobacco, she most probably had the job. To Maizie's credit, she came in to the interview in a cream-colored linen suit, with a scarf of bright greens, blues and yellows around her neck to give the outfit a bold splash of color. She had on a simple gold necklace and a bracelet to match. No bling, as she had on the day she first came to his house. Rick hung back in the interview and let the two women do the vast majority of the talking. He was absolutely enjoying the fact that this interview gave him the perfect opportunity to watch Maizie's every move without it being apparent that he was staring at her. He was supposed to be staring at her. How good was that! Once in a while, he lobbed a softball of a question to her, so she could really get to expound on the things that interested her and talk about positive experiences with clients and the attorneys she had worked for, and so make her look good. He loved how she tossed her hair back, and he hadn't had an opportunity to look at how long and delicate her neck was.

For the first time in his life, he was disappointed that an interview was over. Usually, he was antsy after the first ten minutes. He normally sized people up fairly quickly, with the exception of Steve. There was something personal with Steve, and Rick had made a mistake with him, a big mistake. Normally, Rick didn't want to waste time going through the niceties if he didn't like the person.

As luck would have it, Dannie was due in the office about thirty minutes or so after they finished the interview. Gwen asked Maizie if she would like to go get herself a cup of coffee and come back in a half hour to meet Dannie. Rick had to restrain himself from winking at Maizie, and he had to restrain himself from saying he'd take a walk with her to get the cup of coffee. Maizie got it right away that being asked to come back to meet Dannie was a very, very good thing. Rick didn't know if he should sit in on the interview with Dannie and Maizie, but it might prove incredibly interesting. Dannie was very sharp and very shrewd, and it would be great to see Maizie hold her own with Dannie. To use sports terminology, if he was lobbing softballs to Maizie for her to hit out of the park, Dannie would be throwing fastballs. He decided not to sit in on the interview unless Dannie specifically asked him to do so. Normally, he wouldn't have sat in on a second interview with a staff member. More importantly, he didn't want Dannie to pick up any vibes between Maizie and him, and she very well could.

Maizie said she had an errand to run and she would be back in forty-five minutes to give Dannie a chance to get settled. Gwen led the way out of the conference room, followed by Maizie and then Rick. Maizie turned around on the way out of the room, so that she faced Rick and mouthed the words "Thank you" to him. He gave her a nod and a big smile in acknowledgment.

About forty minutes passed, and Maizie returned with a shopping bag and a large iced coffee. So she really did have an errand to run. Gwen told Maizie that Dannie was on the phone and then she'd be available. Rick decided that he'd leave the office and make it seem that she was just another employee who would need the final approval from Dannie.

Once Rick saw her settle down on the couch to wait for Dannie, Rick called her on the cell phone. He guessed that she would turn the cell back on when she left the office, so he was prepared for what he wanted to say to her.

"Hey, Maiz, it's me. Don't say anything or say my name; just listen. I'm going to get my car washed, and I have my cell on. When you finish with Dannie, why don't you call me and we can have a drink or a cup of coffee. I told Gwen how much I liked your résumé, and she liked you in the interview, so I think meeting with Dannie will pretty much be a formality. So call me when you leave the office."

"Got it, I'll give you a call after I'm done with my interview. Bye."

About five minutes later, Gwen came out to find Maizie in the waiting room and told her Dannie was ready to see her. Maizie left the shopping bag on the couch and followed her down a long hallway. Gwen explained the configuration of the office as they walked.

"As you can see, Maizie, we're getting close, but we're still not quite ready to move in. Dannie wants all the associates to move in at the same time. Dannie is getting really impatient with the delays, but we have to have the final inspection from the building department, which seems to be taking their good sweet time getting here. What they don't know is that Dannie knows the mayor quite well. She's holding off calling him, but God help the building inspector if she does. Dannie can rattle off names and dates like an encyclopedia, so she'll be able to make them look bad. We're trying to keep her calm for a few more days. You never want to use up a chit if you can avoid it."

Gwen knocked on the door and waited a fraction of a second before proceeding into the office. Maizie took a quick glance as she walked into the office to try to take it all in, but she was surprised at her first glance at Dannie. Dannie had on a pink Oxford cloth shirt with the sleeves rolled up, and a pair of white shorts and sandals.

Dannie got up from her desk and walked toward Maizie to shake her hand.

"Come over here and sit down on the couch; I don't have to sit at the desk. Sorry about the informality," she said as she pointed to her shorts and sandals. "I wasn't expecting to see anyone here today, but I couldn't see any reason to drag you back for an interview simply because I wasn't dressed for clients. I know that Rick and Gwen had already interviewed you and liked what they saw. They were also impressed with your résumé."

"I really appreciate it your seeing me today on such short notice. That's very nice of you; I know you have a lot to do with the move and the new firm, Ms. Bevan."

"Maizie, Ms. Bevan is my mother-in-law, and God knows, I don't want to be her. If you're going to work here, I want people to feel as if this is a team, all pulling in the same direction. We don't need to set up artificial barriers. I want people to respect me because they think that I'm a good lawyer, not just because I sign the paychecks. So if I'm going to call you Maizie, you can call me Dannie. If there are clients around, then you can fall back on Ms. Bevan."

She looked down at the folder in her lap with Maizie's résumé and a few other pages of information that Maizie had filled out.

"So we're in agreement about salary and benefits? Did Gwen talk to you about a starting date?"

"Yes, Gwen was very thorough about all the details. The only thing she wasn't sure of was who I would be working for. She said you would make that decision."

"Actually, it's one of two people. The associates are all still working at the firm in New York City, so none of them is here for you to meet. Would you like to come back in next week and meet the attorney you'll be working for? We can certainly arrange that."

Maizie hesitated for a second. Should she say she wanted to meet the person or not? The thoughts exploded in her head. If she said she wanted to meet the person, did that sound like a pain in the ass? If she said no, did she seem like a dummy who was just going to sit at a desk and type? She quickly decided on the former.

"If it wouldn't be too much trouble, I would really like that. I know you mentioned it before, but I have always thought that the attorney and the paralegal are almost like two people dancing. You get to the point where you know what your dance partner is going to do and what they need you to do in response."

Dannie smiled a broad smile. "I like that analogy. I'll have to remember that. I'll give you credit the next time I use it. I'll have Gwen call you and set it up. Thanks for coming in. I look forward to your working here with us."

With that Dannie stood up and extended her hand to Maizie.

Maizie was so happy that she had the job, and it was so easy. She hated being unemployed and she hated feeling useless. Now it was over and she could exhale.

"Thank you, Dannie, for seeing me and for hiring me. I look forward to getting started. If you need me to come in early and help get things settled, I'd be more than happy to do it. I know it sounds crazy, but I really like working."

Dannie laughed. "I hope you can say the same thing about six months from now. Can you find your way out and tell Gwen you're leaving, so she doesn't think you're wandering around the empty offices aimlessly."

And with that, the five-minute interview was over. A new phase of Maizie's life was about to begin, and she was so ready for it. You never knew what challenges life had in store for you, but for the first time in a long time, she was sure it was going to be good.

CHAPTER 32

Rick went to the storage facility in Yonkers with Gwen to make sure the file transition went smoothly. He knew he didn't really need to go, but since everything had been going well, he felt he ought to finish the job in case Steve Goldrick had a surprise in store for them and decided to make it difficult. Everything had gone well with the new office space, but there was still fighting going on in the old firm between Dannie and Steve—two pigheaded people who would rather butt heads than find a way to compromise. Under normal conditions, Rick would have volunteered to try to mediate a deal between Steve and Dannie, but he realized that he was so disgusted with Steve for stabbing him in the back, he knew in his heart of hearts he couldn't be objective.

Two days before the move of the files from storage, Rick called Dannie and said, "Let's be proactive in case Steve is going to be a prick one last time, because he can. I'm going to prepare an Order to Show Cause and have it with me in case Steve thinks he's going to stick it to us one more time, just for spite. He probably knows the movers are on the clock, and so he can cost you more money and make them come back another time. With the Order to Show Cause, I can go to one of the judges you've appeared before many times, who knows you, to order the old firm to let us have the files."

Dannie agreed, and so Rick went to the storage facility armed with the Order to Show Cause in his briefcase. Surprisingly, there was no saber rattling by Steve or the firm, and after close to an hour of watching files move on gurneys to the moving truck, Rick told Gwen that he thought it was safe for him to leave.

"I'll have my cell phone on, so call me if you need me to come back. Maybe Stevie Wonder decided he has better things to do with his time than hassle us. He's probably focused on screwing someone else. There aren't that many more boxes left to move, so I think it will be fine."

Gwen agreed and so he left. After another two hours passed without a call, Rick realized that the boxes must all be on the moving truck, so he could exhale.

The following morning, Rick arrived in the new office to find a number of boxes with a green tag designating that these were his files. He hesitated to go to the file room, knowing it would look like a bomb had gone off. Thank God, that was not his job. As he went into the file room, it reminded him of the catacombs. There were boxes everywhere with small aisles to walk through. Man, all lawyers do is generate paper and denude the forests, he thought.

Rick thought that some of his active files had been moved by mistake to the file room. He was a little afraid that this was going to be the proverbial needle in a haystack, but he did have some hope of finding his files with the green tags. He wandered through the catacombs, looking for his files. After a few minutes, he was getting exasperated and about to give up when he saw a number of boxes with green tags on them.

"Shit, of course, these damn boxes are in the corner and under a mountain of other files. Stupid ass movers. How hard is it to get the boxes with the green tags into my office?" he growled. "I'll probably get a hernia from moving these boxes. I hope the medical insurance is in place."

After a few minutes of shuffling boxes, which were packed full and heavy, Rick was sweating and cursing simultaneously.

He had five boxes with green tags that he had now freed, and he picked them up, stacked them on to a hand truck and rolled them down the long corridor to his office. He went back for the other two boxes and looked at the mountain of file boxes he had created in the file room.

"I'm not moving them back to where they were. Let one of the clerks get the hernia."

On the way back to his office the second time, Rick grabbed a bottle of cold water. Once he was back in his office, he sat in the client chair next to the boxes. He opened up the first box, and the name on the first file was an Eastern European name he didn't recognize. Strulovic. He was looking for a file with the last name of Davis on it, who was his client. Shit, now he had dragged a file or files to his office for no reason, and they would have to track down whose file this really was. He opened the second file and saw Steve Goldrick's name on it. Crap, now we have to return files to, of all people, Steve himself. He'll probably want a full investigation into all the files that were taken, just to make our lives miserable.

As Rick moved through the files in the second box with his fingers, he saw the word "Adoption" written on every file. These were recent files, and all the names designated as "Birth Mother" were Eastern European women's names. Steve didn't do any adoption work that Rick knew of, nor did he ever remember any of the associates doing that kind of work for him.

Now his curiosity was piqued. He pulled out a handful of files. Every single file had the same front label, presumably the name of the Birth Mother on the front. As he opened the first file, stapled to the left-hand side of the file, were copies of three checks, all made out to Steve Goldrick. Each check was for $33,333.33—a neat $100,000. Rick threw the file on the floor and reached for the second file. Again, there were copies of three checks all for the same amount as were in the first file, and all made out to Steve Goldrick. A cardinal rule of being a partner in any law firm is that the checks for fees are made payable to the law firm and not to any individual attorney. Fees are the property of the law firm. Lead us not into temptation, as they say.

File after file in the box was identical to the one before it. An Eastern European name on the front of the file, three checks made payable only to Steve, presumably from the proposed adoptive parents and pictures of newborn babies.

Rick threw these files on the floor as well to designate which files he had gone through. He used the keys to his car from his pocket to remove the protective moving tape from the box lid. He again grabbed another handful of files, but he was certain as to what he was going to find. He moved through these files more quickly than the first set of files, because he knew what he was looking for. Every file he looked at was set up exactly like the one before, and each file had the same set of checks stapled to the left-hand side of the folder.

Rick now sat down at his desk and opened one of the files to read it thoroughly. What he saw shocked him. It was obvious that Steve could not have pulled this off without help, but it would be interesting to see who he trusted to do this and for how long this had been going on. One of the co-conspirators did not surprise him, but two of them did. Steve's longtime and very trusted secretary, Helen, didn't surprise him at all because she was extremely protective of Steve, and she wielded considerable power in the firm with Steve's blessing. This made a lot of sense to Rick. She was the perfect person to be in on this, and no one ever questioned Helen about what she did, because to question her was to question Steve, the consummate sin.

The two other co-conspirators surprised him. They were none other than Steve's daughter and son-in-law! Keep it in the family and presumably keep all the money in the family, too. A husband-and-wife team was brilliant as a front to establish legitimacy with the Birth Mother. His daughter, Gabriella, would gain the trust of the Birth Mother in a way that a man alone could not do. Gabriella had inherited Steve's charm and personality. She had a way about her to convince people to do what she wanted them to do. Rick had met her number of times before and had seen her in action.

Rick also knew that there had to be doctors on both sides of the Atlantic involved. He saw the names of two doctors with unpronounceable names with lots of consonants, attached to hospitals or clinics he had never heard of. Rick's guess was that the women were impregnated in their own countries and then flown to the United States for the deliveries. There was a doctor in Miami who did the deliveries. Most probably, Steve's daughter and son-in-law were the couriers of the money for the babies. Rick put the file down on his desk, leaned back in his chair, put his hands behind his head, and took a deep breath. A million questions raced through his mind, and he could feel his heart pounding. How long has this been going on? How much money had Steve pocketed individually that belonged to the firm? What would Steve's partners, or soon-to-be former partners, think about how much money had been siphoned off? With Steve, it was always about the money. Steve was trafficking in babies! What the fuck was he thinking? The goddamn guy had more money than you could ever need or use, and he still wanted more. He would be convicted of a felony and go to jail. The bastard deserves it. With that, Rick picked up the phone and started dialing.

CHAPTER 33

C'mon, c'mon, Dannie, pick up the phone. "Dannie, it's Rick. Call me as soon as you can. I have something to tell you that is extremely important and will blow your mind. I mean it, Dannie, you've got to call me immediately." Shit, Dannie, where the hell are you?

Rick paced up and down in his office, not quite knowing what else to do. This was monumental and he had to tell Dannie. There was no one else he could tell right now, and he needed her input. His heart was pounding from adrenaline.

He decided to take two boxes with him and put them in the car. The other three boxes he put on the side of his credenza against the wall, where the boxes were hardly noticeable. He also put other boxes on top of these, so that these were at the very bottom. For the first time in a very long time, he locked his office. He knew he was being ridiculous, because to a casual onlooker, these were just more boxes of files along with the other boxes of files in his office that had yet to be put away.

As he carried the two boxes to his car, he still couldn't decide why he was getting in the car or where he was actually going. He popped open the trunk and put the two boxes in and slammed the trunk. He got in the driver's side, but didn't start the engine.

He just sat there, as if slowing down and sitting in the car was somehow going to help him process this better. After a few minutes of sitting there, maybe that was right. There were two trains of thought racing through his mind. The first was this would spell the end of Steve Goldrick's partnership and, hell, his career. He'd probably go to jail and get disbarred. The second train of thought was the question of how could they use this to their advantage?

He started the engine and drove toward Dannie's house. He didn't know if she was home yet, but maybe he'd wait for her or maybe she would call him while he was on the way. As he exited I-287 in Rye, his cell rang. He looked down at the phone, and saw it was Dannie.

As he clicked the phone on, he heard Dannie's voice and there was real concern in it. "Rick, it's me. Are you OK? Did something happen? I've never heard you sound like that on the phone."

Rick realized that he might have sounded on the edge of being hysterical. He knew he sounded somewhat breathless. Perhaps Dannie thought he was having some sort of relapse and was having a breakdown.

"Dannie, everything's fine with me. Where are you? I need to show you something about Steve Goldrick. Where are you? You're going to be more ecstatic when you see what I have."

"Can't you tell me on the phone? This is nuts. I just dropped off Rob and the kids at Westchester County airport. They're flying down to Florida for the weekend to see his mother. I begged off because I have so much going on with the move. Plus, I hate my mother-in-law. She's such a bitch. I couldn't bear to be in her house for three days unless she was already dead. I can be home in fifteen minutes. Can you meet me at my house, or do you want to meet somewhere else?"

"I'll meet you at your house. I'll probably be there before you." With that, he hit the off button and continued toward her house. He pulled into the driveway and knew he was there ahead of her. A few minutes later, he saw the garage door go up remotely and knew that Dannie was turning into the driveway. He got out of the car, opened the trunk and carried the two boxes into the garage behind Dannie's car. Dannie jumped out of the car like she had been shot from a cannon. She turned to look at Rick, and her glance dropped to the two boxes he was holding. Dannie's expression reflected a moment of disappointment as she looked at the two boxes, but then as she glanced at Rick, and he was actually flushed, she realized that these were not just ordinary boxes, but something akin to liquid gold. Dannie adeptly moved past Rick in the garage, opened the door to the kitchen, and turned off the alarm system, practically in one motion.

Rick put the boxes down on the kitchen table, and Dannie threw her purse onto the chair and spun to look at him. "Fire away. I can't stand the suspense. What's in there—a dead body? Am I going to need a drink, perhaps a shot of tequila?"

Rick said, "Maybe after I tell you. Dannie, I have five boxes in my possession that came out of storage with green tags on them, which should have made them my closed-out files. Only these five file boxes are Steve Goldrick's."

Before he could get another word out, Dannie groaned in much the same way he had when he thought that the movers had mistakenly pulled files that belonged to Steve, of all people, who would make a federal case out of the fact that some of his closed files were taken by mistake.

"Don't groan, Dannie, that's what I did originally. But we have the proverbial gold mine here. These are adoption files that prove that Steve was illegally trafficking in babies, and he was raking in a cool hundred thousand dollars on each adoption that was going directly to him and which he was not turning over to the firm. He's got his daughter and son-in-law involved and helping him move money and the girls from Eastern Europe. Steve's secretary, Helen, is also involved. God bless her that she's so anal that every file is set up precisely the same way with copies of the checks all stapled neatly on the left side of each file jacket. Take a look at these files. You can read a few carefully and then skim through a bunch of the others."

Rick reached into the top box and pulled out a generous handful of files. Rick walked over to the refrigerator to grab a soda for himself while Dannie put on her glasses and sat down at the table to read. She did what Rick suggested and read through three files slowly and carefully. Then she leafed through about eight others.

"How many boxes of these did you say there were?"

"Five."

"Are they all the same?"

"I think so. I've skimmed through about three boxes, and they all appear to be set up exactly the same and with the same payments. I will read the others, but I assume that they're all the same. Even if this is all we have, we have more than enough to take Steve down."

Dannie threw her glasses down on the table and took a long gulp of Rick's Diet Coke.

"There are so many ways to play this; we need to think this through. Let's be smart and get the most we can out of an incredible situation. Revenge is a wonderful thing, but so is money."

"What are you saying, Dannie?"

"I'm saying that it's a slam dunk to call the DA and to call my former partners, who will have their own sense of righteous indignation about his abuse of the law, but mostly the indignation will be about his abuse of their wallets. I don't know which group of vultures will be all over him first. I'm still working this out in my head, but I think there should be something in this for us for doing 'our civic duty.' A mere thank you is nice, but certainly not enough."

Rick swallowed hard and said, "What are you suggesting?"

"I'm suggesting that Steve stole hundreds of thousands of dollars from his partners, from the adoptive parents, and from the birth mothers. He's got to have a huge pile of cash stored somewhere or in many places. I think Steve would really like to share some of that money with us. He just doesn't know it yet."

"Steve is going down, and so are his daughter, son-in-law and his secretary. He's going to jail, and his soon-to-be former partners are going to have him tied up in court forever, and then they'll have judgments against him in every state. He'll be disbarred, and the gravy train will be stopped dead. I think we should get a little of that gravy before it dries up."

"We talking blackmail here?" The tone in Rick's voice was like something he had never heard before in his own voice. He sat down on one of the kitchen chairs, feeling a little sick at the thought of what Dannie was suggesting. Dannie was looking at him and waiting for him to continue. "Dannie, I think this is a big mistake. No matter what we call it, it's still blackmail! This makes us no better than Steve."

"No, no, it's not blackmail because that would implicate us. I think we should ask Steve if he needs a little time to get his affairs in order before we blow the whistle. He may need to move money, and perhaps he might want to take a 'long vacation' overseas. I think we should give him ten days to do what he needs to do, and then we go to the authorities and the firm. In the interim, we are holding onto very valuable property for him, and we'll probably need to hire security guards and get a vault. I think that service is so important that he should pay us fifty thousand dollars a day each to coordinate that service for him. What do you think, Rick?"

"I'm trying to digest this. Part of me thinks it's brilliant, and part of it says this makes us accessories to a crime."

"Au contraire, we are going to turn him in as we are ethically bound to do. We're just going to do it in ten days. Who could possibly know when we found these files? With all that is going on with the new firm, it could have been months before we got to unpack all the files. Steve certainly isn't going to tell them when we found them."

Rick countered, "I don't have a good feeling about this at all. I hope this doesn't come back to haunt us. Considering how ruthless he is, we need to move these files to someplace safe before we contact him. I wouldn't put it past him to hire somebody to break into the office or our houses to try to retrieve the files. Dannie, we have to be really careful of our every move; he's going to be like a caged animal."

"Rick, go rent a storage unit in Stamford, or even farther up in Connecticut. We'll put the files in the storage unit, and let's move a few more boxes in there as well. Let's make about three or four copies of about four files to show him we have the goods on him, but obviously, he'll realize the original files are tucked away some place safe."

"How are you going to pull this off, Dannie? Are you going to ask him to meet with us?"

"Yeah, I'll call him."

"Suppose he won't meet with us. He isn't exactly someone you'd call and say come meet me for a cup of coffee or a drink. He double-crossed me, and he hates you."

"I'll give him enough information to let him know what we have. He'll come to a meeting. He'll be cursing us out, but he'll come once he realizes what's at stake. I want us to move forward on this, but we need to be very careful because Steve is ruthless and shrewd."

Dannie got up from her chair and walked over to where Rick was leaning against one of the kitchen cabinets. She leaned forward and hugged him. He hugged her back. She pulled herself away from him and looked up into his eyes. Each smiled at the other, and Dannie noticed that Rick had a few crow's feet around his eyes that she had never seen before. She stood on tiptoes and leaned in to kiss him. He kissed her back. They pulled away, looked at each other, and then kissed again. This kiss lasted longer and was more passionate as each explored the warmth of each other's mouth. Rick reached down and put his hand on Dannie's breast. She opened the top two buttons on her shirt for him.

Dannie pulled back from the embrace and said, "Let's go upstairs. We have the whole house to ourselves."

He nodded, and she grabbed his hand and led him out of the kitchen, to the foyer, and up the stairs.

As Fannie listened to their conversation, she was pleased that they had found the adoption files. Thanks to her. She was equally pleased with herself for manipulating the manifest the movers had. Now as she observed Rick and Dannie on their way up the stairs to the bedroom, Fannie thought to herself, "In the words of Ricky Ricardo, 'You've both got some 'splaining to do.'"

CHAPTER 34

Rick opened a storage locker in Bridgeport and moved the five boxes into it along with a few other boxes of files. Once that piece of the puzzle was completed, he called Dannie to tell her. She said she was planning to start moving in to the office, so she would be there in about an hour. As she was about to hang up, she said, "I really enjoyed the other night. It was quite a victory celebration."

"Yes, it was," Rick answered, then thought, and a big mistake. In fact, Rick thought the whole plan might be a very big mistake.

As Rick sat in his car, he began having serious second thoughts. This is ludicrous! We could end up in jail alongside Goldrick, or even worse, dead. Who knows what he's capable of? This is not me; what the hell am I agreeing to? I almost ended it before, and now that I'm just starting to get my life back...and then there's Maizie. She makes me feel alive, like life is worth living again. Am I my own life's wrecking ball?

Dannie arrived at the office about fifty minutes thereafter. She buzzed Rick on the intercom a few minutes later and asked him to come in to her office.

"Hi, Rick, come on in and shut the door." Once he had shut the door, Dannie continued, "One of the weird things about being in a partnership is that you get to know the idiosyncrasies of your partners, whether you want to or not. I've figured out the next piece of the puzzle, which is how to get Steve to meet with us. Steve is always bragging that he leaves his house at precisely seven o'clock every morning, gets in his Jaguar, and is standing in the office at seven fifty. We're going to call him at seven ten and tell him to turn his Jag around and meet us. He's going to try to blow us off until he realizes what we have on him. Can you meet me in the parking lot at the diner at about seven tomorrow, so we can make the call while he's driving? I so hope that Little Stevie doesn't get himself into an accident while he's on the phone. That would be so tragic."

The following morning Rick pulled into the diner parking lot and saw Dannie's car parked toward the back of the lot, with the windshield wipers going. It was drizzling, and there was a chill in the air. Rick parked a few spaces away and jogged over to Dannie's car. He knocked on the window, and Dannie unlocked the doors.

"It's not even seven, and you're already here."

"It's a lot closer to get here from my house than yours, and I've been up for a long time. I was too keyed up to sleep well. It's kind of the same feeling I have when I'm starting a trial. Actually, this is sort of like a trial. You have to get yourself pumped up. So, Rick, are we ready to take down this prick? I'm going to put him on the speaker, but I think it would be better if he doesn't know you're here. I had an old client who owed me a favor, so I took the precaution of getting a burner phone from him that we'll get rid of when this is over."

They waited a few minutes in silence in the car until the clock on the dashboard said 7:10. Rick knew that the clock was digital, but he could swear that he heard ticking. Then he realized that it was his own heart pounding. Dannie pulled out a piece of note paper from her purse with Steve's phone number on it. "Well, here goes."

Rick was frankly surprised how calm Dannie sounded. There was not the least bit of nervousness in her voice that he could detect.

Dannie punched in the numbers and hit the speaker option. Steve answered on the third ring.

"Hi, Steve, it's Dannie Bevan. I figured I'd catch you in the car on your way to work."

" Ah, yeah, Dannie, you did catch me in the car."

"Did you get on the Hutchinson River Parkway—or should I say, 'The Hutch'—yet?"

"How do you know I take the Hutch?"

Steve definitely sounded off balance, and Dannie had taken him off guard. Dannie ignored the question.

"Steve, I'd like to meet with you at the diner in Larchmont now."

Steve was beginning to regain some of his composure and now was a little bit wary of what was going on.

"Can't do it, Dannie. I have a big meeting with some A-list clients in my office this morning. Call Helen and set up a meeting for later in the week. Actually, I'm pretty busy this week. It might even have to be early next week."

The arrogance had returned. Have your girl call my girl.

"I don't think so, Steve. This can't wait. There are babies being born every day and money to be made."

"What are you talking about, Dannie?"

"Don't try to play innocent with me. Your innocence went out the window the first time you took a hundred thousand dollars."

There was dead silence at the other end of the phone. Steve was either digesting what Dannie had just said, or he was choking on it.

"Steve, turn the damn Jaguar around and meet me at the diner in Larchmont in fifteen minutes, or it will be the biggest mistake you ever made. And, I daresay, you have made hundreds of thousands of them...if you get my drift. See you in a few minutes." With that, she hit the off button with a flourish.

"You are one cool character, Dannie. You sounded as calm as if you were ordering a pizza. How do you do it?"

"Many times I've made demands of my opponents and then walked out of a big meeting, and I was bluffing. This was a piece of cake. We hold all the cards, and now he knows it. I gave him fifteen minutes to get here in case he needs extra time to stop to throw up."

With that, she leaned across the seat and kissed Rick. Another long kiss. Rick kissed her back, and he had to admit that the thrill of this was adding to the sexual tension. The problem was he was thinking of Maizie as he was kissing Dannie. Rick then thought to himself, "What the hell am I doing? As hot as Dannie is I'm messing with fire, and it can only lead to disaster. I'm going to have to end this."

They walked into the diner as if nothing had happened. Dannie asked for a table instead of a booth and told the receptionist that they were meeting a tall man who should be coming in shortly. She seated herself so that she was facing the door.

"I want us both to be facing him, so we can see his expression. I don't think he has any idea you're going to be here."

When the waiter came over to the table, Dannie ordered coffee with skim milk. Rick ordered coffee with regular milk. Frankly, Rick could barely get the coffee down. If he had to eat something right now, it would be all over. A few more minutes elapsed, and again they sat in silence. Rick thought, "What was there to say now, anyway? In what piece of literature was the phrase 'the die is cast'? Oh yeah, *Julius Caesar*. Don't want to end up like him."

Rick saw Dannie's tension and her body stiffen. He knew that Steve had come in. Steve came over to the table and seemed clearly surprised to see Rick sitting there. With Steve standing up and their sitting down, he towered over them. He sat down quickly, without saying hello.

He growled, "What do you want?" Rick pushed a manila file in his direction without saying anything. Steve looked ashen when he sat down, and Rick had some time to study him as Steve slowly opened the file. Steve had on a dark gray suit, but for the first time, Rick noticed that Steve's tie was partially undone, and the top button of his shirt was open. Rick couldn't remember ever seeing Steve with his tie undone. The most Steve would ever do to be casual was to take off his suit jacket.

Steve leafed through a few pages of the photocopies but didn't even go halfway down the pages. He most probably knew what was in there already. He pushed the file back in Rick's general direction.

"Where did you get these?" He looked from Dannie to Rick.

"It really doesn't matter now; does it, Steve? There are several sets of copies safely stored away in a number of places in addition to the originals. Dannie and I just wanted to have insurance. These are for you, but they only encompass a portion of all the files we have."

Steve looked at both of them with hatred emanating from his eyes.

"What do you want?" This time it was more of a hiss than a growl.

Dannie answered this time. "Here's the deal. We will hold off for ten days before taking these files to the D.A. and to your partners. We figured you're going to need some time to get your affairs in order, and perhaps you and your daughter and son-in-law might need to take a trip overseas. I think you'll probably need to move some money out of the country in addition to the money I assume you already have out of the country."

At the mention of his daughter and son-in-law, Steve actually winced.

Dannie continued, "Since these are such sensitive files, we'll need some remuneration for their safekeeping. We think one mill ought to do it. You can pay it to us tomorrow morning."

"Look, I don't know that I can come up with that kind of money by tomorrow morning or at all."

"Don't play us for fools, Steve. You've got money stashed away, and I'm sure you have money in some off shore accounts. You were collecting one hundred grand per adoption, and we've got five boxes of files, but I'm sure there's more. Surely, there has to be a little cash left over for us."

The sarcasm was dripping off her words. All three of them at the table knew it.

"How do I know that even if I can come up with this kind of money, that you won't double-cross me and go to the D.A. an hour after I give you the money?"

"Frankly, Steve, you don't. But what you do know is if you don't give come through, we will definitely go to the D.A. tomorrow and call your partners. This way you have time to do what you need to do and keep most of your money. You can figure out somewhere to go where they don't have extradition. Maybe you can have one of the associates in the firm research that for you."

"Shut the fuck up, Dannie."

"Now, Steve, we were partners until recently, and now we're going to be partners again for a day. You weren't exactly gracious to me when I was leaving. You kind of unceremoniously dumped Rick, and so he needs a little help from your personal resources since you were unwilling to help him before when you had the firm's resources at your disposal."

"So this is what you're going to do. You're going to get the money together today. I'll call you tomorrow at seven ten and tell you where to meet us. Bring it in a briefcase or two, and nothing larger than Benjamins. And by the way, there are affidavits in several centrally located places stating that if anything should happen to either or both of us, you are the person who caused our demises. I'll also save you some trouble and tell you not to bother to have anyone break into our new office or either of our houses because the files are certainly not there. Do I make myself clear?"

Steve knew he was defeated, but he was still sending death rays across the table to both of them.

"Both of you can go fuck yourselves."

"We'll see you tomorrow morning, then."

Steve nodded. He was not only ashen, but he was sweating. He lumbered to his feet and turned to walk out. He bumped into one of the waiters, who spilled a plate of sunny side up eggs on Steve. An appropriate metaphor for Steve in this situation. Before the waiter could react or say anything, Steve sped out of the diner.

Dannie looked at Rick. "Well, that went well, don't you think? I really couldn't have eaten anything before, but now I'm starving."

With that, she called the waiter over and ordered a ham and cheese egg white omelet, whole wheat toast, and home fries. And a refill on her coffee.

CHAPTER 35

Rick answered the front door and gave his brother, Jason, a hug. "Hey, Jas. How ya doin', bro? How's the hand?"

Jason made a guttural sound and a fake karate chop with the hand with the cast on it. "Still fighting for truth, justice, and the American way." They both laughed, knowing that Jason had broken it playing basketball.

"When is the cast due to come off?"

"Next week I go to a soft cast. It still really throbs in the damp weather. I feel like the old guys who do nothing but complain about their aches and pains."

"If you're one of the old guys, what does that make me? I'm right behind you. How are the kids?"

"They're fine. If you feel up to it sometime, Julie is becoming quite a good softball player. She's a really good lefty first baseman. You should see her hit. She's fearless. Leans right in over the plate. She's gotten hit a few times on the elbow because of that lean in, so now she's wearing a big elbow guard."

Jason hesitated, watching for Rick's reaction. A shadow clearly passed over Rick's face, even though he tried not to have a reaction.

"Better an elbow guard than a cast," Rick said with a little smile.

"This is fall ball, and we have, I think, six more games. I sure hope you get a chance to see Jules play; she misses you. We all do."

"I know I've been absent from your lives. I needed some time to sort through things and get my act together. I've missed all of you, too. I promise to come see Jules play; you can count on it."

As they sat down in the kitchen, Rick asked Jason if he wanted a beer. "Help yourself in the fridge."

"What are you making?"

"I thought we'd start with mussels. Then your favorite—steak, which is apparently still moving it's so rare—and salad with pears and Gorgonzola cheese."

"Wow, what happened to hamburgers and hot dogs? I'm not knocking it. You've become quite the foodie."

The conversation moved through the obligatory recitations of people they knew in common and what they were doing, who was getting divorced and who was changing jobs. Politics was also a hot topic with the way the economy was tanking.

The talk then moved to sports, the Yankees and Mets, and the Giants and Jets. It sounded like a kid's nursery rhyme. They were both Yankees fans, but Rick was a Jets fan and also had a liking for the Packers. He had always thought that Vince Lombardi was the epitome of a coach's coach. Jason was a Giants fan, and so the rivalry continued. Rick and Jason both liked college basketball, but they couldn't agree on those teams either.

Jason asked Rick, "How's it going with the new firm? Things working out OK?"

"We're just getting started, but it seems to be working out well. You'll have to come over and see the new place. It came out looking great. The old firm was just such a rat race, and I didn't realize how much I hated it until I was away from it. The time away gives you perspective. The Managing Partner, Steve Goldrick, turned out to be a real prick. I'm glad to be away from him. For some reason, I think he was sabotaging me so that I never would have made partner."

"That's really shitty after all you did for that firm. Talk about no gratitude."

"Steve thought the firm was 'entitled' to that because they were paying me well. They wanted to own me. Nothing was ever going to be enough."

"It always comes down to money with guys like that, Rick. It's a shame, but it often does. Do you think the new situation is going to be better?"

"I really do. I can see the kind of work I'm handling is going to lead to being a partner, and I think pretty soon. Remember that I went to law school late, after I already had an MBA, so I'm older than people who went to law school right out of college. Anyway, there are the two partners, Dannie and Chris, and they set it up that I'm the most senior person. Then there are the associates, some of whom report to me as well as the two partners."

Jason nodded in agreement. "Sounds good for you."

"Listen, I need to talk to you about two issues, Jason, and you gotta swear to me that you won't tell Beth. I really mean it: you have to keep your mouth shut. Promise me."

Jason's face clouded over with concern, but he was also happy that his brother was going to confide in him. It had been a long time.

"I promise; we've been brothers forever. You know that you can count on me for anything. I won't say a word to Beth. I love her with all my heart, but you and I both know it's hard for her to keep a secret. Whatever it is, it stays between us. I know you've been through a lot, and I kind of felt helpless to do anything for you. So, shoot, what is it?"

Rick looked down into his glass as if he was going to find the words written there.

Jason waited, looking at him, and Rick took the last swig of his beer and got up to open another bottle. He was fidgeting with the bottle cap just to do something with his hands.

Rick began to speak and said, "I met this really nice girl. She's bright, she's gorgeous, and she likes me. Her name is Maizie. She's the daughter of my friend, Abby."

Jason looked a little puzzled. "Is the problem that Abby likes you, too?"

"Hell, no. She's old enough to be my mother. I actually think she wouldn't mind it if Maizie and I hooked up. In fact, she was pleased that I helped Maizie get a job as a paralegal in the firm. But I feel really guilty that I'm even interested in her, as if I'm being disloyal to Jennifer. She hasn't been dead all that long. I loved her so much."

"Look, Rick, I know you loved them. We all loved Jen and Adam. I know you somehow felt responsible for their deaths. You can't control fate. It was an accident, and whether you were with her in the car or not, that guy might still have hit them. You can't be certain things would have turned out differently. I believe it wasn't your time to go. We don't get to decide that stuff. You will always love her, but you're still here on this earth, and you get to have a life."

Jason continued, "Maybe it wasn't a coincidence that Abby helped you. Maybe you are meant to hook up with Maizie. You should chew on that for a while. The fact that you're even willing to think about getting involved with someone is a good thing."

"That's what the shrink says, but I still can't help feeling guilty that I'm here and Jennifer's gone."

"What about the fact that Maizie is now your employee? Is that going to create a problem?"

"She's not going to be working for me, so that's one thing. She really needed a job, and I think she's a good paralegal, so I was helping both sides. I haven't even been out on a date with her, and I may not, so I saw no reason not to give her a chance." Rick paused and then continued, "Jason, there's something else. And more serious."

"Oh, God, what else?"

"I think I told you about Dannie Bevan—what a smart and terrific attorney she is, and a fiery redhead. At the time the old firm was going to cut me loose, she offered me a job, and a good one, at the new firm. She's put me in a position of authority and backed me up on everything."

"So far so good, Rick. I'm waiting…and…?"

"We had a victory…uh, a big victory together." The words exploded from his mouth like a shotgun blast. "Then we slept together. Honestly, for me it was fine. Not really much more than that. I think that's why I don't feel guilty about it. As I was screwing her, I kept thinking that I'd much rather be in bed with

Maizie. And then there's the whole guilt thing with Maizie and Jennifer. I feel like I'm a hamster on a wheel. I keep going round and round."

Jason let out a low whistle. "Jesus, Rick, can you possibly have made this any more complicated? There are about a thousand things wrong here. Dannie is your boss and now Maizie's boss. What happens if they find out about each other? If you stop screwing Dannie, will she be vindictive? What would you have said if a client told you he did this? What about if you stop screwing her and then she finds out you're screwing Maizie? Your career in this firm may be circling the drain before it even gets off the ground. You couldn't have kept it in your pants? This certainly doesn't sound like you. I've always been the wild one."

"Like you said, I'm here on this earth, and it just happened. And I didn't want to stop it. It felt good to do it. What can I say...I'm fucking human."

"Actually, Rick, it was both. You were fucking and human. A beautiful red headed one!" Jason continued on, partly kidding and partly sarcastic, "Well there's always the Food Network if the law firm doesn't work out."

"I know I screwed up, no pun intended. Let's hope it doesn't come to that."

Rick didn't feel the need at this point to tell Jason the other part of the secret—that he was about to come into a considerable sum of money courtesy of his former "friend" Steve Goldrick. Maybe dropping this bomb about Dannie was enough for now.

CHAPTER 36

The following morning was still cool, but the sun was trying to break through the clouds. Dannie was glad it wasn't raining, because the rain would definitely have hindered her plan. Dannie was waiting for 7:10 to show on the clock in her car. She made a mental note that she should bet 710 in the daily numbers because it appeared that this was turning out to be a hell of a lucky number. As the number changed to 7:10 on the clock, she looked down at the same piece of paper she used yesterday to dial Steve's cell phone number. She dialed and Steve picked up the cell on the second ring.

"Hello," he growled.

"Good morning, Steve; it's Dannie. And how are you this morning?"

"Go to hell!" he answered back.

"Steve, where are your manners and that charming disposition we have all come to know and love? You do not want to piss me off, because you certainly wouldn't want me making any calls today." Dannie was being very careful about what she was saying on the phone to him today in case Steve was taping the conversation. Dannie was, however, enjoying taunting him.

Steve didn't respond to the sarcasm or the taunt, but he did say, "Where do you want to meet?"

"Meet me at the ball field on Gedney Way in White Plains. I assume I will have the pleasure of your company all by yourself."

"Yeah, by myself."

Dannie waited a few minutes and then called Steve back.

"What the fuck do you want? I'm on the way."

"We've had a change of plans. Meet me in the park at Saxon Woods. It's right off Mamaroneck Avenue near the field at Gedney Way, but farther south. Just drive in and make a left after the field house and park there." Then she hung up.

Dannie was already in Saxon Woods and waiting for him. She was supposedly part of an exercise group that was starting to form. There were a number of people arriving and getting out of their cars and walking toward the field house. Some were already limbering up. Dannie thought this was a perfect place because it wasn't isolated and, from where she was standing, she could see everyone coming up the driveway. Rick was seated in a car halfway up the driveway, and he could see if anyone was following Steve. Rick was sort of slouching down in the seat, and he had on sunglasses and a baseball cap pulled down to the sunglasses. Rick was somewhat amused at this. He felt like a character on *Hawaii Five-O* on a stakeout. He mused about how many lawyers could say they had really been undercover or had been on a stakeout.

A few minutes later, Rick saw Steve's big, black Jag pull in. Steve slowed down to check where he was going. Rick kept one eye on his car, but kept watching the driveway to see if Steve had someone follow him. Dannie was in a pair of sweat pants and a Gore Tex jacket, and she blended right in with the exercise group. Steve pulled into a parking space, rolled down the window, and turned off the engine but didn't get out of the car. He really didn't know what to do, so he stayed put, figuring Dannie would find him or call him back on the cell. Little bitch! Why hadn't he read her correctly for what she was before this? And how the hell did they get their hands on those files anyway?

Someone knocked on the passenger-side window and jolted Steve. It was Rick. Rick motioned him to roll down the window. Rick leaned in and put his elbow on the car where the window was down. With the other hand he reached in and handed a backpack to Steve. "Fill them. There's one inside the other." Steve motioned with his head toward the floor of the car on the passenger side. Rick saw two briefcases on the floor.

"Oh, for Christ sake, just take the briefcases. This isn't some spy movie."

Now it was Rick's turn to growl. "Fill the fucking backpacks. You're not in a position to argue."

Steve shot back, "You have no idea who you're fucking with and what I can do to you or Bevan!"

"Just fill the backpacks with those bills, Stevie, that's all you need to do. No threats," Rick responded calmly.

Steve made a face and yanked the top briefcase onto the seat. Steve snapped open the briefcase and picked up a large handful of bills and dumped them into one of the backpacks. Steve tossed the filled backpack in Rick's direction across the seat. Rick grabbed it and zipped it up. Steve started filling the second one. The second one was about three quarters filled, and the two briefcases were empty. It had been Rick's idea to use the backpacks and ditch the briefcases in case Steve had a GPS put in each briefcase. They would never know for sure if he had placed the GPS in the briefcases, but who wanted to chance it.

Rick nodded to Steve, leaned all the way into the car and grabbed the car fob out of the ignition and turned and walked away. He got into his car, started the engine and drove away. Rick replayed the scene in his head. He didn't think that they had said fifty words each. He drove a few miles and then pulled into a CVS parking lot. He got out of the car and looked around. No one was in the parking lot. Rick stomped on the fob and crushed it into several pieces. He picked it up and wrapped it in a piece of newspaper and walked over to the garbage can outside the door. He casually dropped the paper in the large garbage pail. He then walked back to his car, got back in and drove off. He called Dannie and she picked up on the first ring.

"Everything went perfectly, and I just broke the fob, so I had to throw it away."

Dannie knew exactly what he was saying because they had talked about it in advance. Dannie said she had driven past Steve, but he was standing outside the car screaming into his cell phone with his back to her. Dannie had also been careful to use her son's car, which Steve had never seen before.

They were going to meet at the rendezvous point as planned, to split the money. It was all so cloak-and-dagger.

CHAPTER 37

As if to prove that there was indeed honor among thieves, Dannie waited for the ten days she had promised Steve she would before she called the District Attorney's office. She wasn't quite sure why she had waited and kept her word to Steve. Did she want to give Steve a running start to get out of the country, most probably with millions? She also thought that he had most of his money out of the country already. In point of fact, she really was surprised that Steve had a million dollars in cash that he could lay his hands on in twenty-four hours. She thought he'd have some money socked away in a safe deposit box, just not that much. If he had come up with a lot less money, she would have taken it. As she mused on this, she thought that Steve was not at all certain that she wouldn't just take the money and call the D.A. that same day. He had gambled that if he truly didn't piss her off and perhaps had appeared to acquiesce to what she wanted that she might wait the ten days because she might think that she was in control.

The next day after Steve reluctantly gave them the money, Steve called his secretary, Helen, at about eight o'clock in the morning and asked her to meet him at a coffee shop about two blocks from the office. When she hesitated with him on the phone,

Steve said, more quietly than she had heard him in years, that it was extremely important and not to ask questions. When she walked into the coffee shop, she saw Steve sitting in a booth near the back. As she approached, she took in a lot more information about him than she could verbalize. Steve looked pale and tired and this surreptitious meeting in a coffee shop had her on edge from the first minute.

Steve had a mug of coffee on the table and nothing else. "Helen, I don't know what to say to you except to say that we're all in deep trouble. I don't know how that bitch, Dannie Bevan, got her hands on the adoption files, but she did. She's blackmailing me—ah, she's blackmailing all of us. She said that if I paid her off, which I did, that she'd wait ten days before she went to the D.A. I can't be sure that she'll wait the ten days. You've been loyal to me all these years, and I am not going to hang you out to dry."

The waitress came over to the table at just that moment, and Steve waved her away. By now, Helen had turned a complete shade of gray. She picked up Steve's mug of coffee and took a huge gulp. Steve was taken aback by her action. Helen, who was so deferential to him, now had the look of a wild woman, and in a million years Steve could never have imagined Helen taking anything of his, no less grab his mug and take a drink.

"Helen, listen to me. I need you to get a grip on yourself. I just told you that I will not hang you out to dry. I'm going to help you. He reached into his jacket pocket and handed her an envelope. There are two tickets to Mexico in there for you and Jack. They're for tomorrow night. But I need you to go into the office today and act like nothing's going on. Just take messages for me today and tell people I'm at a meeting with clients in Philadelphia today and tomorrow. Tomorrow morning you call in sick, and tomorrow night you're on the plane. Then it's the weekend, and you've bought yourself another two days before anyone thinks anything is wrong. There's also a hotel reservation for you. You can then decide where you want to go after that. It's too suspicious if both of us just don't show up in the office today. Can you do this, Helen?"

No answer. She continued to stare at him.

"Helen, can you do this one thing for me?"

Slowly, Helen nodded her head yes.

"Good, but you need to act a little more like yourself. Pull it together; I know you can." Steve said with a little more conviction, "We can sit here for a few minutes until you can compose yourself."

"What am I supposed to tell Jack?"

"Helen, Jack knows what's been going on. There's no way in hell that you could have had a house like yours on a secretary's salary. Realistically, we knew there was a possibility, however small, that no matter how careful we were that something might go wrong. Well, it has gone wrong, and we have to deal with it. Do you want to call him now while I'm here, or do you want me to call him? You obviously can't call him from the office, and you can't be crying in the office."

"Can you get me a cup of tea please, Mr. Goldrick? I'm going to go to the ladies room and then call him. Can you wait here for me? What happens if he wants to talk to you?"

"Well, I don't think I can come into the ladies room, but you can come out and I can call him. I'll order the tea in the meantime."

More than twenty minutes passed, which seemed like an eternity to Steve. He had picked this coffee shop because he knew that even if Helen panicked, she could not slip out the back without his seeing her. Finally, she returned to the table and sat down. She looked more composed than when she went to the ladies room. Apparently, Jack got it. He hadn't upset her, and in fact, he probably calmed her down a little.

"Mr. Goldrick, what do we do when we get to Mexico? Where do we go from there?"

"That's entirely up to you. I know you have that off-shore account we opened for you, so you can decide once you're in Mexico. It might be better if I didn't know where you're going."

"What are you going to do?"

"I think we'll be taking a vacation, too. It's probably better that you don't know where we're going either. So do you think that you can go into the office and act normally for just today?"

"I looked at myself in the mirror in the ladies room, and I think I look horrible. It will be plausible if I call in sick tomorrow."

"It's all right, Helen, this is all going to work out. You'll be sipping margaritas on some beautiful beach somewhere and delighted that you're out of the rat race. I have always taken care of people who have been loyal to me. You're at the top of the list."

Helen's eyes welled up.

"C'mon, Helen, don't fall apart on me. Think of that white sand."

He put one hand on hers and looked into her eyes. With the other hand, he reached into his jacket pocket again and took out another envelope. He pushed it toward her and said, "Here's some cash to get you started and you won't have to take any money out of any bank account for a while. You're the best, Helen."

Steve got up to leave and bent over to kiss her on the cheek. He turned and walked out. Another instance of honor among thieves.

CHAPTER 38

"I don't mind telling you, Dannie, that I feel like the world's biggest hypocrite. We're going to the D.A. to blow the whistle on Steve, when we, ah...you know." Rick couldn't bring himself to say the words out loud to her, and he thought he probably would never say them out loud to any other living soul. He had always thought of himself as a person of integrity, and he had tried to live his life that way. He actually marveled that it had been so easy for him to blackmail Steve. True, Dannie had been a huge motivating force, but he had done nothing, absolutely nothing, to try to talk her out of it or stop her. Was it the money, or was he exacting revenge on Steve? In either case, it hadn't been very hard for him, and he felt he needed to do some more soul searching. He didn't want his values to merely be something he paid lip service to, but apparently that was precisely what he had done. He couldn't tell anyone, even his shrink, so he was left to work this out alone. Would it make it better if he donated the money to charity? It was really bothering him, and now this whole charade with the district attorney's office...

Dannie, on the other hand, seemed to have no qualms whatsoever about what they had done. Her response was almost laughable.

"Rick, he stole from the adoptive parents. He stole from the birth mothers. He totally circumvented the law on adoptions. He stole from his partners. In fact, he robbed us blind, because he was raking in hundreds of thousands of dollars—literally—and keeping it all for himself. The firm obviously couldn't have been a part of his illegal activities, but the time he spent concocting this whole adoption thing and carrying it out was a total misuse of the firm's time and resources."

"Hell, he was the managing partner of the firm! He was the face of the firm and now he absconds with millions of dollars to God knows where. The firm might very well go under if they can't do some serious damage control and do it fast. The clients are going to be apoplectic. The partners aren't going to know what hit them. They're in shock and the shit is just beginning to hit the fan."

Dannie almost made it sound believable, except that she couldn't contain herself and threw in one final statement. He knew she was being sarcastic. "We are merely carrying out our civic duty as concerned citizens and as officers of the court as attorneys." Even Dannie couldn't say that with a straight face.

The Westchester County District Attorney's office called Dannie to set up an appointment with her and Rick for Wednesday afternoon. Dannie and Rick parked in the underground parking lot near White Plains library and walked across the plaza to the courthouse where the district attorney's office was housed. Rick had a rolling suitcase, which held copies of two and a half of the boxes of Steve's adoption files. Dannie had the balance of the contents of the third box. The other two boxes were still on the floor of Rick's office tucked away in a corner by his credenza, but there were copies of all the files. Dannie had painstakingly copied them herself, so no one was the wiser. As long as it took to copy all the files, there was one she noticed and decided to hold back and not divulge the contents to the D.A. She would show that file when the time was right.

The files were tucked away in a storage facility as insurance against Steve. Rick had not yet looked at the contents of the fourth and fifth boxes, and both he and Dannie believed there were more boxes to be found…somewhere. Rick presumed that the other two boxes contained similar documents. Now the D.A. would have a set of documents as well. The D.A. could hash out with the remaining partners in the firm or subpoena any remaining files. There could be nastier surprises among Steve's current or closed-out files.

Dannie and Rick went through the security checkpoint without incident since both of them had SecurePass, which allowed attorneys to go through security in the courthouse without getting on a line and going through metal detection. They then walked toward the bank of elevators. They got off the elevator at the third floor, where the district attorney's office was located and identified themselves to the receptionist behind the bulletproof glass. After a few minutes, a young woman whose name tag said "Bonnie" came out to meet them. She gave them each a visitor's pass and escorted them to a small conference room.

Just prior to this, Dannie had called one of her former partners, with whom she still had a decent relationship, Ted Schoeneman. She sort of hated to drop this bombshell on him, because they had always gotten along well, but she wasn't sure who was actually "driving the train" now that Steve was gone. Let Ted figure out who was now in charge. Dannie called Ted about an hour before their appointment with the D.A. so that there would not be enough time for anyone in the firm to do something to stop her from going to the D.A. She also made a point to monitor her cell phone calls and only answer it if she recognized the phone number.

Dannie had an amusing vision in her head of the partners piling onto a yellow school bus for a fieldtrip to the storage facility in Yonkers and then clamoring over each other to get out of the bus and be the first ones to rip open Steve's closed-out files. She could envision a feeding frenzy as the partners rifled through the files, sweating and screaming at what they found. This was actually a situation where your worst fears about a problem might not be as bad as the problem truly was. It was not inconceivable that the end of the firm might be in sight.

The firm was already in a frenzied state when people realized after the weekend that Helen was nowhere to be found, and then no one could get Steve on the cell phone or receive a return text message, a phenomenon so unbelievable as to be akin to the sun rising in the west. Two of the partners paid a personal visit to Steve's house, and two other partners were dispatched to Helen's house. The partners couldn't decide whether to file a missing person's report for each of them; but there had been no ransom calls and everything looked in order as far as anyone could see by peering through the windows of their houses. No broken locks, no sign of forced entry, no signs of any blood in either house or signs of a struggle. But both Steve and Helen had vanished. No signs of their spouses either.

A few of the clients were at first annoyed that Steve was not returning their calls. That could be covered by the other attorneys picking up their matters and saying Steve was tied up in court, but that would only last so long. Some of Steve's long-time clients were beginning to get suspicious when Helen wasn't there holding their hands and passing messages back and forth to Steve while he was "in court." One enterprising senior associate who had been shanghaied on one of Steve's files suggested that Helen could have walking pneumonia and was therefore too sick to be in the office. He said it tongue in cheek, meaning that Helen had "walked" off. It was better than any other explanation that anyone else had come up with, so Helen "officially" was diagnosed with "walking pneumonia."

It appeared that Steve had disappeared into thin air. Not an easy phenomenon for someone with a persona and ego as large as Steve's. Dannie's call to Ted took him so off guard that he was stammering on the other end of the phone.

When Ted finally regained some measure of composure, he said, "We thought this situation couldn't get any worse, and now apparently it has. We were just about to give the police in Larchmont the go ahead to break into Steve's house to be sure he wasn't lying dead upstairs on the second floor. I guess we can certainly call off the dogs now on this missing person's thing. He's almost certainly absconded to someplace where we won't find him for years. Do you think Helen and her husband are with him?"

"Honestly, Ted, I have no way of knowing, but she was certainly every bit the co-conspirator. I feel awful about this too; Steve was my partner for almost eight years. I'm furious about what he did; he's going to drag all of us into this mess to a greater or lesser degree. I assume you guys want to look at the files? How do you want to handle looking at them? Do you want to come to my office, or do you want to go to the D.A.'s office?"

"Dannie, couldn't you have given us a heads-up on this situation before you went to the D.A.?"

"Look, Ted, we only found these files among some of our own files. We've all been scammed here and it really doesn't matter if you looked at the files yesterday when we found them or today or tomorrow. It's not going to change anything."

"Did Steve know that you had these files? Is that why he took off?"

"I don't know what he knew or when. He or Helen may have gone to look for something in the files and realized they were gone. They may have realized that they were about to be found out. That's my best guess."

There was a heavy sigh at the other end of the phone from Ted.

"Well then, Dannie, let me go break some more good news to my partners, and I'll get back to you about coming to see the files. I personally would rather come to your office. I can't imagine anyone wanting to go to the D.A.'s office, but right now there are a lot of people in the firm who aren't thinking straight. Thanks, Dannie."

With that, Ted hung up the phone, and a whole new chapter began for everyone.

The woman named Bonnie in the D.A.'s office said to Dannie and Rick, "Liz McCormack will be with you in a minute." Shortly after Bonnie left them, the door to the conference room opened and in walked Assistant District Attorney Liz McCormack, a woman about forty-five years old with curly dark hair. She had porcelain-white skin in sharp contrast to her hair, a good-looking woman of Irish origins. Or so people thought because of her complexion and last name. Her maiden name was really Messina. Liz had joked when she was married that she didn't even need to change the monograms on her clothes.

Liz extended her hand to both Rick and Dannie. "Thank you for coming in. I know you're both busy attorneys, so I promise I won't keep you long. From what you've told me on the phone, it seems this adoption scam had been going on for years and then Steve Goldrick just moved into his predecessor's shoes. He walked away with millions from all these adoptions. You were both in the same firm in New York City. Did you ever have any suspicions of anything going on?" Both of them shook their heads no.

Liz McCormack continued on with the questions. "He couldn't have done this alone. He had to have help. Who do you think that was?"

Dannie volunteered, "Well, as you review his files, you will see the role Steve's secretary, Helen, played in all this. She was like Cerberus, the mythological dog who guarded the gates of hell. Helen protected his business and his files, and he, in turn, protected her. I don't think the woman ever took a sick day. No one else worked on his files but her. They had the ultimate symbiotic relationship. She disappeared right before he did, so he must have tipped her off."

Liz said, "The firm in New York City has circled the wagons. I'm not getting any help or cooperation from them. That makes me suspicious that someone else from the firm was involved. We are going to start issuing subpoenas, but we're going to have a hard time with them moving to quash the subpoenas because of attorney-client privilege. Any ideas of where we should start looking?"

Rick said, "Steve was a very powerful force in the firm and was the managing partner. He was a big producer, a big source of revenue to the firm. He had a lot of clout. Dannie was one of the few people who bucked him, and Steve didn't like that. My impression is that the partners liked the money and the clients he brought into the firm."

"Do you agree with that, Dannie?" Liz asked.

"Well, there were a few of the partners who did buck him occasionally, but they had to be careful and pick their battles on a subject where there would be a lot of support from the other partners. It was pretty hard to fight him alone. Steve was smart enough to realize that one of the ways to keep the other partners loyal to him was to spread the wealth around. He did that by using formulas to let some of the other less productive partners get a bigger share of the revenues, but Steve also made sure that they knew it was his doing to ensure their loyalty to him. I really can't say if that loyalty extends to this day, or if they're just trying to cover their own asses."

Liz now directed her focus back to Rick. "So you were one of the associates. What was your interaction with him?"

Rick thought for a moment and said, "It was very obvious to me and to all the associates that he was in charge. He's a very smart and savvy guy, but he comes across as a dictator, which I believe he is. Every move Steve makes is calculated—and calculated for his benefit. He couldn't have kept this whole black market operation going for so long unless he was very smart."

Rick continued, "One place to start looking would be with the associates. If Steve took a liking to one of the young associates, it would certainly be really great to have Steve as a mentor. He could easily put some associate's career on the fast track to partner. Someone had to make court appearances for him and deal with the clients and the clerks in the courts on these adoptions. A good place to start looking might be with the associates who did a lot of work with Steve."

Dannie added, "Another thought might be to look at a solo practitioner outside the firm and see if there's anyone you can identify to whom Steve was funneling work. You might find out that these black market adoptions are still going on, and if that attorney is still doing them, you could shut down a big black market operation. Wouldn't it be something if that person actually led you to Steve Goldrick? He still is on this planet, and you know he's not living in a slum."

Dannie took the conversation in a different direction. "I'm not really sure about the jurisdiction in this case. Some of the victims involved lived in Westchester, and Steve lived in Larchmont. However, the law firm is located in New York City, and some of the victims are in New York. We weren't quite sure what to do about this."

Liz said in response, "We'll make some decisions after we've had an opportunity to review the files carefully."

Liz had been nodding her head in agreement with what Dannie and Rick had been saying. She asked a few more questions and then said that she didn't want to keep them any longer. She thanked them again, and the meeting came to an end.

As Dannie and Rick walked across the plaza to their cars, Rick said, "I gotta hand it to you. You made it seem to Liz that we were all about cooperation and that the firm is a bunch of lying thieves. How did you manage that?"

Dannie replied with a smirk, "Did you forget, Mr. Singleton, that we are attorneys and officers of the court? We are merely fulfilling our obligations as such. If we send Little Lizzie off in another direction from us, so much the better. It's all about perspective."

CHAPTER 39

A few days later after the trip to the D.A.'s office, Rick buzzed Maizie on the intercom and told her to make sure that she picked up the phone and didn't leave it on speaker. Rick told Maizie to meet him at a restaurant a few blocks from the firm. When they were alone and out of earshot of anyone else in the restaurant, Rick told Maizie all that had gone down with the D.A. about the baby brokering ring—all except the money he and Dannie had acquired for giving Steve the heads-up. He could never tell Maizie that. It was time to focus on other things for now.

After they had discussed the meeting with the D.A., Rick then changed the subject. "Hey, Maiz, the realtor called and found a few houses and condos for me to look at. Want to come with me? I'd really like it if there were two of us there to see them. I told her I'd get back to her as to what night. Any night work for you?"

Maizie was secretly very pleased that Rick was asking. She wanted to be with him and support him after all that had happened.

"Wednesday or Thursday night would work for me. Any ideas of where the condos or houses are?"

"I'll find out and have her send me the information from the Multiple Listing Service before we go and look at them. I'll send them to your personal e-mail. No sense in having anyone else here see them."

Maizie knew exactly what Rick was saying between the lines. She wasn't quite sure yet where this relationship was going. Office relationships were messy even if they worked out. The rational side of Maizie was rapidly being swallowed up by her emotional side. Her rational side was screaming that this was risky business. She was new to the office, and her worth unproven to the firm. Rick was an attorney and clearly in a position of authority in the firm. Although he was not one of the partners, he was the only other attorney, except the partners, to whom the associates reported. If it came to a showdown, Maizie had no illusions that she would be the one cleaning out her desk. However, there was the emotional side of her that, even after such a short time, felt very comfortable with him. She had had this feeling before about him—that they were similar to each other and very compatible. The only way to find out if the water was warm or cold was to jump in and see how it felt. She knew she was going to jump in to the water, and her instincts told her it was going to be fine. In fact, she felt it was going to be much more than fine.

Thursday night they met the realtor at her office, and all three of them drove together in one car. They saw a few condos that were nothing special. They were fine and nothing more. Rick really didn't seem to be settled on a condo, although that was what he said he wanted originally. He said he didn't want to be bothered with snowplowing or lawn maintenance, yet he didn't seem to be too excited about the condos, which would have taken care of that. He said he wanted to downsize, yet he turned up his nose at the smaller places.

The last place the realtor showed them was a detached town house in Purchase. It was a good deal larger than the other houses and condo they had seen, but it was also much more expensive. They entered the kitchen. It had enough counter space, made of speckled Italian marble, for a small restaurant. The kitchen also had the most up-to-date appliances, well suited for a master chef, and all the cabinets were made of rich walnut. It gave the cabinets a completely different look, not a dark walnut as on a floor, but lighter with darker hues. The handles, knobs and faucets looked like a burnished copper. Maizie thought that the décor gave the kitchen a combination of southwest and Asian flair. Maybe it was the glass and lighting, she wasn't sure, but it was a beautiful kitchen, and Rick saw that, too. Maizie said to Rick, "Now this is the kind of kitchen you could really thrash around in and whip up your culinary creations." Rick looked at her, smirked and nodded.

Rick asked the realtor to show them a few more places because none of these really intrigued him, well maybe one had. Maizie was beginning to get a headache from the huge disparity between what Rick said he wanted and then what he actually wanted. What the hell did he want? Maizie was thinking to herself.

When they returned to the realtor's office, Rick guided Maizie around to the passenger side of his car, and said, "I'm starving! Want to get some dinner?"

"Yeah, that sounds great. This house hunting has been a real workout."

Rick said, "I know of a good Italian restaurant in Rye. I feel like pasta."

They were a little on the late side, and so they were able to get a table in the restaurant without waiting. Once the waiter brought the wine, Rick took the glass and held it out for Maizie to toast to their "house hunting outing," and then he took a huge swig of his wine. He then said to Maizie, "You were unusually quiet tonight. I'd like to hear what you think."

"Well, it's your decision, so I wanted you to get an unbiased view of the houses."

"Thanks, but if I had wanted no comment whatsoever, I might have asked Helen Keller to come with me." He smirked at her again. "Maiz, you're a perceptive person, so I really want to hear what you think."

"Hey, don't knock Helen Keller. She probably communicated better than the two of us together. But if you must know, I liked the house in Rye Brook, and it had a new kitchen and a beautiful family room. I think people do a lot of living in those two rooms. The house in Rye Neck was nice, too. The town house was my favorite. I could have lived in that kitchen alone, but I have to believe that the town house was much more expensive than the others. You know the realtors do that sometimes to make you fall in love with a house, even if it's out of your price range."

Rick listened intently to Maizie as she spoke. Then he pulled out a small notebook similar to the ones a reporter uses and made some comments to her based on what he had jotted down as they walked through the houses and condos. Abruptly, he said, "Enough. Let's just talk about something else. I'm tired, and this is making me crazy."

Maizie didn't know what to make of this sudden change of subject. It was fine with her. As they talked about other subjects and ate dinner, Rick seemed to calm down and was more like himself.

When they finished dinner and got in Rick's car, he sat there for enough time that Maizie turned to look at him, since he hadn't made any motion to start the engine. He drummed his fingers on the steering wheel and then turned to look at her.

"Maiz, I can see why you were confused tonight, because so was I. All the things I told you I originally wanted were true when I said them. But that was quite a while ago. It was also when I thought that I would be living by myself and throwing myself into work. I wanted to get away from the big house and the memories. I thought I was going to be a hermit. You know the expression that man plans and God laughs. Well, I'm sure God is laughing right this very minute. As we looked at those places tonight, I kept saying to myself that I didn't want to live there alone, but that none of the places were nice enough for two. I kept envisioning myself in those houses or condos with you."

Maizie actually drew back in her seat, because although she knew that the relationship with Rick was going well, she hadn't expected this much from him so fast. In truth, she was somewhat surprised by the intensity of his feelings for her.

Rick continued, "I know we're nowhere near that far in the relationship, but I want us to try. I never thought I would have any interest in being in another relationship, except that I can only think of trying again with you."

With that Rick leaned across the seat and waited to see if Maizie would lean toward him to kiss him. She did.

Their lips touched, and then their tongues explored each other, slowly and with desire. All of her senses felt as if they were in high gear. A deep warm feeling rose in her; she wanted, and she wanted him.

Rick wanted this kiss to last. He pulled her to him and he gently brushed the hair away from her beautiful face and gorgeous green eyes. He lovingly looked into her eyes, and he felt a connection, a longing as if they had an unspoken past. He then took her face in his hands and kissed her. Perhaps it was now all right to move on. The shrink kept telling him so, and maybe this was the first time Rick really believed it himself, in his own heart.

CHAPTER 40

Rick had been moving things around in his office, so one night he moved the last two of the five boxes on the adoptions out of his office and into the trunk of his car. He sort of forgot about them, or maybe he wanted to forget about them. He wasn't exactly proud of what he and Dannie had done, so he let the whole matter drift into the back of his mind.

He had more than enough on his plate with the new firm, selling his house and buying the new place. His relationship with Maizie was going along better than he could ever have hoped. He did have the nagging feeling that he was somehow being disloyal to Jennifer, but now that he was feeling better, he could see that he wasn't going to be able to live in the past his whole life. The shrink had appropriately pointed out to him that it was the other way around. Since he was able to see that he couldn't live the next forty years of his life alone and in mourning, he was feeling better. He would always love Jennifer and Adam and they would always have a special place in his heart. He also had to admit, however begrudgingly, that the shrink was right again when he said that each person had an unlimited capacity to love. He wanted to love again, and maybe kids were in the future as well. It wasn't like slices of a pie where there was a finite object that could be divided only so many ways.

Rick surprised himself with how well things were going with Maizie. Once they started dating, even though he originally wouldn't have admitted to himself that that's what it was, *dating*, he was so happy. It felt like a long time since he could honestly say he was happy. He liked his work and Dannie had given him some great matters to work on. He liked the associates they had chosen to come to the new firm, and the associates looked to him as a more senior person to whom they could turn to for help. It was one thing to ask a more senior person for help and say you didn't know what the hell you were doing on a matter. It was quite another to admit that to one of the partners. He was doing some mentoring and this was a new and refreshing role. Dannie realized what was going on; she remarked to him that the stream of questions from the young associates to her had lessened immeasurably. There wasn't the oppressive pressure to produce and do billable hours that there had been at the old firm in the City.

Maybe because he was more relaxed at work, Rick was much less on edge in his personal life. He knew he was falling, and falling hard, for Maizie. It dawned on him one day when they went food shopping and he realized he was having a good time. He laughed to himself that he was so pathetic. He was having a good time in Whole Foods only because he was with Maizie! He started reading movie reviews again, because he was interested in seeing the new movies. Before Maizie, there had been a long period when he couldn't sit still long enough to go to a movie. It wasn't any fun to schlep to New York City when you had to go into the City every day for work, but now that he was working in Westchester, they went into the City to see both Broadway and off-Broadway shows.

They both liked sports, so they went to Mets and Yankees games to keep some balance. Rick really didn't care if he paid scalpers' prices for the tickets, as long as he and Maizie were going together. Maizie seemed to be having as much fun as he was. She never said no to any activity. He took her fishing one day and realized that he had finally found an activity she hated, even with him. Maizie was totally grossed out by baiting the hook and refused to try doing it. She was even more grossed out, if that was possible, when he caught a fish and had to remove the hook from its mouth. By the time he caught the second fish, he realized that this activity was on borrowed time, and he should wrap it up—immediately.

At first when they were dating, Maizie seemed a little reluctant to stay the night. Rick wasn't sure if the reluctance was due to the fact that this had been his house with Jennifer and Adam or if she just wasn't ready to stay over. This made him all the more determined to sell that house and buy a house that would be theirs, so that they could furnish it, decorate it together, and make it their own. Rick didn't push her, sensing that it had to feel right for her, and pressuring her to do something that she was uncomfortable with would not be good for the relationship. Maizie arrived one Saturday morning at Rick's house about eleven o'clock with a large tote bag and deposited it with a very loud thump on the floor on the front foyer. Rick merely looked at the tote bag and then at Maizie and winked.

"Is there anything else in the car you want me to bring in, Maiz? Anything you want me to hang up for you?" They both laughed, and the ice was broken.

Maizie didn't seem to be bashful about having sex with him. Anywhere would do, and Rick was all in favor of that. The only exception was the bed Rick had shared with Jennifer. So they took the large guest room and made it their own.

Rick would never forget the first time they had made love. It was an ordinary day, or at least it had started out that way. He and Maizie had gotten up, gone for a run, showered, dressed, had breakfast, run errands and done just ordinary things on an extraordinarily hot day. Rick knew to take it slow with Maizie. He didn't want it to be the quickie he had with Dannie. He and Maizie had slowly developed a relationship that was evolving into a deep love. Rick wanted to take in every moment with Maizie. Rushing things with her was the last thing he needed to do, not just for Maizie but for him as well. He certainly didn't want Maizie to know about Dannie. It was a damn good thing Dannie hadn't pushed the envelope on that "one-nighter." Rick and Maizie came home, and they both decided that the pool was a good idea in the muggy heat. Maybe they'd invite Jason, Beth and the kids, and they'd barbecue out by the pool.

They had been in the pool, lying around on floats and then cooling off by overturning the other's float. At one point during the afternoon, Maizie got out of the pool to get something else to drink. When she came back with the pitcher of iced tea and two glasses, she also came back with nothing on! She looked at Rick with those eyes and a raised eyebrow and a seductive smile.

Rick wasn't quite sure he was seeing what he thought he saw and hoisted himself out of the pool with powerful arms and shoulders. He wiped his face and hair on a towel never taking his eyes off her. Not knowing what he should do at that point, but knowing full well what he'd like to do, he took the pitcher of iced tea from Maizie and poured them both a glass and handed one to her, smiling. Rick raised the glass as if to toast, but Maizie stopped him. She put a finger up to her lips and said, "Shh, don't say a word." She took the glass of tea she had and Rick's hand and walked over to the chaise lounge. She pointed for him to sit down, and he did. Maizie then put a finger to his chest and gave a gentle push signaling him to lie back on to the chaise, and he did. She then undid the string on his swim trunks. Maizie motioned with one hand as if she were a magician ready to make something disappear and said, "Off with those," in a breathy whisper. Rick made those trunks disappear. Maizie then straddled him in one fell swoop without spilling a drop. Rick lay there looking at her, still not saying a word, and that was the easy part. The other part was very much aroused. Maizie began to tilt the glass that was full of ice tea. Drop by drop the cold tea fell on Rick's chest, his soft chest hair catching some of the droplets while the others created a path down along his sides. A stream of tea made its way to Maizie's equally soft mound of hair that was pressed against Rick's growing desire. The tea was cool and wet. Maizie took the glass of tea tilting her head and arching her back let the tea stream down her neck to her breasts and below her navel. What she wanted to be was wet. She took Rick's hand as he slid it up from her hip to her breast. She put the glass down on the little table next to the chaise, and Rick pulled her down to him, pressing her body against his. He felt her firm breasts against his chest as he moved his hands to her ass and squeezed tightly, helping her slide up and down his body until he was rock hard and deep inside her. "Oh my God," she moaned, "you're so deep. I can't wait, please." Maizie's breath became short, quick and louder. "I want to feel you come inside me. Do it now, Rick, now." Rick then lifted her up with his hips as he plunged even deeper. She grabbed him as if to hold on, riding him up and down. He let out a groan as he came. He couldn't stop. They continued to explore every part of each other. After they were done, hot, wet and spent, they lay wrapped in each other's arms. Maybe inviting Jason, Beth and the kids could wait for another day.

CHAPTER 41

Abby was sitting at the kitchen table, which seemed to be the gathering place for almost everyone in her family. The kitchen was the place to be for food, conversation, drinks, problem solving and almost everything else. Go to anyone's house for a party, and everyone ends up there. It must be a universal phenomenon. Since finding the letters and discovering her mother's secret, Abby had been wrestling with the idea of having to, and needing to, tell Maizie and Scott. Why hadn't she confided in Jerry? Not only was he her husband, but he was also her best friend. God, how she missed him! Why *did* she keep this secret? First her mother and now her...Abby thought, "Am I really like my mother? Am I becoming my mother?"

The phone rang and startled her from her thoughts. Abby was pleased to hear Scott's voice on the other end of the phone. Scott was exceptional not only because he was Abby's son—a mother's bragging rights—but he also had a photographic memory, which was a huge advantage as a doctor. He was able to quote pages from medical treatises much to the astonishment and sometimes annoyance of his professors. Instead of going to the medical library, his friends and fellow residents would merely call Scott for answers to perplexing questions. Despite his gift, he was not taken with himself. He had compassion and a genuine sense of humor. Scott often answered the phone, "Doctor Know-It-All, how can I help you?"

Scott called once in a while, but primarily it was Abby who did the calling. She knew she had to cut him some slack because of his grueling schedule as an orthopedic resident, but she still missed him because he rarely had a big block of time off from work for them to get together.

"Is this the very famous and prominent Dr. Evers?"

"Indeed it is. You are one of the fortunate few who are allowed to speak to Dr. Evers directly without having to go through layers and layers of personnel first," he joked.

"How are you, honey? How's it going?"

"Same old, same old. Too much work, too little sleep. I have something to tell you that is going to make you happy. There's an orthopedic conference in New York City starting this coming week for three days. One of the attendings was supposed to go, but he was just diagnosed with pneumonia and is in the hospital. Guess who was asked to take his place?"

"That's great, honey. When is the conference starting?"

"I'll save you the trouble of trying to be nonchalant and beating around the bush, Mom. I have the weekend off, and then the conference starts, which the hospital, in its infinite wisdom, counts as workdays. I can come down for the weekend and stay with you and then go to the conference Monday morning."

"That's a wonderful surprise. Does Maizie know you're coming down?"

"No, I'm telling you first, so you can do a Paul Revere and announce to the whole lower Hudson Valley that I'm coming."

"Can I plan that you're going to spend the entire weekend with us, or do you have other ideas?"

"You've got me captive for the entire weekend. One thing I was thinking, is there any chance we could get tickets to a Knicks game for the three of us?"

"Actually, Scott, I think it will be the four of us. I assume that Maizie has mentioned Rick to you. They're getting pretty serious, so I'm sure she'll want you to meet him."

"Yeah, she's mentioned him, but I didn't realize it was that serious. Do you like him?"

"I really do. Wait until you see the two of them together, how they look at each other. I think this is Mr. Right."

"Wow, the Maiz, found Mr. Right, and Mom approves. We might be headed for the end of the world as we know it. Maizie told me she had started dating Rick. I hope this Mr. Right thing turns out well."

"So do I, Scott, and in all honesty, in my heart, I think it will." There was silence on the phone for a few seconds between them. Abby was waiting to see if Scott had anything else to say on the subject. Since he didn't say anything, Abby broke the silence and said, "When will you get here?"

"I'll let you know how early I can get off Friday night. If it's reasonable, I might drive down then, if I'm not too tired. Otherwise, Saturday morning. I have to see what's on the schedule for Friday. I'll give you a call to let you know."

"This is great. I'll call Maizie and let her know. Love you bunches. 'Bye."

Several days later, Scott rolled in Friday night about ten thirty, looking tired and pale, but otherwise happy. Abby was waiting up for him and like any good mother of a "boy," wanted to know if he was hungry. The answer was always yes.

The next morning Abby let Scott sleep until he was ready to get up himself. She knew in the life of a resident, sleep was a precious commodity. About nine twenty that morning, she heard the key in the back door and in whooshed Hurricane Maizie.

"This is a surprise. I didn't know you were coming this morning."

"I figured that we've given him enough time to sleep, and you don't get him all to yourself. When did he get in?"

"About ten thirty."

"And how long did you two stay up talking?"

"Until about quarter to one when neither of us could keep our eyes open any longer."

With that, Maizie turned on her heel and headed for the stairs.

"Why don't you let him sleep a little bit longer until he wakes up by himself?"

"Nope, he's slept enough, and we only have him here for two days before he goes to the conference."

Hurricane Maizie bounded up the stairs, and shortly thereafter, Abby heard laughter coming from the bedroom.

Saturday morning breakfast was one of those family times that fond memories are made of. Once Abby heard Maizie pounce on Scott's bed and startle him awake, and then she heard lots of laughter and mumbled conversation. She was thankful and happy that they had become so close. Abby often wished Jerry had lived to see his children grow up. She really missed the idea of growing old together with him. Abby then heard running around from upstairs and she thought they had morphed into ten year olds again. It was her cue to start making the breakfast that had been Scott's favorite since he was a little boy—a buckwheat pancake sandwich. She made bacon and eggs and sandwiched them between two buckwheat pancakes. Maizie came downstairs to help Abby.

"Scott and I knew that you would definitely be making buckwheat sandwiches. Some things never change. In this case, it's a good thing."

Scott came downstairs dressed in a pair of jeans and a Boston College T-shirt.

Abby looked at Scott's T-shirt and said, "Boston? Are you kidding me?"

"This is as much of a concession as I will make to the Boston teams. I will never wear a Red Sox or Patriots T-shirt."

They talked about so many things and reminisced about people who had lived in town when the kids were young. Abby glanced back and forth at her son and daughter, thinking just how lucky she was. She realized, sitting there at the table, how quickly time goes by. Time certainly never stands still, no matter how much you wish you could at least slow it down. God, how she loved her children—all three of them.

Abby and Maizie wanted to know all about what was happening with Scott and the residency. Scott told them that he was considering doing a fellowship after his residency and that both of the ones he was interested in were in New York City.

Scott had saved this surprise to tell them in person. If he was accepted to either program, Scott would be moving back to New York in the summer. Abby jumped up from the kitchen chair and wrapped her son in a bear hug. Her eyes were moist with tears. Both Maizie and Scott looked at one another as smiles broke out on their faces. "Mom, at least let him breathe!" With that Abby let go and Scott took a deep breath.

"Look, Mom, I still have to come back here for interviews in a couple of weeks, so try not to break my ribs, even though I'm going into orthopedics. I will definitely let you know as soon as I hear when the interviews are scheduled. Let's just keep our fingers crossed that things work out. I feel fairly confident that I will be asked to interview."

Changing the subject, Scott said, "How's Rick? When am I going to get to meet him?" Scott had a little attitude in his voice.

"You can meet him tonight," Maizie replied.

"Sounds good, but I hear there's news on Channel 4, that perhaps this guy is the one. I know you told me he was the 'special one,'" he said, making finger quotes in the air. "You conveniently *forgot* to tell me the two of you are buying a place together! When and where? You didn't bother to run that by me before you put in an offer? It better well have an extra bedroom for me!"

"Oh, bro, you will always have a place to stay. We'll build a big dog house and I'll even throw in a pillow."

"Real funny; you know I want some extra bones, too. Get it—an orthopedic joke!"

"A lot of the time when I talk to you, you're half asleep, so I don't know what you hear or remember."

"So is he the real deal?" Scott asked.

Maizie stole a quick glance at Abby. "Obviously, Mom has told you about him, and she was the source for the Channel 4 news flash."

"Yeah, but I want to hear it from you."

"Well, you know that he's a lawyer, and a pretty successful one at that. But that is not what I love about him. He's so down-to-earth. What you see is what you get. I feel like I've known him my whole life and it hasn't been all that long. It's like the pieces of the puzzle fit together. I'm so comfortable with him, and I don't think I have ever felt that way about anyone else. I really love him. I think you two will like each other a lot and get along very well."

"Wow, that's a pretty glowing endorsement. Rick is the guy who tried to commit suicide, right?" Scott had a concerned look on his face. "Is he OK? Is this guy stable? Normal people don't try to commit suicide."

Scott probably shouldn't have, but he looked directly at Abby. His unspoken message was, "Is he OK?"

Now both of them were staring directly at Abby. Abby looked from one to the other and said, "Rick had an awful shock when he was told about the death of his family. I can't even imagine how he felt. Look at how it affected all of us when your dad died. We were all devastated. Believe me when I say there were days when I wanted to end it, but the difference is I still had the two of you. I had to keep going; you kids were depending on me, and I could see how much pain you felt. His death was a crushing blow, so I can understand what Rick felt."

Before either Maizie or Scott could say anything, Abby continued, "Rick has survived. In fact, he's done much more than that. He put the pieces of his life back together and has been able to grab on to life again and find a beautiful and smart young woman. I can see that Rick loves you, Maizie, and you love him. Not much else to say besides that."

Fannie was sitting on the other side of the room. She thought to herself, "Not exactly, Abby. There still is more to say, only you don't know it yet."

CHAPTER 42

Two weeks after Scott's visit, Abby hung up the phone with Scott and felt like a breath of fresh air had come into the room on this rainy evening. Scott told her that he was coming for two interviews next week for the two fellowships in orthopedics. Abby could tell that he was trying very hard not to be too overconfident, but that he was so pleased to have been asked to interview at both hospitals. She was about to call Maizie to tell her the news when she heard Fannie's voice.

"That's a wonderful opportunity for him. He deserves it. He's worked very hard. It will be good for you and Maizie too; I know you both miss him a lot."

Abby looked at her mother and almost spat the words at her. "Why are you here? I really don't want to see you, and I don't want to talk to you! Go away! You screw up my life. You just disappear when we get to the tough subjects. I'm done with you!"

Since there was no response from Fannie, Abby continued,

"Do you hear me? I can't believe you had the nerve to appear!"

Fannie stared at Abby for a few long seconds, and Abby waited for Fannie to speak. Fannie said in a voice much more muted and much less emphatic than she normally used, "Abby, yes, I hear you. I'm going to say something to you, not to be sarcastic or to be a know-it-all. Just as you felt that there was never a good time to tell Jerry, whom I'm sure would have understood, and then there was never a good time for you to tell the kids—that's what happened to me. I know you are furious with me for never telling you that I knew where your son was, even as you got older and after you married Jerry, but now maybe you can understand what happened with me, because you couldn't bring yourself to tell anyone either. Neither of us did it to be mean or malicious, but that's how it played out. Does that make sense to you now?"

Abby never took her eyes off her mother. She was biting her lip, trying very hard not to cry. She could feel her eyes well up, and then she could feel the tears streaming down her face. "I hear you, and I didn't do the right thing either. The decisions that you and Aunt Rita made and your secrets started this whole problem. You could have given me a choice as to whether I wanted to know where my son was and how he was doing. You made that choice for me; you never gave me an option. Do you think you made the right decision to keep my son a secret from me?"

Fannie sidestepped the question. Instead she answered, "I'm sorry, Abby. I'm sorry you think I made the wrong decision. What I am most sorry about is the pain I caused you throughout your life. No one can change the past, but going forward, it's your reaction to the situation that can change its outcome."

"You didn't exactly answer the question, but it is the first time I heard you say you were sorry."

A few seconds ticked by and Abby said in a calmer, more forgiving tone, "Mom, I've been giving this a lot of thought lately, and I'm going to tell Maizie and Scott that I had a son that I gave up for adoption. I'm really sorry that I never told Jerry about the baby. I was going to...I really was, once we were engaged. It just never seemed to be the right time. The longer it went, the harder it was. Then Scott and Maizie came along and we were so absorbed with them. I could just never find the right time with Jerry, and so I could never, ever find the right time with the kids. First they were too young to understand, and then they were teenagers, and that certainly wasn't a good time. The time was never right." Abby sighed and looked at Fannie. "In some respects, I see I repeated your mistake."

Fannie had a wistful look on her face. She said in a softer tone, "Look, we did what we did. We often wish it, but we just can't change the past. Hopefully, the pain you've known will give you the strength to go forward." Fannie was silent for a few seconds and then continued, "What do you think Maizie and Scott's reaction is going to be, Abby?"

"My hunch is that it will mostly be curiosity. About a lot of things. If it were me, I think I'd have lots of questions about him and what happened to him and where he is now. I've made up my mind that I am going to try to find him. I want to meet him once and see what he's like. He may not want to meet me, but that will be up to him. It may just be a one-time thing, but we can decide what to do after that."

"Abby, it's your decision. I don't know if it will turn out to be a good thing or not. This is a risk, but one you seem pretty sure that you want to take. Do what you need to do. I think it's better if I don't have an opinion on this issue."

Abby nodded. The thought that flashed through her mind was that this was probably the first time she could remember in her entire life in which her mother did not have an opinion. Usually, it was a very strong opinion.

CHAPTER 43

Scott arrived early Sunday afternoon at Abby's house the day before his first interview for the fellowship. Abby watched as he carried in two suit bags with two different dark suits and a white shirt and a light blue shirt on hangars in plastic bags.

"I'm impressed—not one, but two, dark suits!"

Scott shrugged and said, "I bought one and got the second for fifty percent off. I brought both suits with me so I don't have to get the first one pressed between interviews, or in case I spill something on the first suit. This is really important to make a good impression, Mom. Some people even practice for the interview, but I didn't go that far."

"Do you have any idea of where you stand? How many people are being interviewed?"

"I really don't know how many people are being interviewed. One of the attendings at the hospital likes me, and although he would like me to stay put, he knows that I'd like to come back to New York. He knows these two programs are more what I'm looking for. He made a call for me to Columbia where he has a friend, and spoke to them about me. Hopefully, that will do some good; he said they were impressed with my credentials. Where's the Maiz?"

"Maizie and Rick are going to come for dinner tonight. Rick went to see the Rangers, so he'll come over when he gets back. Maizie has no interest in hockey, so he went with his brother, Jason. I expect that Maizie will be here shortly."

Scott came back downstairs a few minutes later after he'd hung up his clothes.

"So it's pretty serious with the Maiz and Rick?" he said, as if they had been having this discussion before he went upstairs.

Obviously, the subject had been on Scott's mind, and Abby didn't hesitate in her answer to him. "Yes, I think it is. When you see them together, you'll see that they're both very happy. He's a good man. Maizie deserves that."

"I didn't want to ask you in front of Maiz, but do you really like him? Do you think that he's all right after an attempted suicide? That really worries me."

"I told you the truth about what I thought when you asked me in front of Maizie last time you were here."

"I don't know, Ma; I wanted to hear what you really thought. People suffer all kinds of trauma in their lives and they don't try to kill themselves. Look at what you said about how distraught you were when Dad died, but you never actually tried to kill yourself."

"The difference is Rick lost almost everyone he loved. That's the difference right there. The pain has got to be so intense. The answer I gave in front of Maizie was the truth. Maizie and I discussed her possibly getting involved with him before she ever went out with him. I told her of my concerns. It's bad enough that his wife and son died, but he blamed himself for their deaths. He carried a tremendous amount of guilt. I can see what a difference Maizie has made in him. He's happy. I haven't seen him that way for a long time. Why don't you ask Maizie about him yourself?"

"How can I possibly do that, Mom?" he said with more than a little annoyance in his voice. "I'm a couple hundred miles away, and I don't think this is the kind of discussion you can have on the phone. Plus, she's living with Rick. How can I get a straight answer out of her when he's right there?"

"Well, he isn't there every minute, so you could try talking to her on the phone, or ask her to call you. You still think of Maizie as your little sister, but in reality she's a grown woman. Pay attention tonight with how they act with each other. But I definitely give my approval, and you love her too, so you need to satisfy yourself."

"She'll probably be offended that I'm meddling in her life."

"Excuse me, Doctor, but isn't it part of your job to talk to people and get them to tell you the truth about what's hurting them? Use your same brilliant powers of persuasion and throw in a little bit of that charm."

"All right, all right, but I'm only asking because I love her, and I don't want to see her get hurt big time. Is there any possibility that a starving resident can get some lunch in this establishment?"

Shortly after they finished lunch, Maizie breezed in wearing very large sunglasses and a bright red sweater and jeans. Today was a very big bling day. Maizie had a way of making an entrance into any room if she wanted to, and apparently today was one of those days. Abby knew that Maizie really, really liked jewelry, and she had apparently communicated that to Rick, who was only too happy to oblige. He had bought her quite a few pieces in recent months, many of which were in evidence today.

Maizie asked Scott about the upcoming interviews and the fellowships, and Scott was more than willing to tell her the same story about the applications and interviews he had told Abby earlier. He finally admitted that he was very nervous about the interviews. Scott really liked basketball, and there were various games on TV as they talked. Mostly they were providing background noise and every so often, Scott clicked the remote to glance at a new station and a new basketball game.

Abby put the cake in the oven and came into the family room to sit with Scott and Maizie.

Abby asked, "After you have these interviews, what happens next? How long does it take before you hear?"

"It probably could be a few weeks because they interview residents from all over the country. If things are going well, I'll get called back for a second interview. I'm not sure of the exact timetable."

Abby took a deep breath and decided she was going to jump in; she wanted to act on her decision, and she didn't know how long it would be before Scott was back in New York. She had put this off for so many years now, and she couldn't stand it any longer.

"I want to talk to you both about something." Scott rolled his eyes at Abby's tone of voice and looked at Maizie to see what she knew. Maizie shot a glance back at Scott and shrugged. Usually that tone of voice meant that someone was in trouble, or Abby had some serious announcement to make. Neither of them had any idea of what was coming.

Abby shifted in her chair uncomfortably and looked from one to the other. "I have something to tell you that I've never told anybody else." Abby stopped and then started again, stammering a bit. "I…I want to tell you this from beginning to end, and then you can ask me whatever you want. But please let me finish. I…I never even told your father, and I deeply regret it."

"When I was fifteen, I got pregnant with the boy I was dating. He wanted me to have an abortion, and I toyed with the idea, but my mother talked me out of it. I had a son, and I gave him up for adoption. Nana thought it was the best thing to do, to give him up for adoption, and I was a high school kid. I couldn't support myself, and I was certainly ill equipped to care for a baby and try to finish high school. Nana definitely pressured me to do it, and at fifteen, I didn't feel I had any choice. I suppose it was best for him, too, because he was going to a couple that couldn't have kids and had the means to take care of him and give him a good home."

"I was going to tell your father when we got married, but honestly, I was just too afraid to bring up the subject. Your father was an understanding person, and he was kind, so I'm not a hundred per cent sure why I never told him. I kind of think I had put that chapter of my life behind me, and I didn't want to resurrect the painful memories. I also think I was afraid that he would somehow think badly of me."

"Then you two came along, and we were so involved with raising you. I didn't think it was a good thing to tell you as little kids, for fear that you might think I'd give you two up. By the time you were teenagers, you were impossible, as each of you asserted your independence, so that wasn't a good time either."

Abby stopped and took a sip of her wine, as much to moisten her mouth as to gauge their reactions. Maizie was sitting opposite her, and her mouth was literally hanging open. Scott had been lying on the couch propped up by pillows. He was now sitting bolt upright on the couch.

"What made you decide to tell us now, Mom?" Maizie asked.

"Well, I recently found some letters that belonged to your Nana, and I learned something that totally shocked me. I never knew that Nana arranged with her friend, Aunt Rita, that Aunt Rita's daughter and son-in-law would adopt the baby. There are a lot of letters from Aunt Rita to Nana telling her all about him because they lived in England. She kept that secret from me her entire life. As much as I knew it was the right decision to give up the baby, I always worried about him, and wondered if he had a good home with people who really loved him and took good care of him. It would have given me so much peace of mind had I known that he was with Aunt Rita's daughter and son-in-law."

"I have some pictures of him as a little boy that Nana saved, and what gave it away was that he looked exactly like Maizie in the pictures. I'll never know why Nana never told me, but it would have saved me a lot of anguish that I bore alone."

Maizie, who usually had no trouble finding words and expressing herself, sat there in stunned silence.

Abby took another sip of her wine. "I've made a decision that I'm going to try to find him. I hope I can. I'm hoping that I can find him with all the resources available on the Internet since the court records are sealed."

Scott said, "What happens if you locate him and he doesn't want to meet you?"

"I suppose that's a chance I'm willing to take. If nothing else, I hope that he's secure enough in his own family that I won't be a threat to him or his parents. He's a grown man now, so it's not like I've come to take him back from his parents. I'm hoping he will be as curious about me as I am about him. If we meet each other, and that's enough for him, then it will be fine with me. But I so want to meet him."

Scott asked another question, "What about the father—your 'boyfriend'? Did he care about what happened to you and the baby?"

"Not exactly. He and his parents had high hopes for his future, and neither I nor a baby was part of that equation. He signed off his parental rights."

Maizie finally seemed to regain her power of speech. "This is such an emotionally charged situation for both of you. I can understand why you want to find him. But Scott's right, it's risky. You might not have the reaction from him that you want. He could be open and want to meet you, or he could be hostile that you gave him up."

"I know, I know. Believe me, I have wrestled with this since I found the letters. I know this sounds corny, but there has been a hole in my heart for him for many years now. This is something I need to do. I wonder if he's ever curious about me or if sometimes he wonders what I'm like or if I'm still alive."

Scott was processing the information and later on would have some comment. Maizie, on the other hand, was much more impulsive and explosive. After she got her jaw back in place, she blurted out, "I want to go, too."

All three of them burst out laughing. That comment was so like Maizie. As a kid, Maizie never wanted to miss anything and always wanted to tag along with Scott and his friends, who were older than Maizie. Scott didn't want his little sister tagging along, but Maizie was adamant, and the comment was always, "I want to go, too."

"Where exactly is it that you want to go, honey?"

"With you, Mom, I want to go with you. To meet him."

"I don't know. We'll have to cross that bridge when we come to it. I don't even know if he'll want to meet me. We'll have to gauge what kind of reaction we get from him before we overwhelm him with Hurricane Maizie."

Maizie said, "Rick is going to be sorry that he went to the Rangers game and missed this news."

The usually reserved Scott said, "You certainly know how to drop a bombshell, Mom. I thought I was the one with the big news about my interviews, but that's nothing by comparison with this."

Abby responded, "I know this whole thing may take some getting used to, so it's all right if you two don't know what you really think about it. I've had a very long time to mull this over in my mind, so I'm sure you're going to need some time to process this."

Maizie let out a low whistle. "It's hard to believe that Scott and I have an older brother. Scott and I could have nieces and nephews. If we meet and we get along, there will be a lot of catching up to do." Maizie thought for another moment and said, "Is it OK if I tell Rick about this?"

Abby said, "Yeah, it's OK to tell Rick about this."

Abby took a few seconds and added, "I think we should keep this among the four of us for now. Let's see how this whole situation progresses before we involve anyone else. I haven't even started to look for him."

CHAPTER 44

Maizie and Rick had waited long enough for the closing on the house. Rick now understood why clients were so antsy about their closings. Once you signed the contract and gave a very large chunk of money to the sellers' attorney for the down payment, you started thinking of the house as yours. The closer the date got to the closing date in the contract, the more excited you became. At first Rick had downplayed his excitement, even to himself, but he was looking forward to being in the new house with Maizie in their new relationship. Now he was getting downright exasperated with the sellers' attorney, who was getting in the way of something very important to him.

"Listen to me, Bob; tell your clients I'm through with moronic excuses. We close by next Thursday at the latest, or I'm sending you a Time is of the Essence letter!" Rick screamed into the phone.

Bob must have answered something because Rick screamed into the phone again, "Goddamn it, exercise some client control. You have to tell your clients the facts of life here. If they don't close, they're going to be in for a world of hurt. I'm coming after them for damages and attorneys' fees if I have to start an action for specific performance to make them close. I have never been more serious in my life. Get them to stop playing games. You're the attorney here. Start taking control. If I don't hear from you by five o'clock today that we have a firm closing date, I'm sending out the Time is of the Essence letter."

Rick slammed the phone down so hard that it bounced off the cradle and onto his desk.

A Time is of the Essence letter advises one party to the contract that if they don't close on the real estate deal by a particular date, the other party will hold them in default.

Rick's secretary heard the whole conversation. There was actually no way for her to miss it with Rick's decibel level being what it was. Rick stormed out of his office and mumbled something as he strode past her. She just kept typing; it was easier that way. This was very unlike Rick to be screaming at another attorney on the phone and to be so out of control. She had mentioned to him at the beginning of the real estate deal that perhaps he might want to have one of the associates handle the deal for him, but he didn't seem to want to do that, so she dropped the subject.

About twenty minutes after Rick stormed out of the office, Maizie stopped by to see if he had made any progress with the sellers' attorney.

"Was there bloodshed, or did Rick get anywhere with Bob about the closing?" Maizie asked Lauren, Rick's secretary.

Lauren rolled her eyes and told Maizie about the screaming and the gist of the conversation. "He stormed out of the office so fast I really don't know where he said he was going. I never got a chance to ask, and then he was gone. I don't know if he went to Dunkin' Donuts or if he's sitting in someone else's office. I swear I have never seen him this upset. Maybe he should have one of the other attorneys take over the deal. He's making himself sick over this."

Maizie winced when she heard what Lauren had to say. "I know this is making him crazy. He's taking this as a personal affront. It's not as if we're going to be out on the street if we don't close. Can you give me a heads-up when he comes back and if it's safe to talk to him?"

Lauren said that she'd be more than happy to let Maizie know when Rick returned. About a half hour later, Lauren buzzed

Maizie to tell her that Rick was back in his office but that he was still not in a very good mood. Maizie decided that it was much safer to finish her work on the Probate Petition now and try to go in and talk to Rick later.

About two hours later, Rick let out a sound that could be described as nothing less than a tribal scream, akin to the sound of the fans watching their team score a touchdown and clinch the Super Bowl. The sellers' attorney sent Rick an e-mail agreeing to a firm closing date for the following Thursday. Rick poked his head out of his office to let Lauren know the good news. Then he walked down the hall to find Maizie and tell her the good news.

"Hey, Maiz, that miserable little weasel, Bob, finally sent me an e-mail agreeing to set the closing for next Thursday." Maizie was startled as she looked up at Rick to see him standing over her at her desk. Rick continued on at a frenzied pace before Maizie had a chance to respond to the great news. "He's afraid to tell his clients something they didn't want to hear, but I let him have it on the phone, and I think he was more afraid of my threat of litigation than anything else. I can't believe we're finally going to close." Rick finally finished his diatribe.

"That's awesome! Yeah, you made it happen! I can't wait to get into the house and start doing some painting and decorating. I'm going to call Mom and tell her. While we're eating lunch later, let's decide on when we should schedule the painters and then the movers. We have so much to do, but it's going to be wonderful to do it with you. I know you wanted us to have a house that's ours together. It means so much to me."

"I know it does, and that's why I was pushing so hard to get this done for you. No, I wanted to do this for us."

Maizie looked up at him and said, "Rick, I think I'm falling in love with you. No, I know it absolutely." Maizie's heart was racing. She had no idea whether what she had just boldly stated had come out right. This was not the time or the place she would have chosen, but it was the way it happened. "Rick?"

Rick looked into Maize's eyes, and he didn't give a damn if they were in the office or who saw them. He cupped her face in his hands and kissed her on the lips. He then picked her up in a big squeeze and whispered in her ear, "I am absolutely in love with you Maizie."

After Rick got back to his office, he sat down in his chair and reflected for a moment about when he bought his first house with Jennifer. It was a bittersweet memory because he could remember everything about that day. He could remember with such clarity walking through the house the morning of the closing to do the final inspection. It was a gorgeous day. He kept thinking that it was the perfect house for them. They had contractors ready to tackle the big renovations, and they were going to tackle the little jobs together. The first house with Jennifer was so full of possibilities and dreams about the future. God, how life changes in an instant. Now he was being given a chance to start again. Let it be different this time; let it be different.

CHAPTER 45

After all the histrionics before the closing, as so often happens, the actual closing was very uneventful. Rick insisted that he and Maizie take Abby, his brother and sister-in-law, Jason and Beth, out for dinner to celebrate.

Rick had picked a quiet place in White Plains not too far from the office. He liked it because there were several midsized rooms that made it seem that you were alone with your party in the restaurant. Maizie hadn't realized that the delay in the closing had taken this much of a toll on Rick.

Tonight he was grinning from ear to ear, something he hadn't done in a very long time, and he hadn't even had a glass of wine yet. As crazy as it sounded, somehow Rick had made this closing into a battle of wills or a test of manhood. Rick was also insightful enough to know that he saw Maizie as a symbol of his new life. Dr. Burke, his psychiatrist, was helping him to get over his guilt at still being alive even though Jennifer and Adam were no longer here and that it was all right for him to start a new life with Maizie. The weasel attorney, Bob Lonergan, was standing in the way of his new life, and that was why Rick had reacted so strongly. Now that the closing was history, he was much more relaxed, and tonight he was going to have a good time.

Rick and Maizie wanted Abby to get to know Jason and Beth. Maizie was just sorry that Scott couldn't be there for the dinner. Maizie also didn't want to say it out loud because she knew it would upset her mother, but she also wanted her father to be there for the happy events. She had been thinking a lot about him lately, especially since she was thinking of her wedding and had always wanted her father to walk her down the aisle.

Maizie and Rick arrived at the restaurant, Torino, before anyone else. Abby came in shortly thereafter and hugged both Maizie and Rick. "Congrats to both of you. You must be so relieved that the closing is over."

Maizie said, "We've already got the painters lined up. It's such a relief that we've closed and can get working on the house. I don't know how Rick got these painters to start on Monday, since we've had to stall them because we couldn't get a definite closing date."

Abby looked at Rick over Maizie's shoulder as she was hugging her. Rick winked at Abby and rubbed his thumb and forefinger and middle fingers together in the air to indicate money. Abby nodded in response and smiled.

"We have the luxury of getting the painting done without having the furniture in the house or having them drip paint on the new rugs. Rick keeps assuring me that he can handle the expenses of the two houses for a while until we're ready to move into the new house and sell the Jersey house, but it seems expensive."

Rick looked at Maizie and Abby and said, "I had an investment that exceeded all my expectations. A former colleague gave me a tip. What can I say? I'm certainly not an investment guru; I took a chance, and I was just lucky."

Rick felt like a kid lying to his mother with his fingers crossed behind his back. The former colleague was Steve Goldrick and the "investment" was the money he and Dannie had received from blackmailing Steve. Rick had tried multiple times to rationalize his actions to himself. The best he could come up with was that Steve had more than enough money to live on for the rest of his life, as did his former secretary, Helen, who had miraculously disappeared as well. Rick also believed that at least he was doing something good with the money for someone he loved. It was the best he could come up with that he could live with.

Jason and Beth walked in about twenty minutes late. "Sorry, the traffic on the Tappan Zee was horrendous. Whatever happened to the plans to build another bridge?"

Jason took a seat between Abby and Beth. All the hellos were said, and the conversation began. The waiter arrived at the table to take orders and filled all their glasses with champagne.

They were seated at a round table with Abby facing the wall across from Rick, and Maizie was sitting next to Abby. Jason raised his glass and proposed a toast. "To my younger brother and my best friend: I compliment you on your good taste for finding such a wonderful woman as Maizie, and to Maizie, for being the woman that you are and for making my brother happy. Congratulations on your new home. I can certainly give you the name of a good architect who's very creative, but not cheap!"

"Nothing like shameless marketing, huh, Jas?"

Rick strode around the table behind Jason and thanked him for the heartfelt sentiments. Rick continued, "Now I have something important to say." He stood directly across from Maizie as he spoke. "I never expected to find someone who could make me feel this happy again. I realize we put the cart before the horse by buying this house. Even though we love the house, it is our love for each other that will turn it into a home. Maizie, I have something to ask you."

Jason piped up, "You're not going to ask her to foot the bill tonight, are you?"

Rick replied in an even tone, all the while keeping his eyes on Maizie, "Jason, shut the hell up."

Rick walked over to Maizie's chair, and he knelt down on one knee. Everyone watched in hushed silence as Rick pulled a small box from his pocket. Maizie looked at Rick and it took a nanosecond for her to realize what was happening. Rick opened the small box, and a sapphire and diamond ring sparkled like stars in a Colorado night. The ring was the one she had seen in a magazine one evening at home, and she had marked the page by folding the corner.

Maizie looked at the ring and then to Rick. She had tears forming in the corners of her eyes and she said, looking at Rick, "Yes, yes, and yes. I will marry you, if that's what you're asking! It is what you're asking, isn't it?"

Rick answered, with a chuckle and a grin, "Yes, Maiz, it absolutely is what I'm asking." He then took her hand and slid the ring on her finger.

The surprise from Rick really had everyone a little stunned until Jason started to clap. Then everyone clapped and got up from the table to hug each other. The conversation was then a little louder and the champagne flowed even more freely.

Abby was sitting next to Jason, which was the first time she had had an opportunity to talk to him since Rick had been in the hospital. This was certainly a much happier occasion. Jason was more outgoing and talkative than Rick, who was a little quieter. Jason was an architect, and he had the table in stitches with stories about the crazy things his clients wanted in a house. There was one couple who wanted the house moved after the foundation had been laid because the Feng Shui master told them that the house had not been angled properly to take advantage of the good chi. Their insistence on that had cost them a small fortune, and the builder wanted to kill them.

Jason had another client who insisted that he plan a separate bathroom and shower next to the master bedroom so that the potbellied pigs could have their own place to shower. The client was more concerned about the colors in the pigs' bathroom, so that it would be soothing, than she was about the colors in her own bathroom.

There was yet another client who asked Jason to meet him in the partially constructed house. Shortly after Jason arrived at the house, they were walking through the rooms on the second floor when the client stripped naked to see if he liked the feel of the house with all his clothes off. He wanted to know if Jason thought he looked good naked in the room. Jason really didn't know what to respond, so he said, "I think the lighting is perfect and hits you in all the right places. Now put your damn clothes on before the glare off your skin blinds me." Jason said he couldn't get out of the house fast enough. The next day he sent the client a final bill, and they never "saw" each other again.

The stories went on and on, and by the time the main course arrived, they were crying from laughing so hard.

During the main course, someone mentioned London, and Abby asked Jason and Rick if they liked growing up in England. They said that they loved it because they had traveled extensively in England, Scotland and Ireland. Both Rick and Jason said that although they loved England, when they travelled to the United States to visit family, they realized how much they missed some things from American pop culture like baseball, really good pizza, bagels and American football. However, they always had Frosted Flakes from their grandmother.

Jason encouraged Rick to tell the famous "high tea story." Rick actually got a little tongue tied and embarrassed, so Jason picked up the ball and ran with it. "My mother made friends with a few women who invited her to be a member of some British historical society. Before she could join, they wanted to meet the entire family. My father was able to beg off because of work, but we were sitting ducks. We had to go with her to high tea at the St. James Hotel, not too far from Buckingham Palace. Both of us had to come home from school and get dressed up in suits and ties. You can imagine how much we loved that. I think I was about nine and Rick was about six. We're sitting in this stuffy dining room with these English ladies in their fancy dresses and hats, and every goddamn one of them had to pinch us on the cheek."

"After what seemed like an eternity, the waiter brought the scones, clotted cream and the tea. I wanted a Coke, but my mother gave me a look that basically said, 'Shut the hell up.' As we were putting the jam and clotted cream on the scones, Rick's elbow hit one of the spoons with the clotted cream, which acted like a missile and hit one of the ladies right in the boob. There the cream sat, hanging on precariously from her ample bosom. She, of course, jumped up and screamed and knocked into an oncoming waiter, who dropped an entire tray of scones, clotted cream and jam on her. Everyone started screaming, and my mother got up from the table to try to help the lady. My mother slid on the mess on the floor and landed right on top of the 'clotted cream lady.' My mother hustled us out of the hotel, and she never saw the ladies from the British historical society again."

Everyone at the table was now laughing hysterically, even Rick. "You should have seen what my mother looked like—all gooey and slimy—and she was yelling at us for laughing at her. The car smelled like clotted cream for days." Rick continued, "It really reminded me of something from *I Love Lucy*."

Maizie looked at Rick and said, "We have to get Jason here more often; I'm sure there are more stories like this, and you're holding out on us."

Abby said, as she raised her glass, "Since you are now officially engaged, I have a wonderful story about my parents' honeymoon. Hope this doesn't happen to you, but I hope you have as many laughs."

"I found two eight-by-ten pictures, one of my mother and one of my father. I asked my mother where these pictures were taken because Mom had kept them in their own separate manila envelope. I handed her the pictures and she looked at the first picture for a very long time. It was a black-and-white picture of her alone in the foreground, holding onto a wrought-iron fence attached to a stone and mortar wall. In the background, there were boats, some moored and some looked to be moving about. There was a long pier with a boathouse at the end, which appeared to be some distance away. Mom was looking directly into the camera."

Abby continued as she reminisced. Everyone at the table could almost see the conversation unfold so many years ago between Abby and Fannie.

'So, Mom, where were you in this picture?'

'We were in Provincetown on Cape Cod, and we were on our honeymoon.'

'Honeymoon! This was taken on your honeymoon? Mom, tell me more. I didn't know you went to Cape Cod on your honeymoon. And Provincetown of all places.'

'Well, that was long before they had all those hippie types in Provincetown. And, yes, there were honeymooners even when your father and I married in 1938.'

'All right, no need to get testy; tell me about where you got the dress for the honeymoon.'

'Well, I went to Macy's in Herald Square one night. I wanted new clothes to start my new life with your father. I fell in love with this dress the moment I saw it. It was the most beautiful cream-colored linen with a collared V-neck with cap sleeves. I had a teardrop pendant necklace with an opal in it that was my birthstone. Fred had given me this necklace as a Christmas present, and it was perfect for that neckline.'

'Anyway, the dress was all one piece with a pleated skirt. As you can see, the hem was way above my knee, which was somewhat risqué, but what the hell, I had great legs, and I was now a married woman. It was like the forerunner of a tennis dress. The dress had a zipper up the front, and it had a belt that was my favorite. The belt was navy blue woven canvass with a leather belt buckle. I was really thin in those days, and so when I cinched the belt, it really showed off my waistline. Your father thought I was a stunner in that dress.'

'Mom, where were you when the picture was taken? You look like you're high up.'

'We were in the lighthouse at Race Point; once you climbed to the top, you could see for miles. It was the most gorgeous day. The truth of the matter is I was afraid of heights. I went up there to please your father because he wanted a picture of me from up in the lighthouse. If you look really carefully in the picture, you can see that I'm holding onto the wrought-iron fence. Actually, I was holding on for dear life. As soon as he took the picture, I made a beeline out of there and down to safety on the pier. God, the things a person does for love as a newlywed.'

'When we left the lighthouse and walked down to the pier, they had the remains of a sunken ship that had been raised from the bottom of the ocean bed. That's where I took the picture of your father.'

"Then Mom asked to see the other picture. She said," 'Do you know who that handsome devil is? It's your father. Looks a lot like Gregory Peck—tall and tan, only better looking. He looks like Calvin Klein or that Ralph something or other guy. Look at him standing there in his khakis and his polo shirt with a pipe in his hand. He really should have tried for a modeling career.'

"Mom said, 'I remember everything about that day. It was about eighty degrees with a light breeze. Your father decided to rent one of the boats and take me out. I was a good sport. It was only later that your father found out that day that I was afraid of heights and only went up to the top of the lighthouse to let him take some pictures of me. It didn't dawn on him that I was a little bit hesitant when he suggested going up there.'

'Then I agreed to go out in the motorboat with him. He figured since the height thing hadn't worked out too well, and he knew I was a good swimmer, he thought a boat ride would be terrific. Little did he know I got motion sickness. We were about ten minutes out when I became really quiet, which was totally unlike me. I didn't even finish the sentence. In the split second that it took your father to turn to look at me, I was leaning over the side of the boat, heaving up breakfast, and leaving a stream of chum for the fish. He really wanted to be sympathetic, but he had all he could do not to laugh. He knew if I saw him laughing, he would be the chum for the fish. OK, so that was strike number two.'

'Your father suggested that we just take the boat back as quickly as possible. All I answered in response was a loud moan. He assumed that meant yes. As he tied up the boat to the dock, I couldn't get out of the boat fast enough. Your father said he had never seen a person who was that sick move so fast to dry land. I'm surprised I still don't have the splinters in my fingers from clawing my way up the ramp to the dock.'

'After two disasters in the same day, your father thought it was wise to allow me to decide what we'd do next. We went back to the hotel room and I got cleaned up. After a while, I felt a little better, and we thought we'd take a stroll around town, and if I felt up to it, maybe we'd get some lunch. Your father suggested that since I liked animals so much, maybe after lunch we'd go whale watching. It's a good thing that he had great reflexes and ducked in time not to get hit by the pillow I threw at him in the hotel room. He finally realized that I didn't want to go back on the high seas.'

'Your father always tried to make people think I was exaggerating. He'd say, "Don't listen to her; she's exaggerating. It certainly wasn't that bad. The way she tells it makes for a good fish yarn." 'How's that for a good pun?'

'When we were at the Jersey shore, and you girls were young, I rarely came out in the boat with you and your father. I mostly sat at the beach, smoking my cigarettes and reading novels.'

'Let me tell you what happened next.' Abby then said, "Mom groaned audibly."

'So we left the hotel room and went for a stroll. Finally, I felt well enough to eat, so we sat in an open-air café. They brought us a big basket of bread and I wouldn't even let your father eat a roll. I wrapped up all the bread and rolls in a napkin and stuffed it in my purse because I wanted to go back to the scene of the crime on the dock and feed the birds. It was a really nice restaurant. I can still remember those crab cakes. Your father never ceased to be amazed by me. One minute I'm puking my guts out and the next minute I'm eating crab cakes and having cocktails. What a woman I was! So we finished eating lunch and took a walk back down to the pier.'

'We sat down on one of the benches, and I proceeded to pull the bread out of my purse and rip it into small pieces and throw it on the ground. In less than thirty seconds, we were surrounded by a flock of seagulls. With every passing second, more seagulls arrived. There probably wasn't a seagull on the whole Eastern seaboard that didn't swoop down on us. The next thing I knew there was a seagull sitting on my lap, and I heard screaming. It was like a scene out of Alfred Hitchcock's, *The Birds*. I swatted at the seagull to get him off my lap and grabbed your father's hand to get up off the bench and out of there. We couldn't walk because the seagulls were all around us and screeching. I realized it wasn't the seagulls screeching so loud, it was your father. Big, strong man like him afraid of a few birds!'

'When we finally got off the pier, one of the locals who had watched this whole fiasco said in his New England twang, "Not a real good idea to feed those damn gulls. Last person I saw do it was almost covered in as much bird crap as you." I looked at your father, and he looked at me. The local was right. We were covered in bird crap. This was turning out to be some honeymoon. I was almost afraid to leave the hotel for fear of what natural disaster would befall us next.'

'Your father said, "You know getting hit with bird crap is a sign of good luck. If that's the case, we should win the Irish sweepstakes."

Everyone was laughing as Abby ended the story, and Maizie said, "As much as bird poop is supposed to be good luck, I think we'll pass on that for our honeymoon." Abby then looked over Rick's shoulder to the empty chair sitting in the alcove and saw Fannie sitting there. Abby did a double take to make sure of what she saw. Sure enough, Fannie was sitting in the chair, taking everything in.

Fannie said to Abby, "You really told the story the right way. Your father always said I was a character, and you captured me perfectly."

Maizie saw Abby do the double take and said quietly to her, "You OK, Mom? What are you looking at?"

Abby caught herself. "Nothing, I guess that it was just the shadows in the corner."

"All right then, you jolted like you saw a ghost."

Abby couldn't help but realize the irony. "I'll have to drink a lot more wine or Irish whiskey before I start seeing ghosts."

Fannie gave Abby a nod and a smile and Abby returned the smile. Abby wasn't sure why Fannie chose this time to be here, but in point of fact, Abby was never sure why Fannie picked any given time to appear. Abby presumed that Fannie was here to see her granddaughter get engaged. Abby wondered if Fannie knew about the ring and the engagement in advance. Abby wasn't about to have any conversation with her now. Abby didn't want to be distracted with Fannie tonight; she wanted to enjoy the moment and enjoy the company.

Fannie looked around the table at the five people who were sitting there. Fannie realized that this was her family, and these were the people who brought her the most joy. Fannie wished that she and Fred could really be there sitting at the table like everyone else enjoying this night.

It turned out to be a wonderful evening with a lot of good food, wine, and hilarious conversation. When they finished sharing cannoli, *tartufo*, and cheesecake for dessert, and coffee and cappuccino, everyone decided it was time to call it a night, especially since all the other patrons in the restaurant had left, and it was close to eleven o'clock. Abby looked at Maizie and saw the sheer joy on her face, and Abby was thrilled for that. Abby thought to herself that Fannie had been right that some good had come from Abby finding Rick on the bridge on that fateful night. Rick and Maizie were in love; that was so apparent. Abby liked Jason and Beth. Jason was charming, self-assured, and extroverted. Abby was glad her little family was going to expand.

They all walked out to the parking lot together, and Maizie and Rick made sure Abby was in her car before they left. As she started the car and made a right turn out of the parking lot, Abby almost jumped out of her seat and looked straight at the GPS at the sound of Fannie's voice.

"Did you have a good time tonight, Abby?"

"I did, Mom; you saw that. What made you show up tonight?"

Once again, Fannie sidestepped the question and replied, "Rick is going to be a good choice for Maizie. I was worried about his being able to deal with the past and not being chained to it. It seems the good doctor and Maizie have helped him move on. You were right when you were thinking that it will be nice to see the family expanding. You're so used to it only being just you, Maizie, and Scott. You could be pleasantly surprised with the adjustment to more people in the family."

"What adjustment? I get my house back and Maiz gets a much larger space to fill up with her stuff and what I'm sure will be her future purchases. It's a beautiful thing. "

"What do you think of Jason and Beth?" Fannie asked.

"I think they're engaging, fun, and seem to be very good parents, considering the way they spoke about their two daughters. It's wonderful to see how close Jason and Rick are. Now that I see the two of them together, they have many similar mannerisms and expressions, which sort of make them look alike. I guess that's the nature versus nurture thing. It will be good for

Scott to have some other young men around if he comes back here to do his residency."

Fannie said, "I got a kick out of those stories from when Rick and Jason were growing up in London. Jason's descriptions of having to sit through high tea were hysterical."

Abby volunteered, "Maizie had already told me the story of Rick refusing to eat anything for breakfast but Frosted Flakes, but Jason's way of telling it was much funnier. I can just imagine Rick's grandmother dragging cartons of Frosted Flakes on the plane between New York and Heathrow to get him to eat anything. I guess that was long before the days of Federal Express."

"So, Mom, was there a reason for gracing us with your presence at dinner tonight? You didn't answer me when I asked you before."

"No particular reason. You know me; I don't like to meddle, but I thought I'd like to be around for a happy event."

"Yeah, right, you don't meddle—give me a break. You always have a motive, so spit it out."

"You exaggerate that I meddle. I would call it concern for my daughter and granddaughter. You should be happy that someone is looking out for you and the family. I think good things are in store for this family. Remember you heard it here first."

"Oh, what the hell does that mean, Mom? Is Maizie pregnant? Mom, is she pregnant? Will you answer me? This is so infuriating that you do this to me. You drop some tidbit of information in my lap, and then you leave. I swear if you do this now, Mom, I won't speak to you again!" No voice from the GPS; Fannie was gone again.

As Abby drove home, questions began to form in her head. They were like bubbles that appeared and then burst. Do you think…? Could it be…? Is it possible…?

Just then, Abby heard the chorus on the radio of the song from the Goo Goo Dolls, "Scars are souvenirs you never lose; the past is never far."

CHAPTER 46

Dannie Bevan had been in Los Angeles for the better part of two weeks working on a deal with two movie studios. She had only been back in New York for a few days, but it felt as if she had been gone forever.

She was looking at the pile of work on her desk and was methodically separating the files to parcel out to the associates to work on. Gwen had done a good job of holding the fort in Dannie's absence, but there were matters she wouldn't know how to deal with.

There had been one thing that was weighing on Dannie's mind for a while, and she had put it off until she came back from the West Coast. Dannie was a master of compartmentalizing matters in her own mind, and she dealt with the task at hand and pushed other things to the back of her mind. She needed to speak to Rick about the nagging thing.

She had to admit, but only to herself, that she was sorry that Rick was involved with Maizie. Dannie would have liked things to have worked out with them. Rick was a good lover, and she had so enjoyed him. Dannie's husband, Rob, was boring and was more than a tad obsessive-compulsive. Clearly, Rob didn't have the good abs that Rick had. She and Rick could really have been a power couple, plus they were bound together by the dirty little secret about Steve Goldrick. Rick actually seemed to be perplexed about the situation, but Dannie was much more of a pragmatist, or perhaps a capitalist. She chuckled to herself. Yes, a pragmatic capitalist. She saw a pragmatic way to earn capital. Dannie mused about whether Rick and Maizie had been together before Maizie came to work at the firm, but she could never really be sure. Perhaps it was for the best that she didn't get involved with Rick. It might be too obvious—and grist for the gossip mill. No one interesting presented himself to her in her two weeks in Los Angeles, which was too bad, because Dannie was getting a little restless with only work and Rob. No matter, Dannie would find someone rich, interesting and handsome for her next conquest.

Dannie still liked Rick and so she was going to compartmentalize that part of her life so that the business relationship with Rick would be OK. The guy deserved a break after all he had been through. She thought he was going to have a heart attack with the situation with Steve Goldrick. He couldn't seem to see it as a thrilling problem or as a way to live a little dangerously. There really wasn't any way to lose. It was just a matter of how big they were going to score.

Dannie felt bad that she had to lay this on him, but she had been thinking about it for a while. What he chose to do with the information was up to him. She felt that in one respect she was doing Rick a favor, but on the other hand, she was dumping something in his lap.

She waited until about quarter to five and figured that, when they were through talking, Rick could go back to his office without having to deal with clients or other people demanding his attention. The staff would be winding up for the day and getting ready to go home.

Dannie buzzed Rick on the intercom and asked him if he could come into her office when he had a minute.

"Dannie, can you give me about ten or fifteen minutes? I have to make one phone call. Or do you need me right now?"

"I'm going to be here for a while. Have you seen what my desk looks like? Take your time; I have plenty to do. I want to talk to you about the Goodman matter and a couple of other things."

Rick buzzed Maizie and said, "Dannie has a few things she wants to talk to me about. I'm not sure how long it's going to take. Why don't you head home, and I'll catch up. I'll call you when I'm leaving."

Rick arrived in Dannie's office with the Goodman file in one hand and a legal pad in the other. Dannie looked tired and even though she had done some work on other pending files while she was in California, Rick knew that it was no picnic coming back to what had piled up on her desk. There was only so much she could delegate to other attorneys in the firm.

Dannie described the posturing and negotiations that had gone on with the studios and how a lot of time was wasted, which made Dannie crazy. "I suppose it was good that I was there and held the clients' hands and they had my undivided attention."

After they talked about what was happening on the Goodman case for a few minutes and what the next step would be, Dannie said, "I'm starting to fade. I'm going to ask Gwen to set up a meeting tomorrow afternoon with you and me and Bill, Allison and Tim. I need to get some help with these files, or I'm going to keel over." Dannie gestured in the direction of the files on her desk and credenza. "They're the three best associates we have, right?" Without pausing or waiting for Rick's answer, Dannie continued. "There's one more thing."

Dannie got up from her desk, closed the door to her office and walked over to the highboy opposite her desk. She opened up one of the doors and fished around in the folders piled in there. Dannie retrieved an old-looking manila folder and went back and sat down behind her desk. Rick was watching her every move like a hawk, but he wasn't sure of the import of what he was watching.

"Rick, I've done enough trial work to know that you better have looked at every piece of paper in every file so that you're not blindsided by your opponent. Well, I followed my own rule with Steve Goldrick's files. I went through every file in those five boxes before I copied each and every one of them. After the initial shock of what Steve was doing wore off, the rest of the files were pretty ho-hum.

"That was until I got to the last box and looked at this file." Dannie tapped at the file on her desk. Dannie never took her eyes off Rick, and Rick never took his eyes off Dannie. Rick still didn't know where Dannie was going with all of this, but whatever it was Rick didn't like it.

"I held this file back from all the files we gave to the District Attorney because I don't know what an ambitious DA would do about opening an investigation. I really think that the decision about what to do with the file and the information should be made by you and your family and not me. I hope you understand that I was trying to help you."

Dannie continued to look directly at Rick. "Rick, you have to look at this file and you need to read it."

Rick answered in a perplexed tone, "What are you talking about? I don't understand."

Leaning closer to Rick from across the desk, Dannie said, "This is about your parents and your brother."

Dannie held out the file to Rick. Rick didn't move a muscle and he didn't reach out his hand to take the file. After a few seconds, Dannie leaned a little farther across the desk and extended the file to him again.

Rick seemed to be stunned, but he finally took the file. "Thanks, Dannie. I really appreciate it." With that, Rick got up from his chair, opened the door and walked out.

Dannie was normally quite sure of her actions, especially those to which she had given a lot of thought, as she had with this one. Dannie leaned back in her chair and closed her eyes. For the first time in a long time, Dannie started to second-guess herself. Should she have given the file to Rick? Too late now. She was getting a splitting headache.

Rick walked down the hall and back to his office. He was glad there weren't many people left in the office that he'd have to talk to. It was just as well that he had told Maizie to go home. He put the file down on his desk as if it were toxic. He stared at it for a minute, and then he took a deep breath and opened the file. Rick thought he knew the worst, but the worst was yet to come.

Rick had seen the setup of a file like this numerous times from the other files in the boxes. Rick saw the checks with his parents' name on them. While his parents had told Jason and him that Jason was adopted, they had never gone into any of their motivation in adopting a child. Rick assumed that desperation to have a child after so many failed pregnancies must have been an extremely compelling force that made his parents deal with a scumbag like Steve Goldrick. Why didn't they go through a reputable adoption agency instead of going black market? Rick really didn't have any insights or answers. After looking at the other adoption files, Rick knew that long-deceased corrupt judges and corrupt clerks in the courts had also lined their pockets based on couples' desperation to have a child.

Rick continued to peruse the file when he literally bolted upright in his chair. He blinked and looked again, but what he had seen was still there. "Holy fuck. Are you kidding me?"

The birth mother of his brother, Jason, was Abigail Ann Parker! My God, the birth mother was his soon to be mother-in-law, Abby. How could this possibly be true? It was like the line from *Casablanca*: "Of all the gin joints, in all the towns, in all the world, she walks into mine." Rick noted with some irony that the main character in Casablanca was also named Rick.

Rick didn't know what to think or what to make of this. He knew from Maizie first, and then from Abby herself, that she had made a decision to find the son she put up for adoption when she was a teenager. Rick had no idea what Jason would say when he found this out. Rick racked his brain for any conversations he had ever had with Jason about his being adopted. Jason seemed at peace with the fact that he was adopted and Rick wasn't, but Rick had never heard Jason express any interest in finding his birth parents. Now his birth mother had practically been dropped into their laps, whether they wanted it or not.

Rick wiped a bead of sweat from his forehead. This had all the earmarks of a messy and very awkward situation. Even if everyone knew it, it could always be the elephant in the room. There was no getting around the fact that Abby and Jason would undoubtedly be together at family gatherings. How would that play out? Oh, God. Rick tried to decide what he should do now. To make matters worse, Maizie was waiting for him at home. He needed to think this through before he mentioned this to Maizie. He needed to know how he felt before he had to deal with Maizie's view of this. Shit, was life just one big mess that wanted to dump on him?

Rick sat in stunned silence for what seemed like an eternity. His mind couldn't comprehend what he had read in that adoption file. His pulse was racing, and his thoughts were racing even faster. So many random thoughts were swirling around in his head as if all his thoughts were stuck in a whirlpool. The whirlpool effect he was feeling reminded him of the night he attempted to end his life on the bridge.

He had discussed more than a few times with the shrink why Abby had shown up on the bridge exactly when she had. Rick was pretty sure he would have jumped if Abby hadn't come along. But Abby had been so damn persistent and refused to leave. Then there was the whole thing about her climbing up on the bridge and falling over the side and practically getting killed herself for her good deed. He'd read in the newspapers many times about people stopping their cars on a bridge and talking someone down or at least getting the person not to do anything rash, and then the police took over. So her coming upon him on the bridge that night was not all that remarkable in and of itself. However, her climbing up on the bridge was a different story!

He really, truly, liked Abby as a person. He had wanted to stay connected to her and the same seemed to be true for her as well. It wasn't an act or anything trumped up. Then Maizie came into the picture...

Hadn't he had enough grief in his life already? He lost Jennifer and Adam, and now that he was finally picking up the pieces of his life and was starting to be happy again, this bomb exploded in his face.

CHAPTER 47

Abby was at Rick and Maizie's house and had been there most of the day, waiting and waiting for the new furniture and the Verizon installation. Tina had accompanied Abby, brought along not just for company, but Abby thought it was wise considering all the workmen coming and going. She felt a little safer with Tina there. Tina had checked out almost every room. She eyed every workman and on occasion received a pat on the head and "what a good dog" praise. Abby had been noticing recently how hard it was for Tina to get around. Her hip dysplasia had become troublesome and painful. The vet had put Tina on Tramadol, a pain suppressant, and non- steroidal anti-inflammatories. This cocktail had worked for about three years, but Abby and the vet knew that Tina had reached the maximum dosage. Tina had been by Abby's side since shortly after Jerry's death. The ugly truth was Abby would soon have to make "the choice," or she hoped, Tina would let her know when the time was right for Tina to die. But until that time came, Abby paid extra special attention to Tina and made her as independent and comfortable as possible. Since Abby didn't have any clients on Wednesday afternoon, Maizie had asked Abby if she would sit in the new house and take delivery of the furniture from Pottery Barn and wait for the "Cable Guy." Some of the rooms were almost done, but others still needed the carpenter to finish or the painters to prime the walls and paint. The house really smelled of paint, and Abby had the windows open in the rooms she was in. Maizie and Rick had decided to wait a few more days before moving in to let the paint smell lessen and have the contractors finish and get rid of the ever-present dust and construction debris.

Abby also told Maizie that she would start unpacking some boxes of linens and towels and then start on the boxes with dishes and glasses for the kitchen and whatever else she had time for. Abby finished putting away everything in the linen closet and moved on to the other boxes in the great room.

This next box contained pictures, all carefully wrapped in bubble wrap. Abby sat down on one of the chairs and put the box on the table. As she unwrapped each picture, she carefully laid it on the table. Abby had never seen most of these pictures before, so this was a chance to really look at them. Some of the pictures were so poignant that Abby felt a lump in her throat. There were so many pictures of Rick with Adam as a baby, Adam as a toddler, and Adam as a three and four-year-old. Abby could feel the pain of his loss. It reminded her of her son that she had given up for adoption some many years ago. It wasn't quite the same, because hopefully her son was still alive and doing well, but it was still the pain of loss.

As Abby continued to unwrap the pictures, she came across a picture of what looked to be a young Rick and Jason at a black tie event, perhaps someone's wedding. They were seated at a table with a group of people and smiling at the camera, most probably a paid photographer at the event. As Abby looked more closely at the picture, the smile on her face evaporated. Holding the frame in her hands carefully, she looked at the picture again, squinting to see if all of the people she was looking at would become clearer. Out of frustration she grabbed her glasses from her sweatshirt pocket and looked again. "I can't believe this... This can't be true. Oh my God."

There right before her eyes, staring back at her from the picture were Aunt Rita and Uncle Tom, and Caroline and Jonathan. What were they all doing together? Why were these six people together?

Abby felt a little sick to her stomach. This was Uncle Tom and her Aunt Rita, her mother's best friend from high school. Although she didn't want to believe it, there was one and only one conclusion that she could draw from this. Rick's older brother, Jason, was her son! Jason...Jason is really my son—really my son. How could this be and I not have known it? All these years, worrying and wondering about him...He's so close; he's so close, and yet what can I do? All of these thoughts whirled around in her head like a tornado, bits and pieces thrown about. When I met him at the hospital, there was something familiar about him. How could I have not picked up on it...even when we were all out to dinner? How could I not even know my own son when I saw him?

Abby had been enraged that Fannie had known all these years where her son was and never told her. Now Abby could feel the blood pounding in her temples. Not only had Fannie known where her son was, but he was practically under her nose. Goddamn it, Mom, how could you do this and get away with this for all these years?

Abby's brain came to a screeching halt from that avenue of thought and then jumped to Jason. What would Jason think? How would he feel about this? Had he ever tried to find her? Did he want to find her? Abby had wanted to find her son and meet him, but only if he had wanted to meet her as well. Now this was thrust upon them all whether they liked it or not.

As Abby's brain raced along with all the permutations, she also realized that this could be the proverbial elephant in the room. They would undoubtedly be together at family functions going forward. Rick and Jason were close. Maizie and Rick would probably have children. Abby would be at birthday parties and Christmas and Memorial Day barbecues for her grandchildren, and Jason would be there as their uncle.

A second, more potent thought popped into her head. Jason was her son, and he and Beth had two daughters. He had two of the cutest little girls she had ever seen. I have two granddaughters that I barely know! Now that she focused on Scott and Jason, she could see the resemblance between them. However, there was no denying Jason had some distinct features of his father, but Jason looked more like Maizie than Scott as children. Abby's thoughts were racing so fast that she almost couldn't keep up. It was going to take time for her to process this situation.

Fannie was standing, leaning against the doorway of the great room. She had seen Abby unwrap the pictures and knew precisely what this meant.

"You saw the picture of Rita and Tom with the kids? It's a very good picture of Rita. You know she didn't photograph well."

Abby was startled once again by Fannie's voice. "What the hell do you want?"

The painter, working in the hallway, poked his head into the great room and said sheepishly, "Were you talking to me? Because I don't need anything. I'm just painting the hallway."

Abby realized that the poor guy thought she was yelling at him. Now it was Abby's turn to be sheepish. "No, sorry, I wasn't talking to you. Just thinking out loud really. I've been doing that a lot lately."

The painter gave her a quizzical look and said, "All right, maybe you should have that looked at. I'll be going back to work now, ma'am." With that, he turned quickly and exited the room and continued down the hallway.

Before Fannie could say anything, Abby continued, in a quiet hiss, "Great, now the painter thinks I'm fuckin' crazy. I am—for talking to you."

Abby continued on about Jason. "You think this is some kind of game? You think Jason and I are just pawns? This is my life you've been screwing with all these years. It's not bad enough that you did this while you were alive, but now you have to do it while you're dead, too?"

Fannie saw and heard Abby's white-hot anger, and she wanted to say something that would make her feel better and maybe even calm her down. The problem was Fannie had never been one to mince words, even in death. Fannie also didn't think that Abby would have believed her if she said she was sorry. Actually, Fannie wasn't sorry about the whole thing. She was only sorry about a part of it. That's what she hoped she could get Abby to understand.

"Abby, sit down on the sofa and breathe for a second. Get a hold of yourself. Should we wait to have this discussion when you've had a chance to digest this and you're a little calmer?"

Abby's anger erupted again. "You are really a piece of work, you know that? You've waited all these years to have this discussion with me, and you're only having it now because you have to, since I found this." Abby was waving the picture in the air and pointing it in Fannie's direction.

Now it was Fannie's turn to be defiant. "I don't regret, and neither should you, the fact that you gave the baby up for adoption. You did the right thing for both of you. You couldn't support yourself or a baby. Think about it for a minute. You were able to finish your education and then you married Jerry, and you have two wonderful children. We talked about your possibly keeping the baby when you were pregnant. It just didn't make sense for you to try to raise the baby without a father and your being a teenager. You've had a good life, and you've been a wonderful mother to Scott and Maizie. I also knew that Caroline and Jonathan would love him and give him a good home. Caroline had had so many miscarriages, and they were heartbroken that they couldn't have children. Caroline and Jonathan were able to give him a great home with lots of love. They were able to take good care of him, provide well for him and pay for his education to become an architect. So, no, I'm not sorry that you gave up the baby for adoption." Fannie's tone to Abby was now more strident.

"Mom, we've been over this. You knew he was safe and was being cared for, and I worried about him every day since I gave him up. Didn't it ever occur to you that I might want to have that same peace of mind that you had? Didn't it ever occur to you that I might want to know how he was growing up, and that he was safe, happy and well cared for? No, it was fine that you knew it, but you didn't think about me."

Fannie looked at Abby for a few seconds and said, "You're wrong. You're dead wrong. You've only been thinking about this from your point of view. About what would have been good for you. What about Jason? Would that have been good for him to have you in his life? What about Caroline and Jonathan? Is this all about you? I don't think so. I think it was about what was in the best interest of your baby, and you seem to have forgotten that. He was the innocent one in this situation."

"You can be mad at me all you want, Abby, but I was right. Let's not forget that you never even told Jerry or the kids that you had a son. You kept your secrets for your own reasons, and that's fine. But then you have no right to condemn me for keeping mine."

"Mom, I had my reasons for not telling Jerry and the kids."

Fannie looked at Abby and said in a soft tone, "Precisely my point."

CHAPTER 48

Abby hit the button again on the remote. She hadn't slept since her confrontation with Fannie. This was the third morning in a row where she was awake before four thirty in the morning. Her body was exhausted from no sleep, but her mind was not allowing it as she hashed and rehashed events and conversations in her mind. For what seemed like the fiftieth time she thought she had a plan, but then she discarded it.

Abby trudged through the morning, making coffee, reading mail and doing lots of thinking with little to show for it. She was making herself crazy with all this; she couldn't concentrate on her work and found herself staring at the computer screen without paying attention to a word of what she was looking at.

Finally, Abby decided that some action, any action, was better than being frozen in indecision. That was complete torture.

Shortly after nine in the morning, she picked up her cell phone and scrolled down to a number on her contacts list. She took a deep breath and hit the number on the touch screen. The phone rang twice, and on the third ring, the male voice answered, not the voicemail. Abby was glad he answered because she wasn't sure what message she would have left.

"Morning, Abby, how are you?" Rick asked, seeing her name come up on the screen. In reality, he was a little surprised that Abby, and not Maizie, was calling him. He knew that mothers and daughters were supposed to be close, but since he and Maizie had bought the house, Maizie and Abby seemed to have an inordinate number of things to talk about involving tile, rugs, granite, paint colors and furniture. Rick really didn't mind, because if Maizie obsessed about these things with her mother, then she wasn't obsessing about them with him, which was fine. In fact, it was more than fine.

"Hi, Rick, I was hoping to catch you at a time when you weren't too busy."

"I'm in the car on my way to court, so you've got me with some time to spare. What's up?"

"Rick, something has come up that I need to talk to you about. Is there a time when you and I can get together alone and talk? It's important."

Even though Rick was driving, he picked up on the word "alone," meaning without Maizie. Abby sounded very serious and very subdued. Abby was also the antithesis of the meddling or interfering soon-to-be mother-in-law, so if she was calling him to talk, it wasn't anything trivial.

"I have an appearance in Surrogate's Court, and then I have to file some papers with the county clerk, but it shouldn't take that long. I'm assuming that you don't want to come to the office, correct? What's your schedule like today?"

"I have a meeting this afternoon in Armonk, but I'm free until then. Can I meet you at City Limits Diner in White Plains for a cup of coffee when you're finished with court?"

"Fine, I'll meet you there at eleven. Is everything OK? You don't sound like yourself." Rick was trying to get an inkling of what was the subject of the meeting, so that he'd have some idea of what he was facing.

"I'm OK. I just have something we need to discuss. I'd rather that you didn't tell Maizie we're meeting."

Rick really would have preferred to have some idea of what they were discussing, but Abby was not being forthcoming. "OK, see you at eleven o'clock."

When Rick hit the off button, he considered what this could be. Abby was a very grounded person, so he tried to think of what this could be about. Could she be in some trouble with the law and needed his help? Not likely. Could she have some gambling problem and someone was threatening her? Again, not likely. Abby lived well but not extravagantly, and he couldn't ever remember her going to Las Vegas or Atlantic City. Maizie would know about those things, so what was it? With all the terrible things that had happened in his life, Rick's imagination now began to run away with him. Was Abby sick and she didn't want to tell Maizie yet? A possibility, but he still thought she would have told Maizie. Could Maizie be sick? Oh God, what if there was something serious with Maizie and she couldn't bear to tell him? Now Rick was starting to get upset, because if something happened to Maizie, he didn't think he could cope. Maizie was his life, and she had brought him back from the land of the living dead. The rational side of his brain kicked in and said that Maizie hadn't even been to the doctor…that he knew of.

Another thought came into his head. Could Abby know about Jason? Could she know that Jason is her son? How could she possibly know about this? Rick started to dismiss this thought as being paranoid. This is crazy; it's just a coincidence. But then he started to think about all the coincidences that had occurred with him and Abby's family. Is this some cosmic joke? Is somebody pulling the strings? What if she does know? How do I handle this?

The time inched by in court, as Rick looked at his watch a hundred times before his case was called. Rick went through the motions in answering the calendar in Surrogate's Court. If it had been anything extremely difficult, he would have had a problem because he was now so distracted by Abby's call. He got in the elevator on the eighteenth floor where the courtroom was located, and grimaced when he saw how many lights were on for people to get off. Rick wanted an express to the lobby, but there were more delays as people shuffled on and off the elevator.

He finally got out of the courthouse and moved rapidly across the plaza to the parking garage. He'd probably be close to on time to meeting Abby or maybe a little late.

It was only a few minutes' drive to the diner, and if he caught the stagger on the lights on Hamilton Avenue and then Route 119, he'd be there on time. Mercifully, the parking lot at City Limits was not packed as it normally was, but this was after the breakfast crowd and a bit too early for lunch. Abby was in a booth facing the door, and she saw him come in and waved.

Rick walked to the table and bent over to kiss Abby on the cheek. Rick had been so busy with the office and buying the new house that he had forgotten how much he liked Abby for her own sake, even without Maizie, and how much he owed her. He owed her everything, and he should never let that fact slip to the back of his mind.

Abby had a mug of coffee in front of her, which was about half empty. Abby said, "I'm thinking about a bagel or a lemon poppy seed muffin. Would you like something?" Abby appeared calmer than she actually was. She also thought that a bagel would give her something to do with her hands.

Rick ordered coffee and a cranberry muffin and Abby stuck with the lemon poppy seed one. The waiter returned in a nanosecond with the coffee and a refill for Abby.

After the waiter left the table to put in the order, Rick stared intently at Abby. She looked tired and a little haggard. Rick decided it was her meeting, and he'd let her start.

Abby fumbled with her spoon for a few seconds and then returned his gaze.

"Rick, you know that Maizie asked me to sit in the house and take delivery of the furniture. I also did some unpacking to help out. I put away some linens and towels and then I went into the great room and started with those boxes".

"I started to unpack boxes that had lots of pictures. I was unpacking the pictures, and I was going to start putting them on shelves, but I decided that you and Maizie have to decide where they go. There were some wonderful pictures of you and Adam."

"Then I unpacked the picture of you and Jason at a wedding or some other black tie event. Your parents and grandparents were also in that picture. I have to ask you your grandparents' names."

Rick shifted uncomfortably in his seat. Now his fears were beginning to come true.

"Why do you ask that, Abby?"

"I need to know if your grandparents' names were Rita and Tom Hutchinson?"

"How do you know that? I don't think I've ever mentioned their names to you. Do you know them?"

Abby hesitated again and said, "Your grandmother, Rita, was my mother's closest friend from high school."

"Are you sure you're right? Are you sure that was your Aunt Rita in the picture? You are right that my grandparents' names were Rita and Tom Hutchinson."

"I could pick out those two anywhere. When I was a kid, we spent a lot of time with them. I could never forget them. Aunt Rita was so tiny and had a nose full of freckles and short dark hair. Even when I was ten, I towered over her. She didn't look as if she had aged at all in the picture from how I remembered her."

Rick tried to hedge a little. "Oh my God, I can't believe that my grandmother and your mother were best friends." Rick thought to himself, maybe that's all she knows...I hope.

"You see, Rick, remember when I told you about my child I gave up for adoption? Well, I stumbled across some letters that Aunt Rita had written to Mom telling her about the baby your mother, Caroline, had adopted. There were photos enclosed as well. It was a secret that Mom and Aunt Rita took to their graves. Or so they thought."

"What secret?" Rick asked. He began to feel warm, almost uncomfortable. Here it comes, he thought.

"There's no easy way to say this, but I truly believe that Jason is my son. Your brother, Jason, is the child I gave up for adoption."

Rick had seen his parents' file which Dannie had given him, but he still hadn't made up his mind what he was going to do with the file or the information it contained. It had occurred to him to do absolutely nothing with it and let the sleeping dogs lie. Now it was clear that the sleeping dogs had been kicked awake.

Rick didn't want Abby to know that he already knew this information, so he played along. "Are you serious? Are you sure it's Jason?"

"Absolutely sure! You know I wanted to find my son, but the way I thought it would happen would be that I'd find some stranger and tell him who I was and see if he wanted to meet me. I think the rules of engagement have now changed."

Rick answered her, "Have they changed, Abby? Have they?"

"Yeah, I think they have, whether we like it or not. I can't sit on this powder keg and pretend it doesn't exist. My mother and your grandmother kept this secret so many years ago, and now we're all paying the price for their secrets. What's the expression about the 'sins of the father'? Well, in this case, it was the sins of the mothers. I don't want to do exactly what my mother did, which is lie about one of the most important decisions I ever made in my life. I don't want you to have to lie either."

Rick would deeply regret the next words that came out of his mouth. "I'd only have to lie because you dragged me into this situation."

Abby looked pained, but before she could say anything, Rick interjected, "I'm sorry, Abby. I didn't mean that the way it came out."

Abby wiped a tear out of the corner of her eye and said, "I'm sorry, Rick, that you feel that way, but this is a very complex situation, and it now involves all of us. I can't just sweep this situation under the rug, because it's not going away."

"I think I wanted some input from you about Jason and his feelings about this. I most certainly don't want to usurp in any way the role of your parents. They were your parents. But has he ever mentioned looking for his birth mother?"

"I don't think so. I don't think I ever heard him discuss it. I don't know if he's averse to this."

Abby looked at Rick again. "Even though you and Maizie aren't married yet, I think of you as family. We're in this together. Look at who was present at the dinner celebrating your buying the house. It was Jason and Beth and me. We're going to be at lots of family events together. I would really like to get to know my two granddaughters. I know this is complicated. We can't have this secret lurking just below the surface for the rest of our lives. Maybe this is our shot at redemption. For all of us."

"What if you tell Jason, and he was happy not knowing? What then?"

"Well, then, I guess I just go back to being Maizie's mother and your mother-in-law."

"Don't be naïve, Abby. Nothing is ever going to be the same. As we say in the law, 'You can't un-ring the bell.' This is a perfect example of that."

Abby thought for a moment and then replied, "I've begun to think that it wasn't a coincidence that I was the one who found you up on the bridge, or that I climbed up to bring you the water. You were meant to live, and live your life not only for you and Maizie, but now for Jason and the girls as well."

"Rick, I felt I had to broach this conversation with you first. I'm sorry you have to be in the middle of this, but you're the logical one to tell. I need to find a way to talk to Jason, and I think I have to do it myself."

Abby continued, "For a long time I thought my mother was completely wrong about everything about this adoption. I've begun to realize that it was the best thing for Jason. Your parents gave Jason and you a very good life, and I'm very grateful to them. It also was the best thing for me as a teenager. I certainly couldn't have taken care of or provided for a baby. Hell, I couldn't even have supported myself, no less be a single mom."

For a fleeting moment Rick considered telling Abby that he already knew about her and Jason. He dismissed it because he could see this opening a Pandora's Box about Steve Goldrick, Dannie Bevan and him and the blackmail. Rick realized that he needed to stay as far away as possible from that topic.

For the first time in the conversation, Rick looked pensive and drummed his fingers on the table. He had stopped looking at Abby and was now looking down at the table.

"What are you looking for from me? Are you looking for my blessing to do this?"

"No, I'm not looking for your blessing. I'm telling you because you and I have a bond between us that was forged that night on the bridge. It has nothing to do with you and Maizie. In fact, it precedes you and Maizie. It has to do with you and your family."

Rick nodded his head in agreement. He then added, "I guess our chance meeting on the bridge that night has gotten us to where we are now. Maybe you're right; maybe it wasn't a coincidence after all. Who the hell knows?"

Abby looked at him and saw that he was fighting his emotions. "What do you think is the best way for me to get together with Jason? I thought I'd tell Maizie myself and swear her to secrecy until I speak to Jason." Abby thought to herself, what a mess. Now Maizie would have to keep a secret, even if only for a little while. Fannie looked on from another booth and nodded her head with a resigned smile on her face. "Secrets—just so many secrets. How did one secret kept with good intentions snowball into this?"

CHAPTER 49

Abby called Maizie at her office later in the afternoon on the same day she had met Rick at City Limits Diner. Usually Abby and Maizie spoke when one of them was in the car or already at home. It was a little unusual for Abby to call Maizie at work.

"Hi, honey, how are you?"

"OK, Mom, where are you?"

"I'm in Greenwich and I just finished up with a client. I know you wanted me to look at the fabric samples, and since I'm only a few minutes away, I thought I'd stop by. Want me to pick up dinner?"

"Yeah, that would be great. With all the stuff going in the house—and then we have a big motion that has to go out for the office, I really don't have very much in the fridge."

"So the idea, Maiz, is to let the new refrigerator stay in pristine condition for as long as possible?"

"Ya know, I hadn't thought of it that way, but that's a great idea. Never food shop and never get the refrigerator dirty. I can't figure out what happened to the guy I was dating who liked to cook. Lately, he's too busy with the office."

"What would you like me to pick up?"

"How about the salad from that new salad place we went to? They were great—and that sourdough bread that they have."

"Is Rick going to be home or just us?" Abby knew the answer to the question, because she and Rick had discussed it earlier. They both felt that they had to tell Maizie about this morning's discussion concerning Jason without waiting any longer.

"He'll be home. You can tease him about why he isn't doing the cooking. Can you be at the house about six? That will give us some time to look at the fabric without him. He seems singularly disinterested in the whole decorating process. His main contribution seems to be writing the checks, and he's downright thrilled that's all he has to do."

"That's probably not that unusual. See you around six."

When Abby got to the house about ten minutes early, she saw Maizie's car in the garage. She rang the doorbell and Maizie answered, wearing a pair of jeans and a turquoise sweater.

Abby handed the bags with dinner to Maizie and walked into the house behind her. As Maizie put the bags on the kitchen table, she said to her mother, "Let me go get the fabric samples, so you can help me make some decisions. I'm getting so confused; the samples all start to look alike." As Maizie left the room to retrieve the samples, Abby walked to the family room and reached for a picture on the mantle. She gently lifted the photo holding it close to her, and took it back to the kitchen and laid it facedown by the flower vase on the kitchen table.

When Maizie returned with the fabric books and put them down on the kitchen table, Abby said to her, "Before we look at them, there's something I want to talk to you about."

Maizie noticed that Abby had on her "serious" face and so she sat down in the chair opposite Abby. The "serious" face, as Maizie remembered from when they were kids, was the look when you were in trouble or, as they got older, when some important topic was about to be broached. In any case, Maizie knew they were not going to just be discussing fabrics as she had hoped. Fannie was sitting in the chair with her back to the wall.

"I told you and Scott that I had a son and I gave him up for adoption and that I thought it was time for me to find him. I think that fate had other plans."

Maizie was about to interject when Abby held up her hand to stop her. Fannie leaned forward in her chair expectantly, waiting to hear how Abby would phrase it with Maizie, even though Fannie basically knew what Abby was going to say. Fannie waited nonetheless to see if Abby would put some sort of spin on it with Maizie. Fannie noted that Abby hadn't really put any spin on it with Rick.

Abby continued, "You asked me to wait for the furniture delivery last week, and I said I'd do some unpacking while I was waiting in the house. As I unpacked the boxes of pictures, I was so moved by the pictures of Rick with Adam."

Maizie was watching Abby and listening intently, but Abby could see that Maizie had no idea where this was going, so Abby pressed on.

"I unwrapped this picture of six people sitting at a table at a wedding." Abby then handed the picture to Maizie. Maizie looked at the photo and realized it was the same one she had looked at months ago when she was packing up Rick's belongings from his old house, the picture that gave her the feeling of déjà vu. It was the picture of a younger Rick, Jason and their parents, Caroline and Jonathan, and Rick and Jason's grandparents, Rita and Tom.

Abby continued, "To my utter shock, I realized that Rick and Jason's grandmother was my mother's best friend from high school. She was the woman we called Aunt Rita. My mother, your grandmother, Fannie, somehow worked it out with Aunt Rita that Caroline and Jonathan would adopt my baby."

Abby paused for a second as Maizie digested all this information. Abby plowed on just to be sure she had said it out loud to Maizie. "Maiz, Jason is my son."

Maizie sat all the way back in her chair and let out a deep breath. Maizie repeated the words slowly as if she was hearing words in a foreign language. "Jason is…your son? Mom, I can't believe this. Oh my God!"

A few more seconds elapsed and Abby could see that Maizie was still processing things and was about to continue speaking.

"Does Jason know this? Does Rick know this?"

"No, to Jason; and yes, to Rick. I'm trying to think of the best way to tell Jason. I'm really not sure how to tell him."

Maizie looked at Abby, and her left eyebrow went up. "How does Rick know?"

"I spoke to him this morning to tell him. I wanted to tell each of you myself."

"Shit, Mom, I'm speechless. I don't really know what to say... Jason? What the hell was Rick's reaction?"

"Shock, mostly, I'd say. I wanted to tell him, but since he and Jason are so close, I also wanted to see what he thought Jason's reaction would be and see if Jason had ever expressed any interest in finding his birth mother."

Maizie got up from the kitchen table. She paced back and forth across the tile floor as she tried to digest what her mother had just said and all the ramifications this news was going to have.

"Christ, I can't believe this. Out of all the millions of people in the world, your son and my brother, half that he may be, is my fiancé's brother. This is nuts! How can this be?"

"I don't know, honey. I can't believe it either, but it is what it is."

"Mom, are you sure? You're absolutely sure of this? Could we be getting ourselves in an uproar, and it may not be true?"

Abby looked at Maizie and said out loud what she was thinking to herself. "Maiz, I admit that this is a very, very unusual situation, but it's something we're going to have to deal with because it exists."

As if on cue, Rick unlocked the door and came in from the garage. "Hi, how's it going?" Rick looked from Abby to Maizie. In that split second, Rick could tell from the expression on Maizie's face that Abby had told Maizie about Jason.

Rick looked at Maizie and said, "Well I guess you now know the 'secret,' by the look on your face." Maizie looked at Rick with a somewhat pained expression on her face and said, "Holy shit, I can't believe this. What are we going to do? And how will Jason feel when he finds out we all know before he does? Mom, does Scott know yet?"

"No, Scott doesn't know yet. But to answer your question, someone had to find out first."

Rick thought to himself, "Lucky me. I got to be the first to find out not only from Abby but also from Dannie. Crap, couldn't life have just left us alone?"

Maizie walked over to the wine rack and picked out a bottle of Pinot Noir and handed it pointedly to Rick. "Open, please; I think this is going to be a long night and we're all going to need it."

As Rick walked over to the kitchen drawer to get the corkscrew, Fannie got up from her chair and moved to one of the bar stools near the center island where Rick had put the bottle of wine. Rick poured two generous glasses of wine and gave a glass each to Abby and Maizie. Rick decided that a beer would taste better and grabbed a Fat Tire Ale from the fridge, a specialty ale that one of his friends sent him from Colorado.

Maizie took a long swig from her wine glass and said, " I love Jason and I like it that he's already in my life as your brother, but shit, now he's going to be my brother, too. I think this is a little creepy."

Abby let Maizie vent as she came to terms with this news.

Maizie looked at Rick, who was leaning on the island in the center of the kitchen, and she said, "So what do you think?"

Rick was trying to be somewhat diplomatic in his answer partly because he didn't quite know how he felt about the situation, but mostly because he knew that the inevitable was about to happen whether he liked it or not. Maybe they should all try to make the best of the situation and see how things played out. To a large degree, it depended on how Jason reacted to the whole scenario.

Rick shifted from one elbow to the other as he continued to lean on the center island and said, "Well, it's messy, I'll give you that, but all of us have lived long enough to know that you never know what's going to happen tomorrow."

Rick looked lovingly at Abby and smiled and then turned to look at Maizie. "I'm the living proof of that, and I have your mother to thank. I think that we all need to take a deep breath and see how Jason reacts. It doesn't matter as much what we think as what he thinks."

Fannie didn't think she had it in her, but when Rick finished speaking, Fannie actually clapped since she thought he was correct in his thinking. Now we're getting somewhere. We need to get everyone on the same page before Abby speaks to Jason. Yes, this was probably going to turn out quite well, after all. Fannie was pleased with herself. The plan was coming together. She actually would have liked to have a glass of the Pinot Noir with them, but what she really would have liked would have been to have a beer with Rick. Alas, that was not allowed, since she was dead... what a drag.

Abby had been silent for a long time, and now she spoke. "I agree with you, Rick, that life has really thrown us a curveball. There is a part of me that's always an optimist and says that this may work out well for all of us in the end. If it doesn't work out well, we'll figure out how to deal with that, too. But I'm still hopeful. I think the next question is how to approach Jason and when."

Abby knew that Fannie had been there the whole time, but she had not acknowledged her. Finally, Fannie spoke to Abby and said, "You'll know the right time to approach Jason and tell him the truth."

CHAPTER 50

After the meeting at Maizie and Rick's new house with Abby, the three of them decided that Abby needed to meet with Jason sooner rather than later, especially since Rick and Maizie now knew. Abby didn't want Jason to think that Rick had kept it a secret from him, and jeopardize their relationship.

They also agreed that Abby would call Scott and tell him about Jason, since Scott wasn't due to be back in New York for a few more weeks. Abby had called Scott and left a message for him to call her without letting on what she wanted to discuss with him.

As luck would have it, Jason, Beth, and the kids had been planning to go to Philadelphia for the weekend to visit Beth's parents. They had been planning to leave Saturday morning, when Jason had gotten a call from one of his partners that they had an opportunity to bid on a big commercial project in Paramus, New Jersey. The chance to bid on the project had come up at the last minute, and they had to have the bid in by the following Tuesday morning. That meant that all the architects needed to be at work for the weekend.

Beth seemed to be fine with taking the girls to Philadelphia to see her parents so Jason could work on the new project. Jason called Rick at about four thirty Saturday afternoon and told him about bidding on the new project. He said that they were finishing up for the day. Would Rick and Maizie like to have dinner with him since he was a "bachelor" for the weekend with Beth and the kids away seeing her parents?

Rick said, "I have a better idea. Why don't you come to our house for dinner? You know what a culinary genius I am. Abby might be coming, too."

"Sure, that sounds good, although I'm not sure about the 'genius' part," Jason said.

Rick shot back, "You only wish you had my talents, Big Bro." They both laughed.

"So what can I bring to accompany this lavish feast of yours?"

"Nothing, I have it covered. Just show up…on time!"

They agreed on seven o'clock.

Just as Rick hung up the phone, Maizie strolled in from the laundry room and said, "How in the world do we accumulate so much laundry with just the two of us? Who were you talking to?"

Rick answered, "I just got off the phone with Jason, and he's coming over for dinner tonight. This might be the best time for Abby to broach the subject and tell Jason. Do you think she's available?"

Maiz said, "I think she's around. I'll have to call her to see. This makes it easier, especially since Beth and the kids are out of town. I think this will give Jason some much-needed time alone to deal with this."

"How did you know they were away?" Rick asked.

"Easy, I talked to Beth yesterday, and she told me she and the kids were heading for Philly because Jason was working on a new project. You know this is going to be so difficult for all of us, but especially Mom and Jason. This could turn out to be one helluva dinner. Do you want to call Mom, or do you want me to do it?"

Rick looked a little sheepish and said, "You call her."

"OK, Chicken Little, I'll call her." Maizie walked into the family room and grabbed the phone and dialed Abby. "Hi, Mom, it's me. Rick just got a call from Jason and he wanted to have dinner with us tonight. Beth and the kids went to Philadelphia to see her parents, and Jason has been working all day to bid on a new project, so he's by himself. Rick invited him over for dinner, and we thought this might be a good chance for you to talk to him. Rick told him that you were coming, too. This is probably the best chance you have to talk to him without Beth and the kids, so he has an opportunity to think about this without everyone being involved. Can you come for dinner?"

"This is certainly a shot out of the blue. Yes, yes, I can come. We probably couldn't have planned it any better. Was this your idea, Maiz?"

"No, it wasn't. It was Rick's, but I think he was then too embarrassed to call you himself. Sometimes men are such babies. We told Jason seven o'clock, so we'll see you then. Love ya, 'bye."

As Abby hung up the phone, her hands were shaking. She had been thinking of this for so long, but now that the time was almost here, she could already feel the butterflies in her stomach. Maybe it was a good thing that she only had two hours left before she told Jason, her son, that he really was her son. If she had days to think about it before their actual meeting, she would have jumped out of her skin. Abby looked down at Tina, "You know something, girlie dog, I'm sure glad that you're here with me. Let's get some fresh air before the showdown."

When they came back from their short walk, Abby headed upstairs to take a shower and get dressed. As she walked into her bedroom, Fannie was there. Abby said, "So you undoubtedly heard the conversation with Maizie, right, Mom?"

"Yes, I did hear the conversation. It's surprising how much influence I still have in the real world, or should I say the living world?"

"What does that mean, Mom?"

"Let's just say I can help you when you need it."

"Well, that really clears things up, now doesn't it? Look, I have to get ready for tonight, and no need to tell you where I'm going. I have a question for you. Do you know how all of this is going to turn out for Jason and me? You seem to know what's going to happen before it happens, so tell me."

Fannie replied, "No, I can't tell you because I don't know myself. Whatever occurs tonight will be whatever you and Jason want. I cannot orchestrate the outcome. I'll quote the mystic Julianne of Norwich, "All will be well, and all will be well and all manner of things will be well."

Abby replied, "Say what?"

CHAPTER 51

When Abby arrived at Maizie and Rick's house, Jason was already there. Jason was sitting at the kitchen table talking to Maizie and Rick as they prepared dinner. Rick and Jason had already gone through a few bottles of beer as evidenced by the "dead soldiers" sitting on the counter.

Maizie was making the salad and was in the process of cutting up peppers and tomatoes, and Rick was seasoning the fish before grilling it. As Abby and Jason sat at the kitchen table, and Jason helped himself to cheese and crackers, Abby was watching Jason in a way that she had never watched him before. Looking at his profile, Abby could see that he resembled her side of the family. His complexion and hair were a little darker than Maizie's, closer in color to Scott's. Now that the secret was out, and she was looking for family traits, they were there. Jason had Scott's ears, and their hands were similar, but some of Jason's features, though subtle, were more like Maizie's. Abby found it hard not to watch him, but she had to catch herself to keep from staring .

Jason was always warm to Abby, and she believed that was because he took his cue from Rick, whom she knew definitely liked her. Abby wondered whether that warmth would remain.

Dinner was uneventful as Jason told them about the new project they were bidding on. Jason was a talker, no doubt about that. In fact, sometimes he was even more animated than Maizie, and that was going some. Rick asked about Julie's upcoming softball season, and Rick said now that life was calming down a little at the office and things were getting under control with the new house, he'd try to come to some games. In the past, Abby had listened politely about Jason's two girls; they were cute kids and were very well behaved, but now Abby's ear pricked up because now she was not only listening, but hearing, really hearing about her granddaughters. This is getting so complicated, she thought.

Fannie was sitting at the far end of the kitchen table. Abby had not acknowledged her presence. Fannie was watching Abby watch Jason. She could understand Abby's wanting to take in every detail about him, especially since she had missed so much of his life. Fannie did want to make things right, and she hoped that tonight would go as well as Abby hoped. Perhaps if it did go well between Jason and Abby and they were ultimately reunited as mother and son, Fannie thought that her time with Abby might be coming to an end. Fannie had been given another chance to make things right—in lots of ways.

As they finished eating and were lingering before they started to clear away the dishes, Maizie looked meaningfully at Abby and winked. "Jason," Abby said with a catch in her throat, "I have recently found out some information that involves all of us, but mostly you and me."

Jason looked at her quizzically and shot a quick glance at Rick. Rick returned Jason's glance but then immediately looked back at Abby. The mood in the room all of a sudden changed.

Abby continued as four pair of eyes rested on her. Fannie had positioned herself next to Jason so that every time Abby looked at Jason, she saw Fannie. "I need to tell you a story."

"Not too long ago, I found these letters written by my Aunt Rita who was my mother's lifelong best friend. Aunt Rita wrote these letters while she was in England helping to take care of her daughter and grandson." With that, Abby twisted around in her chair and pulled the packet of letters from her purse and handed them to Jason. They were tied neatly with a green ribbon. Jason looked at the letters and back to Abby. He took the letters and set them on the table in front of him, and he folded his hands on top of the letters.

The mention of Aunt Rita and England made Jason lean forward in his chair. Before Abby could say anything else, Jason blurted out, "Am I getting this right? Are you saying that my grandmother and your Aunt Rita are one and the same person?"

Jason now turned immediately to Rick and said, "Did you know this?"

Rick nodded his head slowly and said to Jason, "Let Abby continue."

All eyes were again trained on Abby, and she continued. "To answer your question, yes they are the same person, but there's also something else. When I was fifteen I gave birth to a beautiful baby boy. My parents thought the best thing was to give the baby up for adoption because I so young. My mother and Aunt Rita made all the arrangements. I signed the papers, and I never saw my baby again. All I had were two photos of him in my arms. Not a day went by that I didn't think of him, and wondered if he was healthy, happy and had a loving family with brothers and sisters. I always hoped his life was filled with joy. My mother called it an 'unselfish sacrifice,' giving my son to someone else, but it was the most difficult decision I ever made. Those letters you have in front of you made me realize what actually happened and who you were. The letters from Aunt Rita to my mother, your grandmother, contained pictures and updates of the little boy that your parents had adopted. That little boy was my son." Abby stopped talking and was looking at Jason and waited for some response, anything, even if it was anger.

Jason, now with furrows in his brow, leaned back in the chair, trying to get a grasp of what Abby had just said. He thought to himself, "Holy Christ, I'm her son—is that what she just said? What the fuck is going on, and how long has she known? Shit, does Rick know?"

"So you're telling me that you are my biological mother, correct?"

"Yes, Jason, I am."

Jason turned to Rick and asked with rising irritation in his voice, "Did you know this? How long have you known this?" Jason's eyes darted back and forth between Abby and Rick.

Jason felt that everything that was happening at the table was travelling at warp speed and that no one was really answering him. Jason then turned his gaze to Maizie as yet another thought pinged around in his brain. His voice sounded bewildered as he started speaking to her. "Oh my God, Maizie—you're my sister."

To try to break the tension in the room, which had become oppressive in a very short time, Maizie looked at Jason with the beginnings of a small grin on her face, and said, "Yep, that's right. I guess that makes me your half-sister, and you are my half-brother. And I'm marrying your brother. It's a little twisted creepy, but in a good way."

Fannie mused to herself that the "twisted creepy" comment was so like Maizie. She had an ability to inject humor to diffuse or lighten up a serious situation.

Jason did not return the grin. He looked shell-shocked. "This is for real? How long have you all known about this?"

Abby responded, "I've known that it was you for a little over a week. But in reality, I've loved you and worried about you my whole life. I absolutely did not know that my mother and Aunt Rita arranged for you to be adopted by your parents."

Now Jason turned on Rick and said with some annoyance, "So how long have you known about this?"

Rick had the thought flash through his head about the adoption file, but he answered, "Just a few days. It wasn't my place to tell you. It was Abby's."

"Abby, I never really thought very much about my biological mother. I had parents and family, and you weren't in that equation. This changes everything. I'm just not sure how." Jason abruptly pushed his chair back from the table and stood up. "Thanks for dinner. I gotta think…I just gotta go…"

In a flash, Jason jumped up from the table, almost knocking over his chair, grabbed his jacket from the foyer closet, opened the front door and slammed it shut behind him. Maizie reacted almost as quickly as Jason. She grabbed the letters that Jason had left on the table and ran out the front door into the driveway after Jason. She clutched his left arm as he was getting into the car and spun him around, "Look, Jason, you forgot these. The letters may help you to understand better. I don't know because I have never seen them. I meant what I said before. This is a little twisted creepy, and it's going to take some getting used to. Hey, look at it this way, you got a sister, a cute one, and a soon-to-be sister-in-law all in one. A twofer! C'mon, Jason, I know it isn't easy; how do you think I feel?"

"How *do* you feel?"

"Lucky, very lucky. And you are too! I am certainly blessed to have found Rick, and now I have an added bonus… you. Another brother I can hang with and laugh with and share my life with. You also have someone else who loves you and has always loved you, and that's Mom…uh, er…Abby."

Before Maizie could say anything else, Jason cut her off. "We'll see. I need to think about this some more—a lot more. I gotta go; talk to you later."

Before Jason knew it, Maizie had her arms around him in a big hug and whispered to him, "We'll get through this. I promise."

Abby and Rick were still in the dining room. Neither knew what to say for a few seconds and sat there in gloomy silence. Finally, Abby broke the silence and said, "That didn't go very well, did it?"

Rick looked at her and said, "I don't know how it was supposed to go. You just turned his whole world upside down. He's going to have to get used to the situation. Frankly, I'm not even sure I'm used to it, and I'm not the one this impacts the most."

Abby answered him with some sadness in her voice, "I know; I agree with you. I suppose some part of me wanted him to be happy about it, but I know that's unrealistic. It's easy to say let's wait and see what happens, but the waiting is hard. Do you think he'll call you tomorrow?"

"I don't know. He's probably going to need some time, and he'll want to talk to Beth first without the kids. My guess is that he's going to want to talk to her in person. She'll be back tomorrow night. Don't forget that they're still working on that proposal tomorrow in the office."

"Great, I hope we didn't screw that up."

Rick shrugged. "This is a big deal. I think this news makes work pale by comparison. Not to make you feel bad, but I never heard him say he wanted to find his biological parents, even after our parents died. This is going to be a huge adjustment, not just for Jason, but for all of us."

Just then Maizie came back in the house and Rick and Abby looked expectantly at her. "So how'd it go, Maiz? How'd he take it?" Abby asked.

"OK, I guess. He's pretty shook up, but I told him that it's going to work out. I told him how lucky he is to have me not only as his sister, but his soon-to-be sister-in-law. I called myself the 'twofer.' I think I got a little bit of a smile on that."

Abby brushed a tear away and said, "I didn't want to hurt him, but he seemed very upset. I knew that was part of the risk, but still..."

"Look, Mom, you did what you thought was the right thing. It's going to take some getting used to. No doubt about that. Try not to torture yourself in the meantime."

CHAPTER 52

Monday afternoon Maizie ambled into Rick's office, and under the guise of talking to him about the McCarthy matter asked him if he had called Jason. Rick made a face and said, "I think it's better if Jason calls me."

"Bullshit, Rick, you're afraid to call him in case he's mad at you."

"Well, he might be. I couldn't tell if he thought I should have tipped him off before Abby spoke to him. Who knows what's the right thing to do?"

"I spoke to Mom a little while ago and she asked if you had spoken to Jason. I really think she wants you to call him and get a read on how he's doing."

"Wouldn't it be better if she called him?"

Maizie gave him the "I'll-turn-you-to-stone look," and Rick said, "OK, OK, I'll call him."

As Rick dialed Jason's work number, he was hoping that he'd get Jason's voicemail. Jason answered on the third ring. "Hi, Jas, it's me. How ya doing? How's the bid coming on the project?"

Jason said, "Slow, but we're making progress. We have to submit it tomorrow, so it has to get done no matter what."

"You doing OK with the Abby thing?"

"I don't know. I told Beth last night, and she was pretty shocked. I don't have time to think about this now. I have to go back to work. I'll talk to you in a few days."

Jason had been thinking about the whole situation with Abby and found himself distracted, much more than he anticipated. His emotions ranged from anger at Abby having told him she was his mother and with everyone else for being so accepting, to God only knows...He had been pondering it at almost every waking moment, except when he was busy with work. Even then the situation constantly crept into his thoughts.

Jason finally called Rick at work after a few more days had passed. Rick answered the phone, "Hi, Jas, how are ya? How'd the client like your proposal?"

"I think they did like it because several of us are being called back to meet with them in person. Listen, Rick, is there a night when you and I can grab a beer together? I gotta talk to you about this whole thing going on with Abby. I'm having a hard time getting a handle on it."

"Sure, when?" Rick said.

Jason answered back, "Tonight sound good? I'll meet you at six at Clooney's."

As Rick walked into Clooney's, a well-established Irish pub, he had the feeling he had been transported back to the old sod: plenty of Guinness, served warm if you wished, and Irish brogues in abundance. He saw Jason sitting at a booth across from the horseshoe-shaped bar. He had a half-drunk beer in front of him, and as Rick slid into the booth across from him, Jason said, "I ordered you a Guinness and I got us some wings."

Not one to beat around the bush, Jason jumped in. "This whole thing with Abby has really gotten to me. I don't know what I think. I haven't mentioned anything at all to the kids yet either."

Rick sat quietly and took a sip of his beer. Jason looked as haggard and pale as Abby had when Rick met her at City Limits Diner. There was no doubt that this situation was taking a toll on everyone. He waited for Jason to continue.

"This is a goddamn mess. I really never had any inclination to go looking for my birth mother. It would be one thing if I had gone looking for her, but then Abby goes and drops this whole mess into my lap. If it was anyone other than Abby, I would have had a choice about whether I wanted to meet her at all. And what about the other half of the equation that was needed to get me into this world? Who the hell was he? I didn't hear Abby mention anything about him."

Rick realized that Jason was going to continue venting for a while and really didn't want any answers from Rick. Rick picked up a hot wing and took a bite.

As if this was a signal, Jason continued on at breakneck speed. "And by the way, how long did you know about all this? Crap, don't you think you could have given me a heads-up?"

"Look, Jason, I told you I only found out a few days before Abby spoke to you. What the hell was I supposed to do? Run and tell you, 'Oh, by the way, Abby's your mother.' It wasn't my place to tell you. Abby needed and wanted to talk to you herself. It wasn't exactly the kind of thing I could have told you and then you would keep quiet about it. Look at your reaction. I really was caught between the rock and hard place."

"Maybe you and Beth should go talk to Abby. It's not like you don't know her. You got pissed off the night she spoke to you and walked out. I think there are a lot of things you guys still have to discuss."

"Jeez, Rick, what the hell is the matter with you? Whose side are you on anyway?"

"Jason, there are no 'sides' here. Don't be juvenile. Act like an adult."

"What's that supposed to mean? It's easy for you to act all high and mighty. Abby's screwing with my life! Why the hell didn't she just keep her mouth shut? She saw that I grew up all right and that my life was going well. She even knew our parents. Wasn't that that enough for her? I guess not!"

"For God's sake, calm down. I suppose Abby could have kept her mouth shut, but she didn't. She wanted to get to know you as her son, and not just as my brother."

Rick continued, "We grew up with two parents who loved us. That will never change. Mom and Dad are gone now. You knew you were adopted, and now you have a great chance for your daughters to get to know their other grandmother…and for you to get to know Abby. That's a good thing."

Jason sat there for a few seconds, without responding. "I dunno, Rick. I still have to think about this. Sure, it's much easier for you if we all end up loving each other and singing 'Kumbaya.' You still get to marry Maizie no matter how much turmoil is happening in my life. Maizie was right; this is 'twisted creepy.' This whole thing was dropped into my lap and now every time I see Abby I have to deal with it whether I like it or not. And I'm not sure that I do like it."

"Jason, you're blowing this up way out of proportion. You'll see Abby a few times a year and that will be it."

"No, she's going to want to have a relationship with my kids. It's not going to be some casual thing."

"You're acting like Abby is some horrible person. You know her. You know she's a nice woman. You've even told me you like her. Where is this coming from? What does Beth think about this?"

"Beth likes Abby. Every goddamn person on the face of the earth likes Abby," Jason said sarcastically. "Beth can't get over how coincidental this is. Of all the millions of people on this planet, we're thrown together through a twist of fate, for lack of a better term. She actually thinks Abby and the girls would both benefit. I don't know. I never expected this. I never wanted to know"—Jason held up his fingers in quotes—'my real mother.' I hate it that I never even had a say in this. Abby decided the whole thing. Now I have no choice but to deal with this. Abby can't take Mom's place either."

"Is that what this is all about, Jas? No one's taking Mom's place. Not now, not ever. Just because you have a relationship with Abby doesn't mean that you stop loving Mom or that Mom stops having a special place in your heart. This is not about divided loyalties. They can both have a place in your heart."

Jason sighed, one hand clutching the beer bottle and tapping the fingers of his other on the table. "Maybe you and Beth are right. I just don't know. I'd like another beer, but I've had enough. I gotta go; I have to be up early for work. I got this; let's go."

"Jason, you OK to drive? I can give you a ride if you need one."

"Nah, I'm OK. I had a lot of wings to soak things up."

They walked out of the bar together, and Rick put his hand on Jason's shoulder. "This is going to work out. Give it a little more time." Jason shrugged and walked toward his car.

Jason got in the car and started it. He rolled out of the parking lot a little too fast for the gravel underneath the tires. He drove about two miles and stopped at a traffic light. He checked the rearview mirror to see if anyone was behind him and then made a U-turn. He made a snap decision that he was going to talk to Abby. Right now! A few beers had given him the false confidence to face her and tell her what he really felt. One part of him really did like Abby. During the times they were together, he thought she had a great sense of humor and made the best cookies he had ever had in his life. No, they were the best on the planet. The other part of him was enraged that Abby so abruptly blurted out that she was his mother. Didn't she have any idea what this would do to the family, especially to me? What the fuck was she thinking?

The more these thoughts raced through his head, the more his foot pressed the accelerator to the floor. The Audi R 8 Spyder was holding the turns, and it was known for blistering speed and awe-inspiring handling. The road twisted and turned as trees loomed up along the sides of the road and the headlights played off them. Jason hit a particularly tight turn, and an oncoming car was over the center line. Jason swerved hard to the right. Before Jason knew it, he was airborne and headed off an embankment. He let out a blood-curdling scream, his eyes closed tightly, fists clenched white-knuckled around the steering wheel, and he braced for the impact. The air bags deployed as the Audi hit the ground and dirt, grass, bushes and tree bark splintered everywhere. The Audi rolled over twice and came to a grinding halt against a downed tree. Silence, dead silence inside the car.

A few seconds later, a voice as if from heaven crackled inside the car.

"Mr. Singleton, this is Audi Customer Care. The air bags in your car deployed. Are you all right?"

No answer. The same question came again. "Mr. Singleton, can you hear me? Are you all right? I'll send the police and EMS. I will stay on the line with you."

Jason, still strapped in the seatbelt and semiconscious, was lying on his right side, with his arms and head dangling. The car was littered with broken glass, and steam curled and hissed like winter breath from under the crushed radiator. Even though the car was badly mangled, the Crumple Zones had worked, and he was still alive, at least for now. With a great deal of effort, Jason opened one eye and groaned out loud. In this semiconscious state, he heard the Audi Customer Care voice, but he couldn't answer. He wanted to wake up. He didn't want to die.

The car was surrounded by darkness and silence. Jason wasn't sure if his eyes were open or closed, but he somehow could see a stream of light that appeared to be right in front of him. He then saw two silhouettes framed by the light. Jason now felt as if someone was holding his hand and holding his head, so they were no longer dangling.

CHAPTER 53

It was Sunday evening, and Dannie had just pulled in the driveway. She had been out to a movie and dinner with some friends, something mindless to take her thoughts away from work for a while. Rob, her husband, had gone out of town for business. He was flying back to Boston and was stopping at the boarding school to see the boys. He'd be home in a couple of days. Dannie unlocked the side door that led to the kitchen; she wondered why the lights weren't on. She walked over to the sink and turned on the light above it. The light cascaded downward and reflected brightly off the deep, stainless steel sink. Dannie heard something behind her. She turned. Within a split second, a tall man with a mask grabbed her, his fingers wrapping tightly around her neck. She tried to scream, nothing but a tiny bit of air escaped. She struggled, knocking over a vase of flowers from the counter. Glass and water sprayed the floor. The masked man and Dannie both slipped and hit the floor—hard! The man didn't let go; he lifted Dannie's head and smashed it into the floor, and shards of broken glass penetrated her skull. Dannie began to slip into the abyss. Her eyes could no longer focus on the man with the mask. She knew she could not fight back; she just could not move anymore. Darkness seeped in to her brain, as blood seeped out.

CHAPTER 54

Rick's cell phone rang shortly after he left the bar with Jason, and he heard a deep male voice at the other end of the phone. "Mr. Singleton, this is Detective Baker from the Rye Police. Do you know a Dannie Bevan?"

"Yes, I know her. Why do you ask?"

"We got your name and number from her cell phone. How do you know her?"

"We practice law together, and we're friends. Did something happen to her?"

"Is she married?"

"Yes, she is. What happened to her?"

"She was assaulted. Do you know where her husband is?"

"Yes, I think he's in Dallas for business. What do you mean, she was assaulted?"

"We received a call from a neighbor that the front door of the house was open. When we responded, we found her in the house. How can we find her husband?"

"You have her cell phone. His cell phone number should be in there. His name is Rob. Where is she now?"

"EMS just transported her to Greenwich Hospital."

"How bad is she?"

"She's unconscious. Would there have been any other people in the house? What about kids?"

"The kids are away at school. I don't think there would have been anyone else in the house. I don't have her husband's cell phone number. When you talk to him, can you tell him that I'm going up to the hospital and give him my cell number. At least he'll know someone is there with her until he arrives. It's sure to take him a few hours to get back here."

"Mr. Singleton, I'm writing down your cell number. I'm going to want to talk to you about her business and if she had any pissed-off clients. You said she practices law with you?'

"Yes, that's right."

"What kind of law does she practice? And are you aware of any threats made against her?"

"Entertainment law, mostly, corporate law and litigation. No one in the firm does any criminal work."

The Detective let out a short laugh. "She doesn't have to do criminal work to have enemies. If I don't see you at the hospital later, I'll call you. Maybe we can talk in your office tomorrow."

"Whatever you want. I'll make myself available."

Rick hung up the phone and immediately called Maizie on her cell. Maizie and Abby were out shopping together, and when Maizie answered her phone, she said, "Hey, sweetie, Mom and I are out picking up…"

Rick blurted out, "Maiz, I just got a call from the Rye Police. The cop said Dannie was assaulted and she's unconscious. She's up at Greenwich Hospital. I'm going there now."

Maizie said they'd meet him at the hospital, and she and Abby jumped in the car and raced up I-95 to Greenwich Hospital, which took about twenty minutes.

As Rick literally ran into the hospital from the parking lot, he was desperately trying to figure out how he was going to get the doctors to talk to him about Dannie's condition; he was aware of the privacy laws, which would make things difficult since he wasn't her husband or family. He found out from the receptionist that Dannie was in the Intensive Care Unit on the third floor. Rick had to restrain himself from running up the stairs to the third floor, and it was fortunate that the doors to one elevator opened as he was about to bolt for the stairs. Rick thought his lungs would explode if he had to run up the stairs.

Miraculously, Rick's cell phone rang in the elevator. He saw Rob's name come up on the phone, and he answered it immediately.

"Rick, it's Rob. What the hell is going on? I got a call from the police." Rob's tone was frantic.

"I don't know yet, Rob. I'm just getting off the elevator on the ICU floor. Stay on the phone with me. I'm going to find one of the doctors to talk to us."

Rick got to the foreboding door with a sign that read, "Intensive Care Unit—NO ADMITTANCE." Underneath those huge letters was another sentence which read, "Pick up phone to the left and dial 100. A nurse will answer."

Rick did as the sign said, and he said to Rob that he'd call him back as soon as he was able to speak to a doctor or nurse because he was only in the ICU waiting room. The nurse who answered the phone said that Dannie was in surgery but that the doctor, called the "Intensivist," would come to the waiting room to speak to him as soon as he was finished with his patient.

Rick was pacing up and down in the ICU waiting room when Maizie and Abby arrived. Rick said that he was waiting for the doctor, and Maizie knew better than to tell him to calm down or sit down. After what seemed like an eternity, the door to the waiting room opened and a bald man with a neatly trimmed salt-and-pepper mustache and goatee walked in. His white lab coat bore the Greenwich Hospital logo on it above his name, which was Ernest Loucas. He came over to the three of them and introduced himself. They explained who they were and they called Rob back on the phone and put Dr. Loucas on the speaker.

Dr. Loucas explained that Dannie was now in surgery because her injuries were so extensive, and she was bleeding into her brain. The surgeons planned to open her skull to relieve the pressure on her brain from the swelling. "This was a very brutal beating and there was extensive damage done to her face and skull. The EMTs think she put up a fight, so let's hope she has a lot of that fight left in her. Your wife will have a difficult road ahead."

They could all hear the fear in Rob's voice on the phone, so Maizie and Rick did most of the questioning of the doctor. Finally, in a choked up voice, Rob asked the ultimate question. "Is my wife going to make it?"

"Right now it's touch and go, Mr. Bevan. We'll know more when she comes out of surgery. The next seventy-two hours will be critical. We may decide to put her into a medically induced coma. She'll be in surgery for a few more hours, so you might want to go get yourselves some coffee if you're going to wait here. If you decide to leave, then tell the nurse and give her a phone number, and we'll call you when she's out of surgery." As the Doctor left to go back to the ICU, Maizie asked Rob if he was going to be all right. Rob said that he was going to call the airlines and get on a flight as soon as possible.

After they hung up the phone, Abby looked at Maizie and Rick and could see the genuine concern in their faces. Maizie looked as if she was about to cry, and she was holding back trying to be strong. Abby leaned over and put her arm around her daughter, giving her a squeeze. "Look honey, why don't I go down to the cafeteria and get some coffee for all of us. I think it's going to be a long night."

"Yeah, a cup of coffee sounds right. Why don't you go with your mom and I'll call Dannie's partner, Chris, to let him know what happened in case the police haven't contacted him yet." While Abby and Maizie left to go get coffee, Rick thought about Dannie. He thought about what she must have been thinking while she was almost beaten to death. Could I be next? Oh Christ!

Not long after Abby and Maizie walked back into the ICU waiting room from the cafeteria, a tall man with a serious expression on his face walked into the ICU waiting room. "Are you Mr. Singleton?" Rick nodded. "I'm Detective Baker. I'm glad I caught you before you went home."

Rick introduced the detective to Maizie and Abby. He explained that Maizie was also a paralegal in the firm as well as being his fiancée.

The detective said, "I'd like to talk to you about Ms. Bevan. Based on what I saw in the house, it doesn't appear that this was a robbery. It doesn't seem that anything was taken from the house: no TVs, no stereos, no money or credit cards from her purse, which was in plain sight. What can you tell me about her practice?"

Rick answered, "She has a very successful practice in White Plains. She does a lot of entertainment law and, as a result of that, a lot of contract law and the litigation that inevitably flows from that."

"Would she have confided in you if she had received threats?"

"Yes, I think she would have. We worked together at our prior firm in New York City. We've been friends for seven or eight years."

"Are you a partner in the firm in White Plains?"

"No, I'm the senior associate."

"So you'd know about the finances of the firm; or, should I be speaking to her partners?"

"I don't have exact numbers at my disposal as to what Dannie and her partner are earning, but the firm is doing well. Dannie took all her clients from the old firm in the city, and we've picked up a number of new clients since then. I really don't think the firm is experiencing any financial difficulties, and I know they recently gave raises to people."

"Look, I know no one – especially attorneys – wants to answer a question like this, but I've got to ask. Any gambling problems? Any drug problems?"

"None, absolutely none."

"And you wouldn't tell me even if there were problems, right? You'd be helping Ms. Bevan if you could tell me anything about this because it could give us a direction. Right now we have none."

"I get it, Detective, but I really am not coming up with anything. Most lawyers tend to be boring people. We're officers of the court, so we pretty much stay on this side of the law. What can I say?"

"Here's my card. Call me if you think of anything. Thanks for your time." With that, he turned and left.

CHAPTER 55

Seconds later Rick's phone rang. He looked at the number; it was Beth. "Hey Beth, what's up? Everything all right?"

Beth replied with nothing short of hysteria in her voice. "It's Jas—he's been in an accident. I just got a call from Audi Customer Care that the police responded to a crash and the air bags deployed. They sent the police and an ambulance! I don't know how bad it is."

Rick, somewhat stunned, said, "What do ya mean an accident? Where is he? What hospital did they take him to?" The questions tumbled out of his mouth like a waterfall, without end. "God, not again," he mumbled to himself.

"He's been taken to Greenwich Hospital. I'm on my way now; can you meet me there?"

"We're here already. I'll go down to the emergency room right now. I'll meet you there." As Rick was talking to Beth, he frantically motioned to Maizie and Abby to follow him.

Maizie and Abby didn't know what was going on, just that Rick was waving to them wildly to follow him. Maizie looked at Abby with a fearful expression on her face and said, "Something must have happened to Jason! God, Mom, can you believe this?"

Abby said with worry in her in her voice, "Honey, I can't believe this either, but we can't get ahead of ourselves. We need to see what happened to Jason first." However, in Abby's mind, terror was closing in on her like a blanket of fog. She had just found Jason after all these years, and now she could barely entertain the thought of losing him again. Abby said to herself and then to Fannie, "Mom, you better be with him; protect him...please."

Beth continued on the phone with Rick, "What are you doing there? Did Audi Customer Care call you because they couldn't get me? I didn't realize my cell was off."

"No, it's a long story. Something happened to Dannie Bevan. Just get here safe, Beth. I'll be here waiting."

As Rick bolted toward the elevator, he turned to Maizie and Abby. "Shit, Jas was in an accident, and he's being taken here by ambulance. We have to get down to the ER to see him. I can't fucking believe this is happening."

They entered the waiting room of the ER and could tell it had been a very busy night, judging by the number of people there. There were people who had hacking coughs, sick-looking kids leaning against their mothers, one person on crutches with his foot elevated on a chair, and two in wheelchairs. This didn't count the people who had been brought in by ambulance for some sort of acute ailment or who were bleeding profusely and were being treated inside the ER itself.

Rick raced up to the receptionist's window and said he was Rick Singleton and was looking for his brother, Jason Singleton. The receptionist looked up Jason's name in the computer and said, "Your brother is here; he was brought in by ambulance. Right now he's being treated and you can't go in there now."

Rick said, "How badly is he hurt? I need to see him."

"I understand, sir, but he's being worked on by the ER staff. You can't go in and be in the way. As soon as they're finished stabilizing him, I will have the doctor come talk to you."

Rick was getting agitated. His wife and son had been killed in a car crash and he hadn't been there with them. And now this, his brother. Rick was in no mood whatsoever for asshole hospital rules. "Look, you don't understand; I'm his brother. I need to know how bad he is, and I need to know right now!" The tone in Rick's voice made everyone in the waiting room look up.

Maizie grabbed Rick's arm and tried to pull him away from the window. Rick yanked his arm away from Maizie and startled her. Maizie said, "Rick, calm down. You're causing a scene." Rick spun around with anger and frustration on his face and growled, "Don't tell me to calm down. I have to see him. You don't understand. You just don't understand!"

Abby stepped between Rick and Maizie. "Look at me, Rick. Jason is going to need you to be calm and in control. Beth is going to need you, too. It's not going to help anything if they call security. We need you to get control of yourself and calm down. Can you do that, Rick? And we do understand. Believe me, we do understand."

Rick took a deep breath and looked at Abby. After a few seconds, he said in a quiet voice, "You're right, Abby." He then turned to Maizie and said, "I'm sorry, Maiz. I didn't mean to lose it like that. I was just so upset. I'm sorry."

They went and sat down in a corner of the waiting room and waited. Rick wondered how much longer before Beth arrived. He hoped it wasn't long.

Meanwhile, in cubicle number seven, there was a flurry of controlled chaos as three doctors and numerous nurses worked furiously on Jason in an attempt to save his life. In the space of a few moments, Jason had been intubated. They had to insert a chest tube because his lung had collapsed. He was bleeding internally; he had severe lacerations on his arm and face and a severe compound fracture of the femur. The goal was to stabilize him enough to get him to surgery. Time was of the essence.

After what seemed like an eternity to Rick, Abby, and Maizie, a nurse came to the waiting room and called the name Singleton. The three of them jumped up to speak to the nurse. She said that Jason had been stabilized enough to get him upstairs to surgery. "You can come in to the cubicle to see him before we take him upstairs." She explained his injuries as she led them toward the cubicle. Before they entered, she turned and said, "Just be aware that he may not look like himself. He has a lot of injuries."

Rick answered, "I don't care what he looks like. I just need to see him."

As they arrived at the cubicle, one of the doctors, a nurse, and the transport team had already started moving Jason out of the cubicle and toward the elevator. Rick ran over to the gurney and grabbed Jason's hand. Rick said in a voice louder than he wanted to, "Jason, I'm here. We're all here. You're going to be OK. You hang in there. You gotta be tough."

Maizie was shocked by how bad Jason looked, and she hung back a little. Abby didn't hesitate and walked over to the gurney and stood next to Rick. She gently put her hand on Rick's. He looked at Abby and a pang came over him as he realized that Jason wasn't just his brother, but that he was also Abby's son. Rick saw the tears starting to form at the corner of her eyes.

As the transport team hurried for the elevator with Jason's gurney, a nurse escorted Rick and Abby off to the side on the hallway in front of the elevator. The doors opened to the elevator, and Abby saw Fannie and Aunt Rita in the elevator. Her heart almost stopped. For a split second, Abby couldn't believe what she saw. "You're here!" Abby gasped. Everyone near Abby looked at her with a startled expression at her outburst. Abby was too focused on what she saw to notice that everyone was looking at her. She could see that Fannie and Aunt Rita were on either side of Jason's gurney, each was touching his head and shoulder, comforting him. They were there, helping him; they were there—that's all she needed to know.

CHAPTER 56

On a brisk day, the wind blew the dead leaves from the trees in swirls. As the mourners trudged from the limos and their cars to the gravesite, the chill in the air matched their mood. Everyone huddled around the grave, where a silver casket hovered over the empty plot. The artificial turf covered the dirt around the plot, and brightly colored flowers were arranged around the grave. The minister waited until all the family and friends were gathered before she read the final blessing at the graveside. She said, "We bring our sister, Dannie, to her final resting place. With faith and hope in eternal life, let us assist her with our prayers. God of the living and the dead, accept our prayers for all those who have died and are buried with the hope of rising again." Fannie had been standing next to the casket as the prayer was read. Fannie said, "Hallelujah, sister! You got that rising from the dead part right."

The minister finished the prayer, saying, "Look with favor on those who mourn and comfort them in their loss. May Dannie's soul and the souls of the faithful departed, through the mercy of God, rest in peace. Amen."

Rick scanned the people standing around the grave, crying, weeping, tissues in hand. He noticed Dannie's two boys. They were standing on either side of Rob. Rick thought the boys had now been thrust into adulthood quicker than they should have been. He hoped they had a very supportive family to see them through this difficult time. The boys stood stoically, but with red-rimmed eyes. Rick continued to look among the crowd. Beyond the crowd Rick noticed a man sitting in the driver's seat of a parked, dark-colored SUV with what looked like a camera with a big telephoto lens. Rick hoped that this wasn't some third-rate photojournalist trying to make a buck over Dannie's sensational death.

The man in the SUV shot a few more pictures. He picked up his cell phone from the seat next to him and dialed a number. A male voice answered the phone. The photographer in the SUV said, "I got what you wanted." With that, he clicked the phone off, opened the door, and got out of the car.

As the wind blew the chill through the cemetery, the funeral director said to the assembled mourners, "Please place your flower on the casket. When we leave the cemetery, the family has asked that anyone who would like to join them for lunch immediately after may do so at Dindardo's Restaurant."

The mourners began to disperse and go back to their cars. Rick was leaving with Maizie and a few other friends and attorneys. As they made their way down the road from the gravesite, a man accidently bumped into Rick. "Sorry, mate, didn't mean to bump into you."

"It's OK. No problem," Rick said.

Rick and Maizie arrived home late that afternoon, totally exhausted from the emotions of the day. The reality of what had happened was absolutely incomprehensible. Everyone always believed Dannie would recover. Now that belief was gone forever. Rick reached into his coat pocket for the car keys and threw them in the wicker basket on the kitchen counter.

Rick felt something else in his pocket. He pulled out a small, black flash drive. Rick knew that he hadn't put a flash drive in his pocket, and he also knew he had worn the coat to work one day the preceding week. The color drained out of Rick's face as he stared at the flash drive. He realized it was the oldest trick in the world. Rick remembered that he had been jostled in the cemetery by the "Mate guy" with the Australian accent. Instead of the man pick pocketing Rick, he had left the flash drive. Maizie walked into the kitchen shortly after Rick noticed the flash drive.

Maizie walked over to Rick and put her arms around him, "You OK, hon? Want a cup of tea or something stronger?"

Rick answered, "No, just tired, worried about Jason and everything else that's going on. No one was in the office today because of the funeral, so I just need to check my e-mails."

Maizie replied, "OK then, I think I'm due for a nap; join me if you want."

Rick answered, "I'm tired, but I'm still too keyed-up to sleep. Why don't you head on up and I'll be there in a little while."

Maizie went upstairs to bed. She could feel how exhausted she was, but she also knew that this had been worse on Rick. As she got upstairs, she plopped herself down on the bed. Although Maizie still couldn't believe what had happened to Dannie, other thoughts came to mind. Dannie had been good to Rick when he needed it, and she had been a real friend to him. Maizie also knew that Dannie had been kind to her. She had given Maizie the job with almost no questions asked. She was grateful for that. Despite her tough persona and heavy workload, Dannie had always made herself accessible. There would be turmoil in the office as the attorneys tried to pick up the matters Dannie had been working on, but a far more serious concern was that Dannie was a big rainmaker for the firm. Would they be able to keep the huge studio clients without Dannie? Maizie also knew that Dannie's death was one more emotional blow to Rick, and God knew, he had had more than enough of them.

Rick waited until he heard Maizie going up the stairs before he took the flash drive from his pocket again. He walked to the desk in the den, opened the laptop, sat down in the chair, and leaned back. Rick looked at the drive in his hand; he turned it over and over thinking about all the events that had led up to this point. With trepidation, Rick placed the flash drive into the port on the side of the laptop. He waited for what was about to come to light.

CHAPTER 57

The computer screen flickered and finally came on. Rick wasn't sure what he was about to see, but he was virtually certain it wasn't going to be anything good. On the screen was a man with his face disguised and sitting in the shadows. When he began to speak, the voice was distorted, sounding octaves below normal. The man said, "Hello, Rick. If you're watching this, you have already met my friend, who bumped into you at the cemetery. I wanted you to know how sorry I am about Dannie. Such a shame, and leaving those two young boys motherless." Even though the voice was distorted, the sarcasm in the message was evident.

The voice continued, "It was horrible the way she was attacked and left for dead. Too bad she lingered on for a while. You see, Rick, I've known you and your family for a very long time. I've even done some favors for your grandmother, and then for you. You've recently made some poor choices in your short, miserable life and there will be a ripple effect and consequences. By the way, how is Jason? I hear he's had an accident?"

Then the voice went quiet for a few seconds. Rick jumped up from the chair and almost knocked it backward. Rick leaned forward on the desk with his hands on either side of the laptop.

His heart began to race, and he clenched his teeth. He was seething with anger and frustration. He wanted to throw the laptop against the wall. Rick said under his breath, spitting the words out, "You bastard—you fuckin bastard! You leave my family out of this."

The voice started up again. "Thought this would get your attention. But there's more. For every action, there is an equal and opposite reaction. Simple physics. By the way, did they ever find the guy who ran Jason off the road? Jason was drinking that night; maybe pounded down a few too many. He was pretty upset when he left the bar. He had only found out a few days before that Abigail Parker was his biological mother. I knew it all along. Guess you should have called him a cab. Accidents happen—well, you know that better than anyone. Yes, accidents can happen at any time in the future, too. If only Abigail hadn't found you that night on the bridge, what would the outcome have been, Rick?"

"Let me fill in the gaps for you. Apparently, you never knew that your grandmother and I were good friends. Very good friends, if you catch my drift. There was a period of time when your grandparents were having trouble in their marriage, and they separated for a short period. Anyway, she was very upset about some of the things your grandfather had done, and she was hurting. But let me digress for a moment. As a young man, I was really infatuated with your grandmother. You could say your grandfather and I were rivals. I was always the better man, and I certainly became much more successful than he. If your grandmother had cared a lot about money, she certainly would have chosen me."

"Well...while they were separated, your grandmother and I spent some wonderful nights together. She found out she was pregnant after she reconciled with Tom. We were both sure the child was ours, and that little girl was your mother. Which makes me your grandfather and your mother is my daughter, just in case you haven't figured that part out yet. I then used my connections and pulled some serious strings with the Court, and Abigail's child became your older brother."

Rick sat there staring at the screen...stunned. He was so angry that he could taste the bile in his throat. He wanted to scream. 'You're wrong!' and yell back at the screen, but he didn't want to alarm Maizie. The voice continued.

"I wanted her to leave Tom and marry me, but for some crazy reason, she couldn't or wouldn't do it. It was one of those things I couldn't control, no matter how much I tried. That may have been one of the very few times in my life that I didn't get what I wanted. Your grandmother and I kept in touch somewhat surreptitiously over the years, and I'd help her out and slip her some money. I'm not such a bastard all the time, you know, and I'm very loyal to the people I love or who are loyal to me."

"I kept track of your mother and you two boys. In memory of Rita, I helped you out and gave you a job with the firm. Ironic, how secrets can change people's lives. If you had known I was your grandfather, maybe the decisions you made with Dannie would have changed and wouldn't have left her boys motherless."

"You knew we couldn't take you back in the firm because you tried to off yourself. So then you went to work for that bitch, Dannie Bevan. I'm still not sure how you and Dannie got your hands on my closed-out files! You could have left things alone, and everything would have been fine. She was one pain in my ass at the firm. But not Dannie—no, not her—she always wanted more. Well, she deserved it, and she got it!"

"Your grandmother and I stayed in touch with each other until her death. Out of respect for her, I think I'm going to give you a free pass. That means I'm 'thinking' about it, and I'll consider the money a wedding present. You gotta live with all this. Go live your life the best you can, 'cause you never know. Ya just never know."

With that, the screen went black and it was all over. Rick sat back down heavily in the chair and sighed. He was sweating, and he wiped the beads of sweat from his face. Was this truly going to be over?

CHAPTER 58

Jason remained in the Intensive Care Unit. Abby, Rick, Maizie and Beth took turns staying with him, but he was in pain, sedated and out of it most of the time. Beth's parents came up from Philadelphia to stay with Julie and Ellie, as Beth commuted back and forth to the hospital. Beth struggled with bringing the girls to see Jason, and she discussed it with Abby, Maizie and Rick. They all thought the girls were still too young to see their father, hooked up to so many tubes, swollen, black-and-blue and sedated. They all hoped that Jason would do better, but the truth of the matter was, he was still struggling. Complication followed complication, and the doctors were still concerned over his lack of progress. However, he was still hanging in there and fighting for his life.

Abby looked at Rick one night as he came into the ICU after work. He looked tired and pale. The stress of coming to the hospital every day was probably worse than the stress of his job. Abby thought to herself that it was the stress of coming to the hospital, compounded by the fact that there wasn't very much good news once you got there. Abby was now spending several nights a week at Maizie and Rick's house because she was just too worn out mentally and physically to make the trip back to Rockland County every day. Some days she felt like she was just going through the motions, because the days seemed so repetitive.

Abby had read quite a few books on Kindle as she sat in Jason's room; she was completely caught up on her paperwork for her clients, and she had read all her professional journals. One night Abby decided to see what, if anything, would happen if she read the novel she was about to start out loud to Jason. She moved the easy chair much closer to Jason's bed and turned off the television that seemed to be perpetually on across the room. The same stories on CNN had now played three times, and Abby thought it was more than enough.

Abby started reading and had completed about a page and a half when Jason's eyes fluttered open and he moved around noticeably in the bed. Abby was somewhat surprised by Jason's movements. Abby leaned closer to the bed and took Jason's hand. It was black-and-blue from all the IVs.

"Hi, Jason; it's Abby. How do you feel?"

Jason stared at her as if he was trying to get his eyes to focus. When he did speak, his voice was very hoarse. "I was coming to see you."

Abby got up from the chair and leaned to within inches of his face. She thought Jason was merely confused or dazed from all the pain medication and didn't really know what he was saying. Abby said, "Me? You were coming to see me? When was that, Jason?"

"Night of the accident."

"You were coming to see me the night of the accident?" Abby asked with a great deal of surprise in her voice.

Jason nodded his head yes.

"Why were you coming to see me?"

Jason didn't answer her, almost as if he didn't hear or understand the question. Abby was about to ask him again, but before she could say anything, Jason said, "Saw her."

Abby didn't know what Jason was referring to, and she wasn't sure he was completely lucid. Abby could see that talking was an effort for him. "Who did you see, Jason?"

"Grandma Rita."

Abby felt a little like she was talking to a four-year-old, trying to pry information out of him in short bursts. The conversation had taken a somewhat bizarre twist, and again Abby wasn't sure if it was the sedation that was making him say things. She was keeping the sentences short, with the hope that he could focus on what she was saying and what she was asking him. "You saw Grandma Rita? When?"

"Night of accident…in ER. Stayed with me…surgery." Jason's voice was barely above a whisper.

Abby swallowed hard and said, "Yes, I know. I saw her, too."

Jason nodded again, with a slight smile on his face. "Loved her."

"I know that Jason, and she loved you very much, too. She was so proud of you. Those letters I gave to you were from her to my mother when you were a baby and then when you were a very little boy in England."

"Other woman?"

"What did you say, Jason?"

"Other woman with Grandma?"

"You saw the other woman with your Grandma Rita? That was your other Grandmother, Fannie. She's my mother. Did she stay with you, too, in the ER?"

Jason nodded again.

Abby spoke, looking into his eyes, "I saw her, too, that night. She loved you, and your Grandma Rita told Fannie all about you. Your two grandmothers had been best friends since they were in high school together. That was a really long time ago."

Jason looked at Abby through a medicated haze and said in a hoarse whisper, "Am I dead? I see dead people."

Abby smiled at Jason, but she was beginning to get choked up. Jason looked as if he was fading, and this had been a lot of exertion for him to talk. "You are not dead, Jason. I saw Aunt Rita and my mother too, and I am very much alive. We all love you, Jason. Beth, Rick, Maizie and I have been here with you every day in the hospital. You need to keep fighting and get better. Your girls miss you."

Jason had closed his eyes again. Abby bent over the bed and kissed him on the forehead. "Just get well. We have so much to catch up on."

EPILOGUE

The Following August

The sun was beginning to crest over the horizon. The ocean was calm, with only a slight breeze blowing, and the temperature was rising along with the sun. Jason got himself up and made his way out to the deck. He enjoyed seeing the new day begin. Since he felt he had a new lease on life, he wasn't going to waste a minute. He tried to be as quiet as possible even though he knew the girls would be up shortly and ready for the beach. That was it—bed to beach! Jason pushed the button to start the coffee brewing. Beth had set it up the night before. Even some of the simplest tasks were challenging.

Rick appeared in the kitchen, saw that the coffee was brewing and decided not to wait until it was finished. He acknowledged Jason, who was sitting out on the deck in the cushioned wicker chair. Rick poured two cups and went out to sit with him.

"You're up early, Jas. How's the pain?"

"It's there. It's tough sleeping. Nothing seems comfortable, but in retrospect it's all getting a little better. I'm here, and that's a miracle, so no use complaining."

"I guess you're right. We are all glad you're here. It was tough for everyone, watching you fighting for your life."

As the door to the deck flew open, the conversation came to an abrupt halt as Julie and Ellie came bounding out onto the deck.

"Morning you guys. We're headed to the beach early to catch the rays. Want to come?" asked Ellie. Julie gave her an elbow and a stern look. "Dad and Uncle Rick will come down later, right?" As they descended the stairs to the beach, Julie said to Ellie, in a muffled tone, "You idiot! Don't you ever think before you open your big mouth? Dad needs lots of help to get to the beach; it's not like before. Come on."

Jason said to their backs as they raced down the stairs toward the beach. "We'll finish the coffee, and we'll be down later. Stay near the lifeguard station." Jason looked at Rick with a pained expression on his face and said, "I really hate this."

Rick answered, "I know this sucks, Jason. It sounds like a cliché, but you have to be patient. You made a lot more progress than anyone thought you would. Give yourself some credit. It's a goddamn miracle that you're even here having coffee with me. I'll get you down to the beach today and every day."

Jason and Rick could hear the rest of the clan starting to move about in the house. "Morning, boys, you're up early," Abby said out the kitchen window. She grabbed a cup of coffee and strolled out to the deck to join them. She continued, "I hadn't planned to be up quite this early, but Julie and Ellie have already been in my room to make sure I got down to the beach—right now! I negotiated a small reprieve to get a cup of coffee, and boy, am I going to need it. They have the whole day planned out all the way until tonight. I hope I last that long." Abby looked directly at Jason as she continued, "But they are so cute. I love being with them. They're not teenagers yet—that's the challenging time." Abby thought for a minute and said, "Maizie was a handful when she was a teenager. She certainly gave me a run for my money."

Both Rick and Jason answered Abby in unison. "She's still a handful."

Abby answered, "Absolutely true, but life would be a whole lot less interesting without Hurricane Maizie. OK, time's up. I had my coffee and Ellie has spotted me. See you later. If I collapse on the beach, can you come rescue me?" With that, Abby headed off toward the beach and her granddaughters, with a smile on her face.

Rick spoke first. "She is something. People just seem to gravitate toward her. It's amazing how the kids have bonded with her. But maybe it's not all that amazing—it's Abby." Rick looked to Jason for some reaction.

There was a pregnant pause until Jason finally spoke. "You know I've had lots of time think about things, first in the hospital and then at home. Life is one weird ride. I think it's actually merciful that you don't know what lies ahead. If so, we might all just lie down and curl up into a ball."

Jason continued, "Who would ever have thought a couple of years ago that all these things could happen to us? I guess there really are no coincidences—maybe just fate, with a helping hand."

Another few seconds elapsed, and Rick could see that Jason was still working on a thought, so he stayed quiet and let Jason continue. "I'm still not sure why I was so opposed to knowing Abby was my biological mother. Maybe it was because it was so sudden or maybe because it was just thrust on me and I didn't have any say if I wanted to meet her. But you certainly see what a problem keeping that secret from Abby caused for everyone. God, what were the grandmas thinking when they did that?"

Now it was Rick's turn to respond, and there was a moment of silence as Rick struggled for the appropriate answer. At first, Rick wasn't really sure if Jason expected an answer from him or if he was just expressing his thoughts out loud. Rick said, "I guess they thought they were protecting everyone. I certainly have a lot of good memories about Grandma Rita. She was a pistol. From what Abby has told us, her mother, Fannie, was quite a character, too. I guess that's why they were such good friends. I wish I had met her."

Jason looked at Rick and said, "I have something to tell, but you gotta promise me you won't repeat it. And I'm not crazy either."

Rick shrugged and said, "OK, fire away."

Jason started to speak and stopped, as if collecting his thoughts or considering the right way to phrase it. "This is what made me really come around on the adoption. The night of the accident, as I was in the ER, I saw Grandma Rita. She was standing next to the gurney in the cubicle with me. Then I saw this other woman. I wasn't sure who she was. I think I tried to ask Grandma Rita, but I never got an answer, or at least I don't remember if I did. I know this sounds crazy, and friggin' bizarre, but they were both there, I swear. They stayed with me as I was in the ER and then when they took me up to surgery. Grandma Rita said that they would watch out for me.

"It seemed so incredibly real to me, but then I realized afterward that I had been sedated, and it was probably the drugs. Amazingly, Grandma Rita looked the same as she did when we were kids. The whole thing just stayed with me, and I couldn't shake it. No, that's wrong. I didn't want to shake it; I wanted to believe it was true. Finally, one night when I was still in the ICU and I felt like I could string a few words together, I talked to Abby about this, and she didn't seem the least bit surprised. She said that she had also seen them that night in the ER. Abby told me that the other woman was her mother, Fannie. I can't believe she saw them, too!"

Rick stared at Jason, almost without blinking, and said nothing, but he took in every word that Jason was saying. Rick said, "Abby saw them, too? For real? Abby actually saw them? Shit, she never mentioned anything about it to us."

Jason caught his breath for a second, and then the stream of words continued. "Maybe she thought you wouldn't believe her. It was like the little kid in the movie, The Sixth Sense, who says he sees dead people. Maybe it was Abby's mom who set this 'thing' in motion. After what I've been through, doing a little research and talking to other people, nothing seems impossible. I think it was very hard on Abby to have made the decision she did. I think seeing Grandma Rita standing there made me feel differently toward Abby. I think I finally realized that there was a connection among us. Grandma Rita, Fannie, Abby and I—I get it now. I was the secret."

Abby, Julie and Ellie were down on the beach, and the girls were trying to teach Abby how to boogey board. After a few attempts, and some good coaching from the girls, Abby finally got the hang of it. After about twenty minutes or so, Abby told the girls that she was going to head back up to the shade of the beach tent. Abby reminded them to stay close to the shore, and stay together. Julie responded in her most adult manner, "Ok Nabbs, I'll make sure Ellie listens and I'll keep an eye on her." Abby looked at Julie, gave her a kiss on the forehead and a wink. "Another fifteen minutes and we head back to the house for breakfast." The girls had given her the nickname of Nabbs, short for "Nana Abbs." Abby loved her new name, and she smiled at how much energy they had, but mostly she smiled at the gift of her two granddaughters. Abby turned toward the dunes and when she arrived, she sat down in one of the beach chairs and watched the girls giggling in the water. It was turning out to be a perfect day with a cloudless blue sky and the temperature warming the day by the minute. Abby was so glad to be exactly where she was at this moment in time. As she was rummaging through the beach bag for her Kindle, she heard a familiar voice. "It's good to see you still have the coordination and balance. Not bad for an old lady. Your years in gymnastics paid off." Abby almost jumped out of her chair.

"God, do you always have to scare the crap out of me? No, Mother, remember I was the swimmer and Donna was the gymnast?"

"Oh, no matter which you did. It was so long ago. But I didn't mean to scare you. How else am I supposed to get your attention? Skywriting perhaps?"

Abby sighed a deep sigh and looked at her mother and waited for her mother to speak. Fannie looked at Abby for more than a few seconds, and it was clear to her that Abby wanted her to start the conversation. Finally, Fannie said, "I'm really pleased that everything worked out well for you. I know you have trouble believing it, but that's what I always wanted for you…for things to work out well and for you to be happy. Your Aunt Rita and I thought we were doing what was best by giving Jason to Caroline and Jonathan. I figured that you were so young, you'd just move on, and we thought you did. I never realized how much of a bond you felt with your baby, despite your age. I was very wrong and I am sorry."

Abby looked at Fannie as she spoke. She could hear that Fannie's tone and her words were conciliatory. Abby's answered with the same tone. "Look, Mom, I believe you're sorry and I understand why you did what you did. I appreciate hearing those words from you. I never knew I would feel the way I did about Jason even though I was so young. Now in retrospect, I know that we all made the right decision. I just wish I had been able to talk to you about it then. I wish we could have talked then like we're doing now. But it doesn't matter now; it's in the past."

For the first time in many, many years, she and Abby were really talking to each other without screaming and without acrimony.

As Jason continued his conversation with Rick, he glanced out the window and saw Abby having what appeared to be a conversation with someone. Jason looked, then looked again. "Oh my God, it can't be."

"What can't be?" Rick questioned.

Jason continued to stare at Abby. "You won't believe this, but Abby is having a conversation with Grandma Fanny!"

"Shit, you can see her! Where is she?" Rick looked intently out the window. "Are you sure? I don't see anyone but Abby."

Jason said, "She's right there and she's holding Abby's hand." With that, Fannie waved and smiled at Jason; he raised his hand and waved back. He was smiling.

Abby spoke again as she looked at her mother and then back to the girls on the beach. She said, "It's been a lot of years since I gave Jason up for adoption. I think I've had my share of grief and heartache, and as I've gotten older I hope that I have gained some wisdom from those experiences. We all have our shortcomings, but the choices we make can take us to new beginnings, and I have you to thank for that. I have to let go of the past, so I can enjoy the present, the here and now. Mom, I do have one question I would like you to answer. I 've always thought you sent Tina to me when I had asked you for help all those years ago with my decision about having to put Dad in a nursing home. Did…"

"Yes, I sent Tina to you. You needed one another."

Fannie reached out and took Abby's hand. Abby looked at her mother and smiled as a tear formed in the corner of her eye. Abby spoke in a whisper, "I can feel your hand in mine, Mom. I love you, always have, always will."

Fannie looked at her daughter, and said, "I know, I love you, too. I have to go. Keep doing what you're doing, because they're all the right things. Enjoy your life." Fannie let go and she was gone.